HONORÉ WILLSIE MORROW

With Malice Toward None

D1363638

William Morrow and Company

Publishers   *New York*

CONTENTS

CONTENTS

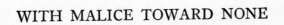

WITH MALICE TOWARD NONE

CHAPTER I

A MAN OF INFINITE JEST

SOME ONE shouted, "Fire! Fire! Fire!"
Lincoln, who was standing beside the turnstile in
the fence between the grounds of the War Department and the White House, talking to Vice President
Hamlin exclaimed, "By Jings!" and pointed to a pink
glow above the roof of the Executive Mansion.

Running figures appeared from nowhere, the vanguard
of that mysterious crowd which seems to exist only to
attend conflagrations. A fire engine belching sparks
clanged up Pennsylvania Avenue. The President leaped
across the snow-encrusted flower borders of the garden.
Hamlin followed. Lincoln's first thought was that here
was more of ten-year-old Taddie's mischief. Tad's
mother had spanked him that very day when she had
found him under her bed smoking one of the cigar ends
Seward always was leaving about. It looked to the
President as if the east side of the White House were
in flames. With Hamlin running easily beside him, he
rounded the south portico and immediately exclaimed in
relief:

"Oh, the stables! Hope the coachman and the horses
are out. There's the coachman, so he's safe!"

In spite of the efforts of mounted guards, people were
climbing the iron fence that bounded the grounds. By
the time the President and the Vice President had passed
the long colonnade that housed the woodsheds and the
other kitchen offices, there was a large crowd watching

the flames shoot up from the stables, lying beyond the kitchen gardens. People gave back slightly as Lincoln and Hamlin appeared in the brilliant orange light.

The two men were, in this year 1863, the same age, fifty-four. Hamlin, a little over six feet tall, was magnificently proportioned and as lean and powerful as an Indian. In fact, he looked not unlike an Indian with a touch of the Roman in the boldness and regularity of his features.

The crowd was not much impressed by the arrival of the Chief Executive.

"King of America!" some one called in a sneering voice.

Lincoln gave the Vice President a humorous glance. "Must be referring to you, Hamlin! *You* look the part."

Hamlin smiled grimly and with a slight jerk of his head remarked, "Yonder is one who not only looks but feels the part!"

Lincoln's gaze followed the gesture. "Why, it's Charles Sumner! What's he doing here? You're right, Hamlin, he'd be an ornament to my job."

In spite of the excitement of the conflagration, the Senator from Massachusetts was making an impressive approach.

"The man who would be king!" cried the same voice that had been heard before.

Sumner did look the part. He was of equal height with Lincoln, six feet four inches. His whole person breathed elegance and authority. His very gesture as he came to pause, of wrapping his blue broadcloth cape about him, was made with an air of superiority that went well with the dignity of his beautiful face and head. He was clean shaven and his eyes were blue even in the fire glow.

As for Lincoln, although the snuff-colored riding

clothes and the high riding boots were of the best mode
—his wife saw to that—there was nothing regal in Lincoln's appearance, unless one caught the noble lines of
brow and cheek, the depth of the blue gray eye. Nothing
of the king, yet Sumner looking at him with a suddenly
appraising eye was moved to say:

"King to the commonalty. Whose phrase is that, I
wonder?"

Lincoln scarcely heard the query for there was a sudden outcry from the stables.

"They *haven't* got the horses out!" he ejaculated.
"They're screeching like women! Burke!" plunging
toward the coachman, who was shrieking something incoherent into the ear of the fire chief. "Burke! Tie wet
gunny sacks over their heads. I'll show you."

Hamlin caught the snuff-colored sleeve and Sumner
put a well-gloved hand on Lincoln's shoulder. He did
not struggle against them but he said pleadingly to the
fire chief, "My boy's ponies are in there! I'd rather
lose the White House than those two little horses,
Chief!"

"We'll do all we can, Mr. Lincoln," gasped the fire-
man whose red shirt was dripping sooty water. "The
heat just drove me out. I'm going right back."

Another dreadful outcry and the sound of beating
hoofs came from the flaming caldron. Lincoln shud-
dered. "I can't stand it! Poor beasts!" He turned
away. "We're no help here, Hamlin. Were you on the
way to my house, Senator?" As he spoke he started
along the path, to the east, thinking to swing round the
colonnade and gain the north entrance to the mansion.

"Yes, Mr. Lincoln," replied Sumner, following through
the snow and slush. "I've been talking with Secretary
Seward about that last note from France on intervention.

Letting the French minister visit Richmond was a grave mistake. I must have a denial of intent on your and Seward's part to present to the Senate in the morning, if you'll be so— Good God!" as Lincoln clutched his arm and pointed.

They had passed the stables and were moving through the north garden before the colonnade which was brilliantly lighted by the burning buildings beyond. A little figure in red was darting across the end of the colonnade which housed the carriages.

As it dropped from sight, "Tad! come back!" shouted Lincoln.

He leaped forward followed by Sumner and Hamlin. Before they had taken half a dozen strides, the child reappeared swarming up a ladder to the roof of the cow shed, adjacent to the stables. Holding his flannel nightshirt around him, he danced up and down on the icy roof, halted for the moment by his father's cry. His chestnut hair was like a crimson halo round his excited little face.

"I'm going to get Willie's pony, Papa day!" he shrieked, his voice thin and hysterical. "I'm going my sec'et way!" Tad could not pronounce his Rs. He turned and with unbelievable swiftness scrambled up the slippery roof to the air vent in the rear wall of the stable. The three men staring up at him roared in chorus, "Come back!" Taddie gave no heed.

"You see, sir, this is what comes of not teaching children to obey!" exclaimed Hamlin.

Lincoln groaned and leaped to the ladder. Being of Taddie's own manufacture, it broke with his first step upward. Hamlin darted away, crying, "I'll get a ladder in a moment."

"Give me a back, Charles," said Lincoln.

The Senator stooped and Lincoln swung up on the roof just as the tail of Taddie's shirt fluttered into the vent. Lincoln was about to drop on all fours for the scramble upward when a little voice arrested him.

"Go back, Papa day, go back or you'll slip and bust yo' neck."

Sumner's voice came from below. "Thomas Lincoln, if you lead your father into danger your mother'll punish you as you've never been punished before!"

"But Willie's pony! Willie's pony!" shrieked Tad. "Excepting Pensacola, that's all the flesh and blood we got left of Willie. I'm going, I tell you, I'm going!"

"Don't move, Mr. Lincoln. I've arranged the ladder and I'm coming up," came Sumner's voice urbanely. "I can manage him."

Lincoln hesitated on the brink of the glowing icy sheet that sloped up to his boy, torn between deadly fear for Tad and chagrin over his own predicament. Here, indeed, was one of the critical moments between him and one of his children that Mary was always warning him would come and would find him impotent. The Senator was now beside him, breathing heavily. He had been subject to attacks of angina pectoris ever since Brooks had assaulted him in the Senate seven years before. His great voice now rolled forth as Lincoln had heard it so often in moments of passionate debate:

"Thomas Lincoln, if you don't come down, I'll come up and break my malacca over your nether end!"

Tad's head appeared in the opening, his face distorted by anger and tears. He edged slowly down to the roof. "Willie's pony!" he sobbed.

"Hurry!" roared Sumner.

Tad slid downward to his father's arms.

A moment later, when Hamlin appeared with a ladder

and two firemen, the rescue had been completed and Lincoln was leading the way once more toward the north entrance.

"Mr. Sumner performed the miracle," explained the President, "but at cost to his poor heart, I'm afraid. Better come in and lie down, Senator."

"No, thank you, Mr. Lincoln," replied Sumner, "I'm quite able to go home. You'll let me have that denial of intent in the morning!"

"Yes! Yes! And a thousand thanks to you!" exclaimed the President.

Sumner moved slowly but steadily enough toward the gates and Lincoln turned to the Vice President:

"He's as irresistible as the Mississippi in flood, isn't he, Hamlin! Come in for a moment, will you, while I finish the sentence the fire interrupted." He led the way into the vestibule and stood beside the little Baltimore heater used by the doorman, still holding Taddie.

"You are warning me that Charles Sumner was my enemy, Mr. Hamlin, and I was telling you that you were wrong. Sumner thinks I'm slow and he doesn't care about my manners. He doesn't agree with me fully on my reconstruction ideas. He's often annoyed by my lack of knowledge about laces and glass pots and steel engravings. But at bottom, he's my friend. He wouldn't work against me in an underhanded way. I love Charles Sumner. My wife and our two boys are devoted to him. He's always round the house, here."

"That being the case"—Hamlin unbuttoned his overcoat, nervously—"why did Sumner come to me to-day and ask me to run against you for the Presidency next year?"

Lincoln suddenly seated himself on the bench opposite the heater. He felt the need of physical support. Had Hamlin told him that his beloved chief secretary John

George Nicolay had turned against him he could not have been more hurt.

"Oh, come, Hamlin! He must have been joking you! I can't swallow that!"

"Then you can't swallow Lyman Trumbull, Ben Wade, Winter Davis, Horace Greeley—" began Hamlin.

Lincoln interrupted. "I know all about those fellows. But not Sumner. No, Mr. Hamlin, not Charles Sumner!"

"Very well, sir!" Hamlin's deep voice was troubled. "I would very much dislike being quoted in the matter, but you'd better tell Sumner what I've said and get the answer from his own lips."

"I don't like to do that!" protested Lincoln. "I don't want to start an issue with Sumner."

The Vice President made an impatient gesture with his mittened hand. "In making no issue, Mr. Lincoln, I beg of you, don't deceive yourself. Sumner would prefer me in the White House, or Chase, or himself, to you. And understand me clearly. I shan't run for the Presidency. I don't want the job. I don't like the one I've got. I'd rather be back in the Senate this minute than anywhere else on earth."

Lincoln loosened his neck scarf with a ruthless forefinger. "This is worse than telling me General Hooker has mired the Army of the Potomac as deep as Burnside did. I need Sumner in Congress. I've hardly a friend up there and I was depending on him."

"Your war with Congress, Mr. Lincoln, is almost as serious in its effect on public morale as the war with the South. You—"

Hamlin was interrupted by the sudden appearance in the inner door of a slender youth in evening clothes.

"Oh, there he is! Father, mother's frantic. She

missed Tad only a few moments ago and she's coming
right out to look for him. *Nothing* can stop her. I'm
sorry, Mr. Hamlin," with an apologetic smile and bow
for the Vice President.

"Coming this moment, Bob!" exclaimed Lincoln, rising
and smiling down at Tad who during the conversation
with Hamlin had been half sniffling, half listening in his
father's arms. "Jings, I'd forgotten the child! Good
night, Mr. Hamlin!" He started hastily into the hall,
followed by his son Bob.

Half way down the private staircase he met his wife.
She was a dignified little person, even in a black padded
dressing gown and with great chestnut braids hanging
over her shoulders.

"What *does* this mean!" she cried. "Bob, I told you
he'd gone to the fire and caught his death's cold, the bad,
bad boy."

Tad's snivelling suddenly changed to hysterical shrieking.

"For goodness' sake!" groaned Bob. "Let's move this
scene of domestic bliss where it won't bring in the newspaper reporters!"

Lincoln, who had been steadily mounting the stairs,
strode down the upper hall to Tad's bedroom. His wife
followed. Bob, who was only nineteen, remained rigid
with disgust at the head of the stairs.

Lincoln dropped Tad down on the bed. Mary thrust
her husband aside, turned Tad's flannel gown up and
spanked him heartily. It was exactly the restorative he
needed. In a moment, he was sitting up, quietly wiping
his face with his father's handkerchief and drinking the
milk his mother had set to heat on the hob the moment
she had discovered his absence.

Lincoln watched the two, smiling. Tad's escapades

and his mother's handling of him were one of his chief
amusements. The large square room was shadowy but
an enormous hobby horse could be seen in the corner
nearest the bed and ranks of toy soldiers marched resolutely across the hearth where the coal fire glowed.
Mary's round cheeks were as pink as a girl's. Her beautiful blue eyes in which, as she ministered to her son, her
irrepressible sense of humor struggled with a temper of
which Taddie's was the replica, were dancing with excitement. Tad, who was like his mother not only in disposition but had also her round face and delicate, sensitive
mouth, gulped his sobs with his milk and proclaimed his
innocence of any desire to drive his mother to her grave
with worry. It was Willie's pony—!

Sudden tears filled his mother's eyes. She stooped and
kissed the child's quivering lips. "If the pony's gone up
to heaven to join Willie, let's be glad for both their
sakes."

"Oh!" gasped Tad. "I hadn't thought of that—"
There was a long silence while he absorbed the idea.

His father tiptoed into the hall and across to the sitting-room where Pensacola and Sumter, Willie's and
Tad's hound dogs, lay as usual asleep on a sofa. He
gathered them up in his arms and made his way back to
the bedroom.

"There," dropping them on the bed. "All you boys
go to sleep!"

A moment of patient waiting on his father's and
mother's part—and Tad was in dreamland with a dog on
either side of him. Mary turned out the light, Lincoln
caught her fingers and they crossed into the President's
bedroom which was just opposite. It was lighted only
by the crackling fire that brought out highlights on the
fine old rosewood and mahogany furniture with which the

great room was filled. Husband and wife stood warming their fingers before the blaze.

"Was there anything especially bad at the War Office, Abra'm, that kept you so late?" asked Mary.

"Nothing unusual. Things look as black as they well can. I believe General Hooker can make the Army of the Potomac fight. Whether or not he can keep tavern for a vast army is another matter. Stanton is dissatisfied with him already. I hope Stanton's not going to get one of his hates against Hooker. I don't know where I should turn."

"You'll have to turn to some one soon who'll lead the Army of the Potomac to a real victory or the country will turn completely against your administration," said Mary, succinctly.

"I can't *create* a general, my dear wife!" protested Lincoln. "I remember one of Speed's stories concerned a fellow who advertised that he could make a new man out of an old one and have enough left over to make a little yellow dog. I wish I had the fellow's address. Perhaps if he left in the material for the dog, he could turn me out a general who could stand on his own legs."

Mary laughed. "Goodness knows you've got plenty of old gentlemen in the army to choose from!—but the fruitless slaughter is sapping the country's morale, Abra'm."

Lincoln sighed and said nothing for a moment as he thought of his disappointment in Burnside, whom he had appointed to succeed McClellan in the Army of the Potomac. However, it was a comfort to remember that though he had dallied long in taking off McClellan's head, he had not closed his eyes to Burnside's weaknesses but had given him only a few weeks of trial before replacing him with Hooker. And Hooker was showing

little genius, thus far.   He shook himself to throw off
the familiar miasma and chuckled as he said:

"Hooker's latest remark is that what the country needs
is a dictator both for the army and the Government.   I
told him that only those generals who obtain success could
set up dictators; that if he'd give me military successes,
I'd risk the dictatorship— He's a handsome fellow."

"So is McClellan," commented Mary, drily.   "They're
all so childish!   As a matter of fact, since you've absorbed
what your General-in-Chief knows of the military art,
you're the best of them all.   Charles Dana told me so."

"Oh, he's just prejudiced by his liking for me."   Lincoln shook his head with a sigh.   "I think Grant is a
coming man in spite of his present unpopularity."

"Grant is a butcher!" exclaimed his wife.   "That's
why the public is against him."

"Grant *fights!*" insisted the President, but with a sick
pang as he thought of the frightful losses that followed
in the little General's wake.

"You might feel differently about him if your own kin
were in his army," protested Mary.

"Has Bob been talking to you again?" asked Lincoln.

Mary turned a startled face up to him.   "No!" she
gasped.   "Abra'm, don't tell me he's talking enlistment
again."

"I haven't had any real talk with him since he appeared
on the scene this morning.   But I reckon that's what he's
come down from Harvard for.   There's blood in the
boy's eye, if I know the boy.   Am I right, Bob?" as their
first-born put his head in at the door.

"You sometimes are, sir," he replied with his father's
own twinkle in his gray eyes.   He was of medium height
with his mother's elegance of carriage, a curiously quiet
face more like his mother's in outline, yet marked by a

baffling and inescapable look of his father. He joined his parents before the fire, slipping his arm about his mother.

"What is it you want, Bobbie?" she demanded, suspiciously.

"Can't I hug you without wanting something?" asked Bob with an injured air.

"Never since you were a baby!" retorted his mother.

"Well, then, I do want something. I want to enlist. I want to go just as a private with no preferment because of father. I can't bear to be cloistered up there at Harvard when all my friends are doing their share at the front. I can't stand it and I won't." He tossed his hair back from his forehead with a jerk. His mother turned to face him, her lips quivering. But before she could speak, Bob went on: "And I don't want to wallow round hopelessly in the mud with the Army of the Potomac, either. I want to go out to Grant."

"No!" shrieked his mother.

Lincoln put his hand on her shoulder. "Don't lose your grip on yourself, Mary. The boy's right in his desire. I'm glad he has it. But," smiling down into Bob's belligerent eyes, "you're only nineteen, son. Wait a year for your mother's sake."

"You can't go! It'll kill me!" sobbed Mary. "Baby Eddie and Willie both in their graves. I can't be asked to spare another son."

"They didn't die to save father's Union," protested Bob.

"If they had, I'd have been reconciled," said his mother.

The boy looked up at his father with helpless exasperation in his eyes. Lincoln shook his head. This was an old scene. A year ago Bob had begun his pleading and now his every visit home was marred by this contention with his mother. He was utterly weary of this struggle between the two.

"Mary," he said slowly, gripping both her shoulders and stilling her sobs with what Mary called his "granite" look, "Mary, we'd better let him go. I honor him for feeling as he does."

"Abra'm! Abra'm!" screamed Mary.

"Hush! O mother, for pity's sake, the servants will hear you!" Bob ran across the room to close the hall door.

But it was not Bob's expostulation that silenced her. It was the continued look in her husband's eyes. She suddenly put her hands before her trembling lips and waited.

"Bob isn't going without your consent, wife. But you're going to be a woman—certainly not less a woman than these countless other mothers North and South. Bob, you go back to Harvard for another year, then I'll give you a commission and mother'll let you go, eh, mother?"

"I—I'll try!" gasped Mary.

"But I want to go as a private!" Bob flushed.

"Never! Never!" from his mother.

"But, mother, can't you see what a position you put me in? It's bad enough up there in Cambridge to be the President's son, but to be the President's son and a coward—it's Hades, that's what it is!"

Lincoln eyed him a little hopelessly. Bob had all his mother's sensitiveness and all her restless energy.

"I swear," he ejaculated, "you two are worse than a pair of brigadier-generals to manage! Every inch of you covered with corns. You say all your friends are fighting, Bob. Yet your buddy, Edgar Welles, is still in college."

"His father's only Secretary of the Navy. So much

isn't expected of him. And besides, he really does some important things for his father and that contents him. Secretary Welles sends him on secret missions that're important." Bob sighed.

"That's true," mused Lincoln, "and Edgar, as near as I can see, isn't one whit steadier than you. It's hard for me to realize you're grown, Bob. You're still the little rare ripe whose nose was always running."

Bob managed a feeble grin. His mother eyed the two with unabated anxiety.

Lincoln went on. "I reckon I haven't been taking advantage of the material in my own family! Bob, you go up to Harvard till the Easter holidays. Don't make any plans for visiting during that time because I'll have an errand for you to do."

The grin on Bob's face widened. "Really important, father?"

"Will it be dangerous?" pleaded his mother.

Father and son looked at each other. "It'll be a full-sized man's job," replied Lincoln.

A sob caught in Mary's throat. She started toward the door that led into her room, hesitated, turned and said, "It's just because I love you both so! I'd give *my* life to save the Union, any time, but I can't spare either of you." Then she left them.

Bob held out his hand. "Good night, father. I'm off early. I'll see you in April."

Lincoln grasped the firm young hand and looked keenly into the clear young eyes. "You go and make it up with your mother, Bob. She carries the dirtiest end of this load in Washington. Don't ever forget that."

Bob nodded and crossed into his mother's room.

Lincoln, undressing slowly, was comfortably aware of their voices but this could not lift his weary depression.

Everything he had touched, everything he had planned and prayed for in the past two years, except the Emancipation Proclamation, seemed to have gone awry. He was a potter who could mold only crooked pots, he told himself grimly. And even the Proclamation was heartbreakingly slow in getting military results. The belief he had had that it would bring vast numbers of negroes over to the Union lines had not been fulfilled. Men, colored or white, were needed so badly by the North that the cold sweat started to his forehead as he thought of the imminence of his having to enforce the draft on unwilling Northerners.

But these facts were no sudden burden. They had been accumulating gradually and somehow his shoulders had developed strength sufficient for the load. It had been endurable. But the fact divulged by Hamlin that night, concerning Sumner, he told himself was pretty near a last straw. As he stood by the fire in his dressing gown the significance of it came home to him, making him feel actually ill.

All his plans for saving the Union included Sumner and Sumner was not his friend! Nay, more, Sumner was seeking to undermine him!

He groaned and, laying his arm on the mantel, dropped his head against it.

A clang of a bell and a clatter of hoofs roused him. The fire engine was going home. He looked at the clock. Ten minutes past two. He hoped the sudden clangor had not wakened Tad. But as he raised his hand to turn off the light, there was a sound of whimpering, the hall door opened, and Tad in the red nightshirt appeared.

His face was screwed into a knot as he rushed to his father. "Papa day, I had a bad d'eam. I thought the stables bu'ned up and Willie's and my ponies—"

Once more Lincoln lifted him. "Sh! Sh! You'll wake mother, darling Tad."

"Let me get in bed with you, else I'll d'eam it again!"

"That's a good notion," agreed his father. "I've been having a nightmare myself. We'll protect each other."

He laid Tad on the bed, turned out the light, opened the window and got in beside the child. Tad nestled against him, and as the moon sank slowly below the window ledge father and son fell asleep.

CHAPTER II

HEEL OF ACHILLES

TAD was in good form the next morning. The family dining-room was a cheerful spot, full of flowering plants and singing birds. With the birds and Tad competing in eloquence, the whole story of the events of the previous night came out. Horror-stricken though she was, Mary laughed immoderately as the little boy lisped through his tale. She seized on the opportunity to produce one of her inimitable mimicries.

"Thomas Lincoln," she quoted, raising both her plump arms in Sumner's familiar gesture, "Thomas Lincoln, if you ever again make such a little fool of yourself, I shall add your father's malacca to the Senator's."

Even James, the colored factotum, passing buckwheats to the President, grinned while Tad and his father shouted. After a moment Mary suddenly returned to her own character and said, thoughtfully, "Mr. Sumner ought to have a dozen children of his own."

"Can't find a woman good enough for him, I suppose," suggested the President, finishing his coffee.

"He hasn't that attitude at all," contradicted Mary. "Mrs. Seward and I have often wondered if he didn't have an unfortunate affair in his youth."

Lincoln replied, as he rose from the table, that he was not inclined to be sentimental over the Senator's past, and added, "I hope Sumner's future doesn't hold an unfortunate affair for Lincoln!" He left Mary blinking.

As he made his way up the private staircase and along

17

the upper hall to his office, he told himself that he'd en
lighten Mary about Sumner when they were alone that
night. Then he tried to put the matter out of his mind.

His office, which was also the Cabinet room, was just
shabby enough to make Lincoln feel at home in it. It
looked south over the marshes to the Potomac. Lincoln
liked rivers. They had belonged to his boyhood. His
desk stood at right angles to one of the windows. The
huge old oak Cabinet table monopolized the center of the
room. Mary had tried to hide its scars with a red felt
cloth which Tad had promptly spattered with ink. There
was a good fire crackling in the grate this morning under
the portrait of old General Jackson. A sleet storm was
beginning; had already obscured the red Virginia hills.
Perhaps the storm would be violent enough to keep people from pestering him, Lincoln thought hopefully as he
seated himself at his crowded desk. He picked up a
telegram and began to wonder before he read it whether
or not Sumner would call in person for the report on
the French Minister's indiscretion. Perhaps he'd better
ask the Senator, point blank—

He was interrupted by Billy Stoddard, one of his three
secretaries. Billy, a tall, slender youth, a good deal
worn by the anxieties of his work as mail clerk and first
buffer between the President and the public, smiled at
Lincoln.

"I know you hoped for a quiet day, sir, but the reception room's jammed already. I was going to hold everybody off for at least an hour but Messrs. Wade, Chandler,
and Trumbull have just arrived and are whanging and
banging and winding the horn for the drawbridge to be
let down."

"I'm sorry my old friend Trumbull's turned on me,"
sighed Lincoln. "He has too much brain to be taking the

course he is with those other two. However, war makes
strange bedfellows. If Trumbull ever makes up with
me I'll ask him if it's because he's heard it's bad luck
to sleep three in a bed. Tell them I'll see them shortly,
Billy." He rose, suddenly determined to tell Mary about
Sumner now. The thing just wouldn't leave his mind and
perhaps she'd have a helpful suggestion. "I'll be back
in ten or fifteen minutes," he added, and, rising, made his
way into the private passage that led to the family sitting-
room. This was the President's favorite apartment in
the Executive Mansion. Oval in shape, it faced south
with a view of the marshes and the Potomac to the
hills of Virginia. Its furnishings were old and hybrid.
Heavily upholstered couches of President Monroe's
régime shouldered the Sheraton chairs of the Adamses'
occupancy and the clumsy Empire tables left by the Van
Burens. The Brussels carpet in faded reds, greens, pinks,
and blues had been laid by the Pierces. It was a rather
hopeless mixture from the artistic viewpoint, but it spoke
to Lincoln of the domestic life of his predecessors and
made them his friends. He was glad that beyond renovating the room, Mary had left it alone. She kept it filled
with flowers. Her rare understanding of plants had
caused the White House conservatories to bloom as never
before.

A bright fire of cannel coal blazed in the grate. Sleet
slashed the windows. The odor of a great bowl of white
freesias filled the air. Mary was arranging a basket of
moss roses on the round table in the middle of the room.
She looked up at him with an interrogatory smile.

"I suppose Sumner would know the name of every
flower and plant in the house," said Lincoln, pausing before the fire. "Confound the fellow! Lord Lyons told
me the other day that when Sumner visits England he

tells the natives more about their trees and shrubs than they know themselves. I reckon when you and he run short on French, you talk the 'language of flowers' to each other!"

Mary laughed heartily. "We haven't run short on French yet but that's a valuable suggestion.—What's on your mind about him, Mr. President?"

"I came in to tell you." And in a few crisp words he repeated Hamlin's statements.

Mary dropped her roses and stood staring at her husband, horror, unbelief, and pain following each other across her face.

"Abra'm, there's some mistake! I can't believe it! What motive could he have?"

Lincoln, pulling at his chin, replied dejectedly, "I think, or rather I hope, that mainly he doesn't understand what I'm trying to do."

"Of course he understands!" insisted Mary. "But he's an Abolitionist, and your slow methods exasperate him."

"There's more fire than that behind Hamlin's smoke," shaking his head. "Mary, I just don't see how I can bind the Union together either now or after the war, without Sumner."

"Do you believe he's strong enough to lose you the renomination?" asked Mary quickly.

"If the Union defeats continue for another year, yes."

"Can't you compromise with him, somehow?" she suggested.

"No!" thinking aloud. "He'll never compromise. If Sumner's my enemy—" He paused, shaking his head.

Mary lifted her chin defiantly. "He's not your enemy! He must have tried to be facetious with Mr. Hamlin. And Charles Sumner trying to be funny is terrible. He says the most insulting and the most insane things, under the impression that he's being playful. You know as well as I do how his lack of humor handicaps him. I don't think he's capable of intriguing, Abra'm. He's as guileless as a child."

"So'm I," declared Lincoln, grimly, "and I'm up to my scruff in intrigue all the time."

"You! Guileless!" Mary sniffed and began to rearrange the roses, but almost immediately dropped them and bit at her fingers, tensely. Then she said, "Is Sumner actually indispensable to you, Abra'm! What worries you most, the fact that he may prevent you having a second term, or that he won't work with you to save the Union?"

"I reckon they both mean the same thing in the long run," replied the President. "You see, I've always counted on him. But particularly since I signed the Emancipation Proclamation last month he's seemed to want to work with me. Mary, I've got to have Sumner."

"Then you shall have him!" Mary squared her small shoulders and brought her small fist down on the marble-topped table. "I don't know how I can help but I will. Incidentally, I've asked him with Alice Hooper and her father-in-law to join us in our box at the theater to-night."

"Do I know Alice Hooper? Any relation to Congressman Hooper from Boston?"

"Only his daughter-in-law!" replied Mary. "Don't you remember her at the Sewards' dinner the other night? She is tall and blonde and young with wonderful yellow hair. Her husband is on General Banks' staff in New Orleans."

"Yes! Yes! Gave me the tips of her fingers and a cold stare! Friend of Sumner's, isn't she? I think I heard some one say so."

"Mr. Sumner almost lives at Congressman Hooper's house. Alice is there with her little daughter during her husband's absence. She's socially very brilliant." Mary tapped her lips softly with a stalk of freesia.

"That lets me out, then," grunted Lincoln. "Perhaps I'd better bring Sumner here after the theater and have Hamlin's rumor out with him."

"No! No! Let him make the first move. Take your own time, my dear!" coming over to pat his arm. "Perhaps when you've had time to think this over it won't seem so nearly fatal."

Lincoln shook his head impatiently and then put his great hand on her shoulder, while he repeated with that enormous earnestness which never failed to convince his hearer,

"Make no mistake about the importance of this, Mary. It was pretty bad when my old friend Lyman Trumbull went back on me and joined up with ultra radicals like Ben Wade and Winter Davis and the rest of those fellows who want to exterminate the Southerners. But I could hitch along without him, as you see. He's no such power in the Senate and the country as Sumner is, though he's a smart man. Sumner, if he wants to, can keep me from saving the Union even though we win the war. Now do you see why I'm so upset?"

"Yes, my dear husband, I see," replied Mary soberly. She reached up to straighten his tie. "I'll do all I can to hold him for you. Perhaps some plan will come to me before a crisis rises between you and him."

"That's what I came in to hear you say, Mary." He smiled down at her, glanced again unseeingly at the telegram in his hand and turned abruptly back to his office.

Nicolay was waiting for him; rather a sallow young man with a little dark goatee and a beautifully modeled

forehead and brow. He wore the same anxious, over-
tired air that had been so marked in young Stoddard
but his smile as he spoke to the President was brilliant.

"Trumbull, Wade and Davis wouldn't wait for you,
Mr. Lincoln. Senator Sumner and General Butler were
here during your absence. Butler wanted Sumner to say
a word to you about restoring his command in New
Orleans. He was in a terribly excited state; talked so
wildly that Sumner dragged him away."

"Afraid he'd kick over a beehive, I suppose," said
Lincoln, as he settled to his desk again. "Sumner's always trying to advance Butler; wants the General's
political support."

"That's just what Butler did—kicked over a beehive!"
exclaimed Nicolay. "I'm wondering if there's anything
to what he said. I think I'd better tell you, sir."

"Fire away, George!" Lincoln waited with interest.

Nicolay walked up and down in an excited way as he
talked. "Well, after Butler had cussed out you and Secretary Stanton for not restoring him to New Orleans in
spite of the French resentment over his Woman Order,
to say nothing of the English, Sumner added fuel to the
flame by saying that you'd told him you could accomplish
more in the way of reconstructing Louisiana through a
soft-spoken fellow like General Banks than through the
fire-eating General Butler. Butler slammed his kepi on
the floor when he heard this. 'God help the Union,' he
roared. 'Soft spoken! Why, those fellows down there
look on softness as fear. We've got to treat them as the
conqueror always has treated the conquered, or there'll
never be an end to insurrection. Confiscate their estates
and give them to the niggers! Transport the Secession-
ists and their families to Texas or Mexico!'—and a good
deal more along that line."

"What did Sumner say to it?" asked Lincoln eagerly.

"Mr. Lincoln," replied Nicolay, hammering his fist into his palm, "Sumner nodded and said that that was the only way to handle reconstruction of the seceding States; to give the land and the vote to the negro and he'd come to full manhood at a single stride. I couldn't stand that so I remarked that no such double gift would be made to the negro while Abraham Lincoln occupied this room. And Butler came back at me like a charging bull. 'Then we'll put Hannibal Hamlin here as Sumner suggests. Hamlin doesn't see the nigger and the alligator as social equals!' Sumner grabbed him then and rushed him out. Do you believe Sumner has turned on you, sir?"

Lincoln did not answer directly. "I'd say the beehive was turned upside down," was his comment as he turned from Nicolay to stare out the window.

It looked as if he'd have to believe that Sumner was about to head the movement of Lincoln's own party against Lincoln. The party and the country were sick of this war of Union defeats. And every day that Grant dallied before Vicksburg, every hour that Hooker held the Army of the Potomac inactive while he waited for the mud on the Rappahannock to dry, added to the general discontent with Lincoln, the Commander-in-Chief, and strengthened Sumner's hands. It looked as if he must face the idea that he'd have only the two remaining years of his term of office in which to end the war and rebuild the Union, only two years in which to purge and purify the conquered States and weld them into the whole so that never again could secession lift its head; Sumner had well named the process reconstruction.

With all possible speed, he must give the handful of Union men always to be found in each conquered State a chance to restore their State governments. But this was impracticable unless he had immediate victories. If only there were men enough to feed to Grant! Grant who fought and slaughtered and attended to his own business. More men and more men—God help the poor boys! He shivered and suddenly was conscious of Nicolay watching him sadly.

"George, this colored man, Fred Douglass. Have you ever heard him speak?"

"No, sir, but I know he's considered powerful by the Boston Abolitionists. Secretary Chase might be able to tell you about him. He had Douglass at his house for tea not long since. Charles Sumner was there."

"Chase is a great Secretary of the Treasury," commented Lincoln drily. "I'd place Sumner as one of the greatest Senators we've ever had. But I'd never take the estimate either one of 'em made of another human being. They've got no feelers. George, I wish you'd arrange for Douglass to come to see me as soon as you can."

"Does he come secretly, Mr. Lincoln?"

"Certainly not. Get Sumner or Chase or Hamlin to bring him to my office here and let me have an hour or two alone with him. Who's outside now?"

"A group of men from Boston headed by Wendell Phillips. They want to protest against your dilatory prosecution of the war. There's a woman weeping her heart out. Wants a reprieve for her son. Half a dozen other women not weeping. Ten or fifteen of the generality as you call them. Better let me take care of the lot of them."

"No! No! I'll see what they think about things. Give me the weeping widow first and the Boston set last."

In spite of the weather it was a particularly crowded day. People's deep depression made them restless, made

them turn to him as the ultimate authority, with every sort
of plea, made them crowd him with impossible suggestions and with preposterous claims and recriminations.
He took dinner about three o'clock on a tray in his office.
and did not stop for supper till Tad came for him at six.

The storm was over when the Lincolns started for the
theater. Their sleigh carried them through a world of
icy beauty until it encountered F Street. This unpaved
thoroughfare was completely blocked by a train of eight-
mule army wagons stalled in the half frozen quagmires
left by gun carriages. The moonlight, the flickering lan-
terns, the kicking mules, the cursing drivers made a more
cheering picture than the President had seen that day.

He called to Burke to stop the sleigh. "I can tell those
contrabands in a minute how to straighten out their
mules," pushing back the buffalo robe.

"Abra'm, don't be a fool," snapped Mary, pulling the
robe back vigorously over her husband's knees. "You're
in evening clothes and you happen to be Chief Executive,
not Chief Mule Driver. Get along, Burke! Turn down
to Pennsylvania Avenue."

"Maybe you're right, wife," agreed Lincoln, amicably.
"But it wouldn't have taken me half a minute to point
out to those drivers that swearing at one another instead
of at the mules is plumb foolish."

"Yes, and you'd have provided the newspapers with
another priceless bon mot. 'Lincoln finds his level, etc.'
Anyhow," snuggling against him, "I want to enjoy this
sleigh ride with my beau. Do you remember our first
sleigh ride?"

"Yes," replied the President, promptly. "I cut Steve
Douglas out and took you home in Steve's own cutter
from Edwards' cotillion party. We drove two or three
miles out into the prairie just from sheer deviltry."

"You do remember!" Mary gave a contented sigh and for a moment they bumped along Pennsylvania Avenue without speaking. It was picturesque and they both enjoyed it; the cavalryman beside each street lamp, the lines of soldiers entering the gayly lighted oyster bars, the ambulances with mounted drivers, street hawkers, newsboys, galloping aides and the glitter of ice on tree and roof.

Mary gave herself a little shake. "Well, I must come back from Springfield and give you a little gossip I've picked up. Mrs. Seward told me to-day that it's being whispered about that Charles Sumner has a very sentimental attachment for Alice Hooper. I want you to watch them together. If this is true there may be a spot in Achilles' heel by which I can get a real hold on him."

"Now, just why should you want me to bother with a thing like that!" demanded the President. "You know as well as I and all the rest of the world that Sumner is so much above an unwarranted interest in a married woman—"

"Who said there was anything unwarranted in it!" interrupted Mary, indignantly. "But if it gives Alice Hooper an influence on Sumner and I can get her ear—"

"Oh, nonsense!" ejaculated Lincoln.

Mary moved away from him. "Very well, sir! You come to me another time for help!"

The President gave a comfortable, low laugh. "I undoubtedly shall!"

"You'd better not!" snapped Mary, and refused to speak again during the few minutes remaining before they reached the theater. They were a little late though they had tried as usual to be a little early, for it was always something of an ordeal for Lincoln to enter the lighted box and there be greeted by the audience coming to its feet. It was worse than usual to-night, for during the rather perfunctory salutation a man in the dress circle shouted, "Nero fiddles while Rome burns!" There was a spatter of "Bravos" at this, quickly drowned by cries of "Shame! Shame!" A group of soldiers in the front row just beneath the stage rushed up the aisle shouting, "Put him out!" They seized the offending gentleman in the dress circle and hustled him to the door, filing back just as all opera glasses were again trained on the President's box. Charles Sumner was entering with Mrs. Hooper on his arm. Lincoln rose and led her to the chair beside his.

She was a truly beautiful woman of the fine blond type that New England occasionally produces; very tall and slender with thick golden hair worn in curls over her shoulders, with large, light blue eyes heavily shaded, with a faultless skin and delicately perfect features. She wore a low-necked frock of pink satin with an enormous skirt caught up with rosebuds. The Senator arranged her ermine coat carefully over the back of her chair then seated himself between Mrs. Hooper and Mary.

Before any conversation could take place the curtain rose on Maggie Mitchell in "The Cricket on the Hearth." Mary had been reading Dickens aloud to Lincoln that winter as a substitute for Petroleum Naseby in those stark night hours when he sometimes appealed to her for help. Nothing could have suited him better this night than this exquisitely homely play. As the curtain went down on the first act, he turned to Mrs. Hooper.

"How that fellow does understand human nature! My wife's read the Cricket to me and the Pickwick Papers. Dickens has a lot in common with Shakespeare, according to my reading of the two men. Old Weller and

Falstaff! Both of 'em tavern clowns of a kind you meet anywhere. Take any character of Dickens or Shakespeare. They're so close to reality you're certain both men picked 'em out of the crowd from actual people. Maggie Mitchell is great. My old, dried, withered eyes are full of tears yet."

"It does seem a pity," said Mrs. Hooper with a sigh, and with one eye on Sumner, "that the British dislike us so when we have such an ardent admiration for their literature."

Sumner cleared his throat but Mary forestalled him.

"One has to distinguish between their literature and their politics!" she exclaimed. "Knowing Lord Lyons has taught me that. Socially, I'm quite in love with him. Politically, I think he's disgusting. When I read British books and plays I admire everything British. When I read their speeches against the Northern cause and see the vile cartoons of the President that *Punch* publishes, I could bite them."

"It's best to base your friendship for men or nations on something that politics can't taint," said Sumner. "Bitterly disappointed as I am in the English attitude toward us, nothing shakes my essential admiration for them. It's their way of thinking that's made England the cradle of the world's liberty. You mustn't let the ebullitions of rather stupid politicians influence you, Madam President!"

"Good heavens, Senator, this from you!" ejaculated Mary. "What of your turning against Mr. Seward and Charles Francis Adams and—"

He interrupted her with a dignified toss of his great head. "Doesn't that prove what I've just said? It's evident I've made no solid basis for my friendship there."

"I shall never dare to differ from you on politics again,

Senator!" exclaimed Mrs. Hooper, touching him archly
with her pink feather fan.

Lincoln, listening with only half an ear, was brought
back by suddenly observing a boyish blush on Sumner's
face as he bent toward Mrs. Hooper and said with great
tenderness: "You'll make me very unhappy, Alice, unless you convince me that you dare to talk to me about
any or everything."

"Jings!" thought the President. "I wonder if Mary's
right as usual!" and as Sumner continued to gaze tenderly
into the blue eyes turned up to his, "Some one ought to
wake him up. Talk about me providing bon mots for
the public!" with a glance at the opera glasses leveled
toward the box. He looked at Mary. She returned the
look with an unmistakable I-told-you-so expression. He
smiled at her and her lips twitched. Peace was declared.

Mary touched Sumner on the knee.

"Isn't that Lord Lyons nodding at you from the dress
circle, Mr. Sumner?"

Sumner with a sigh followed her gaze. A moment
later Lord Lyons entered the box and Mrs. Hooper
devoted herself to him during the remaining intermis-
sions. Just as the curtain dropped on the last act, a
message came from Secretary Seward to Lincoln. The
French had landed an army in Mexico. Lincoln left
Mary in the care of Lord Lyons and hurried off to Seward's house. It was long after midnight when he reached
home.

He sent for Sumner the next morning and gave him
the news.

"I suppose Mr. Seward has already sent off a provoca-
tive note to Louis Napoleon?" was Sumner's first remark.

"Seward'll do nothing without my approval," replied
Lincoln, a little impatiently. The nearer Sumner came

to truth in his comments on the Secretary of State, the more, Lincoln told himself, it irritated him.

Sumner raised his eyebrows and smoothed back his mane of waving chestnut hair with the gesture that was the unfailing joy of sarcastic newspaper men. "This will please the South, inordinately," he said.

"And this will please a lot of fire-eating Northerners," added Lincoln, "that whole set of blind boasters who declare we can lick all of Europe in spite of our difficulty in reducing the rebellion. Mark my word, Senator, some fool will get up in a day or so in Congress and declare war on France. Can you scotch the debate? Better still, can you head it off?"

Sumner spoke quite simply. "I can block the passing of any resolution, of course. Perhaps I can block debate, also, if you think that's advisable."

"With M. Mercier ready to misinterpret and Lyons ready to be grieved—I certainly do think it's advisable!" said Lincoln earnestly. Then he added a little sternly: "Are you whole-hearted about this, Senator? Your sympathy for the cause of liberty in Mexico doesn't give you any desire to help the Mexicans drive the French out?"

"Good heavens, Mr. Lincoln!" Sumner rose from his chair by the President's desk. "I pride myself on being a practical politician.—Good morning, my dear," looking down, with a smile that showed splendid teeth, at Tad who had rushed into the office and seeing his friend had seized his great white hand with both his small grimy ones.

"Senator!" shouted Tad, "the old cat just had fou' kittens in the woodshed and the coachman's dog, Alice, just had nine puppies in the cow shed. Won't you and Papa day—"

Sumner put an arm around the little boy's shoulders. "I don't like Alice for a dog's name, Taddie."

"Don't you?" looking up gravely into the Senator's blue eyes. "He named it after the song, 'Alice, whe' a't thou,' because she is always wunning away. Maybe if I asked him to he'd change the name. What would you like, Senator?"

"I had a very pleasant little dog once named Mischief," suggested Sumner. "She was a brown water spaniel."

"That's a nice name," declared Tad, "I'll go find Pete Kelley and we'll have a cwistening."

Sumner stooped and kissed the eager little fellow. "Thank you, Taddie! And who's Pete Kelley?"

"He's my chum. He lives on 13th Street. His fatha's a wealthy tin man. He twades pots and pans and makes stove pipes and all things like that. I can't say his name well so I call him Pete."

"Perry Kelley," volunteered Lincoln, who sat before his desk watching the little by-play.

"That's Pete!" nodded Tad. "He and I a' going to make a stage in the state bedwoom." He gave his father a violent kiss, rushed across the room and slammed the door after him.

Sumner picked up his tall hat.

"Do you want me to have Seward send you the papers he has on the matter, Senator?" asked Lincoln, following him toward the reception room with a wistful reluctance to let him go.

"I prefer to deal only with you on the subject, Mr. Lincoln," replied Sumner.

"Very well," agreed the President, then he added in a low voice, "Taddie and Bob and Mrs. Lincoln don't complete the list of your lovers in this house, Charles,— without regard to political bias."

Sumner paused and his lips twitched as if with pain. "Thank you, Mr. Lincoln," he muttered, and strode from the room.

That afternoon, Senator McDougall of California offered resolutions in the Senate condemning the French invasion of Mexico and requiring the immediate withdrawal of the French troops. There was an instant eager rousing of the fire eaters. But Sumner with a superb short burst of oratory on the madness of a proposal which would indirectly offer aid and comfort to the Rebels tabled the resolution almost before the Senate as a whole knew what was happening.

Nicolay who had gone up to keep an eye on things for the President described the episode to the anxious Lincoln. "He's the noblest Roman of them all, Mr. Lincoln," he concluded.

"Yes! Yes!" replied the President. "I dread to lock horns with him."

"Humph!" ejaculated the secretary, lifting a huge roll of war maps, "he's the only one worthy of your steel,— just to mix figures of speech a bit!"

CHAPTER III

THE NOBLEST ROMAN OF THEM ALL

LINCOLN did not at once go on with his work after Nicolay had left him. He sat thinking over what he confessed was his cowardly attitude in letting slip opportunity after opportunity to bring into the open the issue between him and Sumner. He feebly tried to excuse himself by murmuring that after all he was like Daniel Webster, who had said so often that he fought principles and not men. This being true, why not forget Sumner's charm and look on him as the embodiment of the danger of disunion; call him to the office and bring him to book, by Jings, as an enemy to the Union!

We-e-ll, perhaps not so harshly as that! Why not try a little of this famous diplomacy of which there seemed to be an oversupply in Washington at present. Let some one else draw the truth out of Sumner. Hah! That was the idea! He brought his fist down on his desk and with a grunt of satisfaction wrote a note to Sumner asking him to come to the Executive Mansion the following afternoon for tea. He next made a careful list of names with a memorandum instructing Nicolay to send an invitation to each for tea at the same time. The list included Seward, the Secretary of State, with whom Sumner was quarreling in a dozen matters, "Father" Welles, Secretary of the Navy, who was irritating Sumner by his attitude on privateering, and Lord Lyons, whose relationship with Seward was marked by a courteous endurance that often disturbed even Seward's suavity and caused the latter to make the eagle scream a little more frequently than good taste required. It had the makings, Lincoln thought, of a party wherein several beehives might be kicked over.

But when the President wandered into the sitting-room at five o'clock the next afternoon, it was Mrs. Seward and not the Secretary of State who stood before the fire. Lincoln liked and admired Mrs. Seward. She was tall and gracious and a philosopher! One would have to be a philosopher, Mary said, to have such utter patience with the brilliant and facile-minded Secretary as did his wife. She wore black, as usual, over a conservative crinoline. Lincoln hated these abortive petticoats.

"I gave a woman a job for her trifling husband this morning," he remarked, as he ranged himself beside Mrs. Seward, "for no other reason than that she didn't wear hoops."

"The first money her husband earns will certainly go for one,"exclaimed Mary, glancing complacently at her own ballooning skirts. "Does Mr. Welles make your life miserable for you about your hoops, Mrs. Welles?" rising to greet this much-loved friend.

Mrs. Welles, whose quiet beauty was Mary's special admiration, smiled as she glanced down at the lavender silk flounces that concealed even the tips of her slippers. "The Secretary of the Navy is a great martinet everywhere but in his own home."

"I don't think Mr. Seward knows the difference between a hoop and a bonnet. You're the crinoline connoisseur of the Administration, Mr. Lincoln!" said Mrs. Seward.

"I've a notion to recommend in my next annual message that they be abolished by act of Congress," declared Lincoln, looking from one attractive woman to another and sipping his tea with great enjoyment. "Not casting any reflections on the delightful nature of this party, as Sumner would say, I'd like to ask what's happened to it? I gave Nicolay a list of men, only, who were to be asked here this afternoon. Who bribed Nicolay?"

"Mr. Welles feared he couldn't get away so I came to bring his probable regrets," said Mrs. Welles. "I always use any excuse to come to one of Mrs. Lincoln's teas. First in the hope that Mrs. Lincoln will be inspired to mimic some one, and second because her cook's a genius at tea cakes."

"Mrs. Welles has spoken for me!" agreed Mrs. Seward. "Ah, here's some one to help balance the crinolines," as Lord Lyons came in.

He was a rather heavy man, smooth shaven, with dark, phlegmatic features, redeemed by very brilliant dark eyes. He wore a black broadcloth coat over silver gray trousers. Lincoln, a little disheveled and in his brown office clothes, shook hands with the Englishman, not entirely unconscious of the contrast between himself and the minister.

"This is good of you, my lord. Was Sumner with you this afternoon, by chance?"

Lyons moved toward Mary and the tea table. "I've just left him, sir. He spoke of coming here, very late. I was to tell Mrs. Lincoln," bowing over her hand, "that he'd promised a little girl, the granddaughter of Representative Hooper, to take her for a ride to Rock Creek. And that promise had to be kept. I hope I've made my answer as meticulous as Mr. Sumner's explanation to me was."

"Isn't that just like Charles Sumner!" exclaimed Mary, as she poured a cup of tea for the minister.

"He's infatuated with the child," said Mrs. Seward. "One can hardly blame him. She's a lovely little thing. She is the image of her mother, so Mr. Sumner, of course—" She paused and a significant smile went around the room.

"Queer he's escaped matrimony so long," said Lincoln. "He's a great hand for the women. I can't reconcile what I see of him round here with what Sam Hooper told me. He said that when Sumner was young he was no ladies' man at all; was just a queer, awkward cockerel, all shank and no crest, like I was."

"But, Mr. President, the ladies always have admired Mr. Sumner, so they must have admired you," said Lyons with a smile. "I hadn't the privilege of knowing you in your youth, but I did know Sumner. I was a mere boy but I remember that on his first visit to us he was the sensation of England. Upon my word, I can't recall a like case. He came to England, a young man in his early twenties, with one or two unimportant letters of introduction. He wished to study international law. Within two months of his arrival he'd become the rage. He must have been overwhelmed with the invitations he received if he hadn't been then, as he is now, of such sound mental integrity. We'd never met an American like him, old or young, so learned, so ardent, so modest, with such a brilliantly acquisitive brain. The men discovered him first and then the ladies! Upon my word, I've heard my mother say he could have had his choice of the best of them. It's a pity that the years have wrapped him in cold dignity."

"He told me once," said Mary, "that his family and most of his friends opposed his taking that trip. I often wonder how our relations with the British would be faring to-day, if the friendships made by that unknown young Charles Sumner weren't alive and vital, a blessed bulwark against complete misunderstanding."

"Hear! Hear!" cried Lyons.

"So I tell my husband," sighed Mrs. Seward, "and he agrees with me and would be so glad to keep friends with dear Charles. But they just can't see eye to eye on our diplomatic relations and I'm always looking out the window to behold the Senator's tall back expressing high dudgeon about something or other!"

"Just now it's privateering!" chuckled Lincoln. "Sumner against and Seward for. They've got the Cabinet taking sides and as usual I've got the thankless job of making a decision."

"I suspect Mr. Sumner of being right," said Mary. Mrs. Seward sighed again.

"Mr. Seward and he are too funny together," Mary went on. "The other day I watched them debating near the turnstile. Mr. Seward with his necktie under one ear— Ah—" interrupting herself, "here is the Senator to defend himself," as Sumner burst into the room.

"A treasure!" he exclaimed to the company at large. "Here's the first three cantos of Henry Longfellow's translation of Dante's Paradiso. I always thought it dull in the original, but Henry gives it true fire and poetic spirit. Let me read you a little of it." Without throwing off his fur-lined cape, he began:

"Longing already to search in and around the heavenly forest . . ."

But his voice was husky and after a page or two he handed the manuscript to Lincoln. "Go on with it, sir, while I clear my throat with tea. Rock Creek was damp."

Lincoln put on his spectacles and moved nearer the

lamp. He read as well as did Sumner although his voice had a less robust quality than the Senator's. Sumner was greatly stirred by the lines, kept murmuring comments to Mary Lincoln, and waved his hands to the cadence of the verse.

"Henry and I always planned to make that translation in friendly competition," he exclaimed as Lincoln came to a pause. "I'm thankful that he, at least, has been able to fulfill the dream."

"I've burst into poetry once or twice myself," admitted the President. "Of the three worst poets in the world I'm at least two, I reckon. It never would have occurred to me, however, that you'd had like aspirations."

"I wished for nothing so much as to devote my life to letters," confessed Sumner, sinking back in his chair with a sigh. "I'm never free of a sense of frustrated hopes."

"And I," exclaimed Mary, "always wanted to be an actress of the Maggie Mitchell type."

"You've real talent for acting, Madam President," Lyons nodded heartily. "As for me, I wished to be a painter, a Landseer, if you please."

"Do you still paint? Have you any of your work in this country?" asked Mrs. Welles.

"Heaven forbid! to both questions, dear Mrs. Welles!" ejaculated the Englishman. "None of my daubs are in existence."

"How do you know your mother hasn't got one tucked away in some obscure bureau drawer?" demanded the President. "Did you ever know a woman not to keep souvenirs of her son's genius? Now, you take Mrs. Lincoln and our Bob— What is it, James?" as the servant hesitated beside him.

"Massa Secretary Welles jus' can't get here, Massa Lincum, sah."

Mrs. Welles rose at once. "He shall not escape the dinner party at our house to-night, if I have to go for him myself!" she exclaimed.

"I think I may as well intrude on the privateering situation," said Mrs. Seward. "The Prussian Minister is dining with us and I must see that Mr. Seward's tie is *not* under one ear!"

Lord Lyons accompanied the two women from the room. As Sumner stood alone on the hearth, Lincoln viewed him with a half sardonic eye. "Lincoln arranges parties," he thought, "and God disarranges them. I feel like a woman who knows her hour has come!" He seated himself beside the tea table and waited for Sumner to speak.

The Senator began the instant James closed the door on Lord Lyons.

"Mr. Lincoln, will you allow me to be utterly frank with you?"

The President felt his muscles stiffen. Was Sumner going to confess and as simply as this? Life, after all, allows very few retreats. . . . Well, better get it over with.

"You're all out of patience with me, eh, Mr. Sumner?" he asked.

Sumner looked from Lincoln, disheveled and weary, to Mary, whose eyes glowed with excitement although she sat calmly enough before her teapot. His throat worked in an unwonted manner. There was a wistfulness in Lincoln's blue gray eyes and a sensitiveness about the thin upper lip that may have made him loath to strike.

"My attitude has nothing personal in it, Mr. Lincoln," said Sumner. "Personally, I have a horror of the task I've imposed on myself this afternoon. Only the same overwhelming conviction that swept me into the anti-slavery fight years ago could have whipped me into the position I'm in now with regard to you."

"Get on with it, Sumner! I accept your apology," said Lincoln, drily. He began to run his little ivory paper knife through his black hair; a sure indication of a moment of stress with him. "Let's not have any elocution about it."

"The better element of your own party as well as the same class of the general public are thoroughly dissatisfied with you as our Chief Executive, Mr. Lincoln. You are not enforcing the Emancipation Proclamation as it should and could be enforced. General Banks in New Orleans and Andrew Johnson in Tennessee are playing with that vital promulgation."

"Here it comes!" thought Lincoln.

Sumner swept on. "You're too fearful of offending different factions. The Northern Democrats, the border States, this, that and the other chimerical consideration holds you back. I agree with the general feeling that while we have entire faith in your integrity, you're too slow of action for the present crisis. While you hesitate and your generals procrastinate, the peace party thrives and at any moment the war may end with slavery still on our hands. We have no faith in slavery being forever destroyed under your rule."

He moistened his lips, glanced at Mary, who sat motionless, and went on. "Knowing, as many of us do, Mr. Lincoln, how utterly impersonal and unselfish your attitude toward the nation is, we ask you to show your patriotism to the full by—" He hesitated, then finished firmly "—by resigning from the Presidency."

Mary gave a little scream. Sumner, the great moral leader of the North, the foremost statesman, the most commanding figure in the whole political field, had turned thumbs down on Lincoln, the President. Perhaps some inkling of the enormity of his request touched Sumner for he was as pale as death and breathed heavily.

Long years before, during one of the numerous wrestling matches by which he had achieved young fame, Lincoln had received a terrific knee blow in the groin. It had been a friendly bout. The youth with whom he was contending was a neighbor of whom the young Lincoln had been very fond. Yet the blow had been given deliberately. If he lived to be a thousand, Lincoln never would forget the shock, not only physical but mental, that this foul had given him. Never since had he experienced anything that approximated a like sensation—until this moment.

He felt the room rock about him. He brushed his hand across his eyes. Then he looked up at Sumner and said quietly, "You've upset me." Sumner would have spoken but Lincoln raised his hand for silence and Sumner subsided. "Before I reply to your request, Mr. Sumner, I'd like to ask a question or two. You've picked on Hamlin as my successor. What makes you think Hamlin can handle the South after the war so that Emancipation won't be a dead letter?"

"You've touched on a vital point, Mr. Lincoln," replied Sumner. "In choosing Hamlin, we choose a man who recognizes that reconstruction belongs to the Congress and not to the President."

Mary started to speak but Lincoln laid his hand on hers and she subsided, cheeks scarlet, blue eyes blazing.

"In other words," said the President, "you'd be able to control reconstruction yourself, Senator?"

"I'd be permitted to do my share, which I'm not now nor would be under your régime," very gravely.

"That is to say," Lincoln suddenly leaped to his feet

and pointed a long finger at the Senator, "that is to say, you think you're better qualified to handle a bruised and heartbroken South than I . . . you who've just admitted you've no bowels of compassion for those who differ from you! And you actually think that an attempt to thrust civic equality of the negro down those Southern throats already choked with sobs is going to insure civic equality to the negro for the future? Sumner, its against human nature. I tell you that every gesture that the Congress will make to confiscate the plantations for the negro sets back his enjoyment of equality another ten years."

"Great God!" Sumner's arms shot toward the ceiling. His face was contorted. "Maudlin sympathy with the greatest crime—"

Lincoln interrupted. "Never mind the oratory, Senator."

Sumner, arms still in the air, stared at Lincoln, amazed and indignant.

Lincoln drew himself to his full height, dropped the ivory paper knife into his vest pocket and said very softly and clearly, "I'm not going to resign."

Sumner slowly lowered his arms and groaned, "God help the negro!"

"He will!" Lincoln nodded. "But I intend He shall help him during the next two years by showing Abraham Lincoln how to save the Union."

Sumner picked up the Dante manuscript and thrust it into the pocket of his cape. Mary and Lincoln watched him motionless. The clock on the mantel chimed six. Sumner bowed.

"Then, Mr. Lincoln, I will wish you good-by. And you, dear Mrs. Lincoln, who have been so kind a friend and hostess, I must say good-by to you also."

Mary made him a sweeping bow and stood with her nose in the air, watching him make his very dignified exist. Then she threw herself into her husband's arms. "Abra'm! Abra'm! What shall we do to him?"

Lincoln held her close and patted her back. "Mary, we'll make him come back to us if we can. In fact there's no if about it. As I've said before, I've got to have Sumner."

"What will he do next?" asked Mary, moving away from Lincoln to look anxiously up into his face. "Will he try impeachment?"

"Not in the midst of war, I reckon," replied the President. "That would be too much like stopping to set a rat trap while the house was burning up. Even Congress must see that. Well, thank God, that's over. Now I know what I've got to fight."

CHAPTER IV

CREATED EQUAL

SHORTLY after supper that evening, Billy Stoddard came into the office and closed the reception room door behind him to say in a low voice:

"Mr. Hamlin has just come in with Fred Douglass, sir, and the other visitors are making it uncomfortable for Douglass. How about taking him into the secretaries' office?"

"Bring him in here," returned Lincoln.

With a little smile, Stoddard went out. A moment later Hamlin entered, followed by a tall, well-built colored man in the conventional black broadcloth frock suit. Douglass was handsome in a brooding and tragic way. The story of his heroic struggle was written in the distrustful curve of his thin, well-cut mouth and in the unbelief of his dark eyes: eyes set far apart under quizzical brows and a broad forehead. His nose was the Indian's rather than the negro's, well arched, with close nostrils. His high cheek bones and hollow cheeks gave his whole face the look of austerity that marks the thinker rather than the fighter. His chin was concealed by a short black beard and his whole aspect was rendered doubly striking by the mass of black hair that stood up like a great halo round his head.

Lincoln shook hands with him. "I reckon we need no introduction, Mr. Douglass. You were a long time getting here."

"I've been up in Canada, Your Excellency. I was in

hopes that some of the fugitive slaves up there would come back and help me preach the gospel of freedom. I was much troubled when I learned I'd been keeping Your Excellency waiting."

"I'd rather be called plain Mr. Lincoln, if you please, Mr. Douglass. Sit down and let's talk. How about the draft bill, Hamlin? Will it go through before the session ends?"

"It'll go through to-morrow," answered the Vice President, sinking into the Cabinet chair next to the one Douglass had taken, while Lincoln took the rocker and slowly elevated his feet to the mantel.

"I sweat when I think what enforcing that measure'll mean," he mused.

"Papa day," called Tad, curled up on a sofa with his kitten, "you wememba what mother said about you' feet?"

"Jings, yes!" exclaimed the President, dropping the offending members. "Will the bill go through as I last saw it, Hamlin?"

"Yes, Mr. Lincoln," replied Hamlin who had twisted about to glare at Tad.

"I've been out of touch with the papers," said Douglass. "Will you tell me if you draw the color line in the bill, Mr. Vice President?"

Hamlin turned back to the fire. "All able-bodied male citizens between eighteen and forty-five are made subject to call after July 1, 1863. Drafted persons can furnish a substitute or pay $300 bounty for exemption!"

"I don't like the bounty idea," commented Lincoln, "but Chase is jubilant over it. Says it will be a full meat course to the Treasury." He turned abruptly to Douglass. "Mr. Douglass, how do you and your colored friends feel about the Emancipation Proclamation?"

"That it's thoughtful, cautious and well guarded," answered Douglass.

"Come now, that's no answer!" cried Lincoln. "The average run of colored man thinks nothing of the kind."

Douglass smiled. "You asked me what I and my friends thought, sir! Most of my people are enthusiastic, if they are anything. I was in Boston on January first with that great mass of people of every color waiting in Tremont Temple to hear by telegraph whether or not you'd signed the Proclamation. It was midnight before word came over the wire, 'It's signed!' People all over the hall began to sob for joy. It looked for a little while as if we could find no other way to express our feelings until a colored preacher with a glorious voice jumped up and began to sing 'Sound the loud trimbel o'er Egypt's dark sea, Jehovah hath triumphed, His people are free—' Everybody joined him. It was superb—this report pleases you more, doesn't it, Mr. Lincoln?"

Lincoln stared at Douglass. This was like no negro he'd ever known. There was no least trace of servility here. Come to think of it, this was the first time he'd ever observed the man beneath the mask of bondage, the first time he'd seen the negro as he showed himself to his own race, never to the white. Douglass actually was sneering at him!

Lincoln found it more stimulating than irritating. He glanced at Hamlin's anxious face and thought with amusement that the Vice President would like to give Douglass an admonitory nudge.

"I'm going to the wrong barrel for soft soap, eh, Mr. Douglass?" he said. "You're not grateful to us for the Proclamation?"

Douglass' tragic face softened. "There's not a col-

ored man who knows of you who wouldn't die for you,
Mr. Lincoln, but we wish you weren't so timid. We
don't believe you'll really finally end slavery when it
comes to reconstructing the Union."

"Et tu, Brute!" grunted Lincoln. "What would you
have me do?"

"Organize colored regiments at once on an exactly
equal status with white regiments. Let us fight for our
freedom ourselves," replied Douglass quickly.

"Colored men have larger motives for being soldiers
than white men," declared Lincoln grimly, "and should
be grateful for a chance to enlist on any terms."

Douglass leaned forward, his hands on his knees and
spoke across Hamlin as though he and the President
were alone. "Mr. Lincoln, this war is something the
white race has brought on itself by its own hoggishness.
So the negro feels. And unless you understand clearly
how we feel you will never be able to enforce emancipation or handle reconstruction. It's very hard for us
negroes to feel gratitude toward any but God. As a
race we have no more inherent loyalty to the whites than
they have to us. But we're not fools. We see in this
war an opportunity to break our chains and you can't
offer us a task too hard for us to tackle. But for God's
sake, offer us tasks as you'd give them to men and not
to beasts of burden."

James came in to renew the fire just as Douglass
finished his plea. His black eyes widened as he saw
Douglass, and as he heard his words he dropped the
tongs with a clatter that caused the kitten to spit and
Tad to giggle.

"Tad," said Lincoln, "you go ask your mother for a
plate of those Vermont greenings."

"I'll fetch 'em, Massa Lincum, sah," proferred James
with alacrity.

The President nodded and looked broodingly into the flames for a moment before he said, "I've never tried to fool myself about this war, Mr. Douglass. I know we're working out in bitter humiliation the sins of two hundred years. We're drinking the dreadful cup to the dregs. But all this being acknowledged, I still in my humility must face facts as facts. And one fact is that white folks up to now have had an insuperable prejudice against using negroes in the army for anything but servants. I've no such prejudice myself but I've felt I must wait until our need for men was so great that colored soldiers would be welcomed before forming negro regiments."

"Surely that time has come now, Mr. Lincoln!" ejaculated Hamlin. "Our regiments hardly average more than four hundred men. The country's in despair over its losses."

"I can't see why you're so sure colored men would enlist," said Lincoln, looking not at Hamlin but closely at Douglass. "All efforts to organize black troops last year proved, if not actually abortive, at least ineffectual. I'd hoped after the Edict of Freedom was signed that Fortress Monroe and Yorktown might be garrisoned by colored troops to free the whites for weak spots where they're badly needed. But out of all the colored population down there, General Dix found only four or five willing to take up arms. They said they'd work but not fight."

"They're too close to their old masters down there!" exclaimed Douglass. "They fear reprisals. Try Massachusetts negroes."

"Why don't they come North?" insisted Lincoln. "Why has the Proclamation failed to bring them over the line?"

"Most of them have never heard of the Proclamation," answered Douglass. "The South would see to that."

"Ah! now we're getting down to the marrow!" exclaimed the President. "Douglass, how shall we get word to those people that it's time to come over into Canaan?"

"More than a word's needed, sir! There must be a promise that they shall not only be free but shall have equality. If you'll assure me of that, I'll go down into the Richmond country myself, even though I'm liable to be taken as a slave, and spread the tidings. You'll see them swarm across the Red Sea then."

"How can I promise any such thing!" ejaculated Lincoln, his heart sinking at this reiterated shortsightedness with all its implications. "Who can know the Southern attitude on that matter better than you? We can free the slaves by winning this war. We could give them the vote. But you know and I know that we'd have to exterminate the whites in the South before we could give the slave the kind of equality you want. I can't give them that equality. If they are given freedom, and when they've had education, the right to vote, the rest they'll have to earn through the generations to come—and that you and I or our children won't see, Douglass."

The colored man twisted his work-scarred hands together in a gesture of despair. "Oh, that Sumner or Chase were here in your place, sir!"

Lincoln shook his head impatiently. "And you actually believe that a scratch of my pen, or Sumner's or Chase's at my desk there, would change your color to the only shade the white has ever been willing to acknowledge covers his social equal? God knows, I want to see the negro eventually enjoy every civic right and privilege, Douglass, but—"

" 'Scuse me, Massa Lincum!" James, almost as black as his clothes, his round face twitching with excitement, appeared before Lincoln with a huge plate of apples which turned to green bronze in the firelight. " 'Scuse me but I got to have my say, sah! An' I'm going to say I ain't one of those niggers that's always wanting to set at the white man's table. I got my freedom and Massa Sumner's fixed it so's my chilluns and all colored chilluns is getting a white schooling right hea' in Washington. If you'll fix it so's my chilluns when they's grown kin hev the vote so's to help make the laws they live under, that's all I want. And what's more, Fred Douglass, his own self, knows if he went down below the line and gathered together all the niggers for a thousand miles and tried to lead 'em North, he couldn't lead 'em. Niggers is so jealous among theyselves they don't want to trust or help out a nigger that's gone ahead like Fred Douglass. There's Massa Sumner! What does he know about colored folks? He's too good to 'em. You're the one that knows 'em, Massa Lincum. Not Massa Sumner, or Massa Chase, or, 'scuse me, Massa Hamlin!"

He paused and banged the apples down on the scarred oak cabinet table, then waved his arm toward the sofa. "You might better give little mischievous Massa Tad over there the vote than the niggers the way they are to-day. Those Southern Massas would make the niggers vote theyselves back into slavery again! I'm telling you truth. Yassa!"

He crossed to the sofa, lifted the sleeping Tad and the purring kitten into his arms and disappeared into the private passage into the living room. No one spoke until Lincoln broke the silence.

"What I wanted to propose to you, Mr. Douglass, is this. Are you willing to organize a group of intelligent colored men into a company of scouts who will scatter themselves through the South and tell the slaves what we're trying to do up here and ask them to come up and help us fight? I'll guarantee to make them into soldiers, eventually, if I can just get the right men to officer them."

"I'll supply you with one white officer now!" exclaimed Hamlin.

"Who's that, Hamlin?"

"My son, Captain Cyrus Hamlin. He and a group of his friends, such as the sons of James Russell Lowell and Thomas W. Higginson, are tormenting the life out of me to get you to let them raise colored regiments and go under fire."

In Hamlin's face was a touching mixture of pride and sadness.

Lincoln felt quick tears flush his eyes. These New England Abolitionists! Of such stuff were martyrs immemorially made. All his caution was not proof against this.

"I'll give you a letter to Stanton to-night to let Cyrus go ahead. The passing of the draft bill to-morrow is going to put a different face on the negro soldier question, anyhow." He took a huge bite out of an apple.

"Do you mean it?" shouted Hamlin, jumping to his feet. As Lincoln nodded, Hamlin placed pen and paper before the President with one sweep of the hand. "Write that order now, sir, and I'll take it to my boy this minute! How about your boys, Mr. Douglass?"

"My three sons enlisted last year, Mr. Hamlin," replied Douglass.

Lincoln wrote the order and signed his name and smiled up at Hamlin who seized the paper and departed almost at a run.

"You haven't answered my question, Mr. Douglass," Lincoln said, when they were alone.

"I'm afraid our friend James answered for me, sir," replied Douglass. "I would need a white man identified in their minds with you to accompany me South, else the slaves wouldn't believe me."

Lincoln finished his apple and threw the core into the fire. "I think I can help you out there," he said finally. "My oldest son Bob is a level-headed fellow, almost through his law course at Harvard. How would it do for him to go along with you?"

Douglass stared as though he couldn't believe his ears. "Will your son agree to that, Mr. Lincoln?"

"If Cyrus Hamlin can do his job, I reckon my son can do his," answered the President.

"Then, Mr. Lincoln," exclaimed Douglass, "all I can say is that all that I have is at your service." He rose as the President rose and after a moment in which he fought to control his quivering lips he added, "Sir, Mr. Secretary Chase has had me eat at his own table. Senator Sumner, John Brown, Wendell Phillips, have fraternized with me. And yet, in spite of our topic of conversation to-day, you're the only man who's ever made me for a moment forget the curse of my color."

"The thing I don't like to remember is that it's we white men who've made a curse of that color," said Lincoln. "But be patient with us, Mr. Douglass. We're trying to make it right—with our heart's blood." He shook hands and added, "You work out a scheme and come to me when it's finished." He walked with Douglass to the door, came back and looked at his watch. He must see the waiting folk in the reception room before reading the despatches on his desk and it was now nine o'clock. He rang the bell for Stoddard.

Although the break with Sumner was now the most consuming of Lincoln's anxieties, it was impossible for him to give to it the best of his thought. The public dissatisfaction with himself and with his generals, particularly with Grant, pressed upon him with ever-increasing violence and would not be ignored for a moment, day or night.

A few days after his momentous five-o'clock tea party, he asked Nicolay to bring him the week's vintage of aspersions on Grant's character and ability. Nicolay's solemn face did not change as he with James' help brought in two great baskets heaped with telegrams and letters.

"Here's a part of 'em, sir," he said as they emptied the baskets on the Cabinet table. "I'll bring more when you're finished. We've divided them into States. These are all from Wisconsin, Iowa and Illinois. The newspaper comments aren't filed as yet."

Lincoln grunted, took a turn or two around the table with his hands clasped behind his back, looked out the window, blurred by rain, and shook his head. "Lord, how I dread to wade in! I don't want to see the newspapers, George. These are closer to the people." He seized a handful of letters and began running rapidly through them. "Looks as if Grant were about as popular as I am! 'Can't hope to keep confidence of nation if you permit General Grant to continue his futile butchery before Vicksburg.'—Grant, a drunken bum—a common roysterer . . . lazy . . . Rosecrans the real general—'" He dropped the letters. "Oh, take them away again, George! They give me the hiccoughs."

Nicolay carefully began to re-stack the letters. Lincoln watched him, talking half to himself, half to his secretary as had become his custom under the influence of Nicolay's understanding and sympathy. "What's the truth about Grant?—I'm not going to get myself into another blind road like I did with McClellan—I never even saw Grant.—He has no personal hold on me.—But he *fights,* though he mostly loses.—Most of 'em don't fight. They argue. I wish I *knew* about Grant. I have a feeling that he's the general I almost think is a fabled giant. George, I'd like to send you out there to look him over. No, I can't spare you. I'll send Charles Dana. You know, that old newspaper man who did such a fine job investigating cotton speculations in the army last year for Stanton?—I'll make my decision as to Grant on Dana's report on him, plus anything Grant may do in the meantime, plus my own feelings about him—"

He fell into silence, watching Nicolay pile the letters with a growing unease. After all, he ought not to put these messages by with nothing but a grunt.

"The thing I get most strongly from those messages, Nicolay, is that the people are in a dangerous state of gloom. They feel ugly because they feel helpless. They've found their military leaders and they've found me continually failing them. Confidence in man is dead and suspicion reigns. It's a time when every foul bird comes abroad and every dirty reptile rises up. The people need a new sign-post. The only one I can refer them to is the One above—and that's a preacher's job. I'm no preacher, God knows, but perhaps if I tell them how my own mind runs just now it would help. I can put it into the proclamation of the national fast day the Senate has asked for."

He had forgotten Nicolay. He walked to the windows and stood staring out blindly at the dim top of the half-finished Washington monument. Nicolay dropped

the packets of letters and listened eagerly to the muttered fragments that reached him. After a moment, he
took out his pencil and began to jot them down in his
notebook.

"—And insomuch as we know that by his divine law,
nations, like individuals, are subjected to punishments
and chastisements in this world, may we not justly fear
that the awful calamity of civil war which now desolates
the land may be but a punishment inflicted on us for our
presumptuous sins to the needful end of our national re-
formation as a whole people? We have been the recipients of the choicest bounties of Heaven. We have been
preserved these many years in peace and prosperity. We
have grown in numbers, wealth and power as no other
nation ever has grown, but we have forgotten God. We
have forgotten the gracious hand which preserved us in
peace and multiplied and enriched and strengthened us;
and we have vainly imagined, in the deceitfulness of our
hearts, that all these blessings were produced by some
superior wisdom and virtue of our own. Intoxicated
with unbroken success, we have become too self-sufficient
to feel the necessity of redeeming and preserving grace,
too proud to pray to the God that made us:

"It behooves us then to humble ourselves before the
offended Power, to confess our national sins and pray for
clemency and forgiveness:

"Now, therefore . . . I do by this my proclamation
designate and set apart Thursday, the 30th day of April,
1863, as a day of national humiliation, fasting and
prayer. And I do hereby request all the people to abstain
on that day from all their secular pursuits and to unite at
their several places of public worship, and their respec-
tive homes to keep the day holy to the Lord and devoted
to the humble discharge of the religious duties proper to

that solemn occasion.—All this being done in sincerity and truth, let us then rest humbly in the hope authorized by divine teaching that the united cry of the nation will be heard on high and answered with blessings no less than the pardon of our national sins, and the restoration of our now divided and suffering country to its former happy condition of unity and peace—"

He experienced a peculiar relaxation of the nerves as he turned from the window to his desk. In uncovering the sign-post for the people he had once more given to himself the final justification of the dreadful responsibility he had assumed.

CHAPTER V

THE RAPPAHANNOCK

THE Lincolns missed Charles Sumner. It had been his custom to drop into the White House daily and to stay frequently for a meal; breakfast, dinner or supper. His hours were entirely uncertain. He and Tad were devoted friends and it had not been unusual for Lincoln or Mary to come upon the huge Senator in Tad's bedroom, boy and man on the floor intently reproducing Bull Run with toy soldiers and the contents of the wood and coal baskets. He had discovered that the President's most relaxed moments were during the hour before midnight. He had been apt then to appear at the door of Lincoln's bedroom, a little apologetic but full of some problem of state, usually connected with England. The dearest thing to Sumner, after negro enfranchisement, was the maintaining of peace with this country which he loved so well.

All these delightful moments now ceased.

Lincoln missed him. There was more than deep anxiety in his dismay over Sumner's dereliction. His affections suffered. Mary's sorrow was mixed characteristically with exasperation, but she fully recognized the gravity of the situation and kept her sharp and witty tongue well under control as far as making comments outside the family circle was concerned. She used her husband as usual, as a safety valve.

"How can you delay so long in doing something," she urged at breakfast one morning in April, "about—" a glance at Tad, "you know what?"

"I'm doing something," replied the President. "I've agreed we'll leave on the sixth on the *Carrie Martin*. General Hooker is all ready for us."

"What do you mean, Abra'm?" signaling to James to bring her Lincoln's coffee cup.

"Hoo-way!" shouted Tad, spilling a spoonful of corn-meal mush over his new black Eton coat. "That means we'll see the A'my of the Potomac!"

"You've been hacking at me to get away from Washington for a while, Mary," said the President. "What do you say to four or five days in Virginia with General Hooker?"

"Just the thing for you!" replied his wife with a sniff and a twinkle. "It will be an exquisite rest for you to listen to General Hooker's troubles and quarrels, amidst the dogwood and magnolias of old Virginia, with John Hay at one elbow, introducing the three thousand officers, each with an ax to grind, and Nicolay at—"

"John Hay's gone to do an errand for me in Florida," Lincoln smiled.

"The principle remains the same," replied Mary, airily. "However, I'm grateful even for that much. At least I shall have the ride alone with you to and from the steamer—except for Tad, the coachman, the footman and the cavalry guard.—What I really referred to was Charles Sumner. Why don't you talk to Representative Hooper about him?"

"I don't make a big move there till I see light, Mary. I reckon my cue for a while is to piece along, a little here, a hint there," declared the President. "Isn't that a new flummydiddle you're wearing?" nodding at the little lavender silk shoulder cape of many ruffles.

Mary looked extremely gratified. "Yes, Lizzie Keckley's introducing them over my shoulders as it were!

You really are becoming quite extraordinary, Abra'm!
You've observed crinolines and capes in a single month.
Do you like this?"

"I do!" thinking how pretty she was with her cheeks
flushed and pleased with himself for his unwonted gal-
lantry. "I like to see you having what you want after
all your years of pinching and going without. You were
as good a wife as any poor man ever had, my dear,"
going round the table to kiss her with the homely sense
of comfort that meant Mary to him.

Her suggestion with regard to Sam Hooper remained
with him as he ascended the stairs and was still fluttering
in the background of his thoughts when General Butler
was announced later in the morning. Butler, a small
bald-headed man with a large sword ornamenting a magnificent major-general's uniform, entered with his usual
pomposity and in a voice that could be heard at the
Capitol demanded to be sent back to New Orleans.

"General," said Lincoln, taking off his spectacles and
running his fingers through his black hair, "I'd like to
send you back there. You're a first-rate executive and
you've a big political following. But until the Woman
Order's forgotten I don't dast uncover you."

"Seward, again or still, I suppose!" ejaculated Butler.
"Why in the name of God don't you get a statesman
instead of a peanut politician into his job? Sumner's
the proper person to be our Secretary of State. But, of
course, you've been so unwise as to break with Sumner."
Suddenly he leaned confidentially across Lincoln's desk
beside which he was sitting. "Mr. President, I wonder
if you realize that there's a particularly nasty kind of
gossip going about concerning that?"

Lincoln eyed the General a little wonderingly. Butler

was impetuous and said to be none too scrupulous politically. But it didn't seem probable that he was an idle tale bearer.

"I hope you aren't going to make me plug up my ears this very busy morning, General," he suggested.

"It's whispered about," blurted Butler, "that you've forbidden Sumner the house because of his attentions to Mrs. Lincoln."

Lincoln could feel his gorge rise. He came to his feet and glared down at the little military man with extreme distaste. "I've a good notion to show you out the door with my foot, Butler, the way I do Tad's pup when he throws up his bone. Maybe you'd better leave before the notion gets the better of me."

"I know I'm making a disgusting impression," admitted Butler, rising but not moving toward the door. "But in spite of that, sir, I'm a gentleman, a gentleman driven to use an extreme remedy for an extreme case. Some one has got to be willing to risk his reputation, sir, to save yours. I am that unlucky man, it seems. But I insist that you allow me to say that you ought not to allow the break with Sumner to last another hour. I can mend the breach for you. I have great influence with Sumner. He and I go arm-in-arm on reconstruction. You permit Sumner and me to work out the Louisiana problem together and I'll guarantee that Sumner will appear at the White House as of old."

Lincoln stood motionless, struggling for complete self-control. Political bargaining was common enough and did not offend him. But no one before had dared use in this way the outrageous gossip that was embittering Mary's days in Washington. After a moment he walked slowly to the door, opened it and stood waiting.

Butler measured him with a long glance from head to foot, then moving, Lincoln thought, like a figure on a stage, he stalked out of the room.

Secretary Chase passed Butler on the threshold. The two men bowed but did not speak. Lincoln closed the door, seated himself on the edge of the Cabinet table and waited for the Secretary of the Treasury to make known his errand. Chase stood upright on the hearthrug, his six feet of height as impressive as though he carried Lincoln's extra four inches; a handsome man of fifty-five, of pure Anglo-Saxon type. Lincoln always watched him with a combination of amused tolerance and admiration. Chase with his petty intrigues and his vanity, his dignity and his high ideals—another of his enemies, Lincoln told himself but, O, what a superb Secretary of the Treasury!

"General Butler isn't happy away from New Orleans, I fancy," said the Secretary.

"He's as full of poison gas as a dead dog," was Lincoln's deliberate comment.

Chase winced. "He's a very able man. Would do well in Grant's place but of course, as this war is being run, he's too able to be put there." Having delivered this shot he drew a document out of his green bag. "You're not reconciled, I understand, Mr. Lincoln, to the workings of the legal tender act of March third."

"It's too late to be worried about that one. It's the third act you contemplate pushing through Congress, Mr. Chase, that I want to get expert opinion on. I have great confidence in your ability but I think you ought to have an outside expert's report that can be used in the newspapers to make people understand that the acts are a military necessity as well as sound finance."

Chase nodded. "Senator Fessenden or Representative

Hooper are the best financial men in Congress. Both
have the confidence of the public."

"Excellent!" exclaimed Lincoln. "Let's get Hooper
at it. He's a genial fellow, while Fessenden is as bitter
as one of his own wild Maine apples. Tell Hooper to
come up here for a talk with me. And now, give me
some details about the working of the bounty idea. I'll
have Nicolay bring in some sample protests that we've
had from the West."

The remainder of the morning the two men spent on
the bounty and its attendant evils. Lincoln worked with
the taste of Butler's nasty proposition still in his mouth.
He believed that even Chase, who was devoted to Sumner and to Butler, would have sympathized with his sense
of insult. But Chase was the last man in whom he would
have cared to confide. He could not, in fact, see how he
could speak of the matter to any one.

Late that afternoon, Congressman Hooper called.
He was a man of about Lincoln's age, conspicuously
well dressed, wearing a high black satin stock which added
to his smooth-shaven dignity. He had inherited wealth
and was a highly successful importer and banker. The
President listened to his dissertation on the green-back
with growing satisfaction.

"You put that all into an essay, Mr. Hooper," was
his comment, "and we'll get the *Atlantic Monthly* to
publish it first, the newspapers later. Do you know
anybody else who understands money and has a mellow
gift of gab?"

Hooper looked thoughtfully at the open window
through which vagrant tidings of young April wandered
and after a moment said, "Try Chittenden, the Register
of the Treasury. He talks and writes delightfully."

"He's a naturalist, too, of no mean parts!" exclaimed

Lincoln. "I met him through Charles Sumner. He
helped Sumner on the bill taking the duty off ornamental
trees and shrubs. Do you remember that speech of
Sumner's ending with 'Encourage them till Burnham
woods do come to Dunsinane'?"

"I remember," replied Hooper. "Sumner knows
everything."

"The knowledge I most envy his possessing right now
is his familiarity with the British," said Lincoln. "My
wife calls him England's Lone Lover."

Hooper smiled. "The women all admire him. As for
me, he's the best friend I have in the world."

"I wish he were mine!" Lincoln's head drooped
wearily.

Hooper walked over to the window and looked at the
magnolias flushing below and returned to stand before
the empty grate beside which the President sat in his
rocker. "I'm in a delicate position, Mr. Lincoln. I'm
in Sumner's confidence but I don't think I breach it when
I tell you that I warned him that a break between him
and yourself on reconstruction policies was a national
catastrophe. And for all that I love and admire him as
I do no other human being, I cannot go as far or as fast
as he does in vindictiveness toward the South. He needs
you and you need him. Mr. Lincoln," in a deeply troubled voice, "can't I be of service in bringing you together?"

"I wish you could be," replied Lincoln. "But Sumner
wants to get rid of me, not work with me. He asked
me to resign. Did he tell you that?"

"Judas Priest, no!" exclaimed Hooper. He did not
speak for a moment. Then he said earnestly, "Mr. Lincoln, I hope you didn't take that as representative of any
large group."

"Oh, I reckon it's large enough, friend Hooper. You couldn't put it in a pint measure. Would it be in bad taste to ask you what Sumner's doing now?" Lincoln in his turn walked to the window and came back.

"I've heard him say nothing about your resignation, sir. He is, of course, frankly much out of patience with you and is criticizing you freely. That you know." Hooper looked uncomfortable.

"The question *was* in bad taste. Let it go," said the President.

"Did you ever think of Sumner as Secretary of State?" asked Hooper. "His work as Chairman of the Committee on Foreign Affairs has given him such diplomatic prestige that I should think—"

"He'll never bargain with his principles," interrupted Lincoln. "I don't hope for that. What I do hope is to call him off his campaign against me as President.—As to giving him Seward's job, I can't dispense with Seward now, Mr. Hooper. Minister Adams is doing a good chore in England and he and Seward are good friends. A year or so from now, things won't be so critical there. But if Sumner will cease to oppose my Presidency and I'm reëlected, I'll be willing to think of him as Secretary of State then. God knows I'd be glad to loosen his choke on the Senate!"

Both men smiled.

"Are you willing to let me toy with that idea for a little while, Mr. President?" asked the Congressman.

"Yes, I am," replied Lincoln, "and I'll thank you very much for any effort whether it's successful or not." He shook hands with Hooper and went thoughtfully to his room to make ready for a dinner party Mary had arranged for a visiting French prince.

Bob came home the next morning. He had spent a

few hours shopping in New York and presented himself to his father clad in the result. Lincoln looked up from his desk to examine him delightedly. Bob wore a short-coated suit of the largest plaids his father ever had seen, purple and green being the dominating tones. A yellow velvet vest. White spats. A broad-brimmed, flat-crowned hat of ivory white felt.

"Bob, whereabouts are you going to exhibit your beauty so it won't cause a riot?" exclaimed his father.

"I'm open to suggestion. Pretty handsome, eh, Father?"

"Beats a summer sunset. I suggest Ford's Theater, if you can get there without being arrested. At any rate, keep away from timid horses, young children and ammunition stores.—Sit down, Bob, I've a job for you. Pull your chair up close."

He outlined Fred Douglass' scheme which now was well matured. "You're to go down to Fortress Monroe," he ended, "and strike out from there. You are to promise the negroes but two things, freedom and work. The details are your problem, not mine."

Bob sat on the edge of his chair, blue eyes blazing. He said nothing for a moment, then suddenly gave his father a tremendous bear hug. "When do I start?"

"To-night, with utmost secrecy. Douglass is coming in this afternoon and you must talk with him. You're to be gone not over three weeks. My one insistence is that I hear from you at least twice a week. You know how you neglect your mother on that, Bob!"

"Yes, sir," replied Bob as meekly as he could manage for excited joy. "I guess I'll go out and show these clothes while I can."

He rushed away followed by Lincoln's affectionate smile.

Mary, faced with the ultimatum in regard to Bob's errand was, as usual on such occasions, philosophical. She cried a little, said she didn't want to know details as that would give her the more to worry about, and then called Bob's attention to the fact that a youth old enough to be sent by the President of the United States on an errand of importance was supposedly old enough not to torment his little brother.

"I wasn't tormenting him, mother! I beg your pardon," protested Bob. "I'm trying to give him a little training. He's not only pert and spoiled but he has no manners."

"Is that why he's nearly always shrieking, 'Stop it, Bobbie!' when you're alone with him?" inquired his mother. "Just what were you to stop this time."

"This time I was to stop covering his mouth with my hand because he was spitting at me!" replied Bob, virtuously.

Mary threw up both her hands. Lincoln gave a shout of laughter.

"Oh, you're all just children!" cried Mary. "No wonder you men can't end the war. I wish we women folks had the chance just—"

Lincoln flew to his office, leaving Bob half laughing and half protesting.

The following day, in a strange April snowstorm, Lincoln, with Mary and Tad, boarded the little steamer *Carrie Martin* to make the promised visit to the Army of the Potomac.

Try as he would Lincoln could not put on a holiday mood. Mary herself was depressed. She said the snowstorm meant bad news.

"Don't say that! The attack on Charleston begins to-day," protested Lincoln.

"Over your opposition?" exclaimed Mary.

He nodded and then yielded to Tad's demands that they go over the boat together. When they came on deck after examining the engine room, the snow was receding among the rose-colored hills and lovely green orchards twinkled in the sunset. Lincoln took the clearing weather as a good omen but Mary shook her head.

"Snow in April means tears," she sighed.

She persuaded him to go to bed soon after supper. But the berth was too short for him and he spent the hours from midnight to dawn on deck, wrapped in a blanket, dozing and worrying.

They reached Acquia Creek soon after breakfast and made a quick landing, with only a glimpse of placid water and rolling hills before they were packed into an army ambulance and whirled toward Army Headquarters at Falmouth.

Virginia in early spring! Poetry incarnate! Lincoln was in the saddle all day long during the short visit, exploring with General Hooker and his aides the terrain over which the next battle with Lee must be fought. Tad, little gray cape flying in the wind, followed his father hour after hour. The child's presence among the grim impedimenta of war seemed as incongruous as the fact that this delicate fairyland of fragrant woods, budding meadows, and red-plowed fields dotted with young plants must be given over to carnage. But war, after all, was incongruous to all that was best and beautiful in life. General Hooker, to whom Lincoln voiced these thoughts, agreed with him.

Hooker's plan of battle seemed excellent to Lincoln. There were but two weak points, one of which he pointed out to the General, the other to Mary. Hooker did not plan to throw all of his 135,000 men into the fight—

McClellan's old weakness. Lincoln pointed this out to Hooker and to his officers, not only in conferences but at the dinner party given to the President by Hooker the night before the return to Washington. Lincoln's last word to the assembled company was *"Put all your men in!"*

Of Hooker's other weakness Lincoln said to Mary that night in their tent, "Hooker's too sure of his own powers. It's the worst thing about him and will undo him, I'm afraid. I can't make my orders more positive unless I drive them in with a club. I've said to him twenty times, 'Beware of rashness! Beware of rashness! But use all your resources in one great drive.' I can't say it more clearly, can I?"

"Any one who doesn't understand your English is a fool," replied Mary flatly. "If Hooker fails and puts up the usual excuse that your orders confused him, I'd cut his head off at the waistline, instantly. Don't stand round in your stocking feet, Abra'm. This tent floor's as cold as my heart is said to be. Here are your slippers."

"Is Tad well tucked in?" asked Lincoln, sitting down beside the candle with the Richmond *Examiner,* which had been sent over the river that day by a sardonic Rebel. No news had come through from Washington and he hoped to find some here.

"I wouldn't add Taddie to my burdens, if I were you," said Mary. "You've tucked the Army of the Potomac to bed. Isn't that enough?" She kissed him and began to braid her hair.

Lincoln unfolded the paper and gave a start as the headlines met his eye. He devoured the items that followed and then ejaculated, "The expedition to Charleston failed! They beat off the ironclads!"

"I told you so!" groaned Mary.

Lincoln shook his head. "They would do it! I had no more weight than Taddie." He sat brooding. Queer he couldn't harden himself to taking the Union reverses coolly. Heaven knew there'd been enough of them to inure him. Here was another sleepless night ahead of him unless he put Charleston out of his mind. He dropped the paper and opened the Bible. But he couldn't focus his mind on it and shortly laid it aside.

"What are you thinking of, my dear?" asked Mary.

"Of Charles Sumner! I've tried to forget him, but Jings! I can't. Seems he was down here with the Committee on the Conduct of the War last week and every general in the army seized on the opportunity to tell him how the war could be won were I out of the way." He gave her a rueful smile.

"Who told you that?" Mary's eyes were snapping.

"Hooker, when I pressed him pretty hard to-day on putting all his men in, used it as a sort of hint that I'd better not interfere too much."

"I'd hoped we could forget Charles Sumner for a week," exclaimed Mary, indignantly.

"So had I," agreed Lincoln. "But as a matter of fact he's not been fully out of my thoughts. Hooker's remark didn't startle me into any sudden recollection of him. He was there!"

"Abra'm, why don't you do something about Sumner?" urged Mary.

"I'm doing all that I can see to do," replied Lincoln. "I've got the whip hand at one point. I can appoint military Governors to carry on my kind of reconstruction in the conquered States and he can't. That's one of my duties as Commander-in-Chief. I'm steaming ahead on that as fast as I can as the best way to fight

Sumner. I wrote General Banks the day we came down here to begin to enroll the loyalists in Louisiana with the idea of having them hold a fall election. They'll have to form a new constitution and then elect members to Congress. I expect to have things in such shape that in another year I'll have Louisiana, Florida, Tennessee and Missouri functioning again in the Union."

"Don't you think he could be persuaded to keep up even an outward appearance of friendship for the sake of public morale?" asked Mary, wistfully.

"You might try it, through Mrs. Hooper," said Lincoln with a grin. "Here's a chance for you to use your famous plan I miffed you so about."

"I tried it long ago and she found it hopeless," sighed Mary.

The conversation lapsed into a brooding silence on both their parts that lasted until they had gone to bed.

They returned to Washington the next night and Lincoln began at once to work on Stanton to make him send every possible aid to Hooker, and for days the muddy roads of the city were blocked with troops.

On the morning of the 25th of April, Stanton asked the President to review Burnside's 30,000 men who were going down to the Rappahannock from Annapolis. Until noon, Lincoln stood on the east steps of Willard's Hotel, bareheaded, as the troops tramped by him through Fourteenth Street. Many of the soldiers wore sprigs of dogwood which they tossed at his feet and by the end of the review he stood knee deep in blossoms which smelled to him of the fairy woods around Falmouth. The last of the passing soldiers he could not see for tears.

CHAPTER VI

BOB MAKES A CALL

HOOKER'S long fight on the Rappahannock, centering on Chancellorsville, began the last of April, and Lincoln gathered himself together to endure what he called his death sweat. During that week of dark messages he enjoyed but one brief hour of respite. Bob returned, tanned and dirty, one night, just as his father was going to bed. The recital of the boy's experiences Lincoln found as enjoyable as an evening at the theater. He gathered that Douglass had done his part nobly and that during the month over two thousand slaves had seen Bob and spoken with him.

"Not many," said Bob, "when you consider your need for them, but Douglass says that that two thousand will be multiplied by fifty as the word spreads. I'm returning to the job in June. And I'd like to take Edgar Welles along. He'll be useful."

Lincoln smiled and nodded. "The enlistment itch cooled for a while?" he asked, an affectionate arm over the shoulder of his first born.

"I haven't had time to think about it," replied Bob. "This is very important work, father! And its unique in that only your son will be accepted by the slaves. I wish you could have seen them! I swear I didn't know whether to laugh or cry."

"It has its drawbacks in that the public must still look on you as a coward," said the President, watching Bob's face. The boy had his mother's extreme sensitiveness.

"But any one by the name of Lincoln must get used to being misunderstood."

Bob nodded. "I don't mind too much, now that my conscience is clear—" He hesitated and under his tan grew a little pale. "But that isn't saying I don't mind the things they say about you, and as for mother—" He broke away from his father and took a turn up and down the room. "Father, I don't see how I can stand the kind of things they're saying now. If I could get at the originator of this latest lie, I'd kill him as I would a skunk!"

Lincoln paused in drawing on the old red dressing gown and looked at the boy a little anxiously. "I'd have said you were located the past few weeks where you couldn't hear anything, son."

"I was. But on the boat to-day I received an anonymous letter saying you'd booted Charles Sumner out of mother's room." His young voice broke miserably.

Lincoln suddenly hurled the dressing gown to the floor. "Now, by the eternal Heavens!" he shouted—then paused, arrested by the look of agonized shame on his son's face—Mary's face—tormented, quivering. "Jings, Bob! Have I got to explain to *you*—"

"Explain!" interrupted Bob, tensely. "Don't affront mother or me with that word!"

"Right!" agreed Lincoln. "Except as they cause her pain, they're beneath notice."

"You don't mean she's been told?" groaned Bob.

"I don't know. I suppose so. She doesn't tell me these things any more. Thinks she's protecting me, bless her," answered his father. "It's one of the prices we pay for the passions roused by slavery, Bob."

But Bob could not be philosophical. "Does Senator

Sumner know what's being said? Is there a break between you and him, father?"

"I don't know: to the first question. To the second: sit down and I'll give an answer in detail," picking up his dressing gown. He began to describe the last interview with Sumner, feeling that it was the best way to calm Bob.

The boy listened with his usual intelligent concentration. "I heard in Boston," he said when his father had finished, "that the Boston set was working to get you out and that Sumner was the leader. But I didn't believe it. Are you doing anything to offset them, father?"

"Only a little, here and there. Looks to me as if winning a few good battles would be the only final quietus I could put on the situation. If Hooker loses this fight—" He sighed and sank into a dreary review of the battlefield and plans. Every outline of both was graved on his heart.

After an uncounted passage of time, he found Bob still pacing the floor. "Go to bed, dear Bob. You'll be returning to college in the morning, I suppose."

"Sometime to-morrow," replied Bob vaguely, as he kissed his father good-night."

Lincoln spent the next morning in the War Office, receiving with Secretary Stanton and General-in-Chief Halleck the telegraphic reports of the fighting around Chancellorsville. Bob bade the family farewell at breakfast and started off, ostensibly to take the train for college. But as a matter of fact, he made a call first which delayed his journey for an hour.

He went to see Charles Sumner.

With or without John Hay, he had called on the Senator many times. Sumner's rooms were filled with choice engravings and objets d'art that fascinated this small-town boy who had inherited his mother's taste for fine things. So outwardly there was nothing unusual, save the early hour, about this visit.

Sumner, in a gray velvet dressing gown, was at breakfast trying to eat and at the same time dispose of the enormous pile of mail which heaped the empty spaces on the table, trespassed on the omelette platter, and overflowed to the floor. He jumped to his feet with his usual cordiality as Bob came in.

"Ah, Robert! Not on vacation still? At least, Easter didn't last so long in my day at Harvard. Will you have some breakfast?"

"No, thank you, Senator," replied Bob, then blushing to his own disgust he drew a dirty envelope from his pocket and laid it on the one Sumner had been reading last. "I—I came in to show you this, sir. It's anonymous."

"You've placed it on one from the Duke of Argyll," said Sumner with an amused grimace. But, as he read the missive, his face changed, his jaw worked, his blue eyes darkened so angrily that Bob was surprised when he said with entire urbanity:

"I suppose it's too much to hope that your mother hasn't received one of these—though I know she's protected from any letters that come through the usual channels."

"My father thought it likely that she had received one," replied Bob, irritated by the Senator's calm. "You take it coolly, Mr. Sumner! It seems to me an unendurable insult to all of you; mother, father, yourself."

"It's anonymous, so it must be endured," replied Sumner. "One hardens to this sort of thing, Robert. Ever since I first showed admiration for your wonderful mother, she and I have been made the subject of gossip.

It's as well that I've ceased to call at the Executive Mansion. The occasion for any such spasm of venom as this has ceased."

"Senator!" cried Bob. "How can you be so heartless! My father told me all about it. Doesn't friendship with a man like him and a lady like my mother mean anything to you? Oh, I know they're not of the British nobility, but they're the rulers of a great country and young as I am, sir, and clearly as I see their gaucheries, I tell you they're wonderful people, both of them! You'll not find their like in Washington or New York or the whole United States for brain and goodness. It's a pity and a shame for you to try to prevent my father from leading this country as he knows is best!"

Sumner, who had seated himself, listened to Bob's outburst with a certain sad patience. When the boy stopped for breath he gathered the letters out of the omelette dish and said slowly:

"I don't know how to explain to a youth of nineteen. You're very young for your years— What is it you want me to do, Robert?"

"I want you to go on being friends with my parents. To stop trying to oust Abraham Lincoln from the White House."

"I must do whatever seems best to me for the negro cause, Robert," in a troubled voice. "My dear boy, don't look at me as if you hated me!"

"I can't hate you, I wish I could!" groaned Bob. "We all love you at our house. Tad was mourning at breakfast because you've neglected him."

Sumner shook his great head and suddenly walked to the mantel and took down a tiny clock in a crystal globe set on the back of an exquisitely carved ivory camel.

"Take this to Taddie. He's often asked me for it. And give him my love."

Bob stood holding the clock, staring at it impatiently. "You just don't understand human love, do you, Mr. Sumner? A clock to solace Taddie's unrequited affection!" he exclaimed wonderingly.

The Senator threw his hands above his head, dropped them, then with a wide gesture of both arms swept the table before him clear of dishes and letters and buried his face in both hands on the table cloth. Bob looked wildly from the leonine head with its mass of chestnut hair to the clock and from the clock to the door. But before he could make an exit, Sumner lifted a tear-stained face and said in a voice of the mellow gentleness that was one of his great gifts:

"That touched me on the quick, Robert. Let me try to tell you something of myself— I had a twin-sister, Matilda, whom I loved to my very soul. I helped my mother to nurse her through a year of consumption. She died in my arms. We were just twenty-one. That was my first lesson in the futility of basing one's happiness on a thing as frail as human life.—Five years later, dear little Jane died of typhoid. She was seventeen—tall, dark, an exquisite musician."

He ruminated for a moment, then went on. "My father was a harsh man. I did my utmost to bring something of gentleness and beauty into our home so that, for a boy, I became peculiarly devoted to my mother, my brothers and sisters.—After Matilda and Jane left me, my dear sister Mary took their place in my heart. She was ten years younger than I. She grew to an extraordinary beauty, tall, stately, with a mind as brilliant and as avid as your mother's, with glorious chestnut hair wrapped round her head. She was a perfect companion, so lovely, so accomplished—"

Bob gently slid the little clock back to the mantel and dropped into the chair beside Sumner. Apparently the Senator did not follow his action, but when the young man laid a sunbrowned hand on the table, Sumner placed his own great white palm over it and clung to it throughout the remainder of his soliloquy.

"Mary too—consumption seized upon her. I remember the day we had to cut her beautiful hair. It hurt me to the soul. She too died in my arms. She was twenty-two. Prescott wrote me to comfort me and said:

> " 'Alas! for love if thou wert all
> And nought beyond on earth!—'

"My brother Horace was drowned in 1850 with Margaret Fuller Ossili. My brother Henry died of typhoid in 1852. Brother Albert with his dear wife and child were drowned at sea in 1856.—Only Julia and George and my dear mother are left me of all that fine household.—There's a blight awaiting every affection that grows within me.—I gave my very soul's soul to another when I was in my twenties. She wouldn't be my wife.—Mrs. Longfellow who was as dear as a sister to me was burned to death two years ago.—And as if death couldn't sufficiently blast me, one by one my ideals have destroyed my friendships."

There was a long silence except for the infinitesimal ticking of the little clock. He seemed to be reviewing the sad roster.

"—Charles Francis Adams whom I cared for as a brother, Richard Dana, the Ticknors—for years I was a social outcast in Boston. Men with whom I'd played as a boy, women who had invited me to their homes,

who had entrusted their children to me, college mates,
old teachers,—all cast me out because I dared to oppose
the institution of slavery. I was pariah—unclean—and
lonely—dear God, how lonely I have been and am. I
am a man acquainted with grief in all its forms, dear
Robert.—You tell me I don't understand human love.
I answer by repeating to you what William Prescott
wrote me of Mary:

> " 'Alas, for love if thou wert all
> And nought beyond on earth—' "

He crumpled the anonymous letter in one huge white
fist and tossed it into the empty grate. Bob did not stir
until Sumner, after a time and with a long sigh, freed his
hand and smiled at him.

"You'll take the little clock to Taddie, won't you,
Robert?"

Bob, with defeat in every line of his face, shook his
head and with suddenly quivering lips rushed from the
room. He *was* only nineteen.

That evening, as Lincoln worked in his office at his
belated correspondence, Taddie, inarticulate with temper, stamped into the room and threw himself on his
father with such vehemence that he knocked the President's arm against the ink bottle. He was followed by
Pete Kelley, a snub-nosed, freckle-faced boy of ten, in a
rusty suit of black. His brother had been killed at Fredericksburg. Lincoln hurriedly scrubbed the superfluous
ink off Tad's velvet Eton suit with his handkerchief while
above Tad's roaring he shouted to the wealthy tinner's
son:

"What's happened, Pete?"

"That there painter that's going to make your picture
has taken our theater to work in!" shouted Pete in reply.

"So Tad had to go crazy instead of going to his mother about it?"

"I tried to get him to go to her but he always runs to you when he wants something he shouldn't have," explained Perry.

Lincoln chuckled and placing a hand over Tad's mouth so as to be heard, said to Nicolay who came in at the moment:

"See if you can't get Carpenter to use some other room. I remember Tad's telling me several days ago he and Pete wanted to use this one."

"It's the state bed chamber, Mr. Lincoln," explained Nicolay with what seemed to Lincoln unnecessary vigor, "and the only space available for the artist's purposes. Brady's men are developing photographic plates in there and Tad has locked them in."

"Tad, go unlock that door!" ordered his father.

"I won't!" gasped Tad as soon as he was released.

Lincoln shook his head wearily, "Tad, you do make me a lot of trouble that you don't need to!"

Tad looked up into the worn face and with a renewed burst of tears handed the key to Nicolay.

"Now, let's go to mother." Lincoln rose and with a boy clinging to either hand, started for the sitting room.

"You mustn't say I made you twouble!" sobbed Tad. "It kills me. Pete, give him the clock. Give it to him so he'll fo'get I've been bad."

Very reluctantly, Pete dug into the bulging pocket of his roundabout and brought forth the ivory camel bearing the tiny clock. The children were the recipients of so many extraordinary gifts that the beauty of this particular one could not surprise the President. But its source did.

"Look, Mary!" he exclaimed as they entered the sitting room. "Here's Sumner's clock out of Pete's jacket pocket."

"'Tisn't Pete's fault," shrilled Tad. "I gave it to him. A man gave it to me just a little bit ago."

Mary took the pretty thing unseeingly. "Tad Lincoln, look at your suit. You'll have a whipping—"

"No! No, Mary!" interposed Lincoln. "I did that with my clumsy elbow."

Mary sniffed skeptically but gave Tad the benefit of the doubt and turned to the clock. "It stood on the mantel under the Dürer's Erasmus. Did a note come with it, Taddie? For goodness' sake, wipe his face, Abra'm."

Before Lincoln could pull out the inky wad in his pocket, Pete thrust a grimy rag into Tad's hand.

"Yes," said Tad, "one came and we tossed it in the waste basket in my woom. Get it, Pete, if the kitten hasn't chewed it. I think the black kitten's motha' plans to have mo' kittens in that basket. She likes it. She goes in it and sings and awanges the scwaps." He blew his nose and stuffed the handkerchief into his breeches pocket. "Does the clock make you feel betta', Papa day?"

"Yes, son, I reckon it helps," replied his father.

"Then come on, Pete, we'll go see what the pitcha' men say to us now," as his friend placed a crumpled note in Mary's hand.

The children departed and Mary and Lincoln deciphered the familiar scrawl. "Dearest Tad: Time heals all things. I shall always love you. Charles Sumner."

Husband and wife gazed at each other. "Shall I acknowledge it?" asked Mary.

Lincoln shook his head. "You might frighten him off. This may mean he's repenting." He placed the clock tenderly on the mantel and stood looking at it. After a moment he turned to say, "Stonewall Jackson was fatally wounded in the fighting yesterday."

"Perhaps since we can't develop good officers of our own, God intends to help us by removing the Rebel geniuses," suggested Mary.

"Hooker is *not* throwing in all his men as I told him to," Lincoln said, laconically.

The two exchanged a long troubled look and left each other, Mary to seek Tad, Lincoln to more torturing hours in Stanton's office.

It was nearing midnight when belated dispatches left him no doubt that Hooker's defeat had been complete. For a moment, as full realization of the extent of the misfortune came home to him, he was panic stricken. He seized his soft hat, jammed it over his eyes and rushed from the War Department into LaFayette's Square where, among the trees, he prayed that he might for a moment be alone. Just to be alone!

He brought up under a magnolia tree, muttering, "What will the country say! What will it say!"

Great magnolia petals showered down on him. He brushed them aside with a groan. They carried the smell of funeral wreaths. A banging door roused him. It seemed that solitude for him was an unattainable commodity. His rush across the square had brought him near to Seward's house. A tall figure strode over the porch down the step, across the lawn, and under Lincoln's magnolia. Even in the dim starlight this was unmistakably Charles Sumner.

The two men clutched each other to keep from falling. Sumner had been in mad haste and the impact of his two hundred pounds was tremendous.

"Lincoln!" ejaculated the Senator. "I tell you I must

and shall know! I will not have your various Cabinet
members refuse to give me the news my own high office
entitles me to!" His voice was trembling with indignation.

"What news are you after, Senator?" asked Lincoln
gently, one arm over Sumner's shoulders.

Sumner answered with extraordinary vehemence.
"What's to be done about the cursed project of privateering? Will the disgusting Charles Wilson be removed as Secretary of Legation in London? But above
all, *what of Hooker?* For God's sake, what of Hooker,
Lincoln?"

"Seward can't answer those questions, Senator, because he doesn't know," replied the President. "Seward's let too much slip. I have to watch him. As for
war news, Stanton has to censor everything. I get most
of my news through Stanton."

"I've been to Stanton and insisted on getting facts,"
his voice rising again, "and he told me to go to the devil."

"And you've run into me!" with a short laugh. "I'll
make a bargain with you, Sumner. You know that's the
devil's speciality! Looks like I'm the only one that has
all the information you need. I'll give it to you any
time, day or night, without reserve, that you'll come to
the White House and ask me for it." Lincoln's pulse
had quickened. It looked like a heaven-sent moment.
He slid his arm down to link it in Sumner's. He felt the
Senator stiffen.

"You're taking an unfair advantage of me, Mr. Lincoln."

"I reckon I am," agreed Lincoln with a calm he did
not feel. "The devil generally does. Are you really
afraid I'll taint you with my doctrines, Sumner, if you

call on me occasionally? Doesn't it occur to you that it might be your duty to try to convert me?"

"It hadn't occurred to me," replied Sumner, slowly, his arm muscles relaxing.

Lincoln began to lead him toward the lighted north entrance to the White House grounds, talking as he did so of what seemed to him the least important of Sumner's queries.

"Charlie Wilson's worst failing appears to be that he sits in taverns with his feet on the table, saying hard things about the British and spitting on the floor," he remarked, smiling to himself.

"Isn't that sufficient to damn him?" cried Sumner. "Don't you realize that for every one that judges us Americans by the perfect manners of Charles Adams, there'll be a thousand who say we're all Wilsons?"

"You're absolutely right, of course," agreed Lincoln, lifting his hat as they passed the sentry at the gate. "What do you suggest I do to let Wilson down easy? He's an able newspaper reporter, remember. And whom shall we put in his place?"

"Will suggestions from me be killed by Seward?" asked Sumner.

"No, sir, they'll be used by me," replied Lincoln.

"Let me think it over until to-morrow," Sumner's voice was mollified. "And now, what of Hooker?"

"I mustn't talk of him until we reach my room. Walls have ears. Stanton's determined the worst shall be held back as long as possible." They were mounting the private stairs now and neither spoke again until Lincoln had closed the door behind them in his bedroom. He turned up the gas. The huge room with its heavy red hangings and massive rosewood furniture seemed oppressive. Or perhaps it was not the furnishings. Perhaps the many hours of travail he'd spent there gave it an imaginary dankness to Lincoln. His dressing gown lay across the bed foot, his slippers beneath. The bed was turned back. A volume of Shakespeare and of Petroleum Nasby lay on the bedside table with a plate of cookies and a glass of buttermilk. Mary!—

Sumner had walked directly to the war map fastened between the two south windows. Lincoln followed and began a rapid explanation of the day's movements at Chancellorsville. The Senator listened, breathing hard, but did not speak until Lincoln stopped. Then he sank into a chair and groaned, "All is lost!" in a voice of despair.

"No! No!" Lincoln patted him on the shoulder. "What're those lines from Milton you quoted to me after the second Bull Run?—'What though the field be lost? All is not lost—the unconquerable will—'" Lincoln smiled wistfully.

Sumner shook his head. "You don't give the whole of the thought:

> "'—the unconquerable will,
> And study of revenge, immortal hate,
> And courage never to submit nor yield.'"

"That's a bad line in there," admitted Lincoln. "We'll leave it to Lyman Trumbull and Ben Wade. By the way, I'd like to tell you about an experiment I made lately. Sit down."

He fetched his tooth-brush mug from the stand in the corner into which he poured half the buttermilk, handing the glass to Sumner. The Senator took it with a nod of thanks and helped himself to the cookies. Both men munched with enjoyment while the President told of Bob's recent expedition.

Sumner listened with absorption, nodding and saying, "Good! Good!" And when Lincoln told of one darky who had remarked that Massa Abraham was God and Massa Sumner the Holy Ghost, he laughed but with tears in his eyes.

It was nearing one o'clock when he rose to go, saying with that half-tender care for his friends which they never forgot nor could withstand, "Your face is ravished with weariness, dear Lincoln. Shall I ask James to give you a rubdown as I pass him in the hall?"

Lincoln shook his head with a "Thank you," and murmured to himself as the door closed on Sumner, "I've had something better than a rubdown."

But he sat long by the window wondering how far the news he had given Sumner about the failure of Hooker had gone to seal the Senator's conviction that he was unfitted to be Commander-in-Chief.

CHAPTER VII

OBERON

MARY was very much excited by Lincoln's account of Sumner's visit when he gave it to her the next morning at breakfast, but the President could not share her optimism. A man like Sumner, obsessed by a crusade, was not to be guided or controlled by ordinary sentiments, nor to be estimated by ordinary standards.

"The more I think about him, the less confidence I have in my ever getting what I call true friendship from Sumner," he told his wife. "I tell you honestly that I'm almost as uneasy as ever about him. I wish I knew what he and his gang are up to."

"Don't you expect him to repeat this call?" asked Mary, anxiously.

"I expect nothing but the unexpected from Sumner," replied the President. "However, I'll go so far as to say that I don't think he'll come unless absolutely driven to it for news."

"I'm going to see if I can't supply a different kind of bait," declared Mary.

Several days later, when Lincoln caught a glimpse of young Mrs. Hooper in the garden, he wondered in passing if the lovely lady was not Mary's "bait."

Alice Hooper had come more or less frequently to the White House receptions but this was her first informal call and she brought her small daughter with her. Tea was served in the garden under a young copper beech, the topmost branches of which touched the windows of the President's bedroom. Blooming pink rose beds lay to the south of the beech and green lawn beyond. A slight haze of gold hung in the air, forerunner of the dust in which the marching troops would shortly veil the city. In the pauses of conversation, the women were conscious of a faint sound as of thunder to the southwest. Hooker was trying to head off Lee's cavalry from a charge up the Shenandoah Valley.

Mrs. Hooper, charming in heliotrope silk, explained that she had called to urge Mary to appear at a raffle which the wives of army officers were holding to raise money for Clara Barton's nurses. The two discussed Miss Barton's work in detail. Little Isabelle, long yellow curls falling over a little pink dimity frock that rippled in so many ruffles over a tiny crinoline that she looked as if she were wearing a huge hollyhock, ran up and down the garden paths talking to herself in some mysterious game of childhood.

This entirely feminine scene had maintained itself perhaps five minutes when a shout was heard from the President's bedroom window.

"Hey! Sissy! Come up hea'! We want you."

Isabella paused and turned a piquant little face upward.

"I hate to be called Sissy!" she shrilled.

"Tad!" called his mother. "Come down here and be properly introduced." Then, to Mrs. Hooper, "I don't know whether he'll come or not. He dislikes girls."

"No boy of any age really dislikes girls of any age," retorted Alice Hooper. "I speak I assure you from a vast and varied experience."

Both women laughed, but before Alice could continue, an alarming sound of breaking twigs and rending gar-

ments came from above and to his mother's consterna-
tion, Tad slid rapidly down the trunk of the copper beech.
His white linen suit was stained and hopelessly torn.
Not at all embarrassed, he placed his dirty little hand
on his heart and made a profound bow to the dimpling
Isabella who had drawn near.

"We want you for Queen Titania in ou' play," he
said. "You a' just a good size and shape."

"Who's the boy in the window?" demanded Isabella.

"My chum Pete. He made the chawiot for the
Queen."

"I won't play with him but I will with you," declared
the little girl, "because you're pretty."

"I'm not," roared Tad. "I never was. I won't be.
You're just a di'ty little—"

Mary clapped her hand over her son's mouth before
his favorite epithet emerged. Isabella giggled and
danced up and down.

"Pretty boy! Pretty boy!" she squealed.

"Isabella!" said her mother reprovingly.

"Aw, come on, Tad!" came Pete's voice from above.
"Bring her along and if she don't stop calling you that,
she can't ride in the chariot."

"Will the chariot really go?" inquired Isabella of Tad.

Mary experimentally removed her hand. Tad replied
with enthusiasm. "It goes like a gun ca'wage with fifty
mules licked by fifty contwabands."

"I'd like to ride in it," exclaimed Isabella.

Tad tossed his head and stood staring at her, obsti-
nately.

"You're as homely as a pig," volunteered Isabella, a
little anxiously.

Tad relaxed and taking the little girl's proffered hand,
led her away.

"Is it safe?" asked Isabella's mother.

"Not usually," replied Tad's mother, with a sigh and rising. "Especially not now as Tad's tutor is down with typhoid. I really don't have an easy moment while Tad's awake. Shall we follow at a respectful distance?"

Alice gathered up lilac gloves and black lace shawl, touched her plumed Leghorn hat with a delicate hand, and followed up the iron stairs to the south portico, thence to the main hall, where they paused for a few moments' laughing conversation with Lord Lyons. In the midst of this colloquy a frightened shriek floated down from above. Both women gathered up their crinolines and flew up the stairs.

"She isn't killed!" called Tad reassuringly as they burst into the room.

Charles Sumner was standing by the bed, holding Isabella in his great arms. Pete and Tad were restraining Nanny, Tad's beloved goat, who seemed to object seriously to a wreath of artificial flowers tied over her horns.

"Nanny is Bottom and Isabella wouldn't let Bottom kiss he'," shrilled Tad. "If she's going to squawk like that she can't play with me and that's final!"

Isabella from her safe haven spoke quite as firmly as Tad. "If you'll be Bottom, I'll let you kiss me. But I won't not let no goat kiss me ever."

"Pete, you kiss he', just th'ough the wall, you know," urged Tad.

"Not me," declared Pete, his freckled face purpling. "I'd rather kiss Nanny."

"I wouldn't let you touch me!" cried Isabella.

"Then I suppose I'll have to," said Tad, grimly. "Come on! We'll put Nanny back in the stable."

"And about time," said his mother in a voice as grim as her son's.

Alice Hooper, who had been standing with lovely eyes

brimming with laughter, now moved toward Sumner.
"Put her down, dear Senator! And thank you for
rescuing her."

"I was coming up the private staircase in an attempt
to see the President alone. Hence my intrusion," explained Sumner, setting Isabella down and bowing.

"But you play with us, Senata'!" cried Tad. "You
be Obe'on since I have to be Bottom."

Sumner, with the enchanting smile seldom seen save
by children, shook his head. "I can't stay this time,
Taddie."

"Oh, stay! Stay just a little while! You've been
away so long!" cried the little boy, running to catch
Sumner's hand.

Isabella suddenly climbed to the bed and thence to
the bureau, from which she could throw her arms about
Sumner and kiss him. Pete was handicapped as Nanny's
keeper and could only add his plea vocally. Sumner, his
serious face transfigured with pleasure, gathered both
children in his arms.

"Just fifteen minutes, then."

Mary smiled at Alice Hooper and they withdrew to
the sitting room, where they settled themselves on a little
sofa from which they could view the hall.

"How children do love him!" exclaimed Alice. "He
and Isabella are infatuated with each other. I tell him
that if she were fifteen years older and he fifteen years
younger, I'd be his mother-in-law."

"I suppose he hates to be teased by you, of all people
in the world," mused Mary.

"Why 'of all people in the world'?" demanded Alice
with a touch of the hauteur for which she was noted.

"It's perfectly obvious that the blessed goose is infatuated with you, too," smiled her hostess.

"Madam!" the younger woman jumped to her feet.

Slender, flushed, beautiful, she swept up and down the room as though fighting to keep down the temper for which she was noted. She and Mary had temperamentally much in common! "Such thoughts should be beneath you. I don't deserve such suspicions."

"Desert has very little to do with what people say of one, I've found," returned Mary, sadly.

Suddenly pale, Alice Hooper came to pause before Mary. The arrogance left her manner and she spoke as simply as a child. "Mrs. Lincoln, is there gossip about Charles Sumner and me?"

"Yes, my dear," replied Mary with equal simplicity, "quite horrid gossip. If it should reach your father-in-law, I fear it might make trouble between him and Sumner. And as for your husband—"

"My husband has perfect faith in me, as well he may have," interrupted Alice vehemently.

Mary nodded. "Of course! Yet he may be convinced that the Senator has been indiscreet in showing his admiration for you so publicly."

"It would break my heart to have Charles Sumner hurt," exclaimed Alice, adding with a little rueful smile, "I want only myself to torment him."

There was a moment's silence during which the children's treble and the Senator's bass floated in at the door.

"Dear Mrs. Hooper," Mary rose to lay a gentle hand on the younger woman's arm, "you're playing with Satan's fires."

Alice gasped as if she had been struck and drew herself up quickly. "I think we'll not discuss the matter further, Madam President! I must fetch Isabella and go home."

But Mary would not allow the conversation to end on this note. "You mustn't be angry with me, my dear. I fear gossip. It has wrecked me socially here in Washington, as you know. Charming and sought for as you are, its clammy hand can beslime you also, make a social outcast of you. Gossip has no respect for place or breeding or wealth. Rather, it prefers them."

Still very pale, Alice had recovered her aplomb. "You are supersensitive for me, dear Mrs. Lincoln. But I'm sure you mean most kindly. I really must beg to be excused now. It's my daughter's supper time."

Mary let her go.

She was standing by the window a little later, thinking over the interview she had forced, when Lincoln came in with Tad, both ready for supper.

"Tad's been describing his afternoon successes to me, Mary," Lincoln said as they started for the dining room.

"Isabella's as much fun to play with as Nanny," declared Tad. "We'll give an honest-to-goodness play soon and he' mother'll let he' come to wehe'sels. The Senata' said he'd come to the play if Isabella's motha' would ask him. She said she wouldn't and the Senata' just picked up his hat and walked out of my room as if she'd kicked him. Can I go to Isabella's house, soon, motha'? She's asked me."

"I'll see," replied his mother. Then to Lincoln, "Did Mr. Sumner have his conference with you, Abra'm?"

The President shook his head. "He must have been too much hurt by the kick! Perhaps he'll come back this evening."

But Sumner did not return and Lincoln spent the evening with Hamlin. Draft enforcement was being met with bitter hostility throughout the North. Lincoln wanted the Vice President to go up to Maine and preach the common sense of this method of raising soldiers.

Hamlin, always glad to get home to his constituents, agreed to do so and proceeded to draw on the President's vast fund of information for material to make into "war medicine," as he called it with a dry Yankee grin.

Just before leaving he showed Lincoln a letter from his son Cyrus. Bob had got in touch with the newly made young Colonel and was sending him a group of negroes to be trained as recruiting officers. The two fathers nodded at each other over the letter with mutual pride.

Lincoln told Mary of Bob's prowess, the next evening. They were standing in the window of Mary's bedroom, looking down on the glory of the garden, ablaze now with lemon lilies.

"I didn't know Bob had gone back to Fortress Monroe!" exclaimed Mary. "How did that happen?"

Lincoln cleared his throat. "Well, he wrote me last week that he'd finished his examinations early by special arrangement with his professors and was going down without stopping here."

"Abra'm," ordered Mary, "you let me see that boy's letter!"

Lincoln took it reluctantly from his pocket. Bob had written that he was not coming to the White House, "in order to avoid making Mother go through the ordeal of saying good-by. It breaks my heart and her's too." Lincoln had not wanted Mary to see those last sentences.

But she was very quiet about it. She read the letter and looked up at him with a pathetic smile. "If the Lord had planned for ages, He couldn't have found a more adroit way to punish me for my lack of self-control than in Bob's constant effort to avoid a scene with me. I *must* be cool and calm with that boy!"

Lincoln patted her cheek. "Don't get *too* calm and collected or I won't know you! As it is, you've changed

so in the last year that often I wonder who the strange
lady is that shares my bed and board."

"Abra'm!" Mary giggled, then gave him a look of
affectionate appraisal. He was wearing a new white
linen suit with a waistcoat of dull ivory silk. The outfit
had cost her many weary hours of conversation and she
was proud of it. "You do look nice! You're going to
have more widows than ever caressing your left hand
while your right signs pardons for their sons!"

"Tut! Tut! Mrs. Lincoln!" He gave a shout of
laughter and they descended to supper with Tad sliding
down the banisters ahead of them.

"What was General Butler raging about in your office
to-day?" asked Mary, midway through the meal.

"He yells louda' than old Stanton but he don't swea'
any betta'," volunteered Tad, his mouth full of green
peas.

Lincoln winked at his wife and said before she could
correct the child, "Butler has changed his mind and wants
Grant's job. Guarantees to take Vicksburg in twenty-
four hours after his arrival on the spot."

"Ask him how soon he could take Richmond!" suggested Mary. "It looks as if Lee didn't want it. I
suppose the way his army is moving up the Shenandoah
he'll be establishing the Southern capital at Harrisburg
before the 4th of July."

"Don't be sarcastic, my dear," protested Lincoln.
"It's too serious a matter."

"And do you think I'm not serious?" cried Mary.
"Aside from my own anxiety in the matter, how can I
see you agonize so and not be serious? But I can't help
wondering with the rest of the public how long you're
going to let General Hooker sit in front of Richmond
while General Lee escapes him into Pennsylvania."

"Let! Let! Good God, Mary, don't be a fool!"—
his taut nerves getting beyond control for an instant.
"Do you suppose I'm not doing all I can to get that army
out of the mud, onto its legs and moving? You, of all
people—"

"Oh, I'm sorry, Abra'm!" contritely from Mary.
"Taddie'll think you're really cross at me. I do try to
mind my own business."

"As far as that's concerned," Lincoln spoke gently
again, "it's as much your business as mine or any one
else's. I'm worried, not cross. Don't hold it against me,
Taddie," with a smile at the staring child. "Butler is
very mad with me. He's staying with Secretary Chase
and I suppose the things they're saying about me would
turn me against myself!"

"Well, I'm not sure but what Butler ought to have
Grant's place," said Mary. "He's a very able man. I
suppose you know how he's got the Presidential bee?"

Lincoln looked at her musingly but made no comment
on the hero of New Orleans. During the remainder of
the meal, he turned over in his mind the probable extent
of Butler's enmity to him and the possible use that Chase
and Sumner would make of it.

After supper, he strolled into John Hay's room. The
secretary was dressing for the evening. The bed, the
chairs, the floor were strewn with garments, while the
young man in his shirt sleeves stood before the mirror
working over an enormous white satin tie. Lincoln sat
down on the edge of the bed after sweeping aside a purple
lounging robe.

"Where are you going to-night, John?"

"I'm going to call on Miss Montgomery, sir, a beauteous damosel from the fair state of my nativity!"

"Do you mind *what* damosel you call on, John, just so she be beauteous?" asked the President.

"Not at all, dear Tycoon! My affections have been blighted so often that I'm no longer capable of real feeling about any of the sex. Have you a lady in mind?" finishing the tie to his satisfaction and turning to Lincoln with his infectious smile.

The years in the White House had taken some of the red from the young man's cheeks, had hardened a little the full curves of his lips. But he still retained the twinkling brilliancy of the black eyes, with their quizzical lift at the outer corners. He still showed untainted his buoyant young enthusiasm for life. Lincoln was always glad to have him back though he was finding the young man's tact invaluable in performing political errands and John was more and more frequently absent from the White House.

The President returned the smile. "John, how does that flirtation of yours with pretty Kate Chase progress?"

The young man shook his head, sadly. "I have no luck with women! I really produced inspired verses for that flinty hearted damosel and she read them aloud with derisive giggles to Governor Sprague."

"Somebody said Charles Sumner was trying to cut Sprague out over there," suggested Lincoln. "She's a handsome, ambitious gypsy. Doesn't like me, much."

"She wants your place for her father," John nodded. "Mr. Sumner hasn't a chance there. Gossip says his heart is in another and entirely ineligible quarter. But he and Chase are very intimate, lately—gossip also. If you want me to go round to Chase's, I'm apt to find Sumner, unless he's at the Hoopers."

Lincoln ran his fingers through his hair, clasped his knee and worked his long body back and forth in thought.

"I reckon you'll have to go round to Chase's house to-night and throw a hand-grenade. I want to find out what they're trying to do to me. You give this message to Sumner if he's there or confide it to Kate or her father for him if he's not. Say I'd like to accede to Sumner's request for a negro department for General Frémont but I just haven't got one handy. That ought to start General Butler off his seat. He's been after me for a department for months. He'll sweep over Sumner like a herd of buffalo when he learns Sumner's been trying to help Frémont out. In the exchange of recriminations you may learn where I stand." He returned John's grin.

"Yes! Yes!" the grin spreading. "Do you desire a report to-night, sir? After the flood gates are open—! Well, outside of Seward, if Sumner's there, the three most rapid fire orators in the western hemisphere'll be gathered at the Chase residence—and I may be late in getting away."

"You come to me to-night, boy. I'm worried. Butler is making bad medicine as sure as Lee is headed for Pennsylvania. Chase is a babe in Butler's hands and so in only slightly less degree is Sumner."

Hay fastened a pink rosebud carefully in his button hole, jerked down his vest, picked up a very tall hat and an enormous cane, bowed formally to the President, shouted suddenly, "Raise the portcullis!" clucked to an imaginary horse and was gone.

"That fellow saves my reason about twice a day," said Lincoln to the empty air and returned to his desk.

Three hours later, John seated himself on the edge of Lincoln's bed. The pink rosebud was wilted. John's lips were drawn but his eyes were vivid. The President pointed to the plate of sandwiches on the bedside table and the two munched while John talked.

He found the party, he said, in the garden, back of
the Secretary's house:—Chase, Sumner, Butler and the
pretty Kate, sitting close together, clapping mosquitoes,
and listening to one another and the whippoorwills. He
delivered the message to Sumner immediately on his arrival, confidentially, as among friends.

Butler roared with surprise and indignation, "What,
Frémont a department while I stand on the doorstep
begging and am denied? What in hell do you mean,
Sumner?"

"I mean," replied Sumner, stiffly, "that Frémont is
notoriously the negro's friend. If giving him a department will draw out the negro troops rapidly, not only for
their own sake but to offset the danger of a draft rebellion—"

Butler interrupted, "That's not the way to do it! Put
me aboard a ship with a white regiment. Land me at
a Southern port. I'll march North gathering negroes as
I come and arming them with their peculiar weapon, as
John Brown planned. I'll give them the spear their
African fathers used. I'll bring through an army that'll
terrorize secession."

"Your plans needn't keep Frémont from having a department," said Chase.

"Frémont with a department means Frémont thrust
forward as dictator by the Abolitionists, eh, Sumner?"
exclaimed Butler. "I suppose that's the latest hope of
the Boston set!"

"Not so," retorted Sumner. "Frémont with a department means Frémont busy and content, leaving you a
free field to show your mettle."

"Haven't I shown my mettle?" demanded Butler
fiercely, and he embraced the opportunity immediately to
utter a long address in which he described at great length

his accomplishments at Annapolis, at Fortress Monroe, and at New Orleans.

After what seemed to John an endless period, Butler was interrupted by Secretary Chase who asked point blank if the General were recommending himself for the Presidency, adding that more than military and legal ability were essential in the Executive Mansion in the present crisis—a broad understanding of finance was required. Followed an address by Chase on his accomplishments as Secretary of the Treasury and they were many and impressive.

Sumner listened to his colleagues, a motionless shadow in the heavy scented garden. When they had finished, he said, slowly, "All conversations are idle which do not include the fact that Mr. Lincoln apparently has no idea of withdrawing and that, as he himself says, only those generals that win victories may think of dictatorships."

"In other words," exclaimed Butler, "Lincoln has an object in not giving able soldiers commanding positions. He's afraid of the dictator. Ha! I see it all now!—Hooker won't head Lee off. You'll see. Lee's going to be allowed to win another victory."

Chase took fire at this evidence of Butler's clear vision. "You're right, General! What blind fools we've been! This is dreadful! Preposterous! My friends, if Lee again defeats the army of the Potomac, I'll publish our discovery to the world and the people will demand an impeachment of Lincoln."

John Hay had dropped into a chair which he had dragged discreetly back of Kate Chase, but he reminded them of his presence at this moment by letting slip an indignant snort.

Kate Chase rose quickly and beckoning to John be-

gan to move toward the house. "You may as well know,
Mr. Hay, that many people can't endure Mr. Lincoln
with your gay insouciance. He's a serious problem to
some of us."

John bowed. "That may well be, Miss Chase, I'm
sure," he murmured and followed her from the garden.

Lincoln listened to his secretary's lively tale without
once interrupting him. When John finished the story
and the cookies together, the President wiped the sweat
from his forehead with the back of his hand and said,
with a twisted smile, "Well, it looks as if any fool could
now understand what they think of me. Contempt has
swamped any idea of secrecy— Seems from most any
point of view, John, as if Hooker ought to lick Lee—
John, nobody knows the strength of the Presidential itch
till he's had it—"

"Interpret for me, sir!" urged John. "The talk of
impeachment is idle, of course!"

"I'm not at all sure that it's idle," replied the President slowly. "Any one of those men would like to impeach me. If I could draw Sumner off, though, he could
control the others."

John's young face showed a growing astonishment.
"Not really, Mr. Lincoln! Why, I was thinking it half
a joke! They haven't a leg to stand on."

"What difference does that make?" asked the President. "Sometimes I'm made mighty uneasy with regard
to our national future when I realize how frequently a
small minority is able to block or wreck the efforts of the
majority. And I'm not blinking at the possibility that a
majority of the people want to be rid of me.—Sumner
may be sitting over there this minute planning to impeach me."

"If I thought that was so I'd go over there and—and—" John looked at Lincoln in perplexity. "What can one do to Sumner, sir?"

"I don't know!" exclaimed Lincoln.

"I do know one thing," said John, "if you'll pardon my saying it, and that is that you are too patient with Sumner. He's the kind of a man that a good swift kick has a salutary effect upon."

Lincoln suddenly laughed. The picture presented was too much for his risibilities, anxious as he was, and John went off to bed, glad to have won the laugh.

The President, after long thought, decided that the most pressing necessity from every point of view was that Hooker should hasten after Lee. Late as it was, he went into his office and sitting in his night shirt wrote a strong letter to Hooker which he ended with this adjuration:

"Lee's army and not Richmond is your sure objective point. If he comes toward the upper Potomac, follow on his flank and on his inside track, shortening your lines as he lengthens his. Fight him too when opportunity offers. If he stays where he is, fret him and fret him."

He sent this off by messenger before going finally to bed.

Then as the hot June days swung toward July, he awaited the result of his order with increasing anxiety. And it was with a painful sort of relief that before a week had passed he observed the slow line of ambulances beginning to thicken on Pennsylvania Avenue. Hooker for once was obeying Lincoln literally and was fretting Lee.

Lee reached Winchester, Virginia, hungry for the North. Lincoln, as he pushed through his daily tasks, wondered how long human nerves could ache as his did before they were exhausted into numbness. But his taut nerves were revealing to the people something of Lincoln's granite, at which Mary rejoiced. He was nervous and impatient. He touched up Banks again about the fall elections in Louisiana. He wrote to the committee which had protested violently against the arrest in Ohio of a well-known Democrat:

"Must I shoot a simple-minded soldier boy who deserts while I must not touch a hair of the wily agitator who persuades him to desert?"

He wrote to Andrew Johnson in Tennessee hurrying him toward the formation of a loyal State Government. He watched uneasily the taking of Mexico City by the French but forced Seward in no uncertain terms to keep hands off. He sent a bitter admonition to the radical and conservative Unionists who were rending Missouri with their disagreements:

"It is very painful to me that you in Missouri cannot or will not settle your factional quarrels among yourselves. I have been tormented with it beyond endurance for months on both sides. Neither side pays the least respect to my appeals to your reason. I am now compelled to take hold of the case—"

And never for an hour could he forget that narrow gray line marching with such incomparable resolution up the Shenandoah Valley. Again and yet again he urged his generals to make haste.

"General Hooker:—So far as we can make out here the enemy has Milroy surrounded at Winchester and Tyler at Martinsburg. If they could hold out a few days could you help? If the head of Lee's army is at Martinsburg and the tail of it on the plank road between Fredericksburg and Chancellorsville, the animal must be very slim somewhere. Could you not break him?"

On and on—that thin gray line! Could nothing turn
it? The people of Pennsylvania were becoming panic-
stricken. Lincoln responded to the Governor's plea for
help by issuing a call for 100,000 State militia:

"I, Abraham Lincoln, President of the United States
and Commander-in-Chief of the Army and Navy thereof
—I, Abraham Lincoln, President of the United States—
God!—" He dropped his head into his tired hands in
pain too deep for tears.

But there was no time for introspection. He could
not pause even to agonize over Sumner. Another message must go to the front:

"Major General Schenk:—Get General Milroy from
Winchester to Harper's Ferry, if possible. He will be
gobbled up if he remains, if he is not already past salvation—"

General-in-Chief Halleck and Hooker quarreled without cessation. Lincoln tried for several days to soothe
both men, then he put his foot down and wrote in terms of
unmistakable harshness:

"Major General Hooker:—To remove all misunderstanding, I now place you in the strict military relation to
General Halleck of a commander of one of the armies to
the General-in-Chief of all the armies. I have not in-
tended differently but as it seems to be differently understood, I shall direct him to give you orders and you to
obey them—"

Early in the afternoon of June 27th, Lincoln called
Halleck to his office. He was utterly disgusted with
what seemed to him the puerile and dangerous friction
between the two generals.

"Halleck!" he began in a high, strident voice utterly
unlike his usual low tones, "I'm ashamed of both you
and Hooker. I've reached the limit—"

The office door which he had ordered to be locked, suddenly banged open. Charles Sumner, white linen coat flying, face purple, rushed up to the President's desk.

"Mr. Lincoln, I've just heard that Lee's army has scooped up all the free negroes in southern Pennsylvania and sent them back to Richmond to be sold into slavery. I insist—"

Lincoln jumped up so suddenly that his chair tipped over. He could not see Sumner for the sudden rage that overwhelmed him. "Insist?" he shouted. "Who are you to insist to the President? Insist? I tell you that I'm so full of 'insists' now that another one will make me puke. Sumner, get out of this room and stay out till you can come in with the respect due my office."

Lincoln turned his back on the Senator and completed the interrupted sentence. "—the limit of my patience with you. Undoubtedly Hooker had sent in his resignation only in a fit of petulance over the orders you've given him about keeping his men at Harper's Ferry. But the time's passed for petulance. This thing is too big for petulance. You prepare an order which I'll sign, accepting Hooker's resignation and putting General Meade in his place."

Halleck, with an expression of satisfaction on his pale, harassed face, hurried from the room. Lincoln turned to behold Sumner still standing by the Cabinet table. Sumner cleared his throat but once more the office door was flung wide and a woman burst into the room; a woman whose black bonnet had fallen back from her gray hair, whose black stuff dress was heavy with dust, whose bare feet were bursting from broken gaiters. Stoddard stood hesitating in the doorway.

"She's back again, sir. I've held her away from you two hours."

"It's all right, Billy," said the President. "What is it now, Madam?"

The woman leaned over the edge of the desk, her face working, her eyes half blind with old weeping. "You remember me, last week, Mr. Lincoln?"

"Yes! You said you had three sons and a husband in the army and not a cent from any of their pay. And would I do something about it. And I did. I ordered part of their pay garnisheed for you."

"Yes, sir, you did. And yesterday I learned that my boys are dead. Two of them of wounds at Chancellorsville and one at Winchester. Oh, sir—Oh, sir—will you let me have my man back? He's all that's left and he's too old to fight. Older than you, Mr. Lincoln. Not much good to me but all I have. Save him for me, sir—"

"Don't cry! Don't cry!" urged Lincoln. "Tears make it hard for me to think. I'm learning not to be softened by tears."

He forgot Sumner—and Halleck—and Meade. Here was the bloody sweat of war, indeed! He arose to remove himself from her working, clinging fingers and stared out the window—that ever thickening, never ending line of ambulances—

After a moment he turned to the woman. "I still have two," he said gently, "and you have none. It doesn't seem fair, does it? So I'll give you back your husband." He dropped to his seat again and took up his pen.

The woman crowded close. She made a peculiar sound, thought Lincoln, like an old cow bereft of her calf. He wrote an order to Stanton. The woman looked over his shoulders, her shaking fingers fixed on his arm, then smoothing his black hair; as though they two were

alone; as though her trouble was the only trouble; as
though the humanness of the thing she sought and Lincoln gave leveled every barrier.

He signed the paper and thrust it into her hand.
"There!" he sighed.

The woman's face twisted. "God will—God will—"
she could not finish but rushed out of the door which
Stoddard still anxiously held open. He closed it after
her and Lincoln sank back in his chair.

Sumner cleared his throat. "Such scenes are very painful. You have my deep sympathy, Mr. Lincoln. I—I
fear I sometimes forget how driven and overworked you
are. I deserved the rebuke. Will you accept my apology,
sir?"

Lincoln looked from the proffered hand to the sincere
face above it. "I'll take it with one understanding, Mr.
Sumner," he said firmly, "that you cease this childish
avoidance of me. Dislike me if you will, impeach me if
you must, but don't be cowardly. I'm not going to bite
you or assault you. Your honor is safe when you're
alone with me."

Sumner, still holding out his fine white hand, said seriously, "You really think I'm afraid of that? Well, since
you are so frank I'll say that it's not been fear but decency
that's kept me away. How can I feel as I do toward your
policies—"

"Oh, come, Senator," urged Lincoln, hoping that he
was not betraying the astonishment he felt at the effect of
the drubbing on Sumner, "what you feel about my policies
isn't a patch to what I feel about yours! I sincerely believe that for the good of the state we ought to put up a
front of at least casual bearing with each other's in-
firmities."

"I'm glad to hear you say that," said Sumner. "It is seriously inconvenient, not to feel free to come to you for information. But my conscience——"

Lincoln seized his hand with a short laugh. "The New England conscience is out of place in politics, Mr. Sumner. What do you hear from John Bright?"

Sumner's face lightened. He took a letter from his pocket and the interview ended with the reading of a delightful message from the great Englishman to the American President.

CHAPTER VIII

THE FATHER OF WATERS GOES UNVEXED TO THE SEA

THE next morning at breakfast Lincoln asked Tad for a report on the progress of the play.

"He'd better give it very soon," said his mother, before Tad could reply. "I'm going to keep our family life as near normal as I can between the heat and General Lee, so you can prepare to move out to the Soldiers' Home, next week."

"Then I gotta see Isabella wight away!" exclaimed Tad, throwing down his napkin.

"Finish your breakfast, Taddie," admonished his mother. "I'm not going to move to-day!" Then turning to her husband and looking anxiously at his careworn face, "You'll be glad of the cooler nights out there, Abra'm?"

"Yes, my dear, to say nothing of being free of poor old Stanton!" answered Lincoln, heartily.

He liked the cottage. It was an unpretentious place of the style made popular by Godey's Lady's Book—a peaked little house, set with many dormer windows of the Gothic type, surrounded by trees of enormous beauty. He loved these trees, and the little dwelling with its meager front hall, its tiny parlor and bedrooms, was more homelike to him than all the grandeur of the Executive Mansion.

But he scarcely had uttered his approval when the Secretary of War rushed into the room—"poor old" Stanton who had had no let-up day or night since Lee had started his promenade northward. He was disheveled, had had no breakfast, but would not accept Mary's invitation to sit down. He needed the President, at once.

A stunning collision had taken place the day before between the head of Lee's column and Meade's left wing, near Gettysburg in Pennsylvania. A battle had developed and was continuing with increasing ferocity. Lincoln dropped his fork, seized Stanton's arm and hurried with him back to the War Office. He hardly left there for two days.

It was not a restful spot under the best of circumstances, for Stanton's irascibility kept every one's nerves on edge. With the stress of the great battle added to the usual routine, Stanton was about as easy to get along with, Lincoln thought, as a swarm of yellow jackets. But here was the best place in Washington to feel the pulse of the fight. A fairly accurate detail map of Southern Pennsylvania had been made hastily for Stanton. A procession of messengers gave tardy but roughly accurate information of division movements. Lincoln was now adept in understanding military formation and phraseology. He set the pins and moved them, ejaculated, protested, approved, forgot to eat his meals. It was obvious that one of the great engagements of the war was in progress. The thought of its importance, its implications, its possibilities, were almost beyond calm endurance.

On the afternoon of July third the dispatches, which had been hopeful in tone, ceased to arrive. Stanton lay on the broken springs of the old horsehair sofa, his black beard drenched with sweat, his eyes sunken with exhaustion, but still dictating telegrams. General Halleck, unshaven, blue eyes bloodshot from lack of sleep, paced the floor. Lincoln in his shirtsleeves sat on Stanton's high office stool, his heels caught in one of the rungs. People came and went. Senator Ben Wade, short, sturdy, and very warm in his black alpaca suit, penetrated the fastness to utter a blighting denunciation of Grant and his protracted siege of Vicksburg. With all the vindictiveness at his command he demanded that Grant be dismissed. Lincoln listened with interest. Wade was one of the Jacobins, one of Sumner's allies, but Lincoln wanted no quarrel with him. So when Stanton uttered a preliminary growl, the President said, serenely:

"Senator Wade, you remind me of a story."

Wade whirled on him, his thick pompadour seeming to stiffen like a cock's comb. "Yes, that's the way with you, sir, all story—story! You're the father of every military blunder that's been made during the war. You're on the road to hell, sir, with the Government and you're not a mile off, this minute."

Lincoln grinned. "Senator, that's just about the distance from here to the Capitol, isn't it?"

"My God!" groaned Wade, striding from the room.

Sumner, in lavender silk trousers and a brown alpaca coat, passed him in the doorway, looked after him with arched eyebrows, then entered slowly. "May I know the latest news, Mr. Secretary?"

"No news for hours. Up to noon, looked as if we'd held 'em," replied Stanton from beneath the handkerchief he'd placed over his face. "I'm going to doze for a few moments, gentlemen."

Halleck, oblivious to all about him, continued to walk the floor. He was like a man in a coma.

Lincoln beckoned the Senator to the map on the east wall. The sinking rays of the sun cast a livid, wavering light on it. Lincoln placed his finger on a blue pin.

"Here's the disposition of our lines at six o'clock this

morning. Meade's been entirely on the defensive. If he can once turn the enemy and actually take up the offensive, we'll end the war with this battle, yes, sir!"

Long after the President had returned to his stool, Sumner studied the map. Then he took up his station on the window seat, looking down on the White House grounds where Tad drove little Isabella Hooper up and down in Pete's idea of a chariot. Stanton snored but roused at dusk to urge Halleck, still silently pacing the floor, to get some rest. Halleck, with a sigh, went out. James came in with an enormous tray of food from Mrs. Lincoln.

The three men ate without appetite, prowling about the office or strolling into the telegraph operators' room adjacent to listen eagerly to the chittering of the sterile instruments. The breathless moments wore away until midnight. Sumner looked at his watch and had just announced that he was going home when one of the operators rushed into the room with a message addressed to Secretary Welles.

"Six P.M. Have just left the field. All is well. Byington."

"Who's Byington?" demanded Stanton.

No one knew. Lincoln took the message. "I'll just slip over to Father Welles myself and inquire," all weariness suddenly vanishing. "I'll bring the information back to you, Mr. Stanton!"

"I'll come with you!" exclaimed Sumner.

They rushed through the breathless summer darkness to the Welles' house. The Secretary of the Navy came down the stairs in his trousers and shirt, his manner as imperturbable as usual. He paused on the lowest stair to hold the message toward the gas light. Then he smiled at the two faces turned so anxiously toward him.

"Then we can sleep to-night!" he said, "This news is undoubtedly authentic. Byington is editor and owner of a paper in Norwalk, Connecticut. I know and trust him."

Lincoln gave an enormous sigh and suddenly felt drowned in weariness. "I shall sleep for the first time in three days," he said. "You're a very present help in time of trouble, Mr. Welles. Come, Sumner, we must go relieve Stanton's anxiety. We have a reprieve, at least."

But Sumner insisted that Lincoln go home, leaving the errand to him. So the two parted, Lincoln crawling up the stairs to his own room with half-closed eyes and scarcely aware that Mary helped him to take off his boots.

No further news came from Gettysburg during the night nor during the early morning hours. Billy Stoddard and Mary had engineered a Fourth of July entertainment before the White House grounds; had planned it to help offset the dangerous depression that was sure to darken Washington did news of a Union defeat come from Gettysburg. They made use of the tremendous troop movement through the city to stage a spectacular parade with much gay band music. A speaker's stand was set up just outside the north gates and Mary devastated the garden and the green houses to decorate it.

At noon, when Lincoln entered the stand to make his speech, there still had come no decisive word from Meade. He was a little aghast at the stupendous size of the audience packed into Lafayette Square. He did not like to address so large a crowd without having written out his speech. But such had been his preoccupation with Gettysburg that he had forgotten completely this morning's engagement until Stoddard had come for him, five minutes before the speech was due.

The sun was brilliant and dust hung motionless and

golden over the crowd as he crossed the stand to the speaker's table with its inevitable pitcher of ice water. A band burst into "Hail to the Chief!" at his appearance. He leaned against the table moistening his lips. What to say to that uneasy, unhappy throng!—as he stood hesitating, Billy Stoddard touched his arm. The boy was as white as his linen suit as he handed the President an open telegram.

Lincoln read it, felt the world turn black with the revulsion of his feeling, then turned blindly to the wavering pink sea below. Here in the dispatch was written his speech and he read it aloud:

"Lee began a retreat toward the Potomac at three o'clock this morning. Meade."

A long sigh swept the square. Then a bandsman brought his sticks down on the bass drum and the storm was released. The crowds, the bands, the regiments at rest became an inextricably commingled, shrieking, huzzaing, weeping, embracing riot.

Lincoln, unheeded, slipped back to the War Office. He feared the inertia that would follow the victory and knew that immediate pressure must be brought on Meade to make him follow Lee and give battle. And such was the stimulation of his relief that he really believed that Meade's army might prove to be almost as fluid as Lee's!

After the excitement of this memorable "Fourth" was over, Mary, looking utterly fagged, remarked at the supper table that perhaps now it would be possible to go out to the Soldiers' Home for a decent night's sleep. Before Lincoln could reply Tad exclaimed in protest:

"But to-night we give the play!"

His father and mother looked at him in dismay. A spoonful of ice cream half way to his mouth, Tad returned the stare and tried to make them understand.

"Isabella said she'd come and make he' motha' come. I wanted Pete's fatha' and motha' but they was going to a funewal. All the help in this house said they'd come and so did Lo'd Lyons and Mrs. Welles and a lot of otha' people. I've been asking them all day."

His mother threw up her hands. "Tad, of all the thoughtless—"

"Don't, wife!" interrupted his father. "Taddie, didn't you realize there'd been a terrible battle and people have been under an awful strain and it's no time for a child's play?"

"This isn't a child's play," returned Tad, his lips quivering. "It's Shakespea's. You' own pet, Papa day, and so—"

"Do you know yet whether or not Mrs. Hooper's coming, Taddie?" asked his mother, suddenly.

"That's what Senata' Sumna' asked me," replied Tad. "Yes, she is. Isabella said she'd make he' because Isabella can't come alone."

Mary's mobile lips flexed from annoyance to amusement. Her tired eyes began to snap with excitement.

"Well, Abra'm, since we've a houseful of guests coming, I think you and I had better take a hand. James," turning to the servant, "you and Ben come up to the sitting room right after supper. Tad, you go see that your theater is all ready for patrons."

Taddie with a whoop of delight ran from the room.

James at that moment laid a note at Mary's plate. She read it with a smile. "Alice Hooper wants to know if the children's invitation is authentic. I'll send a line to her at once, if you'll loan me Louis."

Lincoln nodded.

The guests arrived, most of them in an obviously tentative frame of mind. Baron Gerolt, the Prussian Minister

with the Baroness, Dr. Stone, the family physician, three
of the President's cavalry guard, Pete's little sister
Martha in wonderful pantalettes, Lord Lyons, amused
and affable, Job Cotter, who ran the gingerpop stand
near the White House, lovely Mrs. Welles and a dozen
others were seated in the state guest chamber when Lincoln and Sumner entered the room. As he identified the
silhouettes of most of the guests, against Tad's candle
footlights, the President whispered to Sumner:

"We ought to send Tad as minister to England. He
can handle any combination!"

Sumner, catching sight of Alice Hooper's exquisite
profile in the front row, agreed with an enthusiastic,
"Yes! Yes!" and picking up a chair carried it to an
empty space beside her. Lincoln laughed to himself and
slumped into a seat by the door where a messenger could
find him easily.

If Tad had his father's genius for friendship, he also
had his mother's executive ability. The bedroom furniture had all been removed except the enormous four-
poster bed. From this, Tad had stripped the bedding
and covered the frame with boards to form a solid platform. The bed curtains enclosed all save the front where
he had hung one of his mother's gorgeous red Persian
shawls. Exits were provided by using the closet to the
right and the door of the one bathroom the house contained to the left.

The entertainment was a Shakespeare potpourri;—
bits chosen here and there as Tad's understanding and
liking might dictate. As James drew back the shawl for
the first scene, Lincoln heard his wife gasp with surprise and amusement. Taddie wore one of his mother's
basques of white velvet which came half way to his
knees, a pair of her white knit silk stockings which more

than met the basque, his own toy sword and belt. He
was ridiculously like Booth's Hamlet which Mary had
taken him to see. Ridiculous, yet his boyish prettiness
never was more pronounced than when he stalked across
the stage toward a flag-draped packing case. Here stood
Isabella in one of her mother's night dresses, caught up
by a great blue sash, her hair falling in molten beauty
around her lovely, excited little face.

"He jests at sca's that neva' felt a wound! But soft,
what light th'ough yonda' window bweaks—" began Tad,
in his clear treble.

"Oh, Romeo! Romeo!—" interrupted Isabella.

"Shut up, can't you till I finish?" demanded Tad.

"If I wait, I'll forget, so I won't not wait," replied
Isabella, emphatically and with a resolution that reduced
Tad to silence while she finished the four lines.

"You've spoiled it now. It won't make sense," declared Tad, folding his arms mournfully over the white
velvet tunic.

"Taddie, don't not be cross with me!" pleaded Isabella. Then with happy intuition she added, "I'll sing my
song while you remember," and in a voice like a tiny
silver thread she began, "Hark! Hark the lark at heav-
en's gate sings—"

Tad, still with arms folded à la Booth, recovered himself under the spell of the song and as the little voice died
away he exclaimed:

> "Thine eyes a' lodesta's and thy tongue's sweet a'
>   Mo' tuneable than la'k's to shephe'ds ea'
>   When wheat is gween and hawtho'ne buds appea'."

Some one touched Lincoln on the arm and he followed
Stoddard into the hall. "Secretary Welles is in your

office, sir, and says he must see you." Lincoln hurried
into the Cabinet room.

Father Welles was standing before the war map and
as the President joined him, he ostentatiously moved
below Vicksburg the line of blue-headed pins that crossed
the Mississippi.

"What!" gasped Lincoln.

"Yes, Mr. Lincoln! I've just received a dispatch from
Admiral Porter. Vicksburg fell on the Fourth of July."
Welles gave his rare dry laugh and for a moment Lincoln
thought he was going to try a hornpipe!

"No!" shouted Lincoln. Then words failed him. He
stood staring at the Secretary's smiling face while he let
the good news sink into his blood. "I swear, Mr.
Welles," he brought out at last, "I don't know what we'd
do without Uncle Sam's web feet. I don't believe you've
ever brought me any but good tidings.—And so the
Father of Waters goes again unvexed to the sea!" He
suddenly enveloped Welles in a bear hug. "This is great!
Great! I'll telegraph the news to Meade, myself," re-
leasing Welles to pick up his hat.

As the two men crossed the lawn, another angle of the
glorious news struck Lincoln. "What a relief to General
Banks, down there in New Orleans! What a help toward
renovating Louisiana and bringing her home to the
family!"

Welles gave an enigmatic grunt. "Our friend Sumner
won't find that angle of the event happy."

"I shan't remind him of it," said Lincoln.

"Sumner's no fool, sir," retorted Welles.

The theatrical performance was over by the time the
President returned to the White House. He caught
the first group of departing guests at the stair head and
holding out his arms to halt them, shouted, "Vicksburg

has fallen!" then hurried through the chorus of rejoicing
to his office. Sumner was there, staring grimly at the
gloomy portrait of General Jackson over the fireplace.

Lincoln cried his news.

"Yes! Yes!" said Sumner, sadly, "I heard you, a
moment ago."

Lincoln wondered if the implications of the victory
were responsible for this unwonted apathy. He clapped
Sumner on the shoulder. "Whoever controls the Mississippi, controls the Union! This makes a young man of
me. Come, Senator, the children didn't produce tragedy,
did they? I hated to leave, I'd rather have missed a
performance by Booth than Tad as Oberon. I'm glad
you gave up the rôle."

But Sumner only jerked his head impatiently. "I'm
glad of the victory. None rejoices more than I do in it.
But taken in connection with your known attitude on reconstruction, I could have wished it delayed until you had
reached a better attitude. Come, Mr. Lincoln, do this
for me. Agree that you'll make no move on reconstructing Louisiana until—"

The President interrupted—no use fencing longer.
"I've already ordered Shepley and Banks to get moving
on fall elections down there!" He parted the tails of his
evening broadcloth and sat down on the edge of the table.

Sumner, still standing under General Jackson, turned
on Lincoln furiously. "You have no authority for any
such action, sir! When Louisiana seceded, she committed State suicide. She became a Territory. All local institutions ceased and Congress automatically assumed
jurisdiction over the vacated territory and only Congress
can make a new State there and admit it to the Union."

"My idea is," Lincoln said gently, "that if the majority
of the people in Louisiana transferred their obedience to

a foreign power, the loyal minority constitutes the State and should govern it. I'm merely giving the loyal people a chance to exercise a function they've never lost."

"And do you think the vote can change treason to devotion?" demanded Sumner, excitedly. "Can the wedding veil make a virgin of a harlot?"

"No, but one harlot in a convent doesn't make common women of the whole lot," retorted Lincoln. "There are a good many loyal folks down there."

"Are you looking on the blacks as loyal folks?" asked Sumner, quickly.

"My feeling toward the blacks," replied Lincoln carefully, for here was Sumner's tenderest point, "is that the very intelligent ones and those that have fought as soldiers should be given a chance to prove themselves. These should be given the vote, but by the Southerners, themselves."

"Impossible! Hopeless!" groaned Sumner.

"Not so," contradicted Lincoln, but still gently. "If the loyal people of Louisiana, for example, will make a new constitution, recognizing the Emancipation Proclamation and while they're at it adopt some practical system by which the two races can gradually live themselves out of the old relation into the new it would be entirely feasible. After all, the power or element of contract may be sufficient for this probationary period by its very simplicity and flexibility."

Sumner stared at the President as though he thought him insane. "You don't know what you're saying, Mr. Lincoln!"

Lincoln glanced through the door into the reception room where several people were waiting to see him.

"Let's go where we can have privacy, Senator," he suggested and led the way into the sitting room.

Mary was standing by the table with a book in her hand. She looked up and said as casually as though their entrance were expected, "Carlyle's, 'French Revolution,' in French, than which there could be nothing more amusing."

Sumner's face softened. "Yes, even in July!" He gave no heed to the chair Lincoln pushed toward him but stood staring wistfully at Mary. "Your husband and I are arguing and I'm in no mood to argue. I feel more like—what is it you ladies say?—having a good cry."

"Don't let me interfere!" said Lincoln, glad of this sudden shift in the Senator's part.

"Why tears? Because you've neglected our friendship so cruelly?" asked Mary, quickly.

Sumner did not answer this directly. He looked down at the determined little person in the rose point evening dress and said, "I've missed you."

"Well, whose fault is it?" asked Mary in much the same tone she would have used to Taddie. She seated herself and the lamplight deepened the tender beauty of her blue eyes. "I'm not worrying too much. You'll be back, asking a favor of me. I know men. Helpless creatures!"

Lincoln rubbed his chin reflectively. Sumner, he reminded himself, or any other man, was helpless when Mary was in this archly maternal mood. One felt like melting into tears and telling more than the facts warranted. She could woo a catamount to the confessional. The Senator was no exception. Ignoring the President, he pushed a great stool to a place directly in front of Mary and seated himself on it. Mary folded her hands sedately.

"The Hoopers," began Sumner, opening and closing the feathered fan he took from Mary, "are very old

friends of mine. I've known the family all my life.
Alice was a Mason. Her mother and my dear twin sister
were devoted to each other.—I have almost no intimates
left save the Hoopers and not even them now, for some
time ago Alice sent me to Coventry. I couldn't learn
why. To-night, when I seated myself by her, she made
an excuse and joined Mrs. Welles. When I asked to
see her home, she frigidly said, 'No!' and when I pressed
her for a reason she replied only, 'Ask Mrs. Lincoln.' "

"Reckon he's forgotten me and secession," thought the
President with a sigh of relief. "I don't envy Mary her
job," and he made his way back to his work.

But he gathered that Mary, from her story of the interview at bedtime that night, was well pleased with her
rôle.

"Alice shouldn't have left such a thankless task to me,"
she told Sumner when he made his plaint. "It wasn't
kind of her. But after all, it's not kindliness in Alice
Hooper that fascinates one."

"Kindliness?" repeated Sumner. "I suppose she has
the normal amount of that commodity. I've evidently
offended her seriously. What have I done, Mrs. Lincoln? Do you know?"

"Yes, dear Charles Sumner," very gently. "I know.
You've shown the fashionable world of Washington too
clearly that its most fashionable belle fascinates you.
After all, she *is* married and so there's been horrid gossip
about you both."

Sumner sat perfectly still, his blue eyes fastened on
Mary in growing consternation. "I've caused people to
gossip about Alice Mason? I, who would not let a
harsh breeze stir a hair of her head?"

Mary smiled. "You know as well as I that there's
been a horrid mess of talk about you and me, Senator.

Rightly enough, you've been philosophical about it. Where's your philosophy regarding Mrs. Hooper in like case?"

"But Alice is—" protested Sumner and paused.

"Alice is—" mimicked Mary, then went on earnestly. "Wait a moment, I'll read you what Alice *is* from the *Intelligence* of yesterday. It gives an account of Mrs. Eames' benefit for the Sanitary Commission." She turned the pages of the sheet, Sumner watching her somberly. " 'Mrs. Sturgis Hooper was there with her beauty, grace, slender and stately form, her high bred manners and her aristocratic reserve.'—The aristocratic reserve," commented Mary, laying down the paper, "is a little gratuitous. I've seen her when she showed the bad temper of a spoiled child."

But Sumner was not to be drawn into a discussion of Alice Hooper's character.

"But, Mrs. Lincoln," he asked, "why didn't Alice tell me this herself?"

"Because I think she couldn't bear to hurt you. I think she cares too much for you."

Sumner's great head sank to his breast and when after a pause he looked up, his face was drawn as though by a long illness. "There's a curse on my affection for women," he said. "Well—that's ended! You've been a good friend to me in this, as in many other ways, dear Mrs. Lincoln." He rose. "I'm—I'm not quite myself. This has been a greater blow than you know. Ah," clenching a great white fist and allowing it to fall upon the table, "she is lovely—lovely—"

"Memories are one of life's great compensations," said Mary. "Memories particularly of what never was and could not be. All our poets know that—'Heard melodies are sweet, but those unheard are sweeter'—'The spirit ditties of no tune'—'She cannot fade, though thou hast not thy bliss'—" she paused and sat with brooding eyes in the empty fire place.

"You have a great gift for sympathy!" ejaculated Sumner. "I shall come back to you often, often.—I haven't the resiliency of twenty-five years ago—" He bowed over Mary's hand and went out.

Lincoln, listening to Mary's account of this, made as she brushed her gorgeous chestnut hair before his mirror, bit his thumb and sighed, "Poor fellow! Poor Charles! —Mary, you really feel sympathy for him? Your little intrigue isn't all intrigue?"

Mary paused with the brush posed. "I'm devoted to Charles Sumner. Even were nothing else involved, I'd have wanted to give him this warning. But"—shaking the brush at him earnestly—"I'd stoop to *any* intrigue known or unknown to help you. And there's no use in your looking sanctimonious, young man!"

As there seemed nothing to be said in response to this, Lincoln suddenly kissed her and turned to another subject.

"I have a feeling that Meade is going to sit down and nurse his wounds in spite of all my urging. Lord, send me a general with legs!"

CHAPTER IX

POOR NANNY

AFTER all, Lincoln went out to the Soldiers' Home alone. Taddie had a sharp attack of ague late in July and little Isabella Hooper wilted in the terrific heat of Washington. Dr. Stone ordered both children away. The Hoopers departed for their summer place on the Massachusetts shore and Mary left her husband reluctantly and took Tad to the White Mountains. Sumner started on a lecture trip without appearing again at the White House. Lincoln was glad to see him go.

There was no wooing Sumner by any method he had thus far discovered. One might as well, thought Lincoln, coo to Bunker Hill monument! He was pleased to be left with a few months before him clear of Sumner and Congress in which to speed forward reconstruction in Louisiana and Tennessee. If he was to have only the one term in office, it behooved him not to waste an hour, a moment, in doing all that he could to commit the Government to his own peculiar plans. The need for haste became an obsession with him; an unceasing urge that chafed him day and night. He began a campaign of letter and dispatch writing, in an attempt to inspire Governor Shepley and General Banks in Louisiana and Governor Johnson and General Rosecrans in Tennessee with his own conception of speedy action.

The month of August remained long in his memory as a not unhumorous combination of chills and fever which afflicted his own body and mental chills and fevers which affected the mental processes of the men whom he sought to use for the great cause. Recrimination and indifference, feverish preparations and tardy performances. Rosecrans, slow and querulous. Burnside tardy in crossing from Ohio to Rosecrans' aid and between them the battle of Chickamauga lost. Banks and Shepley snarling over the question of authority—only Andrew Johnson, among them all, showing marked ability. And most heart-twisting of all, Meade losing Lee and settling down, apparently for life, on the Rapidan.

After a few weeks of this Lincoln wrote to Mary and asked how soon she thought it would be safe to bring Tad back to Washington. He was homesick for them. With this same letter he wrote one to Tad telling him news calculated to revive the boy's interest in home affairs. Poor Nanny goat had disappeared. She had been found by the gardener chewing up his pet flower bed and had been dealt with so harshly by him that she had retired to Tad's bedroom. The chamber-maid had found her lying on Tad's bed, chewing her little cud. The chamber-maid, too, had been harsh and Nanny had run away. Perhaps her wounded feelings had driven her to extreme ends such as joining the Army of the Potomac. Perhaps she would return when Taddie did.

The letters had the desired effect. Within a week after they were written Mary and Tad appeared at the White House with many trunks, with a cage containing a skunk, a turtle and a hoot owl, and with the flurry of domestic excitement that Lincoln loved because it meant Mary and Tad.

An hour after her arrival, Mary had completed an examination into the President's ways of eating and sleeping during her absence and repaired to his office with her report. He was a disgrace, she declared, to any wife.

"No! No! Don't break my old heart like that!" he protested with a grin.

"But you are! Even your giant strength can't stand up under Washington, the war and politics, plus your idiotic habits. James says you have attacks of heartburn. I'm going to put a box of saleratus and a teaspoon here on your desk. See that you use it. You haven't been eating enough and you're as thin as a bodkin. Oh, my dear, my dear, you do upset me so! Now, drink this glass of buttermilk and come with me for a ride."

"Where's Tad?" asked Lincoln after he had drained the glass with relish.

"He and Pete have organized a hunt for Nanny. I'm going to order the carriage right now. The horses are positively dying for exercise. Put that letter down and come, my dear husband," laying a tender hand on his.

He rose with alacrity and offered her his arm which Mary took with a sweeping curtsy and a little giggle.

Physically the ride was not particularly pleasant. September was very hot and very dry and Washington was playing host to a pest of flies unprecedented in any one's experience. People said that the proximity of many battlefields and the great number of hospitals in and around the city were the cause. However that might be, no means availed against the dreadful, buzzing, biting swarms that made waking hours a burden and sleeping almost impossible. They settled by the hundreds on the carriage. Mary's veil was a partial protection to her. But Lincoln, the coachman, and the footman were in misery while the horses almost kicked out of the traces in their irritation. In spite of this, Lincoln was glad to get away from his work; glad to see something beyond Lafayette Square; glad to be with his wife again.

"Tell me about the skunk," asked Lincoln after they

were well started. "Is he to be a bedroom pet, also?"

"Good heavens, no! Tad promises to keep him in the stable. For a long time I held out against bringing him home but Tad was so heartbroken about Nanny that I gave in. He bought the beast from a farmer boy up in Vermont, or rather traded for it."

"What did he swap?" asked Lincoln.

Mary's eyes twinkled. "That I didn't discover till we reached here. He gave the boy a photograph of yourself."

"No! Jings! Oh! Oh! Couldn't be better!" Lincoln's laughter caused a cow grazing pensively by the roadside to break her tether rope.

"What's he named it?" he gasped when he could.

"Louis Napoleon! The turtle is McClellan and the hoot owl is General Halleck."

"Better not let M. Mercier hear the first," laughed the President. "Tad's the joy of my heart. We must get him another goat."

"He says he doesn't want it. Nanny was his only love. He's written to all his friends telling of his loss. To Stanton, among others, who curiously enough sent him a wonderful formal letter of sympathy, and to Charles Sumner, from whom he has not heard. But that's not strange. Sumner wrote me from Boston that his brother George is dying in a hospital there. Poor Charles! He'll be the last brother left out of five!"

"That's hard news!" exclaimed Lincoln. "I'd like to write him a letter of sympathy. But if I do, he'll think I'm soft-soaping him."

Mary considered this for a few moments. "Perhaps you're right about it. You usually are in such things. Have you heard that he's joined in a quiet boom of Chase for the Presidency?" Lincoln nodded and she went on, "And have you heard that Butler is talked of as the Democratic nominee? You ought to get rid of Butler by putting him in your Cabinet."

Lincoln smiled. "What a crazy quilt you'd make of my poor Cabinet if I gave you your way! Who next?"

"Sumner next as Secretary of State," replied Mary promptly.

"Sam Hooper's idea, too," said Lincoln. "Another one of those blind boils you can neither cure nor bring to a head. I'm going to use Butler's executive ability by putting him in charge of the Department of Virginia and North Carolina and then pray to God he won't hamstring Meade. Now let me tell you about the good work Bob is doing in bringing his dark children up out of Egypt."

Somehow, in spite of dust and flies, it was a most refreshing drive. Yes, it was good to have Mary back.

With his wife's return and the arrival of cooler weather, Lincoln's wonted intellectual energy revived. This was well, for the annual message must be prepared and he must bring to this work a brain that functioned freed of the fog of weariness, for in it he proposed to take his stand, four square, on his own method of reconstruction. And he proposed in it also to hush for all time the complaint of Sumner and his radical followers that the President was only half-hearted in his efforts to enforce the Emancipation Proclamation; that he did not strenuously desire to free the slaves; that he was willing to make a peace with the South on slavery terms. It was a difficult paper to prepare not only as a state document but as a matter of literary composition—to make it lucid, to make it final, to make it beautiful.

The varying fortunes of Grant's campaign in the West with the thousand pressing details of his position as Chief Executive kept his office in a turmoil and he found it impossible to write there. He formed the habit of stealing away to his bedroom just before supper. Here he would seat himself before a window, feet on the sill, rest his long telescope on his toes and gaze at the Virginia hills. Something in this mild occupation released his mind from other perplexities and allowed it to clamp completely on the problem at hand.

Frequently he sat with meditative eye at the end of the telescope long after dusk had settled, blotting out first the red hills, then, in sequence, Long Bridge, the unfinished shaft of Washington Monument, the marshes, the Mall, his own garden. His mind was refined to an etcher's point as he traced the delicate subtleties of his task.

Tad, the free lance, alone had power to rouse him from his absorption in this work and Mary used the little boy as messenger to summon his father to the evening meal. Tad was still mourning for poor Nanny. He came in one evening at dusk and taking the telescope from his father's unresisting hands applied his own eye to it.

"Maybe Nanny did join the A'my of the Potomac," he murmured.

Immediately Lincoln roused himself. "Poor Nanny! You won't let me buy you another nice she goat, Tad?"

"No!" from lips that quivered. "Nanny was *hand*-twained. She wasn't just a plain she goat, Papa day. She was educated as much mo' than wegular goats as a West Pointa' is than a wegular pwivate. I'm getting so old now I don't feel like I could begin educating anotha' goat."

Lincoln kissed him. "What can I do to ease your heartache, darling Tad?"

"Take me to supper!" Tad wheedled and hand in hand the two descended to the dining room.

"Somebody's got to do something," Lincoln declared to his wife that evening. "Tad's mourning for poor Nanny would draw tears from an army sutler. What do you say we try to locate a she goat that will look like Nanny and, we'll hope, will have better manners? And just thrust it on him?"

"It might work," agreed Mary. "I'll see what James can do."

But James' efforts were forestalled. A day or so after Lincoln had made his suggestion, Tad rushed into his father's office.

"Come quick and see what Senata' Sumna' has given me!" he shouted, ignoring Halleck and Stanton who were seated with the President.

"Is Mr. Sumner here?" asked Lincoln.

"Yes! In my woom! Come on! All of you come," Tad added hospitably.

Stanton shook his head irritably. Halleck did not trouble to answer. Lincoln rose. He always felt a little offended when Tad was slighted. "If you gentlemen will excuse me, I'll report on that matter in person at the War Office a little later." And he allowed Tad to lead him out.

Lincoln paused in the door of the child's bedroom. Two baby she goats, each a tiny replica of poor dear Nanny, were horning each other vigorously on the hearth rug. Senator Sumner, in deep black, held their lead ropes.

"They a' Boston goats!" cried Tad. "I'm going to name one Beans and the otha'—" He hesitated.

"Cod," suggested his father, crossing the room with hand extended to Sumner. "This is like your kindness, Senator! How can we help loving you?"

"Don't try!" heartily from Sumner.

He looked worn and very sad, Lincoln thought. "What's the news from our Boston friends," he asked, aloud. "How is Sam Hooper and Mrs. Hooper—" He paused, conscious that he had been tactless.

But Sumner was cool enough. "I saw Sam, yesterday, but I've not seen Mrs. Hooper or little Isabella since July."

"I heard from General Banks not an hour ago that there was a great deal of sickness on his staff and that Captain Hooper was among those afflicted," said the President. No use trying to be tactful. Sam Hooper was his own friend as well as Sumner's. Not but what it was a queer situation. Perhaps he'd better try to make it sound a little less pointed. "I've got a couple of neighbor boys down there in New Orleans and their folks got me to ask particularly for them. That's how the matter came up. I wonder if Sam Hooper knows?"

"He didn't mention it to me," replied Sumner, slowly. "Is Captain Hooper very ill?"

"Stanton is getting me a report on him, with the other boys," replied Lincoln. "Will you go over to the War Office with me while I get it? If things go wrong, you'd be the one to break the news to Sam. I'll try to head off the regular death notice going to him. Would you prefer to have me bring word back here?"

"I'll wait here with Taddie, if you don't mind, Mr. Lincoln," replied Sumner.

The President nodded and went out. His feelings, as he made his way to the War Office, were difficult to analyze. There was typhoid down there on Banks' staff. Sturgis Hooper and the neighbors' sons had little chance of recovery. If young Hooper died—well, it was like the most of life. One man's loss was another man's gain. Sort of indecent, his own hasty exit to get news for Sumner. When he reached the War Office, he found that Stanton had received the delayed telegram from New Orleans. Sturgis Hooper was dead and so were the two other young officers. Lincoln took the yellow slip from the operator and without waiting to check over the entire list with Stanton, he hurried back to the White House. What a situation! Shakespeare should have had it to play with or Charles Dickens! Sumner still stood quietly on the hearth rug watching Tad with his new pets. Without a word Lincoln handed the Senator the death list. Sumner read it slowly, then looked up at the President.

"I know several of these boys," he said, quietly. But he was white to the very lips. "If you wish, I'll write to their families."

"Check them off and I'll delay the army notices," agreed Lincoln, purposely businesslike and crisp but watching Sumner closely. The Senator looked as if he were about to faint.

But Sumner was steady enough. He folded the tragic slip and put it in his pocketbook. "I'll send this back to you in an hour or so, Mr. Lincoln," he said. His voice was husky. His eyes suffused.

"Thank you again for Tad, Senator," said the President.

"I love Tad," murmured Sumner and he went slowly out into the hall.

On his way back to his desk, Lincoln met Mary and told her the news. She gasped, blinked and exclaimed, "Isn't it ghastly how one man's grief may mean another man's solace!"

"I'd say Sumner had a long hard row to hoe before he found his solace," Lincoln nodded grimly.

"Poor fellow! I'm afraid he has!" agreed Mary.

CHAPTER X

THE EXPLOSIVE

LINCOLN finished the annual message about the middle of November. His preoccupation with this had caused him to leave until the last moment the setting down of a speech he had been asked to make at the dedication of the Gettysburg cemetery on November 19th. He left for Gettysburg on the 18th with John Hay, Seward, Nicolay, Stanton and others, both reluctant and eager to go. Tad was ill, not seriously, but he disliked leaving him. He and Mary since Willie's death could scarcely contain themselves for anxiety if either Tad or Bob so much as sneezed. Lincoln was feeling ill, himself. He was feverish and his head ached and buzzed.

His back ached too. But he was eager to get away from Washington for a few hours. Eager, too, to see the battlefield, every rod of which he knew vicariously as he had known Antietam and Chancellorsville. He was afraid Mary would discover his condition and sic Dr. Stone on him. Then his holiday would be nil.

But he got away without trouble and finished writing the little speech on the train. He delivered it the next day. It sounded flat, it seemed to Lincoln, after Edward Everett's long hour of superb oratory. The people seemed unimpressed and he supposed they looked on his effort as a sort of benediction following Everett's great sermon. He hoped it was not an entire failure, he told Everett, who praised it.

Not that it mattered. Nor did the view of the battlefield later matter much. He felt ill and wanted to get
home. He got there late in the evening of the 19th.
Mary gave him one look, then made him lie down on
the sofa in the sitting room. Then she sent for Dr.
Stone.

The doctor examined the President carefully. When
he had finished he said gravely, "I'm afraid we've got a
case of varioloid here, Mr. Lincoln."

Mary gave a little scream. "Small pox, doctor! My
poor husband!"

"Mild small pox," agreed Dr. Stone. "You must get
to bed, sir, and we must put the White House under
quarantine."

"Has Taddie got this, too? Are you deceiving me
about him?" gasped Mary.

"No! No! Tad only has malaria and is doing well."
The doctor smiled at her. "Keep him away from his
father. Take off your shawl, Mrs. Lincoln, I'm going
to vaccinate every one in the house beginning with you.
We doctors all go armed these days for just this."

"But it took with me, last summer," protested Mary,
nevertheless baring her plump white arm, her voice
steadying as she did so.

Dr. Stone grunted and rubbed the firm flesh with alco-
hol. He talked as he worked. "You must get to bed
and stay there, Mr. Lincoln. Varioloid can be dangerous. I don't want to frighten you. But you're a very
sick man and must take care of yourself."

Lincoln glanced up at the doctor who looked curiously
unreal. In fact he seemed to waver back and forth like
a ghost disturbed by wind. "I can't go to bed," he said
hoarsely. "I've got to finish my annual message and discuss it with the Cabinet. And those poor fellows out at

Chattanooga are beginning a fearful fight. I'm needed at the end of a telegraph wire. I'm not catching, am I, till I begin to erupt?"

"Not necessarily. But you must stay in bed, Mr. Lincoln, or you'll endanger your life. Can't you control him, Mrs. Lincoln?" He looked at Mary. He knew she would rise wonderfully to the emergency, though she might have hysterics afterward.

She gave the doctor a little nod and taking both Lincoln's hands, she gave him a gentle tug. "Come, my dear! You've no excuse for not spending this night at least in bed. You've got a new kind of patronage to distribute now, eh?"

Lincoln staggered to his feet, blind with pain. "Yes," he mumbled, "it's the only time I've had something to give away that nobody wanted."

He passed a wretched night, his fever giving him horrid, inchoate fantasies. But he woke in the morning with brain clear enough to realize that he was going to be very ill and that unless he discussed the annual message with his Cabinet, at once, he might not be able to do so at all.

When Nicolay came in to say that the Cabinet members had convened and wished to know what of the President's work they could perform, he sat up in bed and told the secretary to help him on with his dressing robe. This done, he said:

"Now you go out and ask them if they're afraid to come in here for a little while. I'm not catching yet. And I want to read them the message. Then I can go ahead and be sick right comfortably."

All the seven followed Nicolay back into the bedroom. The sight of them steadied the President to a supreme effort. His brain cleared marvelously. He was even

able, he told himself with a grin, to observe a certain
hopeful aspect in Chase's concern for him, as if the Secretary of the Treasury were wondering how often varioloid proved fatal or if it ever ripened into black smallpox or if black smallpox in a President were grounds for
impeachment. When they were seated around the room,
he took the message from Nicolay and read it aloud.

It was a remarkable state document, more remarkable
than Lincoln at all realized until he saw its effect on this
particularly astute audience. As an annual message must,
it contained the usual report on the condition of the
country, but it contained three other clauses all of which
Lincoln considered exceedingly and equally important.
First it contained a proclamation of amnesty for repentant rebels with the oath of allegience they must
sign.   Second, a succinct statement to the effect that
when ten per cent of the pre-war voters in any rebelling
State should take this oath of allegiance, they could form
a State government which would be recognized by the
Chief Executive as the authentic voice of that State.
Third, he magnificently reassured Congress and the country of his abhorrence of slavery and of his unbreakable
determination to end the "execrable institution."

When he had finished, he dropped the manuscript a
little feebly and took off his spectacles that he might perceive clearly the effect his explosives had had on his
associates.

Seward smiled. "In other words, Mr. Lincoln, you've
forever put to rest the howl of the radicals that you won't
permanently end slavery."

"Yes! Yes!" exclaimed Father Welles. "You've
closed Sumner's mouth for good!"

The other members joined in with enthusiastic congratulations on his restatement of his attitude toward

the slaves.   Lincoln waited with growing surprise for
their comments on his reconstruction program.   To his
utter astonishment none came.   Gradually, it dawned on
him that these men, too, had been skeptical as to his
determination to down the "slave empire"—these men
who, one might have thought, must understand clearly
his every political purpose.   And in the intensity of their
relief and joy, they were ignoring the importance of the
methods by which he proposed to carry out his promise
to end slavery.   It was a staggering thought to Lincoln.
If the message had this effect on his official intimates,
why might it not have the same effect on Congress?
Wasn't it possible that in swallowing his declarations on
Emancipation, Congress would swallow his plans for
reconstruction?   If this were possible, then the message
would go farther than his wildest dreams of its purpose
had carried him.

He listened to the ejaculations of the Secretaries—
even Chase piped up feebly, although the clause on slavery robbed him of his choicest criticism against Lincoln—
tried to thank them and suddenly realized that he had
gone beyond his strength.   The faces about his bed
faded away and when he came to himself, the room was
empty and Mary was holding smelling salts to his nose
the while she chided him.

He was very ill for a few days; so ill that he found
himself during lucid intervals earnestly tabulating Hamlin's weaknesses and strength and wishing that he'd been
able to make the man from Maine more fully his partner in his plans for reconstruction; so ill that, as he
learned later, the whole country was speculating on Hamlin's known and unknown biases.   The fever, the pain,
the almost intolerable itching finally engrossed him and

he was obliged, as he told Mary, to leave the country for a while to stew in its own juices.

But he was splendidly strong and by the first week in December he was mentally himself and able to rejoice mightily in the great news of Grant's victory at Chattanooga. There was no such dearth of information concerning this battle as had been the case with Gettysburg. Charles Dana was with Grant and he kept Stanton informed.

"Dana's reports for six months have been giving us fair warning that Grant's the man," said Lincoln, as he read Dana's vivid story of the battle to Mary. "I reckon that what with Dana's opinion and Grant's vindication of it, the little General's in line for that dictatorship. And what will Butler and his friends say then?"

Mary shook her head. "Butler'll say *he* never had a real chance."

"Then he'll say a lie," returned the President, flatly.

He was chafing now over the quarantine restrictions. He wanted to get up to the Capitol and read the annual message himself to a joint session of the Houses. The more he thought of the reception the Cabinet had given his paper the more excited and sanguine he became about its possible effect on the Congress, the more he grew to believe it might be possible to sweep some of his own reconstruction legislation through on the wave of enthusiasm he was sure now the message would engender.

But when he told Dr. Stone his plan, the physician vetoed it with all the large vehemence at his command. He tried to win Mary, but she became half hysterical at the mere mention of such a strain on his weakened nerves. Still, not till the day the message was due did Lincoln really give up the struggle. Then, while eating his breakfast in bed, he sent for John Hay and dispatched him to the Capitol with the manuscript.

John was gone for hours and Lincoln worked himself into a fever before the young man appeared. He had waited until Congress had exhausted its first comments. The story of the day lost nothing, of course, in John's telling. However, Lincoln was convinced that there could be no question but that Congress had received the message with wild enthusiasm.

Charles Sumner had gone about, saying, "The slaves are free! The slaves are free!" Boutell, the extreme radical, had kept shouting, "It is right at last! The free are forever free!" Owen Lovejoy, the Western Abolitionist, had sobbed, "I shall live to see slavery ended in America!" And Greeley, on the floor for the day, had cried that it was devilish good!

Not a single question had been raised about his reconstruction clauses. Every thought had been focused on the slavery issue. It was astounding! Lincoln felt his physical weakness drop from him like a discarded garment.

"Why, John, the millennium's arrived! The radicals are praising Lincoln!" he cried. "Here, give me a shoulder. I'm going into the office and do an hour's work instead of sitting here like an old lady tatting. Even Lyman Trumbull and Henry Winter Davis approved me, eh?"

"Trumbull did. Davis asked that the reconstruction portion of the message be referred to a special committee and that was done," replied John, as he offered the President his hand.

"Who is chairman of that committee?" asked Lincoln, sharply.

"Winter Davis himself," replied John.

Lincoln sank back on the sofa. "My mortal enemy!" he groaned. "Still, you say he didn't talk against the message?" hopefully.

"Not at all, sir," replied John. "I'm sure you can rest easy. There's a real feeling of loyalty to you to-night in Congress. Davis or Sumner either won't be able to get any dirty legislation through."

"Loyalty!" ejaculated Lincoln. "You poor puling babe! Haven't you learned yet, dear John, that there's no such word in the lexicon of politics? Even Sumner, the finest Roman of them all, can't be loyal. Human nature's a pretty weak thing, I reckon. The world is full of Judases. Come to think of it, the Savior of the world chose twelve disciples and even out of that small number, selected by superhuman wisdom, one turned out a traitor!" Then with a twinkle, he added, "Maybe it's not improper to say that Judas carried the bag, was treasurer to Jesus and his disciples!"

John laughed ruefully, then asked, "Is that why you have no real intimates among the politicians, Mr. Lincoln?"

"I reckon that's part of the reason," agreed the President, a little sadly. He sighed, then looked over the young man appraisingly as he lingered before the fire. "You look as if you needed to get out to grass, John. Being tied to an office job is hard on a young fellow like you. You've got some so-called political friends among the Unionists in Florida, haven't you?"

The young man grinned. "Had a letter from one of them last week. They want me to run as their Representative in Congress."

Lincoln returned the grin, then said seriously, "We'd better work while Congress debates. General Gillmore plans to try to take over the north of Florida, soon.

How'd you like to go down there and try out this oath of allegiance of mine? Fix up some blank books and so on and see how it works."

John's black eyes blazed. "I'd like it above all things, sir! You aren't going to lose any time, eh? When do you want me to go?"

"As soon as you can get ready. I'm going to have one or two tight jobs finished before Winter Davis can get his committee to agree on a hostile program. They won't have the heart to *de*struct a state after I've made it, I'm sure."

"Oh! even Congress isn't that idiotic!" agreed John Hay, as they moved slowly toward the office.

CHAPTER XI

HOPE

SUMNER came up to call as soon as the quarantine was lifted, perhaps a week after the reading of the annual message. He congratulated Lincoln heartily on the stand he had taken with regard to slaves, but made no mention of reconstruction.

Lincoln, who wished to let sleeping dogs lie until Winter Davis reported his program, was glad to have it so. Sumner was looking extraordinarily young. Hope, Lincoln thought, is a great rejuvenator. It was curious finally to have achieved the friendliest of outward relations with Sumner when he never could forget for a moment that Sumner was really his deadly adversary, was at the moment of uttering his perfectly sincere congratulations undoubtedly planning to put Chase or himself in the White House, was figuring how to force Lincoln's resignation, was scheming to block his every effort at rehabilitating the South on lines of mercy! Yet there was nothing dishonorable in Sumner's attitude. All these strange complications belonged to the political game. "No, not game!" Lincoln corrected himself grimly. With Sumner politics was not a game but his very life. Perhaps, he thought more grimly, this was true of Lincoln too!

Not the members of Congress alone reacted happily to the annual message. His stock rose with the whole country. And though the facile pendulum of public approbation began to swing back after a week or so, Lincoln believed that his ideas had made real progress with the nation at large.   The belief became a certainty when, soon after the holidays, Arkansas loyalists began to take the Oath of December 8, as that portion of Lincoln's amnesty clause was called.   Andrew Johnson began administering the oath in Tennessee.   Louisiana was at work on her new constitution along the line of Lincoln's plan.   John Hay left for Florida in January, full of a great faith.   The President was pleased and sanguine.

He said to Mary one night not long after John Hay's departure, "Well, three of my baby States are well on their way to birth and both parents doing well;—myself and the ten per cent loyalists claiming that proud title. I don't believe Congress will have the heart to drown 'em, like blind kittens."

Mary, who was hearing Tad's French lesson at the library table, looked up to say, "You're misjudging the cleverness and the vindictiveness of those men, Abra'm. You're judging them by yourself.   I believe Charles Sumner and Lyman Trumbull and Winter Davis are just hoping you'll take enough rope to hang yourself."

"Nonsense!" replied Lincoln.   "Sumner's so sure he's going to get me out of here by the time the war is over that he isn't going to trouble too much about what I do in the interim."   He seated himself before the fire and Tad at once embraced the opportunity to drop his lessons and crowd onto his father's knees.   He was small for his ten years but still was growing a little large for this old posture.   His mother reminded him of this and ordered him back to his lessons but his father gathered him close and Tad prepared for a nap.

"Father Welles told me to-day," Lincoln went on, "that Sumner lately admitted to him that he had vague dreams of himself for my job but was willing to relinquish them in favor of Chase."

"Abra'm," Mary suddenly leaned toward him, "why wouldn't it be a great move, if you're renominated, to have Sumner run for Vice President instead of Hamlin? You know as well as I do that nice as he is, Hamlin's not a bit of good to you. He's a radical and works with Trumbull and Davis and Wade."

"Sumner would scorn the suggestion," replied Lincoln. "Not but what you're right about Hamlin. I've been feeling round on the subject. Even tried out General Butler for the job, to oblige the anti-slavery Democrats. He thanked us kindly and told us he had a *real* job, now. I've a good mind to try Andrew Johnson in the place."

Mary gave a little scream. "Oh, you great fool! Why, he's nothing but white trash! A narrow, ignorant, hidebound Democrat who gets drunk in public. Now don't do this thing! Don't!"

"He's a true and valuable man," declared Lincoln. "The work he's done has been simply indispensable. His suppressing disorder in Tennessee would be enough to immortalize him. But on top of being Governor and General, he's been a Quartermaster, relieving want and sheltering the homeless. He's re-made that old State and done it intelligently, too. And I tell you, Mary, I'll have to have the help of the Democrats if I'm to have any chance at all of being reëlected. Johnson can swing the border States for me."

"Oh! Oh! Oh!" Mary wrung her hands. "You're wrong in this, Abra'm, indeed you are!"

"I reckon you haven't watched his work in Tennessee," said Lincoln. He was a little uneasy, as he always was when Mary opposed his judgment of men. Mary suddenly burst into tears. "Surely, my dear," he protested, "you don't feel that strongly against him!"

"I feel as if you'd dug your own grave," she sobbed.

He tried to take a light tone. "Come, now! You mean I've nipped some scheme you and Mrs. Hooper had hatched."

Mary, biting her lips, dried her eyes and as she saw Tad stirring, tried to play up to her husband's lead. "Alice Hooper is back looking very handsome in mourning."

"Isabella and me," remarked Tad, suddenly opening his eyes, "a' going to be mawied as soon as I get a new pony instead of a goat. I can't get he' to like Beans and Cod. If poo' Nanny hadn't got lost, she might have liked he'. When I was playing with Isabella yeste'day, Mista' Sumna' said he'd give Isabella a pony but she said to give it to me. But I told him I couldn't take anything from an enemy of my fatha's."

The yawning little boy sat erect, his face rosy with sleep and firelight. His mother crossed the room to sit on the arm of Lincoln's chair. Lincoln rested his hand on hers.

"And what did the Senator say to that, son?" he asked.

"He didn't say anything," replied Tad. "Anyhow, Motha', can I have a pop stand down in the hall to sell to the folks that come to fuss at papa day? I want to make money for the hospitals. I told Isabella she could wash glasses. She said she wouldn't. She'll be a lazy wife but I'll be wealthy so I don't mind. Can I, Motha'?"

"I'll see," replied his mother.

"Isabella's mamma," Tad went on, "is the only one I know who don't like Mista' Sumna'! She's always saying teasy things to him."

"I reckon it would be a wise thing if some one of your parents had the common sense and courage to send you to boarding school, son," groaned Lincoln, gathering the little figure in the black velvet suit close to him.

"I'm not going away from you and motha', one inch," replied Tad with the complacency of sure knowledge. "I don't see why she don't like him. He's stylish and famous and she likes people like that. I asked he' and she only laughed and pulled my ea'. She's so tall and pink and white—" He gave a wide yawn and Lincoln rose, still holding him.

"Well, Taddie darling, seems to me you've given your mother and me enough thoughts to make into cuds for a while. You, to bed!"

Tad spoke sleepily over his father's shoulder. "Motha', will you give me fifty cents to start my pop stand with?"

"If you'll get your French lesson first thing in the morning," replied his mother.

"Ho! Easy!" Tad threw her a kiss which she returned with a smile.

It was the day after this conversation that Henry Winter Davis introduced his reconstruction bill in Congress. Lincoln studied a copy of the bill. It ignored the President's plans and declared that as the Rebel States were out of the Union, Congress was the only agency by which they could be readmitted. It then gave a tight formula for reconstruction that Lincoln knew would enrage the South. For a moment his heart sank, then, as he thought further, he said with sudden relief to Nicolay, who had brought him the bill:

"Sumner won't back this. It doesn't include negro suffrage in its plans. The Senator will inevitably line up against it. I'm not going to worry. Sumner will kill it."

"Perhaps—!" said Nicolay with a doubtful smile.

Tad came in on this conversation demanding to know where his mother was.

"In the garden, most likely. She always tells James where she's going," replied his father. "If you've looked in the garden and she's not there, ask James."

"I have, Papa day," said Tad. "James said he saw her talking in the ga'den to a lady in a black veil and he thinks she walked out the back gate with the lady. He thought it was one of her poo' folks she was going to visit. But Pete Kelley says he saw motha' going into a house way out on Seventh Stweet whe' he was c'lecting old wags. I to'd him he was a big lia'. But he says he isn't."

Lincoln glanced at Nicolay. The threat to kidnap different members of the Lincoln family and hold them until the President made peace had been made so frequently that no one paid much attention to the letters containing the threats. Yet the fear that some one might attempt to do this dastardly thing to his wife or children never was very far from the President's thoughts. So now he said to Nicolay, casually, for Tad's benefit, "This reminds me that I had arranged to go to the hospitals with Mrs. Lincoln this afternoon. Will you tell James to tell her I'm ready?"

Nicolay went out followed by Tad. Half an hour later, he returned without Tad but with Pete Kelley's hand in his. "This small boy insists on his story, sir," said Nicolay. "We can't seem to locate Mrs. Lincoln, nor to extend the facts beyond Tad's account. I've sent him around to visit with Isabella."

"How do you know it was Mrs. Lincoln, Pete?" asked Lincoln, his heart sinking with premonition of evil.

"Because it was, sir," insisted Pete, his freckled face pale with earnestness. "She had on that spotted purple dress she wears in the garden and that big floppy hat with the purple veil. I'd know it in—in—in heaven."

"I think Pete and you and I had better make a quiet trip out to that house," said Lincoln to Nicolay, rising.

"Let Pete and me go alone, sir. I'm sure it would be wiser," begged Nicolay.

"No, sir," replied the President, picking up his hat, "if my wife is in a tight fix, nothing can stop my going to find her. Not Grant nor Meade nor Sumner is big enough for that."

He started for the door, filled with a nameless terror. Nicolay suggested the carriage.

"And have a cavalry guard follow me and a string of reporters later?" cried Lincoln, leading the way rapidly down the servants' path to the rear gate. "No! How far is the house from here, Pete?" he asked, taking the child's hand.

"Just out the Seventh Street pike a little way, that old farmhouse where they raise pigs," replied Pete, at a jog trot to keep up with the President's stride.

"Can you show me a short cut?" asked Lincoln.

"Yes, sir," suddenly turning to a path that led through the pasture lot beyond Lafayette Square.

It was not difficult to avoid passers-by in this direction. Washington was a sprawling wilderness here with no sidewalks and the right of way along the road when they reached it was disputed only by pigs and cows. Fifteen minutes' walk plastered them to their knees with red mud and brought them to a lane at the end of which stood an old red brick house. Its white-pillared portico was falling down. Its front garden was a pigsty and duck pond.

"Here it is, sir!" Pete wiped his nose on his sleeve

and pointed. "I saw Mrs. Lincoln walking up the steps into that house with a lady in black."

Lincoln groaned and Pete suddenly began to cry.

"Hush! I'm not cross. I'm obliged to you, dear Pete. Nicolay, you and the boy stay here."

Nicolay ventured to protest, but Lincoln, still driven by a mysterious certainty that Mary had called him, silenced him sternly.

"I always know when my wife needs me. Let me do this my way, George."

He splashed through the pigsty as certain that Mary was in this ruined farm as he was that the afternoon sky was blue overhead and that blackbirds called from a marsh beside the lane. He banged on the door. There was no response. He thrust it open with his foot.

Mary lay on the floor of the deserted hall. Lincoln leaped to her side. She was unconscious but breathing heavily. He lifted her and rushed from the house.

Nicolay, as he saw the President emerge, sent Pete running like a rabbit with a note to Billy Stoddard. Lincoln did not speak and did not answer Nicolay's questions as he started on a mighty pace along the muddy road. But when the President paused for breath at the edge of Lafayette Square, the secretary produced a little silver brandy flask.

"Try it," ordered Lincoln briefly.

But Mary could not swallow. While they were working with her, the White House carriage galloped up with Pete beside the coachman and in a few moments they whirled through the White House gates.

Dr. Stone was in attendance almost as soon as Lincoln had laid Mary on her bed. To the President's unutterable relief, he announced after a few moments that she was not poisoned but was suffering from a heavy dose of

morphine.   He began at once to work on her, but it was
midnight before Mary recognized her husband's anxious
face beside her pillow.

"Where's Taddie?" was her first question.

"Over on your sofa, asleep," replied the President,
laying her hand against his cheek.   "He wouldn't go to
his own bed until you could kiss him good-night."

Mary raised herself on one elbow and after a glance
at Tad lay down again with a sigh of relief.   "I had a
feeling that something had been done to him."   She
stared at her husband.   "Just what has happened?"

"That's just what we want to know," replied Lincoln.
"I'll tell you what occurred here."

Mary listened intently.   When he had finished his account, she said, "I did call you.   I knew you'd hear."

They gazed into each other's eyes for a moment, then
Mary said, "That Rachel Atkins who's been helping me
with my hospital sewing came to me this morning while
I was at work in the greenhouse and told me with great
secrecy that brother John was in hiding in her house out
on Seventh Street.   She said he'd recently been brought
as a prisoner to Point Lookout, that he had escaped with
the help of her husband, who I knew was a guard over
there, and wanted to see me before he died of a bad
wound he'd gotten last fall at Chattanooga.

"Of course I got excited as usual.   The one thought
I had was that such news about my half brother would
start the gossip about my being a Southern sympathizer
all over again.   But I just had to go to John in his need.
So I told no one and started off with Rachel.   Well,
she had a wounded Rebel there, all right, but it wasn't
John or anything like him.   I was suspicious at once and
accused Rachel of deceiving me.   While we were arguing
I began to feel faint, the way I do so often and Rachel

got me a glass of water. I remember later trying to get out of the house and that's all."

"About enough, I should think!" exclaimed Lincoln, heatedly.

"Don't scold me, dear! I know I was a fool."

"Scold you!" ejaculated the President. "I feel more like weeping over you."

And he did weep, with his head beside hers on the pillow.

The detective police unraveled the story easily enough. The woman Rachel Atkins and her accomplices were Northerners, who had planned to hold the President's wife subject to orders from a group of influential Rebels in Richmond. It was extraordinary how near their scheme came to working. A depot hack had been at the back door ready to convey Mary to parts unknown when Lincoln thundered at the front door. The plotters' escape into the woods had been easy and they were not found until the following day.

Mary was a long time recovering from the morphine poisoning and the shock. It was given out that the President's wife was suffering from an attack of malaria and no one questioned this or asked why the ague should be accompanied by the profound nervous symptoms that accompanied the attack.

CHAPTER XII

A LOVER AT FIFTY

IN one way, Mary's prolonged illness was a good thing for her husband. He alone had power to soothe her restlessness and he snatched many moments from his busy day to go to her and sit beside her sofa talking or reading. These moments, though brief, gave him intermittent respites that helped him a great deal in enduring the frenzied business of the spring.

To every one's astonishment, Charles Sumner came out late in March in favor of the Davis bill. At first, the news staggered Lincoln. He and Sumner had a short passage at arms over it when they met in Stanton's office one day.

"Changed your notion about negro suffrage, eh, Senator?" Lincoln asked, looking up from the telegraph operator's seat he was occupying.

"What do you mean, Mr. Lincoln?" demanded Sumner.

"I mean that I can't understand why you support the Davis bill," replied the President.

"Because it does insure the negroes freedom and I believe that I can amend it to include suffrage." Sumner spoke in a voice that silenced the whole room.

Stanton irascibly asked if it was necessary to bring Senate debates into the War Office and Lincoln at once turned back to the message he had been reading, while Sumner, affronted, stalked out.

Lincoln watched the progress of the bill with anxiety

but, as the days wore on, with a certain amount of philosophy too. The lengthy debate gave him what he needed most—time. Moreover, with the newspapers giving a great deal of space to the speeches, the country at large must inevitably become more or less educated as to this difficult problem of statecraft. He thought that when people understood the matter their common sense would put them on his side. Perhaps this would help him at the polls. And as spring came on his thought as to this appeared to be justified. An astonishingly large number of States were instructing their delegates to the pending Republican convention to vote for the renomination of Abraham Lincoln.

Gradually he became conscious of a thrilling fact; that beyond the yammering, noisy throngs who wrote to him and talked to him and scolded and hampered him with their hates, there was a great, voiceless multitude which believed as he believed. Sumner's phrase, "King of the Commonalty," occurred to him many times that spring as he compared the vicious statements made about him in Congress with the silent comment of the common people sending their delegates to the convention. Perhaps if Sumner did get around to starting that impeachment, the plain folks wouldn't stand for it!

Even when his own plans on reconstruction miscarried, he did not falter as he might have without this consciousness of the backing of the commonalty. John Hay returned from Florida early in April, the picture of despair. Both his mission and that of General Gillmore had failed.

"Pshaw, John!" exclaimed Lincoln. "Don't go round with your tail between your legs! We were merely premature. I'll send you down there later and you'll put it through—after the convention."

As warm weather advanced and roads dried, active
military campaigns pressed upon his attention. He had
to be the main guiding hand of the general scheme, for
Halleck was breaking under the strain—poor Halleck—
and becoming each day more helpless to make decisions,
more sullen and recalcitrant under Stanton's battering
and the contempt of his commanding generals.

It was evident that a firmer hand than Halleck's was
needed at the head of all the fighting forces, but Lincoln
did not want to oust him and hung on to him, trying to
bolster Halleck's weaknesses with his own strength.
However, it was a decided relief to Lincoln when, the
tide of public opinion about Grant having caught up with
the President's, Congress requested Lincoln to elevate
Grant to the grade of Lieutenant General. This was the
highest rank ever held by any American officer save
Washington. Halleck was thus automatically subordinated to Grant, although he retained his position in
Washington.

Grant at once assumed personal command over the
Army of the Potomac and went to Headquarters on the
Rapidan. Lincoln, with a feeling that it was now or
never, girded himself up to watch for signs that Grant
would not be smitten with the lethargy that had over-
taken all his predecessors.

It became obvious in April that the Sumner group was
concentrating its efforts on putting Chase into the
running for the radical nomination. Lincoln hoped that
this meant that they were done, for the moment at least,
with the impeachment idea. The fact that he was fla-
grantly disloyal to his chief did not prevent the Secretary
of the Treasury from clinging with all his brilliant and
vindictive strength to the prerogatives of his office. In-

deed, he so frequently overstepped his prerogatives this spring of 1864 that Lincoln's patience broke.

He refused to ratify a highly improper appointment made by Chase.

Chase immediately sent in one of his periodic resignations.

Lincoln accepted it!

It was not an easy thing to do from any point of view. Chase was superb in his official capacity, but as Lincoln told Mary, after he had made his decision, the Secretary had become so increasingly irritable and uncomfortable that he was making the whole Cabinet irritable and uncomfortable with him. People at large would be bound to misinterpret the act, would be bound to construe it as revenge on Lincoln's part because of those Presidential aspirations. But hardest of all to bear must be the effect it could have on Charles Sumner.

As Lincoln had foreseen, immediately after word had gone out that Senator Fessenden of Maine had accepted Chase's portfolio, Sumner descended on the White House.

It was a lovely May morning, and Lincoln was walking with Mary in the kitchen garden looking for the first signs of fruit in the strawberry beds when the Senator found them. The President almost groaned aloud. His failure to get on with Sumner was becoming a nightmare.

"Shall I stay or disappear?" asked Mary, as they saw the gigantic figure in the checked suit striding over the asparagus beds.

"Better stay. I need support. My moral knees click together like the ague whenever he gets after me, now.— Well, Senator, loaded for ba'r this morning, I see!"

Sumner bowed to Mary, the early sun bringing red lights to his bared chestnut head which was as yet un-

touched with gray. But his face was lined. He looked
as if he had slept little.

Lincoln gave him no chance to speak. "I thought you
wanted Fessenden out of the Senate. You hate him and
are always fighting with him."

"No one can take Mr. Chase's place!" exclaimed Sumner. "Least of all a sick man like Mr. Fessenden."

"If Chase is going to run for the Republican nomination, his resignation is only decent, Mr. Sumner." Lincoln's voice was carefully patient. "I want him to take
a full sporting chance in the race."

"You're playing with me, Mr. Lincoln!" protested
Sumner. "What's back of this? Revenge for Chase's
Presidential aspirations?"

"The study of revenge—immortal hate again, eh?
You don't know me yet, do you, Senator!" Lincoln
stood biting the edge of his forefinger. How to make
Sumner understand! It was the most difficult human
problem with which he'd ever wrestled.

Red birds whistled in the copper beech below his
window. An oriole flickered among the roses. Mary,
moving a little from them, stooped near the strawberry
plants, a dainty figure in her lavender print. Beyond the
iron fence a line of army ambulances was moving. One
heard groans and inarticulate cries as they turned the
deep rutted corners. Lincoln wiped the sweat from his
forehead with the back of his hand. Sumner stood waiting. The fellow was as unavoidable and as inexorable as
fate. He would try the effect of the simple truth on him.

"It was this way, Senator. When Chase again ten-
dered me his resignation I felt bitter chagrin. It meant
that he wanted me once more to go to him and urge him
to remain and that I had accepted what he meant as
disciplining me. It meant that the Secretary of the

Treasury and not the President is top dog, that Chase is no longer subordinate to Lincoln, that the President abdicates his constitutional powers. I have mighty little personal pride, Senator, as I think you've found, but the longer I hold this office, the more sensitive I grow as to its dignity and sacredness. You know as well as I that Chase has crossed the line with me as deliberately and grossly as ever McClellan did. I'm through."

Sumner, cane planted in the garden loam, listened with an unusual expression dawning in his eyes. Unless, Lincoln told himself, he was foolishly vain, that look was one of respect. He was sure of it when Sumner said with his captivating simplicity and earnestness, "I beg your pardon, Mr. Lincoln. I'm afraid we've all been a little intrusive at times. I withdraw my protest."

"Jings," thought Lincoln, "John Hay is right! What the fellow needs is just a good licking every once in a while!" Aloud he said, "Granted, Mr. Sumner! And let me add that no one in these United States has as much admiration for Chase's ability as I have. No one has put up with him as much as I have for the sake of keeping that ability harnessed to the nation's needs. And I'm not going to give up hope of using it again, but in another direction. In case old Chief Justice Taney peters out while I'm still in office, what do you say to Chase on the Supreme Bench?"

Sumner's whole expression changed. His eyes glowed with pleasure. "Is that a promise, Mr. Lincoln?"

"No, it's not a promise—but to this extent—if I can make myself believe that Chase's unfortunate judgments and personal ambition won't sway him in such a position."

This did not dampen Sumner's enthusiasm. "Oh, fine!

Oh, splendid! How you relieve me, Mr. Lincoln!" He held out his hand to the President.

Lincoln took it, thinking in astonishment as he did so that Chase might have been instead of an asset, something of a white elephant on the Senator's overburdened back.

"Come in and have breakfast with us, won't you, Mr. Sumner?" asked Mary.

"Yes, I will, thank you, Mrs. Lincoln," following her along the path. "I wonder if you know the French method of raising asparagus? I have a friend near Albany who uses it with marvelous results."

"I've heard of it," replied Mary. "Do tell me about it."

Lincoln smiled to himself.

The dining room was cool and dim and scented with syringa blooms. Tad, beginning the day in angelic white, threw himself into Sumner's arms with a shout and moved his chair close to his friend's. Mary and the Senator plunged at once into the subject of gardening for which Sumner, who owned no garden, had such a passion.

In the midst of this, as usual, a messenger came from Stanton. Lee had entangled Grant's troops in the wooded swamps of the Wilderness as he had entangled Hooker's a year before. Lincoln hastily finished his meal and left Mary and Sumner debating over the best site for the new asparagus bed. In the War Office, the ghastly details of the unspeakable slaughter in the Wilderness engulfed him and he forgot his mild elation over Sumner.

Mary herself fetched her husband that night from the War Office, a place she rarely visited, though oddly enough with two such explosive natures, she and Stanton got on well together. But James and Tad both failed to bring the President back to supper, and Dr. Stone had warned Mary early in the spring that Lincoln was becoming exhausted. About ten o'clock she appeared carrying a small embroidered pillow and a gray afghan and wearing on her delicate features an expression of indomitable purpose.

Stanton jumped from the sofa and Lincoln turned from the war map.

"Just pull that old armchair to the window, Mr. Secretary," said Mary, briskly. "I've come to keep watch with you and Mr. Lincoln. I can't sleep till he gets home and I'll worry less if I can actually see him."

Stanton gave Lincoln a helpless and humorous glance. Lincoln buttoned his vest and took the pillow and Afghan from his wife. One might as well give in gracefully.

"Very well, my dear," he said meekly, "I'm coming."

He followed her down the hall, through the turnstile and into the garden again. Immersed as he had been all day in the reports of the destruction of the flower of the Potomac Army, he felt as if a century had ground by since he had talked with Sumner. The walks were vague and sweet. They paced slowly, arm in arm. Lincoln began to speak of the horrible losses of the day.

"No, let's not talk about the war," interrupted Mary, flatly. "I want you to sleep to-night. Let's talk about Sumner. Poor fellow! I hope he'll have a garden of his own some day. He was so eager and so pathetic about that foolish asparagus bed. Never has a man needed a home and family more than he."

"How do he and Mrs. Hooper make it?" asked Lincoln, rubbing his head wearily, yet knowing that unless he followed Mary's lead and thrust the war out of his mind, he'd get no sleep that night.

"Oh, he's in a terrible state of mind! Bob couldn't
be more bowled over than the Senator is.—I wish Bob
would write me. Have you heard from him lately?"

"No, but no news is good news. Go on about Sumner. Did he reveal details of his state of mind to you?
Sumner in love rather appeals to my sense of humor."

"Well, if that's the effect it has on you"—indignantly—
"I'll not open my mouth and you can just stay awake all
night."

"Sumner in love is a perfect sleeping potion," he
cried hastily and with a little laugh. "And you know I
wouldn't miss one of your stories of an interview for
six bits, Mary."

She squeezed his arm. "Sit down here under this
magnolia and I'll tell you. No one can find you for a
moment. Put your arm about me and they'll think we're
two of the servants!"

He drew her close against him and she felt his body
relax.

Sumner, she said, selected a spot for the asparagus
trench to the south of the greenhouse, and then gave
Mary the name of an ornamental evergreen shrub whose
identity had puzzled both Mary and the gardener. Tad,
who had tagged after them, announced at this point that
he was going to give the evergreen to Isabella for a
Christmas tree. Then he suddenly added that he was
going to play with Isabella and darted away. Sumner
looked after the little boy, flying along the paths, and
said with a great sigh:

"Oh, for his spontaneity, there! Oh, for his sureness
of a welcome!" Then as if he could not control himself,
he added in an anguished voice, "This is killing me!"

Mary did not pretend to misunderstand him but she
spoke with her usual briskness. "You're so silly in your

attitude toward her. You're much too deferential. Her attitude toward you is just her way of teasing. As a matter of fact, she's deeply interested in you. She talks to me a great deal about your work and has ambitions for you. She's really very clever. Go ask her advice on politics and if she's saucy, squelch her the way Mr. Lincoln does me. You mustn't expect a woman of her social prestige to be overwhelmed by the fact that you're a United States Senator. Let her feel that she could help you to be anything."

Mary paused in her recital and Lincoln gave a sudden loud shout of laughter. "What did he say then?"

"He said good-by and went straight to call on Alice Hooper. Taddie saw him there. I'm dying to know what happened. I'm afraid he was late getting to the Senate."

Lincoln laughed again. "Poor Sumner! Come, darling Mary, you've done your job. I can sleep now!" He took her hand and led her toward the dimly lighted basement entrance.

CHAPTER XIII

MEN—ER—WAR

H E did sleep for a few hours that night, but was roused by the wakening birds to lie and struggle for a long time with what he called his battle horrors. He assured himself that this battle of Grant's in Virginia was actually the beginning of the end if only Grant had the grit to continue until Lee's Army was destroyed. Grant's blood-proof will was what he had been seeking since that April night, three years before, when he had sent the telegram for the relief of Fort Sumter. He must set himself to endure with greater equanimity the sight and sound of those dripping ambulances that filed continuously by the White House.—But Grant's losses were nearing the fifty-thousand mark.—He must gird himself to a new endurance.—God send that the people's nerve stand up under the slaughter! He'd send John Hay at once to the Middle West to see how deep was the despondency there. Mary had said that Grant was a butcher. Well, after all, war was a butcher's job.

The next thing, undoubtedly, would be Greeley yelling for peace. Queer that Greeley couldn't get it through his head that North and South must drink to its dregs the bitter cup. Halleck was claiming that in some of the battles down there Grant's losses were unnecessary and fruitless. Perhaps Grant really was— Well, let that go now. Halleck naturally was disgruntled at being subordinated in rank to the little General. After the Re-

publican convention was over, he'd get down to see Grant
for himself and give him a word of warning.

He rose with a sigh and dressed.

Fred Douglass met Lincoln after breakfast as he was
making his way to Stanton's office. The colored man
was standing by the turnstile, his soft black hat in his
hand, the blazing sun turning his black hair to bronze.
The President shook hands with him.

"Well, Mr. Douglass, what are you and Bob hatching
now?"

Douglass smiled. "Will you allow Mr. Robert to go
with me again this summer, Mr. Lincoln?"

"Let's sit down," suggested Lincoln, leading the way
to the bench he and Mary had occupied the night before.
"Do you and Bob want to carry out the same program
again?"

"No, sir, the colored people are coming over well
enough now. I want you to let Mr. Robert lead up a
regiment of negroes I'll pick myself. Sir, we'll sweep
from Fortress Monroe to the end of Florida with it."

"But, Mr. Douglass," protested Lincoln, "he's only
an untrained boy! Does he know of this?"

"No, sir. But he's your son. That's all that my
people care about. And he's very able. Oh, Mr. Lincoln, don't veto this without long consideration. I want
to hush forever the plea of the whites that negroes can't
stand the gaff of battle. Jefferson Davis says that if
negroes will make good soldiers, their whole theory of
slavery is wrong. Give us a chance to show our mettle,
Mr. Lincoln." Douglass clasped his hands as if in
prayer.

Lincoln stirred uneasily. "But, Mr. Douglass, your
people have already proved themselves nobly. Their
performance with Colonel Shaw alone was enough for

that. My dear friend, you can have no idea of the difficulties your plea presents. It's almost impossible. I
can't undertake it."

Douglass got the note of finality in his voice. "There's
no use in pleading!" he said, heartbrokenly.

"I'm afraid not, Mr. Douglass. Come! Come!"
laying his hand on Douglass' arm. "Don't make me feel
like a criminal. Ask me something that I can grant."

"Give our soldiers equal pay and equal promotion
with the whites," returned Douglass, instantly.

"You've earned it," said Lincoln, "but only Congress
can remove those disabilities."

"If such an amendment is added to the Davis bill will
it stand a chance with you to become a law?" asked the
colored man.

"What, are you so blind as to favor that bill?" Lincoln's voice was astonished. "That bill doesn't grant
you even civic equality."

"But it's at least a guarantee of our freedom!" Douglass' black eyes glowed.

"A constitutional amendment would be a surer way
to get that. The States themselves have to ratify an
amendment," said Lincoln. "I don't mind confiding to
you that I'm insisting that a pledge to pass such an amendment be written into the Republican platform."

"Ah! Glorious! You make me glad!" The colored
man gave a great sigh, then said, abruptly, "But that
means you may veto the Davis bill if it is sent you to
sign? Oh, sir, I beg of you, do sign it."

Lincoln turned in his seat to face Douglass. "I'm not
saying as to that. But ponder this well, Douglass. We'll
certainly assure freedom to your people. But having
done so, I'm not going to try to legislate the former

slave holders into carrying the slaves to the voting booth or sitting down to a meal of victuals with them."

"Then you're going to veto the Davis bill, sir?" insisted Douglass. Lincoln saw suddenly that his sensitive mouth was trembling and that his eyes were suffused with tears.

He slid his hand to Douglass' broad shoulder. "Now, I've hurt you! I'm sorry about that. But I'm getting too old to lie or to give false hopes."

"General Butler said you'd say no to everything," said Douglass with a mournful smile.

"You've been down there, eh? How does the exchange of colored prisoners go on?"

"It doesn't go, of course, Mr. Lincoln," replied Douglass, "and it won't, General Butler assures me, as long as General Grant is in full command."

"Didn't Butler give you Grant's reason?" asked Lincoln, sharply.

"Oh, yes, Mr. President!" replied Douglass wearily, as though, Lincoln thought, the weaknesses of the whites were utterly childish in his eyes. "He says that General Grant's been drinking hard ever since things have gone so badly and he leaves his decision to his subordinates, who are nigger haters."

"And Butler's the man," ejaculated Lincoln, "that they say would be superior to Andy Johnson as Vice President! It's an ornery lie, in plain words, that Butler's given you, Mr. Douglass. General Grant, whether his personal habits are or are not perfect, is a superb military man, and he knows we need all the fighters we can get, without regard to color. He sent me a copy of his letter to Butler. Grant said to stop all exchanges until the South agreed to swap even-steven as to numbers and *without regard to color*. Understand?"

Douglass jerked suddenly to his feet. "But why should General Butler tell me a lie?"

"Oh, that's simple!" The President spoke wearily in his turn. "Butler fancies himself as a military genius when he's really a military fool. He wants to run the Army of the Potomac. But his genius is as a civil executive."

Douglass stared at Lincoln and slowly the expression of alienation softened. "You're the only person of authority in the country who tells me the truth! Mr. Lincoln, do you think Mr. Sumner reads General Butler correctly? They're very intimate. General Butler's planning to swing all his political weight in New England to help Sumner defeat you if you're nominated."

"Did Butler tell you that?" asked Lincoln.

"Yes, sir," replied the colored man. "I like Mr. Sumner and I think I'll warn him as to Butler's character. And I want to say this: If colored men had the vote, nothing could stop your reëlection, sir."

"In spite of my views on reconstruction?" Lincoln smiled as he rose.

Douglass returned the smile. "They only know and care that you've struck the chains from their ankles.— Mr. President"—clasping his hands and speaking with deep earnestness—"isn't there something I can do or say that will persuade you to turn reconstruction over to Mr. Sumner?"

"No!" Lincoln put into the negation all the weight of his months of anxious pondering.

The look of despondency with which the colored man bowed and turned away hurt the President. He didn't want the interview to end in despondency. He had too many such endings lately. He called Douglass back.

"Mr. Douglass," he said, "will you do some recruiting

of your people under General Thomas? I'll try my best
to get you a captain's commission. We need soldiers, Mr.
Douglass. Terribly we need soldiers. When General
Grant once gets possession of a place he hangs onto
it as if he'd inherited it. But he pays a price for his
nighness!"

"I'd be proud and happy to serve under General
Thomas," replied Douglass.

Lincoln nodded. "I'll see Stanton as soon as his mind's
free." He shook hands and hurried to the War Office
more than ever determined to get down and visit Grant.

But he would not leave until the matter of the renomination was settled. He was keeping in touch in
every way possible with the intricate political intrigues
that prefaced the convention and brought to bear all his
hard-won political wisdom on details of the preparations
for the struggle. Once the convention was set at Baltimore, however, he sent John Hay and George Nicolay
to keep him informed of the proceedings and wiped his
mind of active concern for it.

He received the news of his nomination with mingled
gratification and apprehension. The next few months
would make him more than ever the center of unprece-
dentedly bitter political fighting. It was not a pleasant
prospect.

A day or so after the convention was over, the nominating committee waited on him in the East Parlor.—
That little parlor in Springfield where he'd received the
committee of 1861 seemed poignantly remote.

He sent Mary to Vermont shortly after this to finish her convalescence, and then gathered up Taddie and
went down to visit Grant. Charles Dana had told
Stanton that the morale of the Army of the Potomac
was very low. The long-drawn-out failure of the siege

of Petersburg, the frightful losses, and the low type of
men now recruited made it a vastly inferior army to that
with which McClellan and Meade had been blessed. It
was evident too that Lee had not too much respect for
Grant's forces, for just before Lincoln's visit he de-
tached 20,000 men from the Richmond defenses and
sent them up the Shenandoah Valley under General Early
to destroy whom and what they might. Stanton was
worried about this destroying horde. But Grant refused
to share the Secretary's anxiety. One of the many errands Stanton urged Lincoln to do on this visit was to
rouse Grant's interest in Early. But the President, after
thinking it over, told Stanton he didn't feel competent to
argue with Grant over military tactics. He found Grant
as usual, clean-cut as a hound's tooth, not in the least
boastful—sanguine—a very great soldier. The other
officers drank freely at meals. Grant and he turned
down their glasses. The atmosphere was different from
any he'd ever found enveloping the Headquarters of the
Army of the Potomac. Cold efficiency was the watch-
word, and although he rejoiced in it, it depressed him.
He made no suggestions to Grant save that he hoped
he'd accomplish his task with as little bloodshed as
possible.

The one warm memory which he carried back to Washington was of the negro troops.

Some one at officers' mess remarked the night before
Lincoln left that the colored soldiers were strangely si-
lent. There was a division of them camped by the river.
Colonel Thomas, who had a colored regiment, nodded.

"Yes, they learned to-day that they were to lead the
assault on the fortifications east of Petersburg."

"Are they frightened—deserting?" asked Lincoln,
quickly.

"So far, we've never had a negro deserter," answered Thomas, "and they certainly aren't frightened. But where with white troops important military news is received with cheers followed by great argumentation among themselves as to its value, the colored men sit down and 'study.' They're 'studying' now. Later on, they'll sing. That is, some fellow, like a Quaker moved to prayer, will be moved to improvise a chant that expresses the philosophy of the occasion. If the others agree, they'll join him. If they don't, he'll have to try again. No! No! Those men aren't frightened. They're profoundly stirred by this honor of making the initial dash."

When Lincoln left the mess tent, he slipped away toward the section of the camp where the four thousand colored soldiers were living. He made his way well into their midst without being discovered, coming to pause in the shade of a giant sycamore.

There were many campfires gleaming, throwing dusky faces, liquid eyes, white teeth against the spangled sky. And silence. It was profoundly moving. Lincoln wondered what would be the effect if he discovered himself to these men so lost in contemplation. Just as he had concluded to try the experiment, a heavy bass voice at a little distance from his tree began to chant.

> "We-e looks like me-en a-a-marchin' on.
> We looks li-ike men-er-war—"

No one joined him. He changed the melody slightly. In the faces of the groups nearest Lincoln there was no slightest shift of expression, no gleam of interest. The singer changed to a minor key and lifted an octave. A remote tenor now joined him. A baritone came in, then a weird falsetto. As if this last were a signal, there now rose a deep wave of song that increased in volume with each note until with "men-er-war," Lincoln was sure that the whole four thousand had joined.

They chanted the lines again and yet again and again until the President could feel the gooseflesh rise on the back of his neck. He stood with his hands clasped behind him, his heart swelling and suddenly—just for one ineffable moment—he was engulfed with gladness, such gladness, he thought, as Moses had felt when he had led the way across the Red Sea. This, this that he had brought about surely was reparation for the two hundred years of wickedness—

He turned slowly and keeping to the shadows, returned to his tent and went to sleep with that soul-stirring chorus still in his ear, "We looks like men-er-war."

CHAPTER XIV

THE POCKET VETO

LINCOLN returned to Washington the next day still a little uneasy about Grant. It was Grant's stolid countenance perhaps that troubled the President. He did not believe that the little General was as sure of himself as his poker face might indicate. A man sure of himself doesn't bother, Lincoln thought, to build up such a wall of indifference. Grant was a hard man to get at. No commander of the Army of the Potomac ever had treated Lincoln with the cordial respect accorded him by Grant. Lincoln appreciated this deeply. Yet Grant baffled him, held him off.

Thinking his visit over, Lincoln was glad that he'd offered Grant no advice. He had come near to breaking his self-imposed silence only once. He was sure that Grant was underestimating the potentialities for serious trouble in Early's little trip up the Shenandoah. But when he had felt round about it Grant had assured him that Hunter coming in from the West with 10,000 men could control Early's 20,000 and he was glad to have Lee weakened by that many troops. Lincoln had opened his lips to protest but had closed them without speaking.

Lincoln had a feeling that Early was going to knock loudly on Washington's back door before many weeks, and as Grant had all the city's trained forces with him in Virginia, Washington lay naked for the taking. Well, he concluded his thinking, perhaps now was as good a

172

time as any for Grant to learn Lee's possibilities in foot
work.

Stanton alternately cursed and expressed satisfaction
over Lincoln's story of his visit. Both men agreed that
news of Early must be kept as much as possible out of the
local papers while as quietly as possible home guards
should be organized to man the forts that ringed the city.
It was not easy to carry out these plans. Halleck refused to originate anything; would do only the specific
things that the President ordered him to do. Stanton
was not a soldier. Neither was Lincoln. And a soldier
with ideas was very much needed in Washington.

Lincoln worried about this when he was not sweating
over the Davis bill which Congress still debated. Soon
after the President's return from Grant's Headquarters,
Bob came home for the summer vacation, and in the absence of his mother at once constituted himself Tad's
mentor. Tad had not the least intention of permitting
any one on earth to act as his mentor. Nicolay who usually played peacemaker was off to Arkansas to inspect the
progress of reconstruction in that State and John Hay
ardently encouraged Bob in his rôle of disciplinarian.
So, as Lincoln wrote Mary, the siege of Richmond was a
quiet affair compared with what was taking place in the
upper and lower reaches of the White House.

"Bob," he wrote, "is sure enough man's size in his
understanding of many of my problems. He's taking a
great interest in the Davis bill, goes up to the Senate and
listens to the debates and comes back, his eyes crackling
like yours, and tells me about them as intelligently as
Nicolay could. And two minutes later he's fussing with
poor little Taddie as if they both were ten years old.—
Outside of their abortive attempt to reform my darling
Tad, he and John are making an heroic effort at filling

Nicolay's job, but no one can push through the day's run like John George. I reckon you'll have a warm welcome when you get back——"

On July 3, the day before Congress was to adjourn, Lincoln was sitting in his own room just before supper with a heavy heart, thinking over Bob's report on the speeches made that day, when the loud outcry across the hall caused by Tad's refusal to wash his ears at Bob's behest ceased so suddenly that he came startled to his feet and made for the door. It opened before he reached it to admit his wife, in lilac bonnet, sunshade in hand.

"Thank God, Mary!" he ejaculated, gathering her in his arms. A moment later, he said, "You squelched the boys, of course."

"I certainly did——" smoothing his hair with the old loved gesture. "Bob looked so disgusted with me.—— That boy grows handsomer every day, Abra'm."

"He looks exactly like you, my dear," smiled Lincoln.

"You are positively wilted!" said Mary. "I shall move you straight out to the Soldiers' Home the minute Congress adjourns. Have they sent you the Davis bill to sign?"

"Not yet," replied Lincoln. He looked down into her face as she stood leaning against him. "Mary, if I veto that bill, I knock my chances of reëlection sky high. The people can't be expected to understand my reason. They'd have to have been here day by day to see it."

"But I thought you felt the debate helped you with the voters," protested Mary.

"It did, for a while. But they've been at it longer than I anticipated. And constant dripping wears away a stone."

"Are you going to veto it? Does Sumner know?" asked Mary.

"I haven't said I'm going to, have I? I'm thinking aloud to you, that's all. Sumner's pretty mad at me again. He knows I've sent Nicolay out to Arkansas to tell General Steele to give the new State Government the same support and protection that he would have if Congress had seated the new members from Arkansas."

"But that's openly defying Congress!" she ejaculated.

"Only incidentally. Primarily, it's helping Steele do the best he can toward suppressing rebellion. In no event and in no view of the case can it do any harm."

"Except to you, with Congress," sighed his wife. "You poor dear!—I wish Senator Sumner had more common sense. No wonder Alice Hooper—"

"He's in father's office now," said Bob laconically, coming in on his mother's remarks. "He wants to see you right away, sir," turning to his father.

Lincoln threw up both his hands. "Oh, I don't want an argument with Sumner to-night!"

"Then you shan't have it!" and Mary rushed from the room.

As Lincoln would have followed, Bob put his hand out to detain him. "Let her go, father! He was just telling me how much he admired mother's brain. She may make him mad but—"

Lincoln laughed. "But he'll come back asking for more just like the rest of us do." He walked over to the washstand, slipping off his cuffs.

Mary was in her room finishing her supper toilet when Lincoln put his head in a little later.

"Well, you made short work of the Senator. What did he want?"

"I suppose something about the Davis bill. But he put me off with small stuff. Talked about General Banks speculating in cotton and the chance of Banks getting into the Cabinet." She watched Lincoln as she said this, but he made no sign. "I told him he and I agreed about Banks, so that was all right. Then it seems that Stanton doesn't give Fred Douglass his commission and Sumner fears Douglass may make trouble with the Abolitionists for you. I remarked that Mr. Sumner was probably pleased at that prospect and he looked pained. Then before he could start arguing, I asked him how Alice Hooper was. He said they left to-day and asked me at once if I agreed with her that the office of Senator was too small for his powers. I said that I did and he groaned that he was surprised at the lack of vision in women of our intelligence. Good for Alice, thought I. But aloud I bade him good night.—He's tired, poor fellow. Well, you're rid of him, to-night, anyhow."

But as it turned out, Lincoln was not rid of him. Seward, his pale face beaded with heat, his necktie as usual under one ear, rushed in as they were at dessert. Maximilian, Napoleon's man, had reached Mexico City, and MacDougall of California was clamoring for passage of a bill declaring war on France.

"Bob," said Lincoln, "you go fetch Senator Sumner. He'll have to bury MacDougall again. Seward, you go home to bed. You look like Hamlet's ghost."

"Bed! You make me laugh for the first time in a week, Lincoln! Give me something to eat, there's a dear, won't you, Taddie? We don't want bed on an empty stomach, do we?"

They fed him. He talked constantly as he ate but consented to go home and let the President deal with Sumner. The Senator was in a committee conference and came late. He made short work of promising to silence MacDougall, then he asked Lincoln what he proposed to do with the Davis bill. Lincoln refused to be drawn. Sumner, nervously overwrought, walked the floor and harangued. Lincoln, leaning back against the window frame where a rose-scented breeze touched him now and again, heard the Senator's voice more and more remotely. Gradually the tall form in black dinner clothes seemed to merge into the black and white of the slave map behind him. He closed his eyes for a moment.— When he opened them, an hour later, Sumner was gone.

Lincoln rose the next morning with the Davis bill taking precedence over every other anxiety. Congress was to adjourn that day. They were leaving him scant time to study it in its final form. As soon as possible after examining his morning mail, he went up to the Capitol as was customary for the President on the last day of the Session. Bob and John Hay accompanied him in the barouche. It was a heavy sultry day. Small boys added firecrackers to the confusion of the streets. People had hung out flags on Pennsylvania Avenue but in general there was little heart for celebrating the Fourth of July.

Lincoln took a peep at the Senate Chamber before going to the President's office in the same wing. Chaos reigned among the Senators. Several important new bills had been thrust before the body this last morning. Old bills of equal importance still were under debate. Sweating pages rushed up and down. Anxious-eyed engrossing clerks ran about carrying long sheets of parchment for which they were demanding the signature of the Speaker, the Vice President, the Clerk.

No one gave special heed to the President and he was grateful. After one look at the Senate he was glad to withdraw to his own quarters. He seated himself at the handsome rosewood desk beside an open window that gave a wide view of sprawling, half-finished Washington

—an ugly town, he thought, conceived as a city and born as a village without the compactness that gave a village character. Little trees with whitewashed trunks, pigs rooting about them. Pasture lots deep with weeds masquerading as suburban plots. There was something shabby and full of sham about the place. Springfield was much prettier.

John divided himself between the House and the Senate. Bob arranged the bills on the desk and slid them one by one under his father's hand. Lincoln was familiar with most of them and after an identifying glance wrote his signature firmly. It was about 11 o'clock when, after a whispered conference with John Hay, Bob laid the Davis bill before him.

Lincoln stared down at it.

Weeks before he had decided to give it a pocket veto. Yet, in spite of long hours of preparation for it, he found that the act took a supreme effort of will. After all, he told himself, it was bitter hard for a man of his friendly nature to be obliged to do continually these things which roused a frenzy of hatred in men of a fine and ardent patriotism. He knew that under all the confusion, the members of Congress and the visitors in the gallery were concentrating their desires, their prayers, on his signing this bill. He knew that a group of pages just without his door were poised like carrier pigeons, ready to wing with news of his decision to the Senate and the House. Ben Wade's page was there and Lyman Trumbull's and Sumner's and Davis' and the faithful Arnold's messenger.

He laid the bill gently to one side and went on with others. Bob bit his lip and John Hay gave a satisfied grunt. Several members of the Cabinet drifted into the room and seated themselves, waiting. Sumner entered and stood by the window, pale with anxiety. But no one ventured to question the President until Zachariah Chandler came in. This gentleman, who respected nobody's dignity of office, bluntly demanded of the President:

"Mr. Lincoln, are you going to sign the Davis bill?"

Lincoln took off his spectacles and looked mildly up into Chandler's belligerent eyes as he replied:

"This bill has been placed before me only a few moments before Congress adjourns. It's a matter of too much importance to be swallowed that way."

"If it's vetoed," cried Chandler, "the Republican party'll be fearfully damaged! Especially as to the point prohibiting slavery in the reconstructed States."

Lincoln shook his head. "That's the point on which I doubt the authority of Congress to act."

"It's no more than you've done yourself," exclaimed Chandler indignantly.

Lincoln answered with great care. "I conceive that I may in an emergency do things on military grounds which can't be done constitutionally by Congress."

"This is a fearful calamity," ejaculated Chandler. "Your attitude is fatal! Fatal!" He rushed from the room.

Sumner, with a look of unutterable reproach at Lincoln, strode after Chandler. The President turned to Seward and Fessenden.

"I don't see how any of us now," he remarked, "can contradict what we've always said, that Congress has no constitutional power over slavery in the States."

To Lincoln's surprise, "sour old Fessenden" exclaimed, "You're absolutely right, Mr. President! I've even had doubts of the constitutional efficacy of your own decree of emancipation where it hasn't been carried into effect by the actual advance of the army."

The room was full now and Lincoln observed that most of the faces crowded behind the Cabinet chairs were flushed with anger. He tried to marshal his thoughts of the past three months and reduce them to the simplest English at his command. He was determined not to be misunderstood.

"The bill and the position of these gentlemen in asserting that the insurrectionary States are no longer in the Union seem to me to make the fatal admission that States, whenever they please, may of their own motion dissolve their connection with the Union. Now, we cannot survive that admission, I am convinced. If that be true, I am not President, you gentlemen are not Congress. I have laboriously endeavored to avoid that question ever since it first began to be mooted and thus to avoid confusion and disturbance in our own councils. It was to obviate this question that I earnestly favored the movement for an amendment to the Constitution abolishing slavery which passed the Senate last year and failed in the House. I thought it much better if it were possible to restore the Union without the necessity of a violent quarrel among its friends as to whether certain States have been in or out of the Union during the War,—a merely metaphysical question and one unnecessary to be forced into the discussion."

He rose as he finished and bowing, left the office. John Hay followed. When they reached the carriage, Lincoln missed Bob. John explained that the young man was making a hurried tour of the two Houses.

"Looking for trouble," commented Lincoln with a little shake of his head.

"They're all so short sighted," said John Hay, pulling at his tiny mustache in a knowing manner! "People at large aren't interested in the abstruse questions involved."

"If the Radicals try, I don't doubt they can do me harm with the veto," replied Lincoln. "But at all events, I must keep some consciousness of being somewhere near right. I must keep some standard or principle fixed within myself. Here comes Bob, mad clean through! Jings, he looks like his mother! Well, boy, had a good time?"

Bob sank into the seat opposite his father, his lips actually trembling with anger. "Davis is making a speech about you, waving his arms like a crazy man and talking like one, too. He ought to be sued for slander for the things he said."

"What did you listen for, Bobbie?" asked Lincoln, patting the checked linen knee that touched his own.

"I just wanted to measure the depth of his hatred," replied Bob. "And I'd heard him through if Senator Sumner hadn't come up and taken me away. He wanted my opinion on a letter he'd had speaking of the negro's opinion of emancipation—or he said he did. Maybe he was just trying to save me further humiliation. And do you know," with a sudden smile, "he said that if he had your political gifts he'd be Emperor of the world. It was the nearest to a joke I've ever heard from him."

"He wasn't joking! You flatter him!" declared John Hay. "Did you see the pantaloons he was wearing this morning, Bob? They were silk, by Jove, like the lilac checked stuff your mother wears. I dare you to ask him if he has his clothes made by Lizzie Keckley."

Both young men roared with laughter and Lincoln joined them. After all it was a relief to have committed the murder since it had to be done.

But there was no use pretending to himself that he could bring any philosophy to bear on the look with which Sumner had left him. He could not endure with

any sort of equanimity the thought of the Senator leaving
for the summer with bitterness in his heart against him.
He seldom acted on impulse, but now as they plowed
through the dusty road before Congressman Hooper's
house, he called suddenly to the coachman:

"Burke, leave me here and take the two boys home."

"No! No!" protested John Hay. "We'll walk and
leave the carriage for you."

"I don't want my rig recognized in front of here," said
Lincoln decidedly. "I'll walk back, myself," and he
strode up to the door.

The servant showed him into the long drawing room,
draped for the summer closing, but cool and dim and
smelling of rose jars newly filled. Alice Hooper, in a
ruffled white dimity, her golden hair caught back in a
black net, came in at once. She moved down the room
like a naval sloop with all sails set, to greet the President
standing in the window.

"Mr. Lincoln, this is very kind of you! We have only
just finished dinner. May I not—"

Lincoln bowed over her hand and interrupted with his
fine smile. "No, dear Mrs. Hooper! Mrs. Lincoln will
expect me and my business won't take long. I've come
to ask a favor of you."

He seated her close to the shuttered window.
Through the open slats came little hot drafts from the
garden and he placed himself opposite her where he
might share the breeze, for he felt suddenly oppressed.

"I've just come from the Capitol, Mrs. Hooper. I
have given the Davis bill a pocket veto and thereby
finally cooked my goose with the Radicals. I *say* finally,
but I still have hopes of mollifying Charles Sumner."

"Through me?" asked Alice, her blue eyes twinkling.
"But, Mr. President, I'm busy quarreling with him my·

self! He's due here any time to finish a debate we began yesterday."

"Seriously?" asked Lincoln, his own eyes twinkling.

"Well, the Senator takes it seriously. And I'm certain he'd take any championing of you in regard to this pocket veto as a personal affront. He might even wish to fight a duel about it!" She laughed, softly.

"Of course, I don't want to injure the Senator's chances," began the President jocosely, "but—"

"But," Alice took him up, soberly, "as a matter of fact both father and I would be glad to help you, Mr. Lincoln. What may I try to do as to the Senator?"

"Do you allow him to talk politics to you now?" asked Lincoln, running his fingers violently through his hair, then clasping his knee tensely.

"Mrs. Lincoln persuaded me to be less adamant there," laughing again and again sobering quickly to add, "I enjoy politics, as a matter of fact."

"Do you think you could persuade Mr. Sumner to take no active part in calling another convention and nominating another Republican candidate until after the Democratic convention next month? Mrs. Hooper, if the Democrats nominate McClellan on a peace platform, if our military outlook continues black, if the Republican party is split by internal dissensions, McClellan will go into the White House next year and all will be lost." He paused to see if she had taken in his statement.

"Yes! Yes! I see," she said, shaking her pretty head anxiously.

Lincoln thought he could begin to understand Sumner's fascination. "I know what Sumner will say. He'll say that if I'd withdraw the Republican party could unite on some one. When he says that, you tell him that if, after the Democrats have nominated McClellan on a

peace platform, the leaders of the Republican party can
agree on any one man who can be surer of beating Mc-
Clellan at the polls next November than I, I'll withdraw."

The effect of this last sentence on his hearer was
astonishing.

She leaned forward and with great deliberation placed
a slender hand over Lincoln's clasped knuckles. "No,"
she said, quietly, "I'll deliver no such message to Charles
Sumner! I haven't enough confidence in his common
sense. I'm not going to be the one to jeopardize your
tenure of office that way. Why, Mr. Lincoln," rising
suddenly, "I'm surprised at you! Lack of vanity may
be as serious a fault as arrogance. Don't you know that?
And you are *the* friend to the Union in these United
States. I'm descended from men who died in creating
that Union . . . I'll deliver no such message."

Lincoln was singularly touched. Here was the woman
whom he had always found cold and snobbish speaking
with an understanding loyalty that was all the more
remarkable in a woman when one realized that her loyalty
was impersonal. For he knew as well as though she had
said it that his kind of man had no appeal for her. It
was a real triumph of mind over matter! And it healed
some of the hurts he'd felt that day.

He rose with her and walked over to the mantel, looked
into the Chinese dragon jar and with his paper knife
stirred up the rose leaves with which it was filled, then
turned back to the slender white figure still standing by
the window.

"You have confidence in *my* political common sense
have you, Mrs. Hooper?" he asked.

She tapped her lips thoughtfully with the little silk fan

that dangled from her wrist, then a smile broke through her anxiety.

"Even Charles Sumner has that! He often sighs in envy of your riches in that direction."

"Then," very earnestly and walking toward her again, "trust that possession of mine enough to go ahead and do what I ask you."

She was really troubled, but Lincoln held her gaze and would not let it go and after a moment of staring at his sunken, weary, and very tender blue gray eyes, she sighed and capitulated.

"I'll do what I can, Mr. Lincoln. The Senator's not a simple person, you know—and apropos of this conversation in general, I have a great and affectionate respect for him."

"So have I," agreed Lincoln. "And I thank you for— well, for this conversation, Mrs. Hooper. You've cheered me on my way. And now I've got to make tracks for home." He bowed again over her hand and without waiting for the servant to show him to the door, he hurried out into the burning heat. Charles Sumner was just turning in from the sidewalk. The two men lifted their hats and bowed without a word. Then Lincoln made his way to his belated dinner and the Senator went on into the house.

Alice met him in the hall. "Ah, Senator, you met the President!" giving him her hand.

He clasped it in both his, released it and said, "I did not speak to him. I dared not let myself. He turned chaos loose on the Republican party to-day."

"Come in and tell me about it, Senator!" leading the way into the drawing room. "You can't have dined. Let me send for some sandwiches and a glass of wine."

His sober face lightened at this touch of kindliness.

"Thank you, Alice! I was afraid you'd be leaving for Boston on the early boat so I came here direct from the Senate chamber. Lincoln has ditched the Davis bill."

She rang for a tray to be brought, then gave her attention to Sumner's account of the pocket veto. When he had finished, she toyed with her fan for a moment, then told him what she knew he was eager to know,—the reason for the President's call.

He was much agitated by the recital. "Do you mean, Alice, do you actually mean that you're giving me that message with any desire of your own that I'll agree?"

"I told Mr. Lincoln I didn't want to deliver it," said Alice.

"Ah!" in a tone of relief, "then you don't wish me to agree!"

"But why don't you want to do what he says, dear Senator?" She patted the sofa beside her. "Now you've finished your lunch, come here and we won't have to shout."

He obeyed with alacrity. "I don't agree because he's so diabolically clever. I haven't the remotest idea of what he's trying to do."

"He's trying to save the Union," said Alice, "first, last and always. He's as utterly beyond selfish motives as you are. You're the two biggest men I shall ever know, even if I were to be fortunate enough to live in the diplomatic circle of England. It's too bad that Mr. Lincoln can't compete with you in those little elegancies of manner and speech that every woman delights in."

Sumner smiled down at her, the irritated and anxious lines smoothed from his face as if she actually had laid her delicate hand on them. "And why don't you want to deliver the message to me, dear Alice?"

"The saddest thing in our history to-day," she said in a

low voice, "is that Charles Sumner and Abraham Lincoln are not in agreement. I am very jealous of your future! I feared that you'd misunderstand the message and that it would serve only to drive you two farther apart."

He scowled a little and folding his arms on his breast sat in heavy thought. Little Isabella's voice floated down from upstairs. There was a sound of heavy objects being moved. Alice sat in unusual patience. Finally Sumner said:

"If we have a bad war summer, it will be difficult to find any one to beat McClellan, if he's nominated."

"Could you beat him?" asked Alice.

"I? No, Alice, I've too many political enemies in my own camp."

"Who could beat McClellan?" she urged.

"Only some man that the entire Republican party could agree on," he replied, dejectedly.

"Senator, I've hurt you often when I've teased you over your absorption in politics. And I'm sorry about that because I'm really trying to learn not so much politics as statesmanship. Do forgive me enough to explain what would be the result if you agree with Mr. Lincoln's proposal. Wouldn't there be a chance that you'd have him on the hip and be rid of him?"

"Yes, certainly," answered Sumner.

"Then he's willing to take a bigger risk than you are? Oh, don't let him do that! I don't want you to lag one microscopic dot behind him!" She looked up into his face pleadingly.

"Are you trying to influence me, Alice?" he demanded, sternly.

"Yes, I am, Senator! I am sincere and I'm in earnest. I want you to accede to the President's request because I think it's the most statesmanlike thing for you to do."

Sumner moved uneasily and again sat pondering. Then he said, "Never in my life have I been bribed. Any request of this sort from you to me is a sort of bribe because I care so much about your good opinion. Even at that, if this were a question of principle with me, I could hold out against you. But I'm honestly puzzled which way to go, and so for a few weeks I'll agree to go as you suggest. I'll wait to see just how far sighted the President is."

"Now, that is my idea of wisdom and fairness!" exclaimed Alice. "And since you've been such a good little boy, I'm not going to leave until the night boat and you are going to forget all the world of politics and war and play with Isabella and me. We'll go for a picnic supper out to Rock Creek Grove!"

"The world forgetting and by the world forgot!" ejaculated Sumner, rising and offering Alice both his hands.

She accepted them and rose with a smile of such sweet-ness that his pale, tired face flushed like a youth's.

CHAPTER XV

THE REBEL HAVERSACK

LINCOLN did not hear from Alice Hooper again nor did he see Sumner before he left for Boston. He had not expected either event. He could only wait for results. The newspaper reports on his reasons for the pocket veto, in spite of his efforts at clarity, were not satisfactory. He was resolved that this should not be so and on the 8th of July he issued a short proclamation giving a copy of the Davis bill and reiterating his stand upon the method of reconstruction it contained. That done, he felt satisfied to leave the matter to the common understanding.

The family migrated to the Soldiers' Home the morning after the Fourth. On the 6th, Stanton hurried into Lincoln's office and peremptorily ordered him to bring his family back to town.

"Early crossed the Potomac at Shepherdstown yesterday and levied $20,000 on Hagerstown," said the Secretary in reply to Lincoln's protest. "He'll be in front of Washington this week if General Wallace can't hold him. Hunter's asleep somewhere west of Winchester. Can't possibly help. I'm going to put a lookout station at the top of your house at the Soldiers' Home. It commands the best view to the north. By God, you shall not stay out there under Early's guns, Mr. Lincoln!" Stanton wiped the sweat from his spectacles with an enormous silk handkerchief.

"Tut! Tut! Keep your shirt tucked in, Mr. Stanton!

We'll come back! What does Grant say?" Lincoln spoke anxiously but without Stanton's excitement.

"Grant thinks I'm a panicky old woman. You'll have to work on him yourself. Tell him he's got to get some fighting men up here. I've telegraphed the Governors of six States to send us militia, but Early'll be here before the militia arrives, mark my words! If Early frees the 20,000 Rebel prisoners at Point Lookout, hell will be popping here in forty-eight hours."

"I'll wire Grant, Mr. Stanton." Lincoln rose to follow the Secretary to the War Office. "Keep the news as quiet as you can. Panic won't help the city."

"Panic might help Grant," growled Stanton. "He's started one division of the Sixth Corps to Baltimore by boat. That's 5,000 men, and 3,000 cavalry of which 2,500 are sick. Early has 30,000 men. Grant's drunk or crazy."

"He's neither!" snapped Lincoln. "He's a man harassed even as you and I. I'll wire him something that'll get him going."

His protest to Stanton was stout enough yet not wholly stout! Lincoln had more faith in Grant than in any military leader the war had developed, but the past three years had deprived him of the power to feel full confidence in any man. Moreover he had a theory that there was no drinking man who under a heavy strain was not liable to get drunk at a crucial moment.

He sent the little General a strong despatch and made Stanton and Halleck wire to him also. Then he sent a summons out to the Home for Mary to come back to the White House. Mary, somewhat more irritated than alarmed, did not alleviate his general uneasiness by a conversation she held with him that evening. They sat in the kitchen garden. It was Lincoln's idea that they

would here be free of callers. The night was steaming
hot with a thunder storm threatening.

"Fred Douglass came to see me to-day. He's a smart
nigger," began Mary.

"How did he happen to visit you?" asked Lincoln,
with the old wish that Mary would keep out of this kind
of politics.

"Senator Sumner sent him to see if I could hurry up
the commission you said you'd try to get him. Are you
going to give it to him, Abra'm?"

The President chewed meditatively on a stalk of pie
plant. "I've had to put it up to Stanton. If Douglass
comes to you again, bring him to me. While he's waiting
for Stanton, I'll get him to go down to Fortress Monroe
and set his scouts at work again. We are in awful straits
for soldiers. I've got to issue a call for 500,000 more
men. Seems as though I couldn't stand it."

"He's in no mood toward the Administration now to
be sent on any such errand," protested Mary. "And
he's very cross with General Butler. Did you know
Butler is really blackmailing Grant? Grant wants to get
rid of Butler and doesn't dare."

"I don't believe it!" shouted Lincoln angrily. Then
he added apologetically, "Not but what Ben Butler is
capable of trying it."

But Mary gave no sign of offense. She was worried
and merely said, "Well, you'll see!" in the tone that
always irritated her husband; it so frequently accompanied a true prophecy!

"I'll see what, my dear?" he asked.

"Well," veering as she so often did when crowded to
another topic, "you'll see that Grant won't come up here
and take personal command of this chance to destroy
30,000 Rebels."

"Good Lord! How'd you learn about that?" He jerked around on the bench to stare at the diminutive figure beside him.

"I went over to see Secretary Stanton about Douglass to-day and he boiled over to me. Why don't you put your foot down with Grant, Abra'm?" She sounded a little excited.

"I wrote Grant to provide to retain his hold where he is, then bring the rest of his forces personally and make a vigorous effort to destroy the Rebel forces around here. But I also told him it was a suggestion, not an order. I'm not smart enough to give orders to Grant."

"But you are!" Mary almost screamed at him.

Lincoln gave a low laugh. "You do have a tough row to hoe in running this war, don't you, darling Mary?"

She giggled. "It would be simple enough if I could control you! . . . The gnats are eating me up."

"I knew callers of some kind would drive us out of here!" said Lincoln rising and pulling Mary to her feet. "Though the gnats are better than the Temperance women I had with me to-day."

"I suppose the Rebels think they'll get you, if they get Washington," said Mary, uneasily, as they started for the house.

"Maybe they'll be satisfied just to steal Halleck," remarked Lincoln.

"Oh, my dear, nothing so unimportant! Taking Halleck couldn't be considered, even by the North, more than petty larceny," and she laughed at her own tart wit.

Mary's inexplicable intuition proved correct. Grant did not come to Washington. On the 8th, frightened folk began to pour into the town from the north. The Rebels were approaching Rockville and Silver Spring. With their arrival the carefully guarded news broke and

Washington went panic.   Every one that could fled to Baltimore, but in a few hours this route was closed by the Rebels.   The male population of the city was hurriedly armed and sent to reinforce the scant number of soldiers holding the surrounding forts.   Bob, without saying a word to his mother, joined the defense of Fort Stevens just north of the Soldiers' Home.   Tad, however, boasting of Bob's bravery, gave the boy away and every one was surprised but Lincoln when Mary tossed her head and said:

"Of course he's gone!   The Todds were all military men."

"And Bob's father killed mosquitoes in the Black Hawk War," added the President.

Early was putting the torch to the farms and crops of Maryland.   He had laid Frederick under requisition for $200,000.   He had defeated General Wallace and was within a day's march of Washington.   Still no help came from Grant, although he wired that the remainder of the Sixth Corps had left for Washington on the 9th.

On the evening of the 10th, Early's guns fired on the northern defenses of the city.

"It's no credit to Grant that Richmond's safe while Washington's in danger," remarked Mary on the afternoon of the 11th as she came into Lincoln's office with a glass of buttermilk.

Lincoln turned on her sternly.   "Mary, if you think this continual jabbing at Grant helps me or the Union cause, you're mistaken.   If you can tell me something good to do, tell me.   If not, stop this impotent slashing."

"I'm sorry, Abra'm," said Mary, meekly.

Lincoln set down the glass of milk and stared at her. "Are you sick?"

Mary began to laugh.   "Both of us are out of char-

acter, you, cross, and I, humble! Have you heard from
the Sixth Corps?"

As if in answer to her query, Tad, who had been standing at the window with the telescope, suddenly dropped
the instrument with a shout. "Pete's given me the signal.
The vetewans have come!"

Lincoln seized his straw hat and followed Tad.

The city was strangely silent. The streets were half
deserted. Store windows along Pennsylvania Avenue
were boarded up. A great barricade of cord wood cut off
Twelfth Street on the north side. At the intersection
of Seventh Street and the avenue, a crowd had gathered.
Lincoln did not try to pierce it. He lifted Tad to his
shoulder and together they looked over the heads of the
people.

Up Seventh Street from the wharf was marching a
line of soldiers with a single drummer at its head. As
the tanned and seasoned veterans of many battles appeared, the crowd broke into cheers. "The Sixth! The
Sixth! Go get 'em, boys!" Lincoln stayed to watch
several regiments pass, his heart growing lighter with
every sturdy boot thud. Good old Grant! He'd sent
his best!—Then, although Tad protested at his haste he
returned to relieve Mary's anxiety.

The proximity of battle he found curiously exhilarat-
ing. It gratified him to discover that he was not frightened. On the contrary, the next day he tried to slip
away for a visit to Fort Stevens, but Mary caught him
just as he was seating himself in the carriage. She sat
down resolutely beside him.

"Mary, this is absurd!" he exclaimed.

Mary unfurled her little lilac carriage shade and
cocked it over her bonnet. "If you and Bob get shot,
Tad and I want to be also."

"But where is Tad?" exclaimed Lincoln.

Mary's lips quivered and Lincoln now observed that she was pale and that her eyes were dilated. "I've just learned that he left in his goat cart for Fort Stevens, several hours ago. I thought he was at Pete Kelley's house, but Pete went along as Taddie's aide. I don't mind telling you," her voice breaking, "that Tad's going to get a spanking."

"Nobody's going to let harm come to the little fellow, Mary," said Lincoln, more stoutly than he felt, however. And he made no further protests against her accompanying him.

They reached the Fort two hours later, having had to drive round the trenches dug across the various roads from the north. They found Stanton's carriage drawn up before the Fort and Secretary Stanton arguing with a man in colonel's uniform as to the propriety of a civilian visiting the Fort at that moment. When Mary and the President descended from the phaëton and joined Stanton the officer threw up his hands in horror.

"But Colonel," cried Mary, "I came for my little boy, Taddie!"

"We sent him back to the White House an hour ago with a guard, Madam President," the Colonel told her. "One of his hounds got killed by a stray bullet from a Rebel sharpshooter. He insisted on taking the little brute back in his cart. He and his freckled friend and the goats and six privates with a sergeant made quite a funeral cortege."

"Jings!" ejaculated Lincoln. "What'll he do next? My son Robert here?"

"We sent the Home Guards back for city duty as soon as the regulars got here, Mr. Lincoln," replied the officer, moving uneasily. "And now, Mrs. Lincoln, allow me to

show you back to your carriage. This is only a little lull
in hostilities. We've been under fire all the morning."

"But I want to see the Fort under fire," protested
Mary. "Look, you've got some more visitors," as a
handsome span of horses appeared drawing a surrey.

"My God!" groaned the Colonel.

Lincoln slipped away and entered the inner works.
Shortly he reached the gun emplacements where, unheeded in the confusion, he mounted a parapet. The
Fort lay on the crest of a low range of hills. In the
valley below, a line of blue coats advanced toward smoking hills opposite. Minié balls began to sing over the
Fort. A Sergeant standing near Lincoln grunted and
sank to his knees. The President hardly heeded him.
He was watching the line of soldiers. It was like sitting
at a play.

Suddenly a great mass of Rebels rushed from behind
bushes into the road to the north. The Fort guns opened
fire on them at once. Empty spaces appeared in the
Rebel ranks. Perhaps ten minutes of this and the Rebel
line had been wiped out. Silence reigned except for distant rifle fire. Some one grasped the President firmly by
the ankle. A young Lieutenant was looking up into his
face.

"Sir!" he cried, his very lips blanched, "unless you
come down at once, I shall be obliged to bring a file of
soldiers to remove you, though you are my superior officer! I've just forced Mrs. Lincoln to retire from
bullet range."

"Jings!" exclaimed Lincoln, "I thought she was back
there with Secretary Stanton and the Colonel—   I
reckon the kindest thing I can do for you fellows is to
take myself and my family, official and otherwise, out of
here! How does the attack go?"

"They're in full retreat. This is only the Rebel rear guard protecting the movement," replied the young officer. "You will go back now, Mr. Lincoln?"

"Yes, of course, my boy! What State do you hail from?"

"I'm from Pennsylvania. Drop your head below the range of those Minié balls, sir," as Lincoln started to cross the open parade.

Lincoln ducked his head obediently. "All right!" he laughed. "I'm leaving!"

He found his wife and the Secretary in a place of comparative safety under a south abatis. "They're falling back!" he told them.

"Thank the kind Father!" ejaculated Stanton. "I'm going home to get some sleep. Mrs. Lincoln, don't be cross with me," leading the way to a point where they could beckon for the carriages which were sheltered in a little wood.

"But I am cross," returned Mary. "If you continue to be obdurate about giving Douglass that appointment I shall turn as ferocious as you at your worst."

Stanton laughed and Mary exclaimed, "Oh, you men! I'd like to run this government for ten minutes."

"You're not the only one who wants to run things not in your own department," exclaimed Stanton, pulling his black beard with sudden grimness. "Postmaster General Blair is all out of patience with us too."

"What have we done now?" asked the President, his eyes on the efforts of Burke to bring the horses out from the shelter of the wood. The heavy blanket of smoke that lay over trees and buildings was as frightening to the poor beasts as the crack of the Parrotts.

Stanton replied with his familiar note of irritation. "It's a damnable shame the way Postmaster General

Blair is permitted to talk about the army. He's going about now telling everybody that the officers in Washington are poltroons. He means Halleck and me, the coward! He's been my consistent enemy ever since I entered the Cabinet, as you well know, Lincoln. You've simply got to dismiss him."

"*Mr.* Lincoln!" said Mary quietly. Stanton ignored her.

Lincoln took off his soft gray hat and fanned himself with it. He was very tired of the bickering of Stanton and Blair and their unceasing efforts to oust each other from the Cabinet. "On that kind of an order I'm like a woman Speed told me about years ago," he began.

Stanton muttered impatiently, but the President went on, while Burke, who had now driven up, held the prancing horses with difficulty.

"A little lady was sitting in a train when a man with a wooden leg took the empty seat beside her and started to talk. He informed her that at one time he had been the proud possessor of a mechanical leg. All he had to do was to wind it up and set the size of step and she'd carry him round all day. One day not long before, he happened in his travels to come to a fine clear pool of water in a creek and he took off his clothes, unbuckled his wooden leg, and went in swimming."

"Good God, Lincoln!" ejaculated Stanton as the rumble of battle began again in the northern hills. "Let's get home!"

The President went on solemnly and without moving while Mary gazed stoically on the rearing horses, though her eyes twinkled.

"It happened that a raccoon came down to drink while he was in the water. Now a raccoon is a very curious animal. He got interested at once in the wooden leg and what with his sniffing and poking he set the mechanism off and the leg got up and began to run across the prairies. The man yelled and started hopping on his single leg after it. But he'd hardly gone a mile when his single poor old leg got caught in a prairie dog hole and broke. There he was helpless till a tin peddler with a cart came along and rescued him. He never did hear of his mechanical leg again. Now all the while the man was telling this story, the lady kept smiling, so he felt encouraged to add at the end that he was taking up a collection to buy him a new patented leg and would the lady give him a dollar toward it. The lady, still smiling, opened her pocket book and took out a card which she handed to the man. The card read, 'I am deaf and dumb and would be glad for a contribution toward an ear trumpet!' "

With a great laugh, Lincoln offered his arm to Mary and started toward the carriage. But Stanton was outraged.

"What sort of an answer is that, on an occasion like this! Do you call it dignified, Mr. Lincoln?"

The President paused. "I can be harsh if you prefer it, Mr. Stanton," he said tersely. "Blair's house was burned by the Rebels the other day because we had no help to send him. I don't know whether he said those things or not but it's improbable. If they were said, I don't approve of them, but under the circumstances, I wouldn't dismiss a member of the Cabinet for them. Besides this, I propose continuing to be myself a judge as to when a member of the Cabinet shall be dismissed."

Stanton bit his lip, bowed, and entered his own carriage. The President chuckled at intervals all the way home.

Pete Kelley, with a black rag round his hat, met them

at the gates of the White House. He was dust from
head to foot. His blue eyes were dark with weariness
and excitement. He stood on the step of the carriage
and delivered his message.

"Lieutenant Lincoln says you're to come straight up
to his room. Pensacola's got shot, but Tad ain't cried
a tear. Tad and I washed him clean in the bathroom."

When they reached the house, they both obediently
followed the child up the stairs. Taddie's sorrows were
not to be treated lightly. The late afternoon sun filled
Tad's bedroom with rose color. Taddie, his linen suit
incredibly soiled, his chestnut hair in moist ringlets, his
cheeks flushed under the crust of sweated dust, stood
beside the bed leaning dejectedly on a rifle. On the bed
lay the little hound dog, unwontedly white as to hair, a
bandage round his chest. His head was pillowed on a
wreath of Mary's choicest roses. Sumter sat beside Tad
dejectedly scratching fleas.

As his father dropped his hand on his shoulder, Tad
looked up. "Ev'ything of Willie's is dead now," he
said, his cheeks quivering.

"Except mother and Bob and you and me," said his
father. "Well, I reckon he's wagging his little tail off
in heaven now."

Tad looked up into his face. "Do you suppose he's
found Willie, already?"

"Sure he has!" exclaimed Pete Kelley. "He'd find
Willie, if't he was in hell."

"Well, he isn't in hell, you di'ty skunk!" shouted Tad,
"not eitha' of them!"

Lincoln looked helplessly at his wife who had been
eyeing the scene through tear dimmed eyes. She spoke
in a carefully practical voice.

"Have you arranged for his casket, boys? You'd

better go down to the steward and ask him for an empty box. I'll give you a piece of my old white velvet cape to line it with and you'd better work quickly so we can have the funeral right after supper."

"Come on, Pete!" exclaimed Tad. He placed his gun in a corner and ran from the room.

That evening, after little Pensacola had been laid to his long rest, Tad came into his father's office and placed a battered haversack on a letter the President had been reading.

"This is something to wememba' the wa' by, Papa day," he said. "The sa'gent got it off a webel that was shooting at Fo't Stevens. It's fo' you. Open it up."

Lincoln obeyed and emptied on the desk a jack knife, a plug of twisted tobacco, a tin cup, and about two quarts of coarsely cracked corn with a little salt tied in a rag. The corn had been ground up with the cob.

"The Sa'geant said that's all the di'ty webels had to eat now and a good thing too—"

Lincoln sifted the meal slowly through his fingers. "He was a human being, Tad, exactly like you and me. Don't speak of him so. And he had wonderful spunk to march all the way from Richmond and fight on this horse fodder— You'd better go to bed now, my boy."

"Do you like the gift?" Tad asked, anxiously.

"Liking doesn't express it," replied his father with a twisted smile. "Give me a kiss, dear Tad and go, won't you?"

"I'll miss Pensacola!" said Tad, turning abruptly from the room.

CHAPTER XVI

THE TANGLED BURDEN

LINCOLN, after a moment, lifted the haversack gently from the letter he had been reading and finished its excited phrases. It was from Greeley. "I venture to remind you that our bleeding, bankrupt, almost dying country longs for peace; shudders at the prospect of fresh conscriptions, of further wholesale devastations and new rivers of blood. And a widespread conviction that the Government and its prominent supporters are not anxious for peace and do not improve proffered opportunities to achieve it is doing great harm now and is morally certain unless removed to do far greater in the approaching elections. . . . I fear you do not realize how intently the people desire any peace consistent with the National integrity and honor. . . . I have information on which I can rely that two persons duly commissioned and empowered to negotiate for peace are at this moment not far from Niagara Falls and are desirous of conferring with yourself or such persons as you may appoint. . . ."

Lincoln rang the bell for John Hay. "John," he said, when the young man appeared, "you remember I wrote Greeley that if he had any peace envoys from Jeff Davis to bring them here to see me—that is if they had a proposition in writing from Davis asking for peace on terms embracing the restoration of the Union and abandonment of slavery. He's ignored that reply of mine and has sent me another screed. I want you to go to New York and see Mr. Greeley and make him go with you to meet his commissioners. Tell him that if they're qualified, I intend not only a sincere effort for peace but I intend that he shall be a personal witness that it's made."

"But Greeley has nothing bona fide, Mr. Lincoln! He's just a timid little editor!" exclaimed John.

Lincoln nodded. "But he thinks he has something and we'll make him do the investigating himself, which is exactly what he won't want to do. You've a nice job there, John! Get out to-night, if you can. I think the road is clear up to Baltimore. Early is retreating. The Sixth certainly got here just by the skin of its teeth!"

He shook hands with the young man and turned back to his desk to finish a message to General Grant. "In your dispatch of yesterday to General Sherman, I find the following, to wit: 'I shall make a desperate effort to get a position here which will hold the enemy without the necessity of so many men.'—Pressed as we are by the lapse of time, I am glad to hear you say this and yet I do hope you may find a way that the effort shall not be desperate in the sense of a loss of life."

He dropped his pen and stared at the haversack. Tad's memento moved him unaccountably— If only the dreadful trouble would end! If only he could be sure he wouldn't break before the finish! He jumped up and went over to the war map to move a little to the southeast a pin which represented Sherman headed for the Atlantic,—that wild adventure! As for the menace to Washington, *that* was over, but Grant must somehow be made to send up a man right away who would drive Early out of Maryland before his depredations there equaled those of Sherman in Georgia. Stanton had suggested Sheridan. The thought of Stanton made him frown. He went back to his desk and wrote a memorandum for his Cabinet.

"I must myself be the judge how long to retain in and when to remove any one of you from his position. It would greatly pain me to discover any of you endeavoring to procure another's removal or in any way to prejudice him before the public. Such endeavor would be a wrong to me and much worse, a wrong to the country. My wish is that on this subject no remark be made nor question asked by any one of you here or elsewhere, now or hereafter."

Mary came in as he finished this. He showed it to her with the remark that it was a further moral from the tale he had told Stanton that afternoon.

Mary read the statement and smiled complacently. "You really are becoming a tyrant, Abra'm!" Then she haled him off to bed.

It was a relief to have Congress not in session. Before it convened again, he hoped to have Louisiana well on her legs. Banks wrote that there never had been a better constitution than the loyalists had just completed. It embraced all the best points of the old one, and in addition it abolished slavery, making negro suffrage optional with the State legislature. It provided for an election of members to Congress, early in September.

It looked at first as though Lincoln's proclamation on the Davis bill had served its purpose, at least as far as popular acquiescence was concerned. He was relaxing his watchfulness on the matter when he received a terrific jolt. Ben Wade and Winter Davis published in the New York *Tribune* a bitter manifesto concerning the pocket veto and the President.

Lincoln brought the newspaper to Mary's room before breakfast.

"Look at this!" he exclaimed. "Just as I was loosening my galluses a little bit, along comes this! Nothing's hurt me so much since I came to Washington."

Mary read the screed, then tossed it scornfully out the window.

"Well, I don't see why it should hurt you most of anything," she remarked. "It's a horrid document, but it doesn't say things that haven't been said hundreds of times before. It says your attitude on reconstruction is based on your desire to be elected, that it gives you a chance to hold the electoral votes of the Rebel States at the dictation of your personal ambition. They say your motives are sinister and that you want to defeat the will of the people by perverting the Constitution—sickening balderdash! Why let it sting, as you say to me?"

"Because it does, Mary! I've done everything I can to make Winter Davis my friend. I like the boy and I love his father. And he's a Republican. This thing comes, remember, from representatives of my own party. To be wounded in the house of your friends is a grievous hurt, Mary."

She came over to put her arm about him and rub her face against his coat sleeve. "You're tired, Abra'm, or this wouldn't rub you on the raw. I wish you could go away for a few days."

"I hope Charles Sumner didn't back it," said the President.

"He'll live to regret it, if he did," Mary proclaimed, stoutly. "Can this do any real harm?"

"I fear so," replied Lincoln. "It gives a head and a mouth to the impatience of the Radicals with me. But I can do nothing more to counteract that."

For days the sense of hurt clung to him, but his preoccupation with the war gradually overset the pain. It seemed to him during the next few weeks that he and

Stanton and Grant were the only people in the world who could see an end to the war. The depression of the people shown by their bitter criticism of himself and Grant hung about him like an evil-smelling fog. He thought that Grant was affected badly by the hostility, for the General seemed to lack his usual eagerness and activity. He was the soldier of Shiloh, not of Chattanooga. This was alarming. And when Lincoln received a request from General Grant asking that General Butler be demoted, he made a quiet trip to Fortress Monroe and sent for Butler.

Butler came in from camp, sunburned and, for once, shabby. He seemed honestly glad to see the President, and after supper they settled down for a talk. Butler had finished the story of his terrible failure to take Petersburg and the two men had sat in silence for some time watching the moon rise over the black walls of the Fort before Lincoln asked the question he had come down to ask.

"Butler, why do you work against Grant?"

The General's camp chair creaked as he turned on Lincoln. But the President put out a protesting hand.

"For God's sake, General, let's talk without elocution! I like you. I'm not down here to spy. I've come down to see if I can't beguile you into upholding Grant's hands. You know as well as I do you've no business to say Grant's a drunkard."

"I never said so," declared Butler. "I never saw General Grant take a glass of spirituous liquor in my life. I've seen him drink wine at the dinner table but nowhere else. The shoe's on the other foot, Mr. Lincoln. Grant's trying to get rid of me. I tell you, this army needs me. And I tell you, both you and Grant need the support I can give you from Massachusetts and the other New England States."

"The *war* needs the support you can give it," replied Lincoln. "The peace party is almost out of hand. You know you don't want Grant's job. You want to be free to return to politics on short notice."

"What do you mean?" asked Butler, lighting a cigar with a steady hand and showing his aquiline face in startlingly clear profile.

Lincoln was prepared for the question. "It's no secret, is it, that a call has gone out for a new Presidential convention next month. The feeling is that I can't be elected and the Radical Republicans must have another ticket to save it from complete overthrow. They say for the ticket, you and Sumner or Sumner and Farragut. The men back of the call are Chase, Davis, John Jay, Whitelaw Reid, Greeley, Bryant, Sumner. You and Sumner ought to make a very strong run together. . . . Well, you're all within your rights, I reckon. But such being the case, why in the name of common sense and General Jackson, don't you get off Grant's neck?"

"Your political intelligence bureau is good but not infallible, Mr. Lincoln," said Butler, puffing calmly. "I think you're doing Sumner an injustice. I had a letter from him yesterday. I'll just read you a paragraph." He drew a letter from within the breast of his tunic and leaning forward so that the light through the doorway fell on the sheet he read: " 'I do not see how anything can be done except through Mr. Lincoln and with his good will. If he could see that patriotism required his withdrawal, and could sincerely give his countenance and support to a new candidate, I am sure that the candidate of that convention, whoever he might be, could be chosen. But any adverse proceeding would disaffect him and his friends so as to destroy the unity of the party. This unity must be had at all hazards and at every sacrifice. If Mr. Lincoln does not withdraw, then all who now disincline to him must come in to his support. I have declined to sign any paper or take any part in any action because I am satisfied nothing can be done except through Mr. Lincoln and with his good will.' "

Butler finished his reading and returned to his previous position in the shadow. Lincoln listened with mingled feelings of gratification and chagrin. Sumner's attitude toward him hurt in spite of all the philosophy he could bring to bear. He did not propose, however, for Butler to know this.

"He told me some of that months ago, but in what the *Baltimore Sun* calls the scathing and withering style. When he finished with me that time, I was struck blind and found myself feeling with my fingers for my continued existence. A little of the bone was left and I gradually revived. And here I am."

Butler stirred impatiently in his chair. "I was merely trying to do Sumner justice with you, Mr. Lincoln," he said stiffly.

"Oh, you've done that!" The President's voice was bland. "Even at the price of having to wade through the Senator's cursed, unreadable, and ungodly handwriting!"

Butler suddenly laughed and relighted his cigar.

Lincoln laughed too, then asked, quietly, "Cæsar having done all these things, as I've heard Bob translate his Latin to his mother, why can't you leave Grant alone, General?"

"Hah! Let Grant leave *me* alone!" ejaculated Butler.

"General, go to him! Tell him all that's penned up inside your heart and lock arms with him for the re-

mainder of the time you're in the Army. If you'll do
this, I promise you, I'll not lift a finger against your
nomination and if you do win it, I'll do everything in my
power to help you."

"I'll go see General Grant to-morrow," declared
Butler.

"Then I reckon I can go back to Washington to-night
with an easier mind."   Lincoln rose and put on the deer
stalker's cap he wore aboard the boat.

He reached the White House late the next morning
and the following day received a dispatch from General
Grant, containing a withdrawal of the request for Butler's demotion.

Bob, who had returned to his secretarial duties,
brought the dispatch to his father and said, "I didn't
think Grant mixed in politics."

"He doesn't.   Has too much sense and too hard a
job.   This is some of Butler's back-alley calling," replied
Lincoln, reading the message with a sigh of relief.   "I
made Butler straighten it out.   Wish I could do the
same thing by Winter Davis and Lyman Trumbull."

"Well, no one could call their methods of the back-
alley variety."   Bob's voice was rueful.   "What are you
going to do to counteract their thunder, Father?"

"Bob, I'm not going to do anything.   My stock is so
low over the country that even a Papal Bull couldn't
lower me, let alone one from Davis.   I was badly upset
at first but I've reached the point now where I feel like
the man did whose son had a scientific turn of mind.   He
bought the boy a microscope.   The youngster went round
experimenting with his glass on everything that came his
way.   One day, at dinner table, his father took a piece
of cheese.   'Don't eat that, Father,' said the boy, 'it's
full of wigglers.'   'My son,' said the old gentleman, tak-

ing a large bite, 'let 'em wiggle: I can stand it if they can!' "

Bob joined in his father's laughter, then said, seriously, "But are you really discouraged about your reelection, father?"

Lincoln nodded his head. "The only thing that can reëlect me would be a 'return to slavery' plank in the Democratic platform. Even Sumner would stand by me to defeat that— Are you glad to be through soldiering?"

"Oh, of course, being a Home Guard isn't real soldiering! But even at that I can go back to Harvard next month with a fair amount of swagger." Bob smiled.

"I may try to arrange with Grant to take you on when you finish. Your mother's more reconciled than she was, I think," taking up a handful of letters Stoddard laid on his desk.

"Mother's pretty philosophical about anything she sees is inevitable," said Bob with a boyish grin, and picking up a tray of telegrams he went out.

Secretary Stanton entered shortly after. His dark eyes behind his spectacles were red-rimmed for lack of sleep but were full of their usual fiery earnestness.

Lincoln rose to meet him. "Well, old friend, we've weathered through another night, eh? I always tell myself that when I waken.—Anything of the nature of a catastrophe for me this morning?"

Stanton's eyes softened. "You look as if you'd barely scraped through, though, Mr. Lincoln! God Almighty, but you look tired!"

"Same to you!" The President threw a long arm across Stanton's shoulders and the two men stood silent for a moment.

Finally Stanton said, "I've got another letter from

Grant to the effect that Phil Sheridan is expected to do real damage to Early. He gives details as to how the various forces will move. Sensible enough but for one thing. You know as well as I do, Mr. Lincoln, that unless Grant gets up to Maryland to see the ground himself we're in for another damn fool fiasco. The officers will do nothing but quarrel and fight for prestige. They need a head on the spot. And for some reason, Grant won't go. Here, read it yourself."

Lincoln read the message and looked up. "You're right, Stanton. It's good but not good enough. Here, let me see if I can't start him." He seated himself at the desk and wrote, "I have seen your dispatch in which you say, 'I want Sheridan put in command of all the troops in the field with instructions to put himself south of the enemy and follow him to the death. Wherever the enemy goes let our troops go also—' This I think is exactly right as to how our forces should move but please look over the dispatches you may have received from here ever since you made that order and discover, if you can, that there is any idea in the head of any one here of putting our army south of the enemy or of following him to the death in any direction. I repeat to you, it will neither be done nor attempted unless you watch it every hour of every day and force it."

Stanton read the message, nodded delightedly and said, "This is splendid! Of course it's in violation of all official etiquette and propriety."

"I reckon it is," replied Lincoln serenely. "I'm proud of the solid reputation I'm building for just that thing. Get it off, Stanton."

Grant's reply came at noon. He said, laconically, that he was leaving at noon for the Maryland front.

Lincoln heaved an enormous sigh of relief and an-

nounced to Nicolay and Bob that he was giving himself
a treat on the strength of Grant's decision.   The boys
received his announcement with cheers and forthwith he
went over to Chittenden's office and induced the Register
of the Treasury to go with him to visit Professor Henry,
head of the Smithsonian Institution.   "I want to get you
two fellows stirred up to talk.   I want to travel far from
war and politics."

Luck was peculiarly with him, he thought, when they
found in Henry's office the explorer Kennicott, who had
just returned from three years' exploration of the Yukon.
The room was overflowing with pelts, heads, eggs and
other fruits of the trip.   Kennicott was only too glad to
tell his story, and Lincoln put his feet on the mantel and
settled down for a real feast.

It was seven o'clock when the President looked at his
watch and ejaculated, "Jings, I've been in Alaska four
solid hours!   I'm a new man, gentlemen!"   And with a
regretful farewell glance at Kennicott's loot, he rushed
back to his office to make up for his holiday.

It was well past ten o'clock that evening when he decided to go out to the Soldiers' Home to spend the night
with the family, again sojourning there.   He had told
the servants and his guards that he would remain in the
city, but when he passed through the empty sitting room
on his way to bed, he realized that he was lonely.   It
would be good fun to slip out and tell Mary about Kennicott while the story was fresh in his mind.   He evaded
his guard, saddled his own horse, led it out the servant's
gate and was off.

It was over a year since he'd ridden alone.   A thrilling
sense of freedom swept over him.   There was a brilliant
moon.   His horse was fresh and lively and inclined to
shy at shadows.   No chance to worry or think, with this

beast to control, he thought contentedly. He allowed the animal to gallop the length of the turnpike, only slowing him down when he reached the turn into the Home. The August night was lovely—burning stars above and heavy scent of harvest fields on either side the road with locusts droning placidly.

He brought the horse to a full halt as he entered the gates and sat looking at the beautiful view to the north. Suddenly a rifle shot rang out and a bullet whined by the President's ear. The horse bolted, then another shot came.

Lincoln felt as if some one had hit his hat a violent blow. The frightened horse could not be brought up again until his forehoofs struck the porch of the cottage. Mary screamed from above and as Lincoln stood soothing the horse, she appeared on the porch with a candle.

"Abra'm, are you hurt?"

"Not at all," answered the President, still struggling with the plunging horse. "Hold the candle here, will you, Mary? Let's see if this fellow got scratched."

"Who cares about the horse? It's you! Abra'm, what was it? What brings you here?" Her voice rose hysterically.

A yawning colored boy came round the corner and took the reins.

Lincoln lifted the candle from Mary's shaking hand. "*You* brought me here, dearest wife!" He took her hand and led her up the stairs to their little bedroom, talking quietly as he moved. "I had a glorious afternoon in Alaska with Judge Chittenden and Doc. Henry. I came out to tell you about it. A fine fellow named Kennicott—"

As they entered the room, Mary interrupted him. "It's all right now, Abra'm. I'm not going into hysterics. I've learned more self-control in the past three years than in the forty years before. Who shot at you?"

"I don't know that any one did," setting the candle down on the bureau. "There was a shot as I turned from the turnpike that scared my horse. He bolted and jerked off my hat and here I am."

Mary stared up at him. She looked very young with her long braids hanging over her night dress. "Abra'm, how are we going to endure the strain to the end! And you want four years more!"

"It's queer what a man's conscience and vanity working together will bring him to, eh," chuckled Lincoln, sitting down on a stool covered with a cross-stitched tidy and beginning to pull off his boots.

"We'll have a lot of bad news. I broke a mirror to-day!" She stooped to help him with his boots and he saw that her teeth were chattering and her hands shaking. The superb fight she had waged for self-control ever since Willie's death was a constant source of admiration to him. He helped when he could.

"Let's go down to the kitchen and get something to eat, Mary. I'd give five dollars for a cup of your tea. You haven't made me one since we left Springfield."

"Haven't you had supper?" she demanded, straightening up and looking at him disgustedly.

"I forgot to," he replied meekly.

She pulled on a dressing gown, the color coming back to her face. "You are the greatest fool about your stomach that ever lived. I should think you'd learn sense, sometime. I let all the servants go to town except that cotton-headed Jake. You come straight down to the kitchen with me. No, don't start without your slippers. These floors are full of slivers."

She continued scolding as he followed her to the kitchen. She ordered him to sit down at the clean-scrubbed pine table. He did so, watching her contentedly as she manipulated the fire which still glowed. He finally lifted both feet to the opposite chair and interrupted the steady flow of her admonitions with a groan of satisfaction.

"Lord, isn't this fine! Mary, see if those darkies haven't hid some of their own ash-cakes round somewhere. A stone jar they would be in—then some New Orleans molasses, and your tea!—Ah," as she returned from the pantry with corn bread and the molasses jug, "Mary, I wouldn't swap you for Queen Victoria."

Mary dimpled and suddenly laid her cheek to his. "I worship you!" she whispered. Then she poured him his tea.

The next morning he rode back to town accompanied by James and the cotton-headed Jake. When they reached the turnpike, Lincoln dismounted and picked up his felt hat which lay in a clump of goldenrod. There was a bullet hole through the crown. He crushed the hat into the pocket of his coat. He would give it to Colonel Baker of the Detective Police and then forget the matter.

And Mary's prophecy of evil didn't come true that day, for Stoddard met him at the door of the White House with the news that Admiral Farragut had defeated the Rebel fleet and taken Mobile Bay!

CHAPTER XVII

JEANIE DEANS

JOHN HAY, who had returned from Greeley's futile peace mission more than ever discontented with what he called mere clerical work, was eager to attend the pending Democratic convention in Chicago, but Nicolay was better at that sort of thing, so it was he who went. It was John Hay, however, who brought the first news of the Chicago "surrender." He burst into Lincoln's bedroom, showing for the first time since Lincoln had known him, a real despair. Standing by the bed, wrapped in a purple and yellow smoking robe that was much coveted by Bob, his black hair rumpled, his black eyes deep sunk and his lips quivering, the young man read the news aloud to the President.

The Democrats had nominated McClellan on a platform the basic premise of which was that the war was a failure and peace with Unionism the only feasible aim —with no conditions attached to the restoration as regarded upholding the Emancipation act.

John dashed the paper to the floor and kicked it under the bed. "I warned everybody last spring when I came back from the middle West that there was almost revolutionary feeling against continuing the war and a growing enthusiasm for McClellan."

"I know you did, John!" agreed Lincoln. "But I didn't exactly nominate the man!"

John's lips quivered. "I don't know whether the nation's worthy of you for another term, sir. But if the

216

dumb cattle aren't worthy of another term of Lincoln,
then let the will of God be done and the murrain of Mc-
Clellan fall on them!"

He jerked the cord of his robe viciously and banged
out of the room. Lincoln lay for a moment staring
blankly at the ceiling. Then the door again flew open
and John, one broad grin, appeared, followed by Bob and
Taddie. John waved a slip of yellow paper.

"The war a failure, eh! Allow me to read you the
answer General Sherman makes to that! 'September 3.
Atlanta is ours and fairly taken!'—How's that for a
plank for the Republican platform?"

"By Jings!" shouted Lincoln. "What news for a
fellow to receive in his night shirt! How can I do a
hornpipe? Hand me my breeches, Tad."

But instead of dressing himself, he sat on the edge
of the bed, holding the yellow slip and smiling at it.
Finally he said:

"I reckon that this is the moment to call the folks
attention in no uncertain terms to the fact that this war
is not a failure. They've been ignoring what Farragut's
done. And they've got to take notice that Sherman's
army is now substantially the same as it was when it left
Chattanooga. After all the bloodshed—what a relief!
—what a relief! 'A victory is twice itself when the
achiever brings home full numbers.'"

Mary came in on the last of his soliloquy and shooed
the boys out after she had heard the glorious news. But
Lincoln would not allow her to lead him to breakfast
until he had written a proclamation in which he adjured
the people to give thanks to the Supreme Being for these
victories and ordered a hundred-gun salute to be fired
at each arsenal and navy yard of the United States.

Then he ate an unusually hearty breakfast.

"You'd lay on some flesh and be a credit to your clothes if you could get a telegram from Sherman every morning," said Mary as she refilled his coffee cup.

"Or just one from Sheridan! I'm getting discouraged about him," said the President.

For Sheridan still maneuvered for position against Early while Early continued to choke the railroads into Baltimore and Washington. There was now grave danger from a food-and-fuel famine in both cities. Grant had felt that the consequences of a defeat at the moment of the nation's terrible depression would be so grave that he was hesitating to have Sheridan take the initiative. Lincoln had felt the reasonableness of this but now, backed by the news from Sherman and Farragut, he began to urge Grant to take the gamble. In spite of his efforts, however, two weeks went by without apparent results. But on the 20th of September, Stoddard ran all the way from Stanton's office to Lincoln's with Sheridan's reply to the Chicago convention.

"We have just sent them whirling through Winchester and we are after them to-morrow."

Lincoln read the telegram, then looked over his spectacles to exclaim, "Boys, I reckon this will do! We'll shut up shop for the rest of the day."

He spent the afternoon visiting hospitals with Mary.

He awaited, eagerly now, the effect of the Chicago surrender on his own party. The answer came again through the newspapers. On the 29th of September they reported a long speech by Charles Sumner in Cooper Institute, New York, *ardently supporting Lincoln for President!*

From the moment that he read this speech, Lincoln began to cherish a real hope that he might be reëlected.

Sumner first, then Chase!

The former member of his Cabinet dropped into the President's office on the last day of September. He never had seen Chase looking so well, though he was handsome at all times; a big man physically with almost perfect features. What impressed Lincoln most at the moment was the fact that the familiar look of irritation had left Chase's lip and eye. He appeared as urbane as a sleeping child.

"The White Mountains have done you good, Governor," said Lincoln, shaking hands.

"What a pity you couldn't have been up there, too, Mr. Lincoln," replied Chase as he looked from Lincoln's weary face to the shabby, overloaded desk. "We've thought of you and Mrs. Lincoln often, suffering here in this dreadful town."

"I suppose it isn't a dreadful town, really," returned Lincoln, thoughtfully. "In fact, I recall having a sort of affection for the place when I was in Congress. But after this four years' siege— Well, when I leave it, I hope never to see it again.—Sit down and swap a few lies with me. What are you going to do with yourself now, Governor?"

"I'm going to devote myself to your reëlection, Mr. Lincoln," sinking into his old place at the Cabinet table.

Lincoln kept his countenance with difficulty, eased himself onto the edge of the table and clasped his left knee with both hands as he asked:

"You've changed your mind about me, eh?"

Chase looked up at the President and replied slowly, "I don't feel that I really know you and so I can't found my actions on what you say or do. But I've never desired anything but your complete success and I've never indulged in a personal feeling incompatible with absolute fidelity to your administration."

Lincoln bit his lip and told himself that Chase had taken his swapping invitation literally. Aloud he said: "I reckon it's not in the books for you and me to understand each other, Governor! Won't your friends be grieved at losing their pet candidate?"

"I never really desired to be President, Mr. Lincoln;" Chase leaned forward earnestly, his eyes as clear and candid as Tad's. "It's my conviction that the cause I love and the general interests of the country will be best promoted by your reëlection and I've made up my mind to join my efforts to those of almost the whole body of my friends in securing it."

"This is very pleasing to me! Very!" Lincoln suddenly choked, and it was not with laughter. He jumped from the table and walked hastily to the window. Chase really meant what he said. What a strange mind! He stared at the distant Potomac—hopefully—almost cheerfully. The sails were pretty in the September sun. He couldn't recall when he had noticed them before. He went back to the table and looked down at Chase, suppressing a desire to laugh or to weep, he couldn't tell which. "I'm glad to hear this news, Governor."

Obviously moved by the President's emotion, Chase rose and held out his hand. The two men shook hands and Lincoln uttered a silent prayer that the act prove symbolical of a real loyalty from the former secretary.

"My first move will be in my home State," said Chase. "In Ohio I ought to have weight, though I'm ashamed to say that McClellan's strong there."

"But not as strong as Salmon P. Chase," cried Lincoln joyfully. Then with a little hesitation, "Have you seen Charles Sumner lately?"

"I last saw dear Charles at Longfellow's house in Nahant on my way to the mountains," replied Chase, a reminiscent smile lighting his face. "The three of us spent the day on the piazza reading aloud Tennyson's last poem, "Enoch Arden." Longfellow's small daughter nestled in Sumner's lap much of the time. I must remember to tell little Isabella Hooper that. We avoided politics. Of course the Chicago treason hadn't occurred then."

"But he's come out for me!" ejaculated Lincoln. "Now with Phil Sheridan galloping up the Shenandoah valley.—Did you ever see him, Governor? He's not much more to look at than I am, a little chap with a round head, red face, legs longer than his body and not enough neck to hang him by. But he will actually chase Rebels! He and Sherman—after all these years—! Whew! Well, you've brought a fine grade of corn to the mill this morning, Governor," as Chase picked up his hat.

"Perhaps it was time, Mr. Lincoln," said Chase enigmatically.

Lincoln looked at his broad back almost with affection. "Patience is a tired nag," he murmured, "yet will she jog."

Mary was inclined to be scornful of Lincoln's hopes of Chase's personal loyalty.

"It suits him just now to make up to you because Chief Justice Taney is dying. Let's see what he does after the old man is gone."

But though poor Taney obligingly died in late October, Chase made no direct move in relation to the event. However, even before the funeral, a letter came from Sumner reminding Lincoln of their conversation the previous spring. He added his usual few words of admonition.

"I insist that from this time forward, the Constitution

must be interpreted for liberty as it has been thus far for slavery. I remind you also that our war measures must be sustained. A Chief Justice is needed whose position on the slavery question is already fixed and will not need argument of counsel to convert him. Chase's appointment should come hard on the heels of Taney's funeral."

Nicolay gave this letter to the President with a questioning lift of the eyebrows. Lincoln read it, and said, "We'll be swamped with petitions. Every jerkwater lawyer in the country is going to ask for the job. Give them all the same answer: that the President's going to be very shut pan about this matter."

"There's a letter in this mail from Governor Chase. He's still in Ohio," Nicolay grinned.

"What's it about?" asked Lincoln.

"Simply a kind and friendly letter."

"File it with his other recommendations," said Lincoln with his shrewd smile.

Lincoln had no intention of appointing Chase immediately. After pondering on the matter for some time, he came to the conclusion that it would be salutary for this man with his uneasy ambitions, his incapacity for reading men, his unkind tongue, to spend a few weeks in uncertainty. In seeking the reason for the delay it was possible that the Governor might bring his brilliant brain to bear on his own weaknesses of character. Only when he understood these would he be fit for the high office.

So under all the enormous pressure, pressure so widespread that one might have thought that even the war and the pending election were less important to folk than their winning of the vacant place on the bench for themselves or their friends, Lincoln was silent.

He watched the work of his party on his reëlection with deepest concern, gave advice, kept Nicolay on the go. But he made no election speeches himself. When election day came, to his own surprise, he found himself quite calm and going about his routine business with a clear mind. Mary was tense and irritable with anxiety. She finally lost patience with Lincoln's apparent indifference and went off with Taddie to take supper with Mrs. Welles.

A heavy rain came on late in the afternoon. The wind rose almost to a hurricane. It was Cabinet day, but only Bates and Welles were there, for Stanton was down with malaria and the others had gone home to vote. Lincoln dismissed the meeting shortly and as the twilight came on, suddenly realized that he was alone and that he was lonely and uneasy. He prowled about from room to room. The sitting room with a single light burning low and the little dog Sumter asleep on a sofa, Martin Van Buren smirking above him, Mary's room with the faint odor of attar of roses—the toilet things in perfect alignment on the bureau—dear Mary! she'd find Springfield dull, but heavenly dull, after all this. His own room. No, that enshrined too many agonies. He wouldn't go in there. Across the hall to Tad's room. Tad had been playing with his toy soldiers. A pistol, present from some officer, lay on the bed. Lincoln purloined it. He'd had an ugly dream about Tad and his pistol, the night before.

From Tad's room into Willie's. It had been kept without change, though Mary never had entered it from the day of the boy's death. Lincoln lighted the gas and stood looking about. Willie had been Lincoln over again with all Lincoln's boyhood yearnings. Thank God, Willie's father'd been able to satisfy some of them. He smoothed the bed and patted a copy of Scott's poems, still open, face down on the table. Then seated himself on the bed. . . . If it was the will of the people to refuse him this day at the polls—what a relief, what a

tragic relief! . . . Life could compensate him best by
bringing him this refusal. . . . Life, what was it? God
functioning? or man? And who was he, Abraham Lincoln? Who—? President of the United States of
America! God! God! . . . He twisted his hands together and groaned, then sat motionless.

John Hay came upon him, a little breathless from his
search. One never knew when the kidnapers would be
given their opportunity by Lincoln's carelessness of self.
The young man gave a sweeping glance round the room
and his face was very tender but his voice casual as he
said:

"So many wires are down owing to the storm, sir, that
the only news will be in the War Office. Let's go over
there and see what's happening."

Lincoln rose, blinked, and with one hand on John's
shoulder turned out the gas with the other. He twisted
a blue army cape round him and followed the young man
toward the War Office. It was difficult to negotiate the
turnstile, so fierce was the buffeting of the wind.

There was a crowd in the War Office, Welles, Bates,
Nicolay, Stoddard, and several newspaper men. Somebody had treated to an oyster supper on trays. It was
good to be back in the world of men.—

By midnight, it was certain that he had been elected.

About two o'clock Mary sent word that in spite of the
rain that still fell, a huge crowd was serenading his
empty bed chamber. He hurried home through the
kitchen premises, made a little speech from the window
of his room and went to sleep a little later, almost un-
bearably convinced that the Supreme Being was setting
the seal of approval on the thing he was trying to do.

But even now, he did not give Chase the reward every
one said Chase expected. He was waiting to see Sumner. He would not send for Sumner. But, as he ex-

pected, the Senator appeared just before the opening of Congress.

It was a cold, sleety day with Tad lying on the office hearthrug reading aloud from a book of fairy tales while his father worked on his message to Congress. Tad was wild with joy at seeing his friend. Before his father and the Senator could shake hands the boy was embracing him while his shouts of welcome brought James to the door. Sumner hugged and kissed him and exclaimed over his summer's growth. But when Tad had subsided, the two men clasped hands in silence: Lincoln deeply glad to see this man he loved, deeply apprehensive of what this greatest of his adversaries might have in store for him.

Sumner broke the silence, his voice tender and deep. "My dear Mr. Lincoln, you make us all feel selfish, always here, day after difficult day," he glanced around the office as Chase had done, "and the rest of us—"

"And the rest of you," smiled Lincoln, "riveting the chains for another four years. I'm mighty grateful to you for your efforts and your self-sacrifice, Senator. I've followed things with fair accuracy, this summer."

Sumner chose to ignore the implications. "We're all happy over the results, Mr. Lincoln."

"Even Chase?" asked the President, deliberately.

"You must try to overlook the indecorous things Mr. Chase once said about you," said Sumner, drawing Tad down beside him on a sofa and patting the small grimy hand that lay on his great knee.

"Oh! I bear no grudge," answered Lincoln. "They sting but they concern Chase more than they do me. Would he as Chief Justice say indecorous things about the persons and cases connected with the Supreme Court? You perceive that here's where his hens come home to roost."

"I'm sure he won't," answered Sumner earnestly. "It's only where his ambition's concerned that he's unwise."

Lincoln rubbed his head. "Of Mr. Chase's ability and of his soundness on the interpretations of the Emancipation there can be no doubt. But—he's a man of unbounded ambition and he's been working all his life to become President. I'm afraid if I make him Chief Justice, he'll simply become more restless and uneasy and neglect the place in his strife and intrigue to get this job. If I were sure he'd go on the bench and give up his aspirations and do nothing but make himself a great judge, I'd not hesitate a moment. What do you say to this idea, Senator? What if I'd send for Mr. Chase and tell him frankly that the way was open to him to become the greatest Chief Justice the Supreme Court ever had if he'll dismiss at once and forever the subject of the Presidency?"

Sumner raised both white hands in horror. "No! A thousand times, no! Can't you see the construction Mr. Chase and all his friends would put on such a proposition coming from you?"

Lincoln answered thoughtfully, "If he were more my friend, I'd risk it. . . . I'm convinced of his great powers. I hope rather against hope that once upon the bench he'll see in what direction his best prospects of usefulness and fame rest. . . ." He ran his paper knife through his hair several times, Sumner watching him anxiously, then slipping it back into his vest pocket, he said, "Well, Senator, I'll risk it!"

"Thank God!" ejaculated Sumner. "I'm sure you'll not regret your decision, Mr. Lincoln."

"I hope not." The President spoke soberly. "Of course, he'll keep on bringing me up by hand but I'm almost hardened to that."

"Mr. Lincoln," Sumner's deep voice was very soft, "I want to say that I think you're showing fine magnanimity in this. Chase should be most grateful to you. . . . Between you and me, I think this act of yours may save him from political indiscretions that would blast his fame. I wish your treatment of him could be written into history."

"Tut! Tut!" Lincoln shook his head but he felt warmed in spite of his protest. "I don't want praise. I'll tell you a story that will explain why. Do you remember what Jeanie Deans said to Queen Caroline when the Duke of Argyle procured her an opportunity to beg for her sister's life?"

Sumner shook his head and frowned a little. Lincoln went on, serenely:

"I remember it. She said: 'It's not when we sleep soft and wake merrily oursel's that we think on other people's sufferings. Our hearts are waxed light within us then and we are for righting our ain wrongs and fighting our ain battles. But when the hour of trouble comes to the mind or the body and when the hour of death comes that comes to high or low,—oh, then it isna what we hae dune for oursel's but what we hae dune for others that we think on maist pleasantly.' "

There was a short pause during which Sumner patted Tad's hand gently. The little boy broke the silence by asking the Senator if he'd not like to borrow the book of fairy tales.

Sumner accepted the offer, gravely. Lincoln wondered if this were the moment for a few cautious advances on Louisiana but Mary came in with a glass of buttermilk, and a moment later, Sumner, with the fairy tales under his arm and Tad clinging to his hand, followed Mary on a visit to a century plant in bloom in the greenhouse. Lincoln saw him go with a sigh of relief.

CHAPTER XVIII

THE GREAT ISSUE

THE storm for a while after Sumner's departure shut off the stream of callers. Lincoln was glad of the opportunity thus offered for work on the annual message, but he found it difficult to take it up again. Instead his mind ran on Sumner. The thought of the struggle that could no longer be postponed came between him and all his other problems. And suddenly he asked himself why, if he ended slavery and successfully ended the war, he should so seriously concern himself with reconstruction. He would have done his share and he was unutterably weary of strife and contention. Why not let Sumner have his way? Why not?

He tilted his chair back against the wall, put his feet on his desk and abandoned himself to marshaling the thoughts of the past four years. Cleared of the débris of half thoughts, they presented themselves about like this:— The issue embraced more than the fate of these United States. It presented to the whole family of men the question whether a constitutional republic, a government of the people, by the same people, could or could not maintain its territorial integrity against its own domestic foes. It presented the question whether discontented individuals could break up their government and thus practically put an end to free government upon the earth.

Was there in all republics this inherent and fatal weakness? Must a government of necessity be too strong for the liberties of its own people or too weak to maintain its own existence?

There had been many hours when he would have said "Yes!" to this query, but now it looked as if so far as physical force was concerned the answer was "No!"— But "No" only as to physical force. It looked as if the Rebels were not the only enemies to the conception of the Union as the beginning and the end of the nation. Sumner with his contention that State suicide was a possible and an accomplished fact nullified the basic conception of the Union. Once let Sumner put through his idea of reconstruction, based on the admission that the States had left the Union, and the whole Secession contention on State sovereignty was ratified.

The nation had purchased with money the land out of which several of the seceding States had been formed. The nation even now was in debt for money applied to these purchases. It was paying the old debts of Texas. If one State could secede, so could another, and when all were gone who would be left to pay the debts? Then how about the creditor? He must ask Sumner that.

No, he wouldn't ask him that, either! It would get them nowhere. There was no blinking the fact that after nearly two years of effort, he and the Senator from Massachusetts were no closer to seeing eye to eye. Any advantages the President had won had been through luck, the gratuitous gift of the march of events. If he was to go on, he must now make a supreme effort.

Was it worth the struggle?

He recalled his state of mind in '61. He reviewed what the years in Washington had done to his high faith in his fellow man. A throng, more wretched in spirit than those poor fellows he'd seen freed from Libby prison had been in body, filed past his mind's eye; a throng of unequaled sleekness and prosperity of aspect. But in its pettiness, its self-seeking, its dishonorableness, its cruelty and stupidity, this unending file of self-seeking men and women who had passed through his office was leprous.

He wondered if, to the President of a republic, humanity could remain beautiful—or to any ruler of any country. God, how pitiful the human animal was! A bleakness like death horror descended on him. Should he struggle against Sumner to maintain a nation whose citizens had not been made better than those of other nations by its beneficent institutions? Men should become better citizens here than in England or France or Russia. Our initial object was clear on that.

Ah, wasn't that just the point? After all, wasn't the struggle to maintain the Union a plain people's contest to perpetuate that form and substance of government whose leading object was to elevate the condition of men? To lift artificial weights from all shoulders, to clear the paths of laudable pursuits for all, to afford all an unfettered start and a fair chance in the race of life?

From the bird's-eye view, it really mattered little that in the paltry three quarters of a century of the nation's life, so little had been accomplished spiritually. The experiment had only begun. It was an experiment which if successful would have a supremely important effect on civilization. Didn't one then have an unshiftable obligation to carry it on? Didn't the issue have a breadth of aspect that made slavery seem only a local and temporary portion of it? Sumner was near-sighted.

He began to wonder, at this point, just why this vast, impersonal problem of the philosophy of government had taken so vital a hold on him. At what point in his career had its import moved beyond the slavery issue to include the whole theory of human liberty? Slowly he reviewed his boyhood, his memories of his father, his mother. Much that would make a man ambitious there, but nothing to give a man this overweening interest in the great political experiment. His young manhood in Springfield? Mary and Herndon had helped stock his mind with facts, Mary had urged him on—but not from these the vital interest. Washington, the war—Lord, what a long, dusty road!

How unbelievable that he, he of all people in the world, should be the ruler of a great nation! a man of such poverty of opportunity—

Hah! He gasped aloud as understanding swept over him.

In these United States there was no such thing as poverty of opportunity! His own career was proof of that. And in his own career lay the cause of his vital interest in the experiment of government!

He was a living witness that any man's child could look to come to the White House as his own father's child had come. Here at last was the answer to his first query. His absorption in the saving of the Union was based on the desire that any one else might have through this free government an open field and a fair chance for his industry, enterprise and intelligence; that he might have equal privileges in the race of life with all its desirable human aspirations. To save the Union was to secure this inestimable jewel to mankind.

As he reached this conclusion, the sense of depression, of seeing through a glass darkly, that had haunted him so long, melted into thin air. He felt a sudden influx of mental vigor and sureness unprecedented in his experience. The office slowly impinged on his consciousness. The desk took shape before him—the papers—the first sentence of the annual message. He dropped his chair back into position and took up his pen.

He had decided long since to repeat the amnesty offer and to urge again the passing of a constitutional amendment freeing the slaves, thus giving the States a chance to ratify what already had been done as a military necessity. He dipped his pen in the ink but before he had put down a word, Mary spoke from the doorway in a voice of unutterable weariness:

"At last! Do you know that it's midnight, Abra'm, and that you've not been out of that chair for eight mortal hours? Do come to bed! I've a cold supper waiting for you in your room."

"I did take a long trip this time, I reckon," he said apologetically.

Congress made no bones about its intention to fight Lincoln on reconstruction. Just where it would strike the first blow he couldn't be sure, but he took it for granted that the effort would be via Sumner and Louisiana. Sumner went back and forth between the Capitol and the Executive Mansion with great frequency but always on anything rather than reconstruction. Then the newly elected members arrived from Louisiana and presented their credentials and Sumner showed his hand. He rose in the Senate and served notice that he would in a short time outline his suggestions on handling Louisiana.

Thus the storm broke on Lincoln. And he was still without a program!

On the day of Sumner's pronouncement, Alice Hooper gave a tea which Mary attended. Sumner, of course, was there, and Senator Trumbull dropped in. Alice Hooper deliberately precipitated a discussion by saying that she had met the wife of one of the Louisiana Senators-elect and hoped that Congress would admit the new members if all the wives were as charming as this one.

Trumbull said with a grin, "Ask Senator Sumner! I hear he and the President compromised the matter."

"I wouldn't think of suggesting compromise to the President," Sumner shook his head sadly.

Mary spoke quickly, "I would, for you, Senator, if you really have a possible one in mind."

Sumner looked at her thoughtfully. "Perhaps you could get his ear, Mrs. Lincoln. Certainly I've failed for weeks. There's nothing more necessary before the country to-day than that there be no break between Mr. Lincoln and Congress on reconstruction. Much as I am against the premature recognition of Louisiana, I'll hold my peace if I can secure a rule of equality for the negroes of other States."

"Why don't you tell Mr. Lincoln that yourself, Senator?" asked Mary.

"He has made it clear that he won't discuss compromise with me," replied Sumner. "Therefore we can't admit the persons from Louisiana."

"Oh, there are worse things done every day in the Senate than admitting those men would be," smiled Trumbull.

"What's that?" demanded Sumner, soberly.

"Letting fanatics like Ben Wade and Winter Davis get a strangle grip on reconstruction," replied Senator Trumbull, coolly.

A gasp went round the tea table. "What!" shouted Sumner. "After your intimacy there! What do you mean?"

"I mean," retorted Trumbull, flushing but without fumbling his words, "I mean that along with other Northerners with open minds I've been seeing these past months that Lincoln is farther sighted than the rest of us."

"By the living God!" shouted Sumner. "You! You, the Jacobin who scourged Lincoln, the tyrant! You would now join with him to keep the negro in outer darkness?"

"Senator! Senator!" protested Alice Hooper, wiping up the tea he had spilled on the lace cloth.

"I'm sorry, very, very sorry, Alice!" Sumner lowered his voice at once and helped her to repair the damage. Then he turned to Trumbull with his charming, apologetic smile. "Fanatics have no place at a lady's tea table, eh, Senator?"

"Seems to me the ladies put up with a good deal from you, Senator," replied Trumbull. "I suppose it's because you're so ornamental."

"Handsome is as handsome does!" exclaimed Alice. "I've a notion to send you up to the nursery to have tea with Isabella."

"Don't suggest it or we'll lose him, Mrs. Hooper," protested Mary in mock alarm.

Trumbull turned to her immediately and asked her if she had had recent news from her brother-in-law in Springfield, Ninian Edwards. Mary followed his lead and they renewed their old acquaintanceship elaborately while Alice Hooper and Sumner murmured over the tea table. Mary rushed home immediately after Trumbull left, impatient to tell her story to Lincoln. Rarely enough she and the President had the supper table to themselves and she was able to finish without interruption.

Lincoln listened with increasing surprise and pleasure. "Well! Well!" he exclaimed when she was done, "that's a sort of left-handed atonement on Trumbull's part but, to mix figures, I won't look a gift horse in the mouth!"

"Isn't it wonderful? How do you account for the change?" cried Mary.

"I think he accounted for it," said Lincoln. "Trumbull is honest. Mary, I've got my program! I'll execute a flank movement on Sumner. I'll send for Trumbull to-night and get him to head it."

"I don't see," insisted Mary, "why on earth you don't make Mr. Sumner Secretary of State, then he'd be out of your way."

"Because I won't give him the satisfaction of refusing the offer," replied Lincoln. "And anyhow, he'd never bow to the yoke of a Secretaryship!"

"No man can be one of your Cabinet officers and not learn to mind you, Abra'm, I've learned that," agreed Mary.

"Chase never learned to mind," Lincoln pointed out.

"So Chase resigned!" She smiled impishly at him. "But jokes aside, my dear, I'm dreadfully concerned about the men you plan to invite into your new Cabinet. How can you consider General Banks when you might have Sumner?"

"In the first place, Sumner would scorn such an invitation," said Lincoln with dawning irritation, "and in the second place, what makes you think I'm considering Banks?"

"Everybody's saying so, and all sorts of people have been to me with protests," answered Mary, using her finger bowl vigorously.

"I've never thought of him in that connection," said Lincoln shortly. "Nor has any one mentioned him to me. He's gone back to New Orleans."

Mary dropped her napkin. "Good heavens! Then I've put my foot in it again! Has Charles Sumner said anything to you about Banks lately?"

"I said no one had!" looking at Mary with the old uneasiness. "You ought not meddle where you've no authority, wife. You can make me an infinite amount of trouble. Where does Sumner come in on this? What have you been doing?"

"Well, you're so absurdly patient and Banks is such a—"

"Never mind that, Mary!" pushing away his tea cup untasted, "just where does Sumner come in?"

"Well," defiantly, "I wrote him last week asking him to use his influence with you to keep Banks out of the Cabinet."

Lincoln could feel his cheeks burn. "Don't you see that you've put me in a humiliating position before him, Mary? I thought there was one person on earth who wouldn't try to intrigue against me!"

"Nothing of the sort!" Mary's voice was furious. "I'm trying to help you. That letter—I've kept a copy. You shall see it."

"Very well, I'll come with you now." Lincoln rose, more hurt than he could readily explain to himself.

He stood under the chandelier in Mary's room and read the letter. "Hon. Charles Sumner, My dear sir: Our best Republican friends, those who have been the most ardent supporters of the administration through the last trying conflict, are very much exercised over the attempt which General Banks, *himself,* is making most *strenuously* for *imaginary* services; also the leading conservatives who would like to use Banks are urging him for the Cabinet. Our true friends write me frequently and deplore such a prospect. I am sure *such* an appointment would not meet with your approbation. Will you not exercise your great influence with the friends who have a *right* to demand something at the hands of a

Government they have rescued from tyranny? I feel assured *now*, whilst this subject is agitated, your voice and your pen will not be silent. General Banks is considered a *weak failure*, overrated, a speculator and an associate of Secession agents. I believe General Banks would bow submissively to General McClellan if he were in power as to Mr. L. himself. Perhaps you will consider it unbecoming in me to write you thus. But the whole country is anxious about this and it is very natural that discriminations should be made between true, loyal men and those whom the country considers *time servers*. The services of such certainly are not required at a momentous time like this! I can scarcely believe that this news will not meet with your own ideas on the subject. If I have erred, pray excuse me.

"General Banks has been in W——— ten days past, unremitting in his attentions to the President. *You* can do much in this case. Any communication on this subject will be considered private. Your friend, Mary Lincoln."

The President's indignation mounted as he read. When he had finished he dashed the letter to the floor.

"This! From my wife! I thought you had more intelligence!"

"I don't think the letter lacks intelligence," protested Mary, with spirit.

"It's the rambling screed of a woman who'd like to be queen consort but hasn't the requisite training. Now, Mary, I won't have this kind of thing going on. You go over to your desk and write a letter to Sumner, cleaning this up, and let me see it before you send it." He did not raise his voice but he was the more emphatic for that.

Mary stood before him, sparkling with anger. Her

little figure in the purple velvet trembled. Her fine eyes flashed unutterable things.

"Don't speak to me as if I were a Cabinet member, Mr. Lincoln."

"I speak to you as to a woman who's interfered foolishly in her husband's business," he said sadly.

"I thought ours was a partnership," her voice shaking.

"So did I, but it looks as if you didn't understand the word. I'm waiting for the letter, Mary!"

She flung herself down before the rosewood desk, lifted the lid, jerked out a sheet of paper, slammed the lid down, wrote. Lincoln paced the floor. If Mary, who for four years had withstood the wooings and the bribes to which any ordinary woman would have succumbed in a week—if Mary now went to pieces, the one comfort of his life was gone, the one steady solace, the one source from which he never failed to draw sanity, the final support he counted on for enduring this thing to its bloody end. He had used to have, in addition to Mary, laughter. But of late laughter had frequently failed to come when he beckoned. He was tired—strained. God! a man must have peace in his bedroom. It must be his ultimate, never failing retreat. Otherwise he'd break and the cause was lost.

He took with a stern look the note Mary handed him with her finger tips.

"Dear Mr. Sumner: I take this opportunity of offering an apology for having written you so candid, and as it *now* appears, so unnecessary a letter as I did a few days since. Mr. L. now says that no one ever has mentioned the subject to him, he had no idea of it himself and General Banks has returned to his command at New Orleans. And now that I have made the amende honorable for my *sympathetic interest* in General Banks, and with apologies for having trespassed on your valuable time, I remain, respectfully yours, Mary Lincoln."

"That will answer," said Lincoln, dropping the letter into his pocket. "I realize that I've brought a part of this on myself by asking your help with Sumner. Now remember, Mary, you're to promise me to keep out of politics from now on."

"I'll do nothing of the sort!" exclaimed Mary, rushing into her own room and slamming the door.

Lincoln groaned and went into his office to meet a committee from Chicago come to protest against their draft quotas. He gave the note to Bob, who had finished his law course and was awaiting an army appointment. Bob was instructed to find Sumner and to deliver the note into his hands.

Bob traced the Senator to the Hooper mansion and delivered the note to Sumner as he emerged from the door. It was not a fortunate moment.

Immediately after the departure of the President's wife, Alice Hooper had said petulantly to Sumner, "You think more of the darkies, Senator, than you do of your friends."

"You mean that I think more of human liberty than I do of my friends," returned Sumner, gently.

"It amounts to the same thing, my good man," declared Alice. "Will you kindly ring the bell?" She directed a servant to remove the tea tray, then crossed the room to stand with one fine foot on the hearth rail.

Sumner leaned an elbow on the mantel and divided his gaze between the fire and the beautiful woman on whom his heart was set. She was the type for whom men of Sumner's kind are doomed to care. In appearance she was elegant, with an indescribable graciousness and suavity of movement that never deserted her even when

as now she was in a captious mood. She had a genius
for fashionable living that made her, as the newspapers
said, preëminent among all the fashionable women in
Washington. Nor did this preoccupation with society
completely obscure the fact that she had a good mind:
not as keen nor as avid as Mary Lincoln's, but a good
mind nevertheless. Her interest in large political problems was real and highly intelligent and she had an independence of opinion that led back to her Puritan
ancestry.

Sumner admired her much for her intellectual quali-
ties, but her social cleverness attracted him as strongly.
His life as scholar and politician left him little time for
the life of fashion, but ever since his sojourn among the
great families of England in his youth he had yearned
for it. He once told Mary Lincoln that Alice was the
beau ideal of the lady of some fine old English manor.
That she was like the President's wife in some points of
temperament he had observed. But he had so little understanding of women that he did not see that she lacked
the quality that made the Lincolns' marriage sound. She
lacked Mary's understanding of and repentant acknowl-
edgment of her weaknesses. Mary's final charm was
her quick and fiery grief over her quick and fiery temper.

As she stood now with the fire glow in her delicate
face, it seemed to Sumner that Alice embodied all the
beauty, mental, spiritual, physical, that a man could desire in his life. It was over a year now since Sturgis
Hooper's death. She was no longer in mourning; was
leading a gay life. He would wait no more.

He drew himself up, a superb figure of a man, flushing, his moving, tender voice low, a little broken.

"Alice, will you be my wife?"

She looked at him gravely, without surprise. "Sen-

ator, I could give no one what I gave Sturgis. I gave
him all. Yet I made him none too happy. You and I
would both be unhappy together."

"But why, my dear Alice?" asked Sumner, staring at
her with painful anxiety. "Why? Is it the disparity in
our ages that frets you?"

"That's one consideration, certainly," she said. "After
all, you were past your first youth and known to fame
when I was in the cradle."

"There's no denying that. But, Alice, a young man
couldn't give you the prestige that perhaps I may say
without too much vanity will go with my name." He
took a step toward her.

Alice did not move but she gave a little laugh that
halted him. "Without belittling your achievements, Senator, I'll have to admit that a seat in the United States
Senate doesn't seem to me to compass the final glory of
what the country has to offer."

He turned to stone. "You're laughing at me!"

She nodded, her lovely eyes melting in blue fire.
"After all, we're not children, my good man! Even at
that, in some ways, I'm more experienced than you. For
example, I know what marriage is. I know that it re-
quires a deep and common interest to carry it through.
Love is the best interest. If not love, ambition. I'll admit that I've wondered at times, if you asked me to
marry you, what I'd say. And so wondering I've studied
you more closely than you've known. And I've come to
the conclusion that you're wasting your great powers.
You should be Secretary of State, then Minister to England, then President."

"What!" ejaculated Sumner. "Are you asking me
to bribe you to marry me? And at the price of all I
hold most sacred!" He stared at her incredulously.

"Do you know me so little?" He brought his fist against the mantel with a thud that shook the clock. "This hurts most damnably. I bring to you my love. Yes— my love,—all the pent-up emotions and devotions, adorations and yearnings, loneliness and soul hunger of a man who has been denied love all during the years natural to its fulfillment. I tremble like an untried boy at the touch of your finger tips. I flush at the sound of your voice, your very name rings in my ear with all the poetry, music, and beauty that artists have made for us in all the years, and you toss all this aside with a laugh and say, bring me a Secretaryship! It's unbelievable!" His face twitched.

Alice watched him with interest, a little pale, for Sumner deeply stirred was as impressive as a forest in a storm. But there was a curious sort of determination in the set of her lips as if she were forcing herself not to be too much impressed. After a moment she said with her own air of graciousness, touched now with regret.

"I've been archaic and after all, romantic. You must forgive me, Senator. I suppose I had a vague picture in my mind of the knight going out at his lady's behest to bring home the impossible for her, in order to win her hand. And I'd thought of you as romantic—sentimental as a boy. I'm sorry. Let it pass. Will you take supper with us, Mr. Sumner?"

Sumner was breathing heavily. "Thank you, no. I'll wish you good-night, Alice." He bowed and went out.

Bob Lincoln with his note met him as he hurried down the steps to the street. There was only a feeble light from a street lamp near by. Bob could not see the Senator's face.

"I don't want to delay you, sir," the young man fell into step with the older, "but here's a letter my father asked me to put into your hands. It needs no answer."

Sumner looked down at him. "Ah, Robert!" he said gently, putting out a shaking hand for the letter.

"You aren't feeling well, Senator!" exclaimed Bob, perceiving the unsteadiness of the hand. "Can I call a carriage for you? Your heart?"

"Yes, my heart!" grimly. "But I'm only a block from home. If you'll give me your arm—I ought to have a son about your age, Robert. I wish I had one. And like you too, a gentle fellow with a peppery temper." He leaned heavily on the strong young shoulder.

"You've been overdoing," said Bob.

"No! Yes!—I've had a blow, Robert. I've had a blow."

"That's hard! Can I help?"

"Only by getting me to my house, dear boy, and calling my secretary."

He was better by the time the house was reached and able to mount the steps and the stairs without much difficulty. But when Bob saw his face clearly in the light of his bedroom he went off on his own responsibility to find Dr. Stone.

Then he sought his father, but the President, having given the Chicago committee short shrift, was closeted with Lord Lyons. The Englishman looked ill, and in reply to Lincoln's inquiry if this were not true, he answered:

"I fear so, Mr. President. Between its malaria and its typhoid Washington has been a little rough with me." He warmed thin hands at the fire. "I've called for an informal good-by."

"Seward told me to expect you," said Lincoln. "Well, my lord," moving over to stand beside the Minister and warming his own hands, white enough now themselves to bear the contrast with the visitor's, "well, my lord, you

and I haven't been precisely intimate! But we've managed to hitch along, somehow, together, eh? I don't like
to see you leave us. I don't see how any one short of one
of the twelve disciples could have filled the bill better
than you. And come to think of it, they hadn't a cupful
of tact among the lot, while your well of it is bottomless.
Sit down and let's have a talk. You said this was informal, you know!"

Lyons pulled his chair close to the fire. His tired face
was curiously softened. Even his impeccable evening
clothes had a relaxed air, Lincoln thought, or perhaps his
loss of weight made them sit more easily on his big
frame.

"It looks, Mr. President, as if the end were in sight!
I say, thank God for that!"

"It may be a few months off but not longer," replied
Lincoln cautiously. "It's been a great comfort to me, my
lord, that your country and mine haven't become em-
broiled. It was hard sledding for a while, but all's well
that ends well. Seems to me nobody could have done a
better job than Charles Francis Adams has done over
there. Unless Charles Sumner. What do you think,
now that you can speak like a person and not as the British Empire?"

"I think Mr. Sumner would have been a better initial
choice, Mr. Lincoln, because he was already known and
loved there," replied Lyons. "But I doubt if his tact
would have been as unassailable as Mr. Adams' has
proved to be.—Sumner's greatly admired in high places
in my country though, where Adams is unknown. You've
asked me a difficult question, sir," with a smile.

"I've found it so, myself," admitted Lincoln. "How
would Seward have done over there?"

"Oh, not at all!" ejaculated Lyons. "His attitude on

political morals, on statecraft, is utterly cynical. And I'm never sure from one day to the next where I'll find him. I transact all my business with him in writing. This quite aside from the fact that I like him tremendously."

"You've found him to be what our negro James calls sometimey, eh? Well, would you have liked it better if Sumner had had *that* job?"

"Infinitely! There's one appointment that would have been quite perfect! If I may ask, Mr. Lincoln, why did you need Seward's following more than you did Sumner's?"

"Seward's following has much more power within the Republican party than Sumner's. Sumner's gathered about him too many radicals from all parties. What would you think of Sumner in Seward's place next year?"

"Very favorably. Especially if you wish to take advantage of the prestige Mr. Adams has given your diplomacy."

"That's the devil of it!" sighed Lincoln. "Sumner and Adams are at outs with each other."

"Nevertheless, they're both sincere, both brilliantly well trained men, Mr. Lincoln. *Sincere,* sir!" Lyons repeated emphatically. "With the war over, I should suppose the cause for contention between them would be removed. I would earnestly recommend that you make the appointment."

Lincoln gave a low laugh, and in reply to Lyons' surprised look, he explained:

"It's the first time in four years I've ever heard you express a personal opinion. I like it! I'm going to get over to England one of these days myself. I shall do myself the honor of looking you up."

"The honor will be mine, Mr. Lincoln," said Lyons

with unmistakable sincerity. "And as you say I'm being frank for once, will you permit me to add that four years ago I'd not have believed it possible for a man to grow to the terrible task as you've grown. You've reached a point where your imperturbable sagacity astounds me. I only wish my fellow countrymen could see you as I do!"

Lincoln reddened with pleasure. "What! that green fellow from the Sangamon?"

"I'm not at all sure but what much of the greenness was assumed," said Lyons. "At any rate, it's mellowed now into something so rich and original that any Anglo-Saxon may be proud of his kinsman."

"I—I—you mustn't praise me, Lord Lyons," stammered the President, rising and crossing the room to hide his embarrassment before the war map. "I'm not hardened to it, like Sumner."

"You've had all too little of it from your compatriots as well as from others, sir," with a charming air of apology as he rose. "Some day there'll be few, I fancy, self-deprecatory enough to admit that!"

"Oh, come! Come! You'll have me asking for a chance to kiss you, in a moment," protested Lincoln, turning round. "Good-by, my lord, and thank you."

"Good-by, Mr. Lincoln. God bless you, sir." He wrung Lincoln's hand and was gone.

Lincoln stood before the fire reviewing the interview with considerable amazement. He was glad to know the Englishman's opinion of Sumner and he determined that, if Seward would agree, he'd offer the secretaryship to Sumner, when and if the emergency required it. It was very cheering, he thought, to have seen, if only for a moment, the hearty man behind the diplomat. The praise was good, by Jings!

He had a feeling that Lyons' going rang down the curtain on one of the last acts of the drama.

Bob slipped in now and told of his encounter with Sumner.

"Did you tell your mother?" asked Lincoln.

"I tried to.   But she's upset over something"—rue-fully—"and I can't be sure she listened to me.   She's even so unlike herself that she never said a word when I told her that you were going to make a formal request to General Grant to give me a job.   I'm sorry now I didn't say I was going to enlist."

Lincoln put his arm around the boy's neck.   "To tell the truth, son, your mother and I are at loggerheads over a matter and she was probably planning what she'd do to me next."

Bob made a wry face.   "What's the matter with every-body?   Sumner, mother, Tad—"

"What's the matter with Tad now?" smiled the Presi-dent.

"Oh, he got mad at his tutor to-day and fired him. Fractions, I believe, caused the crisis.   Or perhaps it was the sugar scattered in the tutor's sheets, or the pet turkey under Tad's desk.   At any rate, the tutor took his discharge seriously this time, and he's gone."

"When did all this happen?" asked Lincoln with huge enjoyment.   Tutors came and went as frequently as cooks in this household.

"Well, Tad came in and told mother, just now.   But it seems the tutor went at noon and without risking an interview with mother.   Of course, he knew she'd entice him back to the hateful job."

"What did mother say to Tad?"

"Turned him over her knee and spanked him and sent him to bed."

"Taking one thing with another," said Lincoln, thoughtfully, "I reckon I'd better go quietly off to bed, myself. I'm tired."

"'Fraid cat!" grinned Bob. "John Hay and I are going out to see the town."

"If I were twenty years younger, I'd go with you," said the President.

CHAPTER XIX

THE RETURN OF THE PRODIGAL

BUT although he fumbled noisily about his room for an hour, Mary did not, as he hoped she would, burst repentant through his door. It was always harder for him to bear her aloofness than a scolding from her. When he woke the next morning, his first thought was not of Trumbull nor of Sumner nor of Grant, but of Mary. He dressed with great care, put on the gray suit she liked best, and went into her room.

But Bob was there before him, sitting on the edge of his mother's bed, talking rapidly and earnestly. She had been reading "Enoch Arden"—the book lay face down on her knees. She was staring at Bob with tragic intentness. To Lincoln's cheerful "Good morning, mother!" she replied with an icy nod, keeping her eyes fixed on her son. Lincoln stood at the foot of the bed, biding his time.

Bob was pleading, "But to shoulder a gun and face danger, that's the major part of it, Mother!—Last summer when I was a Home Guard you said of course the Todds all were soldiers."

"So I did," retorted Mary. "You proved your steel then. That was enough. I thought you and your father had settled that you were to go to Grant. Why open up the old subject of being a private?"

"Because I just can't be reconciled to sheltering myself behind father's Presidential coat-tails! Billy Stoddard's leaving next month. He's going into the ranks and no favors asked," blurted Bob.

His mother threw up her hands. "Oh, do as you please! You're of age, anyhow!"

"I know that, Mother, but— Oh, pshaw, why can't you send me off freely like other mothers do? We ought to be willing to contribute one man to the Union cause."

His mother sat as erect as a small soldier. "And you think we haven't contributed one man? Would the lives of twenty men be equal to—"

Bob groaned.

His mother stopped short, stared at his angry, mortified young face, then tossed her hands apart and said with a little sob, "Do as you wish, Bobby! I'm ashamed of myself, as usual."

Bob gave a whoop of joy, threw his arms around his mother and kissed her several times, started for the door, then rushed back to say with Mary's own impetuosity, "I'll go to Grant, Mother, for your sake!"

"I'll tell you, Bob," said Lincoln, "let's compromise. I'll ask Grant to take you, and when you get down there with him if you find you aren't really useful, you go into the ranks."

"Fine!" cried Bob. "I'll have to go and gloat over John Hay!" This time the hall door slammed behind him.

Lincoln seated himself in Bob's place on the edge of the bed. Mary eyed him with a cold and appraising air.

"I've shaved," he said meekly.

She picked up "Enoch Arden." He deliberately put out a great hand and took it from her.

"Let's have it out, Mary, without any grand flourishes. I'm sorry I hurt your feelings but I've got to have that promise from you!"

She gave him one of her direct looks. "I can't promise unless you give me a substitute. You admit I've got a brain. You know that all my life I've lived in an atmosphere of politics. I watched my father and mother help Henry Clay in his career. I worked from the time I met you to help you get here. Yet now you tell me to fold my hands and devote myself to my clothes and to spanking Tad. I can't do it, Abra'm. I know my limitations. The very first time something came up, I'd break that promise, unless as I say you give me other work. Three years ago you headed me into hospital relief. But the Sanitary Commission has taken over all that."

Lincoln pondered. All that she said was true. This was the energetic little engine that, for better or for worse, had puffed and pushed and with much shrieking of escaping surplus steam had landed him in the White House. It was too much to ask her to sit idle on a side track, accumulating more steam. It was dangerous too, because, smiling inwardly at the figure of speech, her little boiler was sure to burst, sooner or later.

"Will you promise me this, then, that whatever you do, you'll do only with my knowledge and consent. That's true partnership, Mary."

"But that's only getting at me from an indirect angle," she protested. "You've only to veto everything I suggest and there you have me!"

"Just to prove that I'm *really* compromising," retorted Lincoln. "I've something to suggest, right now. I want to have a resolution introduced immediately in the Senate as well as the House recognizing the so-called ten-percent government of Louisiana. I want to act before Sumner does. The House, I think, is safe, but the Senate—!" He shook his head. "If Trumbull can be got to introduce the bill, it would work miracles."

Mary's sober face quickened. "I thought of that last evening. It would be wonderful!"

"Your news was what made me dare think of it, of course," said Lincoln. "I want you to land Trumbull for me, Mary. You can do it better than I."

She looked at him suspiciously. "You're just soft-soaping me, Abra'm!"

"I couldn't afford to soft-soap you in this issue, Mary, because I've got to make you see I mean business. I've got to have that promise!"

They gazed at each other implacably. The household had roused. Tad and Bob were in altercation in the hall. A broom was thumping intermittently against the sitting room wall. At any moment they might be broken in upon, but the issue must be settled now. Both of them knew that the situation was fraught with more perils than any save themselves could appreciate. Mary sat stiffly erect, cheeks and eyes blazing. Lincoln drooped on the bedside. His face settled into its lines of weary melancholy, but his blue-gray eyes bore a granite gleam in their depths. Yet there was more than granite; there was yearning unutterable. Suddenly Mary threw herself forward and he caught her in his arms.

"Oh, my dear! My dear!" she cried. "Truly I was only trying to save you from an insincere man! But you're right! I should have talked it over first with you. If only I could learn to curb my impulsiveness! It's a curse! I promise! Of course, I promise, if you'll forgive me."

He pressed her close, burying his tired eyes in her hair. "I've nothing to forgive, my darling wife. I reckon we need your impulsiveness in the family to balance my slowness. Only—Mary—if you want my old brain to reel, just let me find that you're really planning to be under-handed with me. Chittenden makes a good retreat for me—so does Dr. Henry—but here—here is my perfect retreat. Keep it for me, dear wife! Keep it for me!"

Her reply was to press her lips to his with a little sob.

A moment later he went back to his room, his heart at rest.

He wrote Bob's letter to Grant, that morning.

"Lieutenant-General Grant: Please read and answer this letter as though I was not President, but only a friend. My son, now in his twenty-second year, having graduated at Harvard, wishes to see something of the war before it ends. I do not wish to put him in the ranks nor yet to give him a commission to which those who have already served long are better entitled and better qualified to hold. Could he without embarrassment to you or detriment to the service go into your military family with some nominal rank, I, and not the public, furnishing his necessary means? If no, say so without the least hesitation, because I am as anxious and as deeply interested that you shall not be encumbered as you can be."

About five o'clock that afternoon Stanton came in to see the President. "I want to make some final disposal of Ben Butler, Mr. Lincoln," he said, dropping into the chair by the desk. "He's made life miserable for Grant and Grant's finally screwed himself up to ask for Butler's removal. Are you willing to consent to it and do you think, if we do, that Grant'll be forced to change his notion within twenty-four hours? My idea is that we ought to back Grant up and send Butler to hell where he belongs."

"Butler should be in town to-day," remarked Lincoln.

"He telegraphed me a few days ago, asking permission to come and testify before the Committee on the Conduct of the War."

"He's down in your parlor at this moment," growled Stanton, "having a dish of tea with Mrs. Lincoln. I put my head in the door and backed out. The Committee on the Conduct of the War has my sympathy! Butler'll stand them on their heads. He's clever as Satan. How much money do you think he's made out of the high offices he's held during this war?"

"I don't *know* that he's made a penny," replied Lincoln with a troubled air.

"I do!" exclaimed Stanton. "I have positive proof that when he went to New Orleans he was worth about $150,000. To-day, he's worth $1,000,000."

Stanton's word on such a matter was not to be doubted. Lincoln's lips tightened. He knotted his black tie which hung loose, smoothed his hair and rose. "I reckon old Ben has outlived his usefulness to this administration. You O.K. Grant's request and I'll go down and break the news to the General before he comes up here and camps. I've learned that it's easier to move myself out of the parlor than it is to move some folks out of my office."

Stanton smiled and patted the President's arm affectionately. "Need any help, sir?" he asked, following him to the door.

"Thank you for nothing!" grunted Lincoln.

Stanton laughed.

He accompanied Lincoln to the very door of the red parlor and left him with a snort compounded of sympathy, approval, and amusement. With a little sense of dread Lincoln entered the softly lighted room. One never knew just how yellow Butler might turn.

Mary with the tea equipment sat before the fire talk-

ing to General Butler, who stood in full dress parade on
the hearth; sword, yellow sash, epaulettes, gold oak
leaves, velvet cuffs, buff gloves, a contrast to Lincoln's
memory of Grant's shabby uniform.

"Well, General," said Lincoln, quietly.

"Not well, at all, Mr. President." Butler shook
hands. "Grant and I are at serious outs."

Lincoln slumped into a rocking chair opposite Mary
and shook his head at her gesture toward the teapot.
Butler resumed his place on the hearth.

"I thought you and General Grant had patched up a
water-tight peace," said the President.

"So did I. Come, Mr. Lincoln, tell me why Grant
has asked for my resignation?"

The President gave him a keen look. "You shouldn't
come to me with questions of that sort, General. Let
your own conscience answer."

"Oh, Mr. Lincoln!" protested Mary. "To a man
who's done such splendid work as General Butler?"

"Conscience?" ejaculated Butler. "Then you too have
a grievance against me?"

"General Grant's grievances are bound to be mine,"
Lincoln spoke coolly. "The only complaint he's made
to me is that you've been letting too much food be traded
into Richmond. He says you and your brother-in-law are
getting rich off it. But if you hadn't failed him in a military way, he could get around the other, I reckon. Has
he gone after you on this matter?"

"I've learned that he's written to Stanton asking him
to retire me. I know I can get nothing from Stanton so
I've come to you. This can't be, Mr. Lincoln. I'll make
it so hot for Grant—"

"Tut! Tut, General! That's childish. Grant is winning the war for us. If he says you must go, you must

go." Lincoln clasped his left knee and looked at Butler with a slight scowl.

"Don't you think General Butler should be told why?" asked Mary.

"Butler knows why," replied the President, quietly.

"The tune is changed, I see, since you won your re-election, sir," sneered the General.

"Yes, the tune has changed. But it needn't have. You've slipped on the banana peel of your own avarice, General. Come now, you've done a great work for your country. Be content to leave the military clean-up to Grant. There'll be plenty of administrative work later that will demand your peculiar genius."

"One needs to be in Congress for that," said Butler sourly. Then he gave the President a wary glance. "Though I have my influences up at the Capitol right now that're not precisely despicable."

"I know you have, General," agreed Lincoln heartily. "I wish I had 'em myself."

"They're at your disposal, Mr. Lincoln," said Butler, "if—"

Lincoln shook his head. "No, thanks, General. One simply can't handle Sumner that way."

"Sumner? Sumner has his price, like any other man!" cried Butler.

"No, he hasn't! Indeed not, General!" Mary leaned earnestly across the table.

"Oh, well, I'm not going to debate with one of his lady friends as to that!" The little officer's voice was mocking.

Lincoln suddenly rose. Butler was going to be nasty. "If you'll come over to Stanton's office, right now, we'll see if he's holding anything up from Grant," he said.

"Oh, but wait a moment!" protested Mary. "Ah, there he is now!"

Senator Trumbull was emerging from behind the red velvet door hangings. Butler's jaw dropped. Lincoln walked slowly to meet his old friend. The two paused under the gilt chandelier. Trumbull was a thin man with sharp features and keen blue eyes behind spectacles. He looked like a village school-master but his air was that of a man of the world.

He looked up quizzically at the President and held out his hand. His voice was preternaturally grave and dry as he said, "Mother, I've come home to die! But I want your forgiveness first."

Lincoln let out a roar of laughter such as the White House had not heard from him in many months.

"Your figure's a little mixed, Senator! What you want is the fatted calf. How about it, Mrs. Lincoln? And here's General Butler! You know the author of the Woman Order?"

Butler shook hands, remarking with a curious smile, "I can fully understand why my poor offer of a few moments ago was refused so lightly." Senator Trumbull gave him a puzzled glance but did not rise to the insinuation. Instead he asked Mary if she was attending the Italian Opera that night. Butler listened for a moment, then bowed and went out. Lincoln wondered a little uneasily what sort of pressure Butler would next exert, then he forgot him.

Trumbull was seated near the tea table and the President joined him. Mary covered what might have been an awkward moment by asking the Senator if he thought this Congress would pass the Thirteenth Amendment.

"We're still doubtful," replied Trumbull. "I don't quite understand Sumner in this, unless he hopes that if it fails he can get an amendment phrased in his own way. He has that kind of vanity, I'm afraid."

"I think you're mistaken there," protested the President. "What does he do or say? Is he actually blocking it?"

"Well, no! He merely refused to help." Trumbull accepted a cup of tea from Mary. "He says he'll *permit* it to pass if it has the strength! But he prophesies that there'll not be enough States to ratify it, even if it passes Congress. If he kills the admission of Louisiana, of course, he may be right."

"No, he isn't!" said Lincoln grimly. "When I fixed it up last year to get Nevada in and on the right side I settled that point. It cost me two internal revenue collectorships and one custom's house appointment to get the requisite votes from certain members of Congress, and was an altogether unmoral proceeding. Sumner twitted me with it at the time, so he's talking nonsense. How much depends on him?"

"The Camden and Amboy Railroad interests," replied the Senator, "promise that if Congress will postpone the Raritan Railroad bill over this session they'll make the New Jersey Democrats help about the Amendment. Sumner's in charge of the Raritan bill in the Senate. His theory is that the bill, in crushing the railroad monopoly, will crush out the last of the States' rights dogma. The Camden and Amboy exacts toll from everything passing through the State, you know, Mrs. Lincoln."

Mary nodded. "Sounds as if Mr. Sumner had right on his side."

"He has," agreed Trumbull, frankly, "but in this instance he ought to let the lesser evil help to wipe out the greater. The monopolies will be crushed in good time.

Mr. Lincoln, we'd like to have you send for Sumner and urge him to be practical."

Lincoln looked doubtful. "I'm willing but useless, Senator. I can do nothing with Mr. Sumner in these matters. While he's very cordial to me, he's making his history in an issue with me on this very point. He hopes to succeed in beating the President so as to change this Government from its original form and make it a strongly centralized power. I think he'd be all the more resolute in his persistence if he supposed I were at all watching his course in this matter. I think the Amendment'll go through, Trumbull. I'm not worrying about it. What I'm lying awake nights over is the recognition of Louisiana."

Trumbull leaned forward to poke the fire. Lincoln and Mary exchanged glances, then Lincoln cleared his throat and plunged.

"Are you still hostile to my ten per cent governments, Senator?"

Trumbull set the poker carefully in the rack and leaning back in his chair placed his fingertips together and said thoughtfully, "What has come to me as I've watched the quarreling of my own committee, the indecision and vacillation of any committee that has tried to draw up a hard-cast rule for all the seceded States, is that it's impossible to reconstruct on any rigid theory of coercion. It has thus gradually dawned on me that your idea of encouraging the loyalists to keep alive a form of State government that shall allow the people to make their own laws is the only feasible plan."

"Yes! Yes!" exclaimed Lincoln eagerly. "Now here's the nub of it! You are chairman of the judiciary committee. Your committee must pass on the eligibility of the Senators elect from Louisiana. Can Louisiana be brought into proper practical relation with the Union sooner by admitting or by rejecting the proposed Senators?

"I believe in admitting the Senators," replied Trumbull cautiously.

"How does your committee stand?" asked Lincoln, his pulse quickening.

"They're doubtful. They're afraid Banks has misrepresented facts. They feel the matter's been too much a personal arrangement between you and Banks."

"That's easy to disprove!" Lincoln rose. "Mrs. Lincoln will excuse us while I take you up to see the correspondence between Banks and me." He led the way out. "I'll show you all of Banks' letters with those of the rest of the Louisiana crowd."

They mounted the stairs rapidly, both men moved by this revival of their old friendship and anxious to avoid showing their emotion. In the office Lincoln placed his files before the Senator. Banks' letters proved him to be a man of parts and Lincoln was glad to have one of his critics read them.

After a few moments, "This is exactly what I need," gloated Trumbull. "Now, to quote yourself, I can ride!"

"How far?" asked Lincoln tensely, his throat suddenly constricting.

"Well," Trumbull was pale, "give me a little time and I'll introduce from my committee a joint resolution, recognizing the Government of Louisiana."

"Ah!" breathed the President, his lips twitching.

Trumbull looked at him. "Of course, you realize, Mr. Lincoln," smiling sadly, "that I'm turning traitor to my old running mates and that they'll fight me to the death, with Charles Sumner leading them."

Lincoln jumped to his feet and put his hand on Trumbull's shoulder. "I know! I know! But you have the strategic advantage of your position.—This—this," he put a hand on Trumbull's other shoulder, "this is a great evening for me, Senator. 'For this my brother was lost and is found—' You know, Trumbull!"

"Yes, I know, Lincoln— I'll just take these along and have copies made."

When Lincoln went into his wife's room later, she was lifting a great sheaf of roses from a florist's box.

"Mr. Sumner's reply to my apology," she said, with a little unhappy smile.

"I told you you'd both resort eventually to the language of flowers!" Lincoln laughed heartily and after a moment Mary joined him.

CHAPTER XX

SUMNER received the news of Trumbull's treason in the cloak room of the Senate. Ben Wade told him. Senator Sumner stared at him, listened with scorn to the oaths that adorned Wade's tale, then stalked out into the Capitol rotunda where he stood wrapped in his blue fur-lined mantle, head bowed over his folded arms—the conventional picture of outraged despair. To do him justice, he was quite unconscious of posing. He had been so long in the public eye that it had become second nature to the Senator to live up to people's favorite conception of him. Men passing to and fro looked at him with interest but no one spoke to him and he was not disturbed until, following an altercation, a man in a wide-brimmed felt hat struck a man in a sealskin cap standing at the Senator's elbow.

Sumner roused and stepped between them, recognizing at once one of the Congressmen elect from Louisiana and a radical member of the House.

"Come, gentlemen, this won't do!" protested Sumner firmly. "Blows will never settle this bitter problem. Think! Think!"

"Think hell!" shouted the Louisianian. "What we should have brought up here is one good nigger overseer. He'd have handled a few of you spouting Yankees so that you'd have known that Louisiana was something more than a State of mind."

The crowd, that had gathered quickly, laughed. Sumner turned away with disgust.   As he did so, he caught sight of Representative Hooper peering over the heads of the crowd.

"I was looking for you, Charles," said Hooper, as Sumner came up to him.   "You've neglected us lately. Come home to dinner with me now.   Yes," as the Senator began to shake his head, "I know you breakfast late, but we don't dine until two.   I want to hear about Lyman Trumbull and what your plans are.   Nothing has occurred, I hope," looking up into Sumner's face a little anxiously, "to anger you with us?   I've always been frank with you about my sympathies with Lincoln."

Sumner jerked his great head impatiently.   "No! No! Don't make me appear too infantile, Sam.   I've not been to see you lately because Alice and I—"

Hooper interrupted.   "Alice told me.   But Alice's vagaries have nothing to do with the relations between you and me.   Alice is a law unto herself."

"Do you think she'd object to my coming?" asked Sumner.   "I—I long to accept your invitation, Sam!"

Hooper thrust his arm firmly under the Senator's. "You come along with me, Charles," and he did not loosen his hold until he had established the Senator in a nest of fur robes in his sleigh.

It was a glorious winter noon and Washington was out enjoying it.   Sleighs and the jingle of sleigh bells mingled with drum rolls and bugle calls.   Even the mud of Pennsylvania Avenue could not tarnish all the bright beauty of the great snowfall of the previous night. Hooper could not resist the temptation to prolong the short drive between the Capitol and his house.   They drove along New Jersey Avenue until they met Alice and Isabella prancing homeward in a gay red sleigh that flaunted a dozen plumes from dashboard and horse collars. Alice, palely magnificent in sealskin, bowed, while Isabella, in white rabbit, screamed:

"Oh, Senator! Senator! Take me in with you!"

"He's coming home to dinner, so calm your ardor, Isabella!" called her grandfather, turning his Morgans cleverly to follow his daughter-in-law's equipage.

Alice met them, later, in the dining room, her manner cool and a little watchful. Hooper kept the conversation in his own hands, made Sumner tell him about Trumbull and allowed the Senator to give vent to his excited irritation only when he told of the fight he proposed to organize against the renegade Jacobin. Alice did not contribute anything but polite necessities to the conversation until Sumner had finished his outburst. Then she said, as she used her finger bowl daintily:

"If I were you, Senator, I'd have a talk with the President before actually going on the warpath. I do still think, as I've said repeatedly, that the most regrettable thing in public life to-day is that Abraham Lincoln and Charles Sumner aren't working in harmony."

"By Judas, you're right, Alice!" exclaimed Hooper. "Charles, do be persuaded! Give yourself and the President another chance. Don't let your personal—"

"Please!" Sumner stretched out a long arm in protest. "I beg of you, Sam, don't insist again on my petulance. No one appreciates Lincoln more than I. I outgrew my prejudices against him long ago. I recognize his essential integrity of purpose. I know he's utterly free of malice and unworthy ambition. I've even come to enjoy his speech. It's logical and spirited and full of quaint humor. His mind works with a sinewy sententiousness that sometimes captivates me. He's an utter original. In fact, he's instituted a new and superb order of state papers that Seward's quite incapable of appreciating. I've learned to love him. But with all that, I cannot and will not agree with him on his way of reconstruction. I must not!"

Alice rose from the table. "Won't you both have tea or coffee with me in the little parlor, rather than wine together here?"

Both men rose, Sumner with alacrity. But Hooper said with an inquiring glance at the other two that he was due at a committee meeting at three.

"Then the Senator must let me continue my pleas alone," said Alice, graciously.

Sumner blinked but opened the door for her with a distinct look of pleasure. He seated Alice before the fire in the cozy little parlor off the formal drawing room, gave her a fire screen, then in the armchair opposite warmed his hands.

"So I'm forgiven, dear Alice?" he said.

She arranged the folds of her dark velvet skirts for a moment before she looked up at him to say, "I thought that I was the one that gave offense!" Her face was sober. "I was sorry that you misunderstood me, dear Senator. I've missed you and your approval."

He leaned forward, studying her face. Then he said earnestly, "Don't play with me, Alice. I shall need all my forces the next few weeks. Even a tragic certainty will scatter them less than an uncertainty with regard to you. And yet," laying his hand for a fleeting moment over hers, "I would to God that I was uncertain!"

She smiled. "Let's leave it that you may be uncertain and go on to consider my request that you go for a final talk with Mr. Lincoln."

"Alice, he and I have talked until neither of us dares say more for fear of an utter break." He leaned back in his chair, his eyes on her delicate loveliness.

"You must promise me not to break with him!" cried Alice, her cheeks flushing. "Senator, a break with him must mean a break with me."

"No!" he winced. *"Don't* say that, I implore you, for I can't promise, Alice. This is a brutal game I'm playing. Don't weaken me."

She tried to press her advantage. "I must say that."

He moved his head uneasily as though in pain. "But must it always be so?" he mourned. "Can't I keep my dearest associations in life untainted by battle? Why must you thrust Lincoln between us?"

"Why did you break with the Adams, the Sewards, the—"

He sighed. "I can't stand this. Will you allow me to go up to see Isabella?"

Alice pulled the bellrope beside the mantel. "I'll have her brought down here. But"—leaning forward in her turn and for a fleeting moment laying her hand over his—"love is a force greater than patriotism and eventually, if you truly care, you're going to give in to me, *Charles,"* accenting his name which she used for the first time in all their long friendship.

His whole face lighted. It was as if his youth had miraculously returned. But as they sat waiting in silence for the child and he turned over in his mind the full significance of her words, the light behind his eyes burned lower and lower, until, as Isabella danced into the room, it flickered out to be replaced by a quiet tenderness for the little girl.

When Sumner started back to the Capitol a half hour later, Fred Douglass, who had been waiting outside the gate, fell into step with him. He, too, had heard of Trumbull's about face and wanted information. When Sumner had told him, he exclaimed:

"Mr. Sumner! I'm more discouraged than ever. If Mr. Lincoln's actually going to back such a bill, we're lost. He's a terrible fighter. The patient, good-humored kind sometimes are. What shall we do!"

"Fight harder than he does," replied Sumner. "I'm sure we'll win in the end because we're right."

The colored man shook his head. "I've learned to know him well and from a side no white man could get. I wonder—his heart is so large—do you suppose if I went to him and pleaded I could get him to give up this bill?"

Sumner, striding over the snowy paths at a terrific rate, gave the matter thought. At first he shook his head, then as if to prove how desperate he actually felt his need to be in the impending struggle, he said, "Well, a good general misses no chances. It can do no harm for you to talk with the President and it might accomplish something. God bless you. Let me know what comes of it."

A little later in the afternoon, Lincoln looked up from his desk to greet the colored leader.

"Ah, Douglass!" he exclaimed, rising to shake hands, then drawing Douglass down into the chair by his desk. "How are you getting on? Tired like the rest of us, I can see. Well, it can't be long, now. Are you moderately well satisfied with the course of events? Are you worried sick like the rest of us for fear General Lee'll escape to the mountains? Guerilla war prolonged for years, that would mean."

"General Grant will take care of that, sir," replied Douglass, twisting his soft hat in his powerful, gnarled hands. "As far as guerilla warfare goes, colored people properly armed have a gift for it greater even than the slave holders have."

"Well," Lincoln rubbed the back of his aching head, "I hope you're right. Did you come with something special on your mind to-day, friend Douglass?"

"Yes, Mr. President, I'm breaking my heart over your pending bill for Louisiana. It leaves negro suffrage out. I can't understand your attitude in spite of all you've said to me."

"Can you understand Mr. Sumner's attitude toward the Thirteenth Amendment?" asked Lincoln slyly.

"No, sir, but I can explain him, in general, better than I can you."

Lincoln laid down his pen and settled himself with his feet on the rim of the waste paper basket.   Douglass always succeeded in rousing his interest.

"Come now, what's the difference between the Senator and my humble self, if the comparison isn't odious?" he asked, with a smile.

There was something dogged about Douglass' manner in replying, as though he was determined to humor the President but equally determined not to be drawn too far from his purpose.

"Mr. Sumner's a lawmaker for all men, white or black. You, sir, are preëminently the white man's President. Mr. Sumner's willing to sacrifice even the Union to free the slaves. You, sir, are ready to deny or postpone or sacrifice the human rights of the colored people to promote the welfare of the whites. You were ready to execute all the supposed constitutional guarantees in favor of the slave system anywhere in the slave States. You were ready to suppress a slave rising for liberty, although his guilty master was already in arms against the Government."

Douglass paused and his piercing dark eyes fastened on the distant half shaft of the Washington monument, softened and dulled until it seemed to Lincoln that the man was in a trance. To rouse him, the President said:

"I had thought the negro looked on me as his friend. Is this name, Father Abraham, mere flattery?"

After a moment, Douglass replied slowly. "They don't know as I do that we're not the special objects of your consideration. Your own race has your deepest solicitude. They're your children. We're only your step-children, children by adoption, children by force of circumstance and necessity."

"The man thinks in straight lines, straighter than most of my associates," thought Lincoln. Aloud, he sought to prick Douglass on by saying, "And with Mr. Sumner it's different, eh?"

"Yes, sir, we come first with Senator Sumner. And yet, it's not strange that it's Abraham Lincoln who set us free."

Lincoln shook his head at Nicolay who appeared with a tray of papers. The sweat was standing on Douglass' forehead.

"The reason for that is that yours is the bigger mind and you have better self-direction. And the very fact that you share the prejudice of your countrymen toward us has made it possible for you to organize them for this war. If you'd been like Mr. Sumner, without prejudice, and had put abolition before the salvation of the Union, your people never would have resisted the Rebellion. The Abolitionists think you're tardy, dull, cold. But for the average slow-thinking white, you're swift, zealous, determined. Your statesmanship, not Mr. Sumner's, has made abolition possible."

Lincoln spoke firmly. "You mustn't speak as if I approved of slavery! I despise it. If slavery's not wrong, nothing's wrong."

Douglass nodded vigorously. "We know that and on that we've pinned our faith. And, sir, I wonder if you realize what a lot of faith we've needed at times. You tarried long in the mountains. You advised us to migrate from our native land. You refused to use us as soldiers. You said you'd save the Union, with slavery, if necessary. You revoked General Frémont's proclamation of emancipation. You clung to General McClellan, who was more zealous to save slavery than the Union. And yet," turning suddenly, his beautiful eyes now burning with intensity, "our hearts believed while they ached and bled that the hour and the man had somehow met in the person of Abraham Lincoln."

"Don't you understand why I did those things, Douglass?" exclaimed Lincoln.

"Yes, Mr. President, to save the Union."

Lincoln jerked his head impatiently and would have spoken but Douglass was before him.

"Aye, sir, you have strained our faith but though the Union is more to you than our freedom or our future, we bow before you when we count the blessings that have come to us under your reign. Hayti's independence recognized, slave trade abolished, and the Proclamation of Emancipation. Sir, having given us all this, why do you continue to deny us the franchise?"

"Still harping on my daughter!" groaned Lincoln. "I've no new reasons, Mr. Douglass. You know them all. I'll add though that I'm very certain that, in the next four years, every slave-holding State will pass laws themselves giving suffrage to the negroes who can read and write; certain if we don't now, by national legislation, try to cram it down their throats. I fear a reign of horror after the war in which your colored folks'll get the worst of it, unless we conciliate where we can conciliate. I'm immovable on this, Mr. Douglass. The part of wisdom for you is to make both your white and your black friends understand this. That is if you've fully grasped my reasons yourself. I sometimes doubt it, because I seem to make no impression on you."

"I understand," still pulling and twisting the soft hat. "But again you're arguing the white cause, Mr. Lincoln, and I'm the negro."

After a thoughtful moment Lincoln rose and held out his hand. "Well, thank you for coming to see me. Good morning, Mr. Douglass."

Douglass took the extended hand and stared up at the President, his eyes slowly filling with tears.

CHAPTER XXI

"STARTING FROM PAUMONOK"

ALICE HOOPER told Mary that she was doing her utmost to get Senator Sumner to compromise with the President but when his wife reported this to Lincoln, he laughed. "Sumner's less apt to compromise now than ever. He's too mad with Trumbull and he's pretty sure we've got him licked. We've got the majority of the Senate with us and the House is going to pass the bill after it finishes with the oratory. Mrs. Hooper has no chance at all to drive Sumner in this."

"But you wouldn't prevent his talking to you, would you?" asked Mary, anxiously.

"Certainly not. He's in and out of the office every day or so on other matters. I'm giving him every opportunity either you or Mrs. Hooper could demand. But," with a cheerful laugh, "I've finally taught him how to take a licking!"

But even this optimistic mood could not do much to mitigate the strain that the march of events was bringing upon him. As Grant slowly but surely closed the terrible jaws of war on Richmond, the President was besieged more and more by excited Northerners demanding that he make peace at once. People were frantic to stop the bloodshed. Lincoln felt the pressure of their outcries more than had been his wont. Dr. Stone warned him again that his nerves were nearing exhaustion. Lincoln, apropos of this, told Mary that he supposed he was like one of the ancient Marathon runners, who, as he neared the goal, eyes popping, tongue hanging out, moved his legs on hope and nothing else.

Lincoln did not believe that Jeff Davis had been licked enough, yet. But, not unwilling to learn the views of the Rebel President, he allowed the elder Blair, who had been a close friend of Davis before the war, to go down to Richmond to feel out conditions there. But he still thought so little of peace probabilities that when, as a result of Blair's gesture, three commissioners from Richmond asked for a hearing on peace proposals, he did not go down to the meeting place off Fortress Monroe himself, but sent Seward. These men were not coming, his intuitions told him, in an attitude of mind that could bear fruit. And anyhow, he could not bear to desert Trumbull in the preparations for the impending struggle in the Senate. Every moment he could spare was given to what he told Nicolay was the conversion of souls.

"Even the war mustn't come between me and Trumbull," with a twinkle of tired eyes. "I often wonder how it'll seem to handle reconstruction without Stanton and Grant on my back: and with Andy Johnson actually helping instead of hindering like dear old Hamlin. I've an idea that any difficulties I'll have with Johnson will be with his disposition. They say he's very irritable. Maybe he does drink too much. I hope the time'll come when there won't be a slave or a drunkard on earth!"

The Thirteenth Amendment passed on the last day of January and this gave the final touch to his optimism. Sumner, after all, was not invincible!

But Seward, somehow, didn't bring events on as Lincoln had hoped he would at Fortress Monroe. Grant, watchful and uneasy and with a growing appreciation of Lincoln's diplomatic powers, urged the President to join the Secretary of State. With the arrival of the General's

message, Lincoln roused from his immense preoccupation
with reconstruction. Perhaps Grant saw a chance for
making an advantageous peace now! He slipped quietly
from Washington and on the army steamer, *River Queen,*
went down to Fortress Monroe.

The three commissioners came aboard early in the
morning of February third, and the conference lasted
four hours. The Southerners, haggard, hungry, their
eyes ravaged by old ferocities, made an enormous appeal
to his sympathies. This then was the look of the cham-
pions of a lost cause! But their requests touched him
not at all. He listened for a time in silence. Seward
liked to lallygag, to talk back and forth, to give here and
take there, quite unconscious of the fact that this verbal
bargain hunting invariably convinced people that he was
insincere.

Lincoln took a grim pleasure in cutting across these
vast vagaries with the blunt remark that he couldn't treat
with parties in arms against the Government. Hunter,
who had aged twenty years in the past four, reminded
him that Charles I had done so when at war with the
Parliament and Lincoln said, "I don't profess to be
posted in history. On all such matters I'll turn you over
to Seward. All I distinctly remember about Charles I is
that he lost his head in the end."

Seward laughed and urged the commissioners to par-
take of the excellent whiskey he'd brought with him.
They thanked him and absorbed the mellow fire with
pleasure. Lincoln sat watching for his chance to strike
a blow for reconstruction. There was more conversation. Stephens was eager to know how Washington had
changed and was the Capitol finished?

Lincoln finally interrupted. "Stephens, if I resided in
Georgia with my present sentiments, I'll tell you what

I'd do if I were in your place. I'd go home and get the Governor of the State to call the Legislature together and get them to recall all the State troops from this war: elect Senators and members to Congress and ratify the Thirteenth Amendment, prospectively, so as to take effect, say, in five years. Such a ratification would be valid, in my opinion. Whatever may have been the opinion of your people before the war, they must be convinced now that slavery is doomed. It can't last long in any event and the best course, it seems to me, for your public men to pursue would be to adopt such a policy as will avoid as far as possible the evils of immediate emancipation. This would be my course were I in your place."

Stephens shook his head, but thoughtfully. It appeared to Lincoln that the seed was going to root and he went on.

"It seems to me that when the war ceases, members of Congress will be received from the Rebel States. Some of your States are now so functioning that when war stops they'll be at once restored to their practical relations to the Union."

"And you think," cried Hunter, "with the temper of Sumner, Wade, Stevens, Trumbull, such things are possible? They'll grind our faces with their heels. They plan to confiscate—"

Lincoln interrupted. "The enforcement of the confiscation and penal laws is in my hands, gentlemen. I shall be liberal. The people of the North are no less responsible for slavery than those of the South. If the war shall cease with the voluntary abolition by the States of slavery, I would favor payment by the Government of a fair indemnity to the owners."

Hunter bit at his nails. There was no sound for the moment but the rush of water past the *River Queen*.

Suddenly the scene seemed utterly unreal to Lincoln; the flickering lamplight in the little salon, with its white painted walls, the red cloth on the round table, the ravaged faces of the Southerners—Stephens, old, old, with a feverish color in his sunken cheeks—Seward with his cigar and with his tie riding over his collar—this was he, Abraham Lincoln, actually preparing the way for peace! The end was in sight, the runner nearing the goal. He must not quicken his pace or all would be lost—

Stephens broke the silence. "We'd like an armistice while we consider these matters!"

An armistice! To end the bloodshed now! God, how he wished he could grant one! For a moment, the desire to do so was almost irresistible. Such a gush of pity and love rose in his heart that he dared not speak lest he show it. He closed his eyes and sat breathing heavily then opened them to say in a voice spent with emotion:

"I'll grant an armistice only to consider the restoration of the national authority. And it is to be clearly understood that any proposals must be made on the basis of the position on slavery assumed in my last message to Congress."

"Nothing for us, in other words," exclaimed Hunter, bitterly, "but unconditional surrender to the mercy of the conqueror."

Lincoln stared at him. The man was dense! Had he not been licked enough? Or was it possible to frame a proposal that would not be a compromise, yet that would entice him out of his battered stronghold. He must have time to consider this possibility. There was no use prolonging the fruitless talking. He rose abruptly and held out his hand to each of the Southerners in turn. As far as Seward and the commissioners were concerned,

the conference had failed. Of course, Seward was sanguine. Good old Seward would have been sanguine if
Noah had refused him sanctuary in the ark.

But Lincoln was not sure that, for himself, the meeting was a failure. It had served to convince him that
it was possible now as it had not been before, to buy
peace—peace and a certain amount of good will. With
a sudden rush of hope and exhilaration he sat up in his
berth that night and, by the light of a wretched lamp,
wrote out again an offer of compensation. He phrased it
as a message to Congress, asking Congress to make a
joint resolution empowering the President to pay four
hundred million dollars, about what it would cost to prolong the war two months, to the slave holders of the
seceding States if they would cease resisting the national
authority on or before April first. If this were done,
"war will cease and armies be reduced to a basis of
peace, all property except slaves liable to confiscation or
forfeiture will be released."

He reached Washington obsessed with the idea that
he had found the answer to all the intricate problems
that blackened the sky. He locked himself in his room
and perfected the message, then called the Cabinet together and submitted it to them. He was keyed to so
high a pitch of hope, he saw the feasibility of his plan
so clearly, that he could not believe when he looked up
from his reading that he was interpreting the expression
of their faces correctly. But when they began to put
their indignant negation into words, he understood that
he'd been living for twenty-four hours in a fool's para-
dise. His high hopes collapsed with a roar about his
ears. He did not listen long to the members but dismissed them wearily. If his own Cabinet reacted thus,
it was worse than foolish to present the idea to the hostile

Congress. He made a memorandum on the back of the document:

"Feb. 6, 1865. Draft of message to Congress not signed or sent. To-day these papers which explain themselves were drawn up and submitted to the Cabinet and unanimously disapproved by them."

He was still staring sadly at the papers when Nicolay came in. "George," Lincoln said in a voice scarcely articulate, "they wouldn't listen to me!"

Nicolay returned through teeth set with disgust, "My dear Mr. Lincoln, you didn't expect them, did you, to recognize pure charity or true wisdom? If I were you, sir—"

He was interrupted by the Attorney General, who rushed in with violent disapproval in every line of his face.

"Mr. Lincoln, I cannot let all these pardons for deserters go through! Indeed I can't! Stanton—"

Lincoln looked up at him and shouted, "If you think that I of my own free will will shed another drop of blood—"

He paused, for the Attorney General's face grew suddenly distorted before his eyes. The walls of the room closed in on the very desk. Lincoln put out an uncertain, appealing hand—and fainted.

A little later he became aware of excited voices and of being carried to his room. When he came completely to himself he was in bed. The fire burned brightly. Winter twilight framed in the windows with the curtains stirring slightly from the draughty cracks. Some one sitting by his bed holding his hand—Mary. Dr. Stone's beard at the bed foot. Lincoln smiled at him.

"Back again, eh!" said the doctor, drily. "Now, I tell you once more, Mr. Lincoln, that unless you have shorter work hours, Andrew Johnson'll be the occupant of the White House before another year's out. You fainted from exhaustion. I'm leaving no medicines, but I'm holding Mrs. Lincoln responsible for the amount of rest you take in the next twenty-four hours."

"How much do I have to take?" asked Lincoln in alarm.

"Twenty-four hours of it. After that, a ten-hour day of work only," ferociously from Dr. Stone. "I'll be back in the morning. Nothing but food and a sniff of your smelling salts, Madam President, remember," and he stalked out.

It was peaceful—peaceful—*had* to stay in bed. . . . After a time, Mary's tender voice, "How do you feel now, my dear one?"

"Well, just about like I've felt every day lately. As if every one of the grist grinding through the office, from Senator MacDougall demanding war with France down to some poor woman after a job, had darted at me. As if they'd taken their thumb and finger, picked out their special piece of my vitality, and carried it off. I feel flabby. Mary, I was in the midst of a talk with the Attorney General. I reckon I can have him in here, eh?"

"I'd shut the door in the face of one of the British Royalty if he tried to come in here to talk to you," declared Mary. "Your next interview's going to be with Mr. Pickwick."

She read Pickwick to him until laughter made him hungry, when she gave him food. Then "Midsummer Night's Dream" until he fell asleep. It was late the next morning when he awoke. After breakfast she sent Tad in with his game of lotto and the two worked happily at this until Lincoln fell into another deep slumber. When he roused from this she was ready with a bowl of broth and a recent volume of Whitman which she had borrowed from John Hay.

"I've found a new way for you to get out of Washington," she said, opening the book and beginning to read to him "Starting from Paumonok."

He lay entranced until she had finished the last fine line. Then he begged for the book and his spectacles and, during the remainder of his second evening in bed, he memorized passages that had caught his fancy particularly. His mind was packed with poetry he had been treasuring since childhood. He told himself he could well move out some of the old lumber to make room for this pure treasure.

CHAPTER XXII

THE BLIND VICTOR

TRUMBULL'S idea was that the chief thing he had to fear for the Louisiana resolution was prolonged debate. This would give Sumner, the arch debater, a chance to delay the voting until the end of the session, March 3. So it was not until the last week in February, when numerous important financial bills were still before the Senate, that he introduced what was called the President's Bill. Lincoln agreed that if the bill would go through at all, it would go in one day's time, perhaps two. He and Trumbull had an easy majority, once a vote was forced.

On the morning of the twenty-third, he sent Nicolay up to the Capitol to follow the course of the battle. Then he set himself grimly to work at his inaugural address. Nicolay came in just before supper. Lincoln looked up at the saturnine young face and dropped his pencil.

"Let's have it, George," he said quietly.

Sumner, Nicolay said, as soon as the resolution had been read in full, rose and stated his position.

"I have joined other Senators who resisted the recognition of the Government of Louisiana because it was initiated by executive and military orders and an insufficient voting population. I insist on these objections in association with these aforementioned Senators. But I stand alone inexorable in the demand that all men, irrespective of color, shall be equal as citizens in the reorganized States. In this stand, I will yield to no asserted urgency, no supposed adverse public opinion, no technical point of constitutional disability, no vote of caucus, no defeats in either House, not even up to the pressure and prestige of the President himself. I have made up my mind to stop the admission of rebellious States to the Union without absolute guarantees of freedom and equality, including suffrage, for negroes upon precisely the same terms as applied to white men. I propose to avail myself of all the resources of parliamentary law to defeat this measure even if, its promoters refusing to yield, the revenue and appropriations bills shall be lost."

As Sumner paused, a stir swept over the Senate Chamber. Senator Trumbull came to his feet but before he could get Hamlin's attention, Sumner, great head stretched forward like a charging stallion, roared:

"You, sir, are keeping strange company and talking a strange language. Why this sudden change of front? By whom or what have you been seduced?" Laughter came at this point from the Democratic Senators, who were delighted beyond measure by this split among the Republicans. Whirling from Trumbull to Hamlin in the chair, Sumner continued, "I move an immediate consideration of the interstate commerce bill, which is a practical measure, while the Louisiana measure will prove a mere dance of debate."

Trumbull's voice, low but peculiarly clear, cut across Sumner's roar: "Mr. President, if a single negro is expelled from the street cars in the District of Columbia, the voice of the Senator from Massachusetts is raised in protest. He will take up the time of Congress about the rights of the negroes, but he will not give a hearing to the 10,000 loyal whites of Louisiana. Let us not waste time, Mr. President. Let us take a vote. There is no need to debate this matter. Every Senator present knows every detail of this bill and already has expressed an opinion on it. The majority here are in favor of it. Let us not permit an infinitesimal minority to block its passage. I assure you, Mr. President, that I shall not speak at length, shall not attempt debate. If the other members will act in harmony with me, it will be a simple matter to pass this bill and return to the financial measures. Let us take a vote now."

Sumner spoke calmly. "I assure the Senator it is utterly impossible."

Senator Wade jumped to his feet. "I refuse to be drawn into debate, but I wish to ask the Senator from Illinois whence comes this new-born zeal for Louisiana? How long is it since he believed it should not be recognized? How long? It is the most miraculous conversion since St. Paul's. You and I didn't differ formerly on this, sir."

Trumbull stood with lips firmly compressed, eyes blazing behind his spectacles. "I am not to be drawn off. I move a vote."

"I move a substitute!" exclaimed Sumner, and began to read aloud a bill forbidding elections in any State until the President had proclaimed that all hostility had ceased within the State and Congress had declared it entitled to representation.

Trumbull was able to cut discussion of the substitute short, bring it to a vote and defeat it. Sumner then proposed an amendment. Senator Howard of Michigan immediately plunged into an elaborate speech, backing Sumner, and for two hours would not yield the floor. When he finished, Ben Wade got through a motion to adjourn, which Trumbull defeated. Johnson of Maryland now made an hour's talk for the bill. The dance of debate was on and was still on when Nicolay left.

Lincoln listened to Nicolay in silence till the young secretary had read the last of his notes, then he asked, "Is Trumbull discouraged?"

"No, sir. Only seven men voted for Sumner's substitute. He thinks you can handle most of them and hamstring Sumner so."

"None of them can beat Sumner in longwindedness," mused Lincoln. "I'm disappointed, but we've still got a fifty per cent chance of winning."

The several recalcitrant Senators called on the President the next morning. He was able to win Howard but not the others. The debate began again that afternoon. Sumner attempted again and again to introduce other business but each time was voted down. The temper of the members grew bitter toward him. Shouts rose, "Don't waste our time, Sumner!" "Give it up!" "Give it up!"

"That's not my habit," answered Sumner and he introduced another substitute, which was voted down. Then he proposed an amendment.

Men went round to his seat and pleaded with him, confidentially, to let the vote on the President's bill be taken.

"But that would be to pass it," smiled Sumner. "And the passage of that bill would prove to be the political Bull Run of this Administration."

He rose to propose a fourth amendment. People in the gallery hissed. Representatives who had strolled over from the House, which had passed the bill, groaned. After this amendment had been voted down, and the early winter twilight proclaimed that the day was done, Trumbull moved an evening session "to give the Senator from Massachusetts an opportunity to say all he has to say."

Amidst sardonic laughter, the motion passed and at seven o'clock the Senate again convened.

The galleries were packed. The moment the session opened, Sumner moved to adjourn. He lost. Ben Wade then repeated the motion and was voted down. Zachary Chandler moved to adjourn. He lost amidst hoots and groans. It was now nine o'clock. Trumbull deliberately rose and accused Sumner of "keeping up a factious resistance in order to feel a spurious authority over the eighteen Senators who desired to pass the bill."

Sumner laughed, sardonically.

Senator Doolittle rose to his feet and called on the American people to witness this scene in the Senate, "particularly the arrogance of the Senator from Massachusetts, who is attempting single-handed to break down the right of every State to judge its own suffrage."

Wade remarked that if the Chief Executive had to depend on poor things like Doolittle to press his measures, the Chief Executive was in a bad way. Doolittle retorted and many precious minutes were consumed before Trumbull could silence the Senator from Wisconsin and plead with Sumner to say his say on the bill.

Sumner rose. It was some time before silence could be obtained from the exasperated members, but when he had done so, Sumner said, "I counsel the Senator from Illinois to look at the clock and to note that it's now twenty-five minutes to eleven with Sunday morning near. An effort to force a vote will be as fruitless as sowing salt in the sand by the seashore. The Senator's attempt to cram this resolution down the throats of the Senate is comparable only to an attempt once made by Senator Stephen Douglas, also from Illinois, who brought in the Kansas-Nebraska bill so proudly, confidently, almost menacingly, with the same declaration that it was to pass in twenty-four hours. I beg of the Senate to devote the remnant of the session to tried measures instead of consuming it with a bantling not a week old."

"Why don't you favor the President's bill, Mr. Sumner?" shouted a man in the gallery. "Because you despise Abe Lincoln, eh!"

"No!" shouted Sumner in reply. And he launched into an explanation of his position that continued until the galleries were nearly empty.

When he at last sat down, Trumbull said, "It's half after eleven. We cannot reach a vote to-night."

"I told you so some hours ago," said Sumner.

And the weary Senate adjourned.

Sunday was spent by Lincoln and Trumbull in anxious consultation, both of them hoping against hope. Trumbull went to see Sumner to urge him to come up to the White House for a conference. But the Senator from Massachusetts was ill in bed.

He was in his accustomed seat, however, on Monday and listened with inscrutable face to Senator Wade's fierce denunciation of the President's work in Louisiana. Wade spoke at enormous length and with the extraordinary vehemence which always was so exhausting on his hearers. Before he had done, men were leaning wearily on their desks. Some of them left the Chamber.

Senator Sherman of Ohio, as the afternoon waned, tried to obtain consideration of a revenue measure, but this only served to change the tenor of Wade's remarks. He began a bitter personal attack on Trumbull who flushed, but sat as grim as any schoolmaster watching the antics of an incorrigible boy. Winter twilight again darkened the chamber.

Sherman appealed to Sumner and Sumner, silencing Wade by a gesture, rose and in a voice of indescribable weariness once more stated his position, ending with a comment which Nicolay took down verbatim for Lincoln's benefit.

"The pretended State Government in Louisiana is utterly indefensible whether you look at its origin or its character. To describe it, I must use plain language. It is a mere seven months' abortion, begotten by the bayonet in criminal conjunction with the spirit of caste and born before its time, rickety, unformed, unfinished, whose continued existence will be a burden, a reproach, and a wrong. That is the whole case."

There was a dead silence after this. Sumner stood immovable, a shadowy giant, and the men staring at him recognized the fact that he could not be defeated. He was arrogant, insolent and implacable. He was as terrible and as splendid as Vesuvius.

Trumbull turned to Nicolay and whispered, "We've lost!" Then he walked dejectedly from the room. His fellows gave the President's lost bill the tribute of a sigh, half of regret, half of relief that the battle was over, and turned to Sherman's bill.

Nicolay dragged unwilling feet back to the White House. As he sadly climbed the stairs to the President's office, he met Mary on her way to serve tea in the Red Room. In response to her eager questioning, he showed her Sumner's final comment.

She read it and looked up at Nicolay, her face slowly losing color. "This will come very hard on Mr. Lincoln, George, in his depleted state. I don't see how he's going to stand it. I've never seen him so wrapped up in anything else but the Emancipation Proclamation. Perhaps I'd better go with you. No"—tapping her lips— "he'll need me more, later."

Nicolay nodded and continued heavily on his way.

Lincoln, who even yet had not permitted himself to give up hope, turned from his heavily littered desk. "News so soon? . . . Ah, George, my boy, don't say we're finally licked!"

"But we are, Mr. Lincoln," said Nicolay, huskily. He gave his account of the afternoon, ending by laying on a sheaf of naval reports the slip of paper containing Sumner's final words.

Lincoln read them. "A seven months' abortion." He covered his eyes. After a moment, he groaned, "Sumner! Sumner! Why, with your other incomparable gifts, weren't you given the prophet's vision! Well—I must think this out again, George. Keep people away for a while, will you?"

Nicolay went out. Lincoln felt a little dizzy, and crossing the room to a sofa stretched himself out on it. Thinking—thinking—he and his soul together again viewing the problem; moving through endless space and gazing down in cold agony on the bloody struggle which it seemed he would not be permitted to shorten or alleviate. Why was this so? Of what use his seeing eye if he could not convince others of the actuality of what he saw. Where was his weak point and what, if any, was the remedy? Hour after hour, he pondered on the panorama of the future which was as vivid and as real to him as the Army of the Potomac on parade.

CHAPTER XXIII

TAD'S LITTLE AFFAIR

MARY sat beside the President all night. She tried, while she knew their futility, all the devices she could invent to rouse him to something more than his gentle "Let me think it out, my dear."

But at the breakfast hour, fate took a hand. James rushed in, his black eyes rolling.

"Madam, Massa Taddie ain't been in his room, all night! We've done searched every inch of this house and grounds, and just now Congressman Hooper's drove up all in a lather to say little Miss Bella's gone too and was she here?"

"Kidnaped!" screamed Mary, leaping to her feet.

"Look for them at Senator Sumner's," cried Lincoln, his eyes opening with a jerk.

"Mr. Hooper did, sah. The Senata's in bed with a heart attack and can't be disturbed. His man says they ain't been there."

"When was Tad last seen?" asked the President.

"He said good night at eight o'clock," replied Mary, adding regretfully, "I didn't leave you to tuck him in. Send some one round to Pete Kelley's to make inquiries, James. And you, Abra'm, had better get in touch with the Detective Police right away. While we're waiting for Colonel Baker to get here, we'll have breakfast."

"Yes, Mary," replied Lincoln, nodding to James, who flew.

A hurried toilet and a more hurried breakfast on

trays in the sitting room were followed by the entry
of John Hay, carrying a bit of greasy writing paper.

"I found this under the blotter on my desk," he explained. "I'm sorry to intrude, Mrs. Lincoln."

"Don't be foolish!" protested Mary, seizing the paper
and reading it aloud. " 'Don't serch. Gone to Urup!' "

It was badly printed and signed with the bloody cross
that adorned many of the anonymous threats which Lincoln and his family received so constantly. As the President studied the message over Mary's shoulder, Hay said,
"Baker is here. I'll fetch him, if you wish."

Colonel Baker scrutinized the note and put it into his
pocketbook. Then, after asking Mary and the President
numerous questions, he called in the household, questioned every one, and enjoined absolute secrecy on each
for twenty-four hours until, he said, he could get his men
planted. He begged Lincoln "to try to continue his
day's routine and Mrs. Lincoln to go to bed with an
opiate." They both stared at him, Mary with contempt, Lincoln with astonishment.

"There's a gang of kidnapers bent on getting your
whole family," explained Baker, rubbing his beard and
shaking his head at once. "You must allow me to protect you."

"I'm going to the home of every child Tad knows in
Washington," declared Mary. "Any one of them may
have a valuable clew."

Baker nodded. "That's good! I'll send a man if
you'll give me a list. But I must ask you not to go out
of these rooms to-day, Mrs. Lincoln, and you too, Mr.
President."

"Oh, come!" protested Lincoln. "I can't stand inactive while my young son is at the mercy of God knows
what villains."

"Where would you go? What would you do?" asked
Baker.

"He's right, Mr. Lincoln. Do both of you be advised
by the Colonel," urged John Hay anxiously.

"I'll stay in only if my wife promises to do so, also,"
declared Lincoln, seeing an opportunity for controlling
Mary's rashness.

Mary stamped her foot. "Oh, I'll agree! Only don't
stop here arguing. Every moment is precious."

Colonel Baker seized his hat and a moment later the
search had begun.

The hours moved with agonizing deliberation, second
merging into slow second. It was a horrible day outside,
with gray lines of sleet cutting through gray fog.
Visitors arrived with faces raw from the slash of the
storm. At intervals Lincoln tried to finish his second
inaugural address, but finally gave it up. He could think
of nothing but Tad and Isabella. His imagination ran
riot. Were they sheltered from the storm or had the
brutes destined them to die of exposure? Was there information they wanted from the children and would they
torture them to get it? Wasn't there an accomplice in
the house who had sneaked Tad out of his room? Where
was Sam Hooper? What was he doing? He rang for
James. The man came in with a swollen eye and cut lips.

"What's the trouble, James?" asked Lincoln.

"Massa Lincum, sah, one of the police that Colonel
Baker's got posted downstairs 'lowed I knew something
more than I was telling about little Massa Tad. I give
him a bust upside of his head. Did you ring for me,
sah?"

"Yes, I did. James, my boy, you look up Congressman
Hooper and see how he feels and if there's anything I
can do. Ask him if it would buoy him and Mrs. Hooper

up any to come over here where we get reports every few minutes of what's being done. . . . James, you know Taddie well. Did he have any enemies? He's been mischievous, you know. I've sometimes wondered if it didn't bother some people."

"Enemies! That little fellow! Taddie! I'm surprised at you, Massa Lincum. 'Deed I am, sah!'"

James gave a great blubber, seized Lincoln's hand, pressed his bruised lips on it, and rushed away.

At noon, Lincoln joined Mary at lunch in the sitting room. Her face was swollen from prolonged weeping, but she was now outwardly calm. As she poured her husband's tea she said, "Abra'm, what puzzles me is why they took Isabella, too. If this is a political kidnaping to bring you to terms, why bother with Alice Hooper's child?"

Lincoln shook his head and stared at his steaming bowl of soup. "I've sent them an invitation to come over here."

"That's a good idea. Eat your soup, Abra'm," setting him an example by forcing down a mouthful.

He obeyed her and a moment later urged her to eat the fish she was eyeing with somber distaste. They finished the meal somehow, and then stood together in the window, clinging to each other's fingers and looking at the storm.

"I've got a part of the inaugural address done," said Lincoln, trying to ease the tension. "Do you think you can look it over?"

"I'll try," biting her lips. "Ah!" whirling as James made an announcement. "Mr. Hooper, what news?"

Hooper looked old and drawn. He dropped his sable-lined cloak and took Mary's hand. "No news. No trace. It's the strangest thing. Isabella was put to bed

as usual at seven o'clock. Her nurse had an evening out.
She went philandering and never got in till near dawn,
when she went directly to bed on the third floor. Alice
and I had been at the opera and afterward at supper
with Mr. and Mrs. Eames. For once Alice went directly
to bed without looking in on Isabella. The poor girl is
bearing up, which it's not her nature to do. Did you
know that Mr. Sumner has gone to seek them on some
private line of his own?"

Lincoln scowled. "I thought that Sumner's recent
victory had put him to bed."

"But he did have one of his heart attacks!" protested
Hooper. "So it's all the more remarkable. He sent
over just before noon to borrow a closed carriage from
me."

He rubbed his chin and looked up at the President,
who leaned dejectedly on the mantel. No one spoke.
The cannel coal made tiny explosions. The sleet beat at
the window. Tears ran down Mary's cheeks as she hud-
dled on an ottoman but she did not wipe them away.

"Mrs. Hooper, Madam President," said James at
the door.

Mary rose to meet the tall figure in sealskin and the
two mothers clung to each other for a moment. Then
James took Alice's wraps and moved toward the door.
As he did so, Sumner's unmistakable tones were heard
in the hall, above a sudden confusion of voices.

"Pray don't crowd us. I must immediately find—"

James opened the door. Mary screamed. Standing
in the hall was Sumner, Tad clinging to one hand, Isabella
to the other.

Lincoln was the first to realize that Sumner was still
by the door, unheeded during all the prolonged greet-

ings. He put Tad into his mother's lap and crossed over to place his hand on Sumner's shoulder.

"Tell us about it, Senator," he said, drawing the tall figure toward the fire.

"My share won't take long." Sumner wiped his eyes. "I didn't hear of the matter until late this morning. When my secretary finally told me I began turning all Taddie's recent pranks over in my mind. Knowing the young gentleman intimately as I do, I didn't believe Baker's theory was essential. I recalled among many things the fact that Taddie had made a great fuss because Isabella's mother forbade the two children to skate on the pool in the garden. He said that when he and Isabella were married they were going to live at the Soldiers' Home where they could skate every day. Isabella suggested that they get married right away. This was followed by a great whispering and giggling."

The two children now devouring the bread and milk James had brought stared at the Senator in wonder. He smiled and added:

"Having reached this point in my deductions, the next step was obvious. I borrowed my friend Sam's horses and set forth for the Home."

"And there we were in the hay loft!" exclaimed Isabella. She was dirty and disheveled but still lovely.

"Why the hay loft?" asked her mother.

"Our cottage was all locked up and we didn't dast go to the house the old soldiers live in," replied Tad, his mouth full. "We was just going to hitch up and come home, because Isabella had boo-hooed he' eyes out.

"Hitch up what?" demanded Tad's mother.

"Pete Kelley's hoss," replied Tad. "He got his dad's old tin pan hoss fo' me, the one he peddles pans with in the spwing. In winta it just stands in the ya'd and Pete has to feed him so no one knew when he loaned the hoss to me. Papa day, I have to pay Pete a dolla' fo' that."

Lincoln slipped his hand into his pocket.

"Mr. Lincoln!" shrieked Mary. "Don't you dare!"

"You're right!" The President hastily withdrew his hand. "Tell us how you managed to get away so quietly, Isabella."

"I did just what Taddie told me to," replied Isabella with a toss of her yellow curls. "I just got out of bed and dressed myself the minute Nurse left me so's I wouldn't go to sleep, you know. Then I went down to the coat closet under the back stairs and rolled up in one of grandpa's buffalo robes there and went to sleep and by and by Tad came and got me."

"Aw, it was easy," boasted Tad. "I just slipped in the back hall and woke he' up and we sneaked out the back alley and Pete was waiting fo' us. We cova'd Isabella up in the bottom of the sleigh and she went to sleep and I hustled that old hoss out to the Home, I tell you. We took about a ton of cookies. They lasted till this noon."

Quite beyond comment for the moment, the dumfounded grown folk listened to this naïve recital. But as Tad gulped the last of his milk, his mother set him off her knee and said, "You go to your room, Tad."

Tad wiped his mouth on his sleeve and looked appealingly at his father. His father returned the look yearningly, but Mary forestalled any appeals for mercy by saying, firmly:

"I hope you feel as I do, Mr. Lincoln, that Tad has got to be taught that he can't cause such agony as he did to-day and not get punished for it. He's too big a boy to do a thing like this and go scot free."

"Exactly!" ejaculated Sumner.

"Amen to that!" cried Hooper.

Tad gave a loud howl and rushed from the room. His mother followed.

Alice Hooper looked from her small daughter, who had assumed an expression of injured innocence, to her father-in-law. "You'd better go up to the Capitol, my dear father," she said, "because I'm in complete accord with Mrs. Lincoln on this and it's not going to be pleasant at our house for the next hour."

Small Isabella flung herself from her mother's lap and rushed toward Sumner, screaming hysterically, "I'm going with you, Senator!"

Congressman Hooper seized his sable-lined cape and he and Lincoln fled while Sumner gathered Isabella in his great arms. He stood, the little girl's face hidden in his neck, looking at Alice pleadingly.

"If I've earned any thanks, Alice," he said, his deep voice tender and a little amused, "pay them by letting off this small sinner. After all, Tad was most to blame."

"Isabella knew she was being naughty. The elaborate secretiveness proves that. I can't risk such a thing happening again."

Isabella turned to show one deep blue eye. "I wouldn't not run away again for a million, million dollars and kisses. It was hoddible. I feel that way now. But if you whip me, you'll make me want to run away all over again."

Sumner and the child gazed at the beautiful woman, anxiously. If Alice was amused, she did not show it. She had suffered a thousand deaths that day. It was not easy to have Sumner plead the naughty little girl's cause.

After a moment, she said, "I recall with vividness the fact that my last very earnest pleading with you for a favor, you refused with implacable firmness."

"But my principles—" exclaimed the Senator.

"To train Isabella properly is my greatest principle," declared Alice. "But I'm going to set you an example of magnanimity."

"You mean you won't whip her!" cried Sumner. "Oh, thank you, thank you, Alice!"

"What a great child you are!" groaned Alice. Then she began to laugh, though with a hint of tears in her eyes. "Yes, I'll let her off, this time."

The child suddenly patted Sumner's cheek and relaxing in his arms began to weep in long hard sobs.

"Give her to me!" demanded her mother, fiercely. And as Sumner obeyed, she clasped the little golden head passionately to her heart.

Sumner eyed them with a soft smile and stooping, kissed one of the lovely hands that supported Isabella. Then he murmured that he'd call the carriage and take them both home.

CHAPTER XXIV

ANDREW JOHNSON

LINCOLN returned to his desk and fell to work on an accumulation of letters. It was routine work and he could think steadily of other matters while performing it.

It was hard to realize that only twenty-four hours had passed since final news of his defeat at Sumner's hands had reached him. Hard, because he now found himself viewing his own downfall not without a certain philosophical amusement. He had been licked in a fair fight and if the cause had not been so serious he could have shaken hands with Sumner, have acknowledged that the best man won, and have set himself to forgetting the battle.

But this he could not do. The battle must be fought again and won. Trumbull, poor fellow, must have more help from the Democrats. Andrew Johnson must be beguiled into putting his own great resources among the Democrats at Trumbull's disposal. Until Congress convened again next December, the new Government in Louisiana must struggle to function without Federal support except such as the President could give. Thanks to Sumner. It was outrageously stupid. And in spite of the Senator's charming and characteristic gesture of the afternoon, a renewed wave of anger against him flooded Lincoln's heart.

He signed papers, rapidly, mechanically, as John Hay and Nicolay thrust them under his hand. He would have Andrew Johnson up for a talk as soon as the Vice President had gotten his bearings in Washington. As long as he was in his present mood, he'd better not see Sumner, though he supposed he ought to thank the Senator more adequately for what he had done for Tad.

As the two secretaries moved out with overflowing mail baskets, Mary entered in evening dress.

"Supper's been waiting a half hour, Mr. Lincoln," she said.

"My dear," he pleaded, "I've only got this supper hour in which to finish a dozen important matters. Won't you let me have it on a tray up here?" He rose and looked down at her contritely. It had been a dreadful day for her. She deserved and needed the sort of quiet hour they might have together if—

She smiled up at him. "Don't make me out such a tyrant, Abra'm," she protested. "Let me have a tray in here with you. I won't interrupt."

"Fine!" settling back at his desk again. "Some day I'll build you a castle on the edge of the Golden Gate, after you've finished buzzing around Europe and California has woven its spell over us."

Mary rang the bell and gave the requisite orders, then seated herself before the fire and did not speak until supper was spread on a little table beside her. When the President had fallen to with a good appetite, she asked if he had seen Sumner again in order to thank him.

"I suppose you'll have to forgive him now," she added.

"I'm angrier at his stupidity than I ever was at anything before in my life, if that answers you," he said. "How's our poor little Romeo?"

"Sound asleep," she replied, complacently. "Sumner certainly loves him."

"So he does and I'm obliged for what he did," agreed

Lincoln, "but"—determined to nip Mary's campaign in the bud—"but he's done the Union a fearful disservice in defeating my resolution."

"Everybody's talking about the break that's inevitable between you and Mr. Sumner. You're immensely strengthening the Democrats by this party split."

"Andy Johnson'll take up that slack," the President assured her.

"I don't suppose you can feel friendly toward Mr. Sumner," agreed Mary. "But I think you're making a mistake in not making some sort of a move that will stop the gloating. Why not ask him to go to the Inaugural ball with us? We'll only be there a half hour but all the world will see and know he's our guest."

Lincoln buttered a roll, thinking this over. It was hard common sense, of course. But it was curious how hard it was to swallow his anger. Not but what somewhere inside him was an unquenchable flame of affection for Sumner!

"Well," he admitted, grudgingly, "I suppose you're right about it. I'll get the note off after supper. I hope," grimly, "that he'll accept it in the spirit in which it's written!"

"Oh! he's not cross at you!" laughed Mary. "He thoroughly beat *you!* Do it as soon as you finish your pudding, my dear. I'm afraid you'll weaken if I leave before it's done. . . . Am I acting the good partner, Abra'm?"

He smiled at her tenderly. "You're my mainstay, as usual."

The next morning, inaugural day, dawned with a heavy downpour of rain that, as the hours wore on toward noon, showed no signs of letting up. Lincoln dressed himself on rising in the same frock suit that he had worn at his first inauguration. It was well made, but he had lost weight and it hung a little loosely on him. Still, Mary looked him over carefully and said that he'd pass muster, so he promptly forgot his appearance.

His office was packed with a portion of the office seekers who were blanketing Washington again like a pest of locusts, but at eleven John Hay moved them all out and the start was made for the Capitol. The mud was so heavy that going would be tedious. Mary had gone still earlier, to sit in the diplomatic gallery of the Senate where Johnson would first be inaugurated. Some one told him that the Vice President was only scarcely recovered from a fearful attack of typhoid. Poor fellow! . . . he must get in touch with him immediately and outline that new battle. Johnson's glorious record in Tennessee proved him Sumner's equal if not his superior in fighting prowess.

Lincoln entered the Senate Chamber at the head of his Cabinet. The dim mahogany dignity of the room had been turned to a mass of brilliant color by many flags, by the gay spring clothes of the women who crowded the galleries, by the splendors of the diplomatic corps in court dress and by the uniforms of naval and army officers with their gold lace and epaulettes and wonderful sashes. The chatter of women filled the great room despite the embarrassed pounding of the gavel by Senator Foote in the chair.

What would Johnson think of it, the poor tailor from Tennessee? The shrill chorus in the gallery rose high, then fell again. The justices of the Supreme Court were entering in their long black silk robes. Chase looked extraordinarily handsome. Then the members of the house. Buzz, buzz! the chatter rose again, then a sudden silence. It was twelve o'clock and Andrew Johnson on Hannibal Hamlin's arm was making his way to the dais.

Lincoln scrutinized his new partner closely; a tall man with fine strong shoulders, black hair, swarthy skin, smooth shaven; remarkable eyes,—not large but piercingly keen and set under a splendid brow. It was evident that he had been ill, for he was furrowed and worn far beyond what even the war strain could have done to him. He was deeply flushed;—embarrassed and excited probably.

Johnson began his speech. It was broken and incoherent. "I am a plebeian and glory in it." He paused, swayed a moment, went on. "Tennessee never went out of the Union. I am going to talk two and a half minutes on that point and want you to hear me. Tennessee always was loyal. We derive all our powers from the people.—I want you to hear me two and a half minutes on that."

Lincoln stirred uneasily. Johnson was always excitable and in the heat of speech-making was said sometimes to be carried away by his feelings. But this! The man's voice was thick, his eyes suffused. Hamlin leaned forward and nudged Johnson but the rambling words poured out in ever-increasing volume. Lincoln half turned in his seat. Charles Sumner covered his face with his hands and bowed his head on his desk. Seward as usual looked bland but Stanton might have been gazing at a specter. Welles, above his whiskers, was blushing. Chase looked like outraged marble. His confrere, Judge Nelson, stared at Johnson with his jaw apparently falling from his face until Chase tapped him on the shoulder, when he closed his lips with a snap.

Drink! Good God! Drink! This was the man he'd insisted on for a running mate, the man who was to defeat Sumner!

Hamlin rose and deliberately interrupted Johnson, requesting him in a half whisper to take the oath of office before he became too ill. Johnson gasped, blinked, then in a low voice repeated the fine words and kissed the Bible, then stumbled to his seat.

Lincoln moved from the Chamber in a daze. What treachery had fate played on him now? No, not fate, drink—

Outside, in the east face of the Capitol where the platform stood, the rain had ceased. Below the platform faces, faces, faces, that familiar pink-tinted sea which had grown so familiar to him in the past ten years. The pink tint reached back and back among the trees. The roar that rose as Lincoln appeared continued until the Sergeant-at-Arms had waved his high black hat and in pantomime bade it be still, and it was still.

Lincoln put on his spectacles, took his little speech from his breast pocket and stepped up to the table.

"Fellow countrymen: . . . On the occasion corresponding to this four years ago, all thoughts were anxiously directed to an impending civil war. All dreaded it. All sought to avert it. . . . Both parties deprecated war; but one of them would make war rather than let the Nation survive and the other would accept war rather than let it perish. And the war came.

"One-eighth of the whole population were colored slaves, not distributed generally over the Union, but localized in the Southern part of it. These slaves constituted a peculiar and powerful interest. All knew that this interest was somehow the cause of the war; to strengthen, perpetuate and extend this interest was the object for which the insurgents would rend the Union even by war; while the government claimed no right to do more than to restrict the territorial enlargement of it.

"Neither party expected for the war the magnitude or the duration which it has already attained. Neither anticipated that the cause of the conflict might cease with, or even before, the conflict itself should cease. Each looked for an easier triumph, and a result less fundamental and astounding. Both read the same Bible, and pray to the same God; and each invokes his aid against the other. It may seem strange that any man should have to ask a just God's assistance in wringing his bread from the sweat of other men's faces; but let us judge not that we be not judged. The prayers of both could not be answered—that of neither has been answered fully.

"The Almighty has his own purposes. Woe unto the world because of offenses! For it must needs be that offenses come; but woe to any men by whom the offense cometh. If we shall suppose that American slavery is one of those offenses which, in the providence of God, must needs come, but which, having continued through his appointed time, he now wills to remove, and that he gives to both North and South this terrible war as the woe due to those by whom the offense came, shall we discern therein any departure from those divine attributes which the believers in a living God always ascribe to him? Fondly do we hope—fervently do we pray—that this mighty scourge of war may speedily pass away. Yet, if God wills that it continue until all the wealth piled by the bondman's two hundred and fifty years of unrequited toil shall be sunk, and until every drop of blood drawn with the lash shall be paid by another drawn with the sword, as was said three thousand years ago, so still it must be said, 'The judgments of the Lord are true and righteous altogether.'

"With malice toward none: with charity for all: with firmness in the right, as God gives us to see the right, let us strive to finish the work we are in: to bind up the nation's wounds: to care for him who shall have borne the battle, and for his widow, and his orphan—to do all which may achieve a just and lasting peace among ourselves and with all nations."

He stood only half listening to the applause. Sumner! Johnson! Would God they could hear his words as he had meant them!

He turned toward Chief Justice Chase and the applause was stilled. The clerk of the Supreme Court, on whose cheeks were undried tears, brought forward the Bible. Lincoln laid a steady hand gently on an open page. The sun gushed forth and for a moment blinded him. Then Chase, yes, Chase (humor in this to be savored later), Chase administered the oath of office which he answered clearly, "So help me God," and kissed the Book.

He asked for Johnson immediately after the ceremony but was told that Preston King had taken him home for a visit.

"He acted as if deranged," said Father Welles, whom he had questioned.

"Oh, no!" protested Seward. "He's sick, and emotion on revisiting the Senate overcame him. I can appreciate Johnson's feelings, myself."

"God Almighty!" grunted Stanton.

The afternoon and evening, a blur of people; an endlessly twisting, turning kaleidoscope of faces—faces, some of them quivering as his speech was mentioned. Mary said that she had seen many people weeping during the last half of the address. They did not meet alone until after two o'clock that night, when they smiled wearily at each other before the fire in the President's bedroom. Mary had with her the inauguration Bible in which Chase had marked the verses that the President had kissed.   Lincoln read them.

"None shall be weary nor stumble among them: none shall slumber nor sleep: neither shall the girdle of their loins be loosened nor the latchet of their shoes be broken."

CHAPTER XXV

THE QUALITY OF MERCY

LINCOLN did not sleep that night, he was too weary. He went to his office after an hour or so and brought back to his bed an envelope of Petroleum Naseby clippings. The man's rough, satirical remarks on politics were the essence of wisdom. Still he couldn't sleep. In the morning exhaustion made him giddy and he was glad to have Mary forbid his rising.

She was not too strict for his peace of mind, however. She permitted the Cabinet to meet in his bedroom. It was pleasant except for the discussion about Johnson, who was reported ill in bed. Sumner had been to Welles and kicked up a great row. Said Johnson must be forced to resign. Hamlin had told Stanton that Johnson was ill in the Vice President's room before the ceremonies.

"Asked Hamlin for a drink of whiskey," said Stanton. "Hamlin told him that one of his first acts as Vice President had been to have drink forbidden in the Senate restaurant and that Sumner had gotten the buffets moved out of the committee rooms. So Johnson sent across the street to a saloon and got a quart of whiskey, of which he drank three tumblers."

"Even at that," said Welles, stroking his beard wisely, "he may not be an habitual drunkard. Did any one ever hear that he was?"

It was agreed that no one had. Lincoln said that he'd had General Sickles investigate Johnson's personal career before his nomination and that it had seemed to be without blemish.

Seward closed the discussion by saying in his usual cheerful, good-humored way, "It will pass! He's a valuable man. Let's forgive and forget."

Lincoln nodded and changed the subject.

The ball was postponed till the night of the sixth. Lincoln felt in fair trim by that time, though a bit unsteady as to leg muscles. After he had gotten himself into his evening clothes, Mary wouldn't let him return to his office; so he lay on the sofa with Tad beside him, reading aloud to his father.

> "When all the world is young, lad,
> And all the grass is green,
> And every goose a swan, lad,
> And every lass a queen,—
> Then hey for boot and saddle—"

Taddie, in his flannel nightgown, ready to go to bed when his parents should leave, little round face unblemished by life—Lincoln watched him and through half-closed lids listened to the verses—

Mary came in. She was lovely; lovelier, he thought, even than on the night of the first inaugural ball. The lines that the four years had etched in her fine skin softened her firmness with a look of sadness. All true loveliness, he told himself, was sad. She wore velvet, of a lavender so delicate that at some angles it was only shadowed white. Her chestnut braids were twined round her head with pansies. Her eyes looked larger and bluer than ever.

She smiled at the two on the sofa. "How do I look, boys?"

Taddie clapped his hands. "You look like Queen Titania. I love you to death!"

"So do I!" with a low laugh from Lincoln. "How

anything as pretty as you could have chosen me—eh, Tad?"

"You're kind of beautiful," declared Tad, stoutly.

The father and mother exchanged an amused glance.

Sumner came in now, carrying a great bunch of orchids for Mary and a new book for Tad. Lincoln had not spoken to him since what he called the Senate murder, excepting on the afternoon when he had rescued the children. Sumner, he told himself, as he rose from the sofa, was a long way from returning to his bed and board. He bowed and shook hands coolly with the Senator, then turned to his wife.

"If you're ready, Mrs. Lincoln, we'll proceed at once. I've an hour's work in the office after we're finished with this affair."

Mary gave him an appealing look. She didn't want him to don his rarely used cloak of dignity with Sumner. But he chose not to see the message in her glance. Mary sighed and called Tad to help her with her wraps. For a moment, the two men stood rigid by the fire. Then Sumner said in a low voice:

"I dread to mention Vice President Johnson's dreadful lapse, but I must. Mr. Lincoln, won't you force him to resign? He's a public calamity."

Lincoln raised his eyebrows. "You seem to be 're-signing' for every one but yourself, Senator! That's a matter you'd better discuss with Andy Johnson, not me."

"I beg your pardon." Sumner spoke stiffly, his face flushing.

Mary came in and with a glance from the President to the Senator, hurriedly announced that the carriage was waiting.

It was a dreadful party. The crush was so tremendous that neither detectives nor police could control it. So many people rushed into the supper room, soon after the Presidential party arrived, that the tables were wrecked and the food trampled on the floor. The confusion was so great that after a short half hour Lincoln insisted on going home. Sumner spent that half hour standing at a little distance from the President, a picture of patient suffering. Acted as if he were enduring a bad smell, thought Lincoln, glancing at him occasionally over the heads of the milling crowd. It was good to get back to the quiet of the White House.

The memory of the evening and of Sumner's attitude was still in Lincoln's mind when he woke the next morning. It had left a bad taste in his mouth. He told himself that the unwonted rôle of being mad at some one he loved was hard on his digestion.

For over a week now, he saw nothing of Sumner, and Johnson also was invisible, taking a rest out at Silver Springs with the Blairs. Lincoln ground the grist of office seekers, keeping the best of his pondering for his relation to Sumner and for the war. The roads were drying up in Virginia now and soon Grant's army must move from its winter quiet. Stanton and Lincoln were beginning to sweat lest Lee should slip away into the mountains before Sherman, coming like inexorable fate from the South, Sheridan coming down the Shenandoah, and Schofield coming from the West had closed every exit and forced Lee to fight Grant.

About the middle of March, Grant invited the President and Mrs. Lincoln to Army Headquarters at City Point, Virginia.—"I would like very much to see you and I think the rest would do you good."

Mary was delighted at the thought of seeing Bob. The boy was, as usual, careless about writing. "But," she added, "I do think you ought to make it up with

Charles Sumner before you go away," reaching up to
straighten his tie as they started down to breakfast.

"But how can I, my dear wife?" he asked impatiently.

She looked at him uneasily. "This is so unlike you!
I've never known you to hold a grudge before."

"This isn't a grudge! Sumner's hurt the Union. It's
not mine to forgive."

"Yet you offer amnesty to Rebels!" she cried.

"After they've taken the oath of allegiance," was his
retort. "Mary, there's no use in my going after Sumner
until I know what I want to do. Just as soon as Johnson gets well I shall have him get to work among the
Democrats and see if Sumner can't be snowed under.
He'll never compromise, any more than I will."

"It's no longer a question of compromise with him,
Abra'm," said Mary. "He thinks he's finished the job.
He told Alice Hooper that after peace is declared the
States themselves will prevent you from carrying out your
theories."

"Ah!" exclaimed Lincoln thoughtfully as he followed
her into the dining room. "That's news! . . . Has
Mrs. Hooper given up hope of making him Secretary of
State?"

"She said she couldn't do much as long as you didn't
seem to support the idea," replied Mary. "My dear, I
could go away with a much freer mind if you'd invite
Sumner up for a political conference before we go."

"Didn't the wonderful one-scene act at the Inaugural
ball satisfy your greed?" asked Lincoln.

"Oh, you know what I mean!" She poured cream
over Tad's oatmeal with an impatient jerk. "Let me
ask him to go to the Italian Opera with us as soon as we
return from City Point. I'll send the invitation before
we go and let it leak out. I can't bear to see the Demo-

cratic newspapers saying the horrible things they do."

"Are they including you again?" asked Lincoln, quickly.

She nodded. "But that isn't my reason, Abra'm. I'm used to that. It's the political side."

"I'm not used to it for you!" His voice was grim. "You send your invitation. He's been trying to see me on some sort of business for a week and I've avoided him. I'll arrange to see him soon and conspicuously. But I warn you now there's going to be no kissing and holding of hands between Sumner and me."

Mary heaved a sigh of relief and devoted the rest of the meal to Tad's outrageous table manners.

Lincoln had no opportunity that day to find the conspicuous moment for seeing Senator Sumner. But on the next, chance arranged the matter with signal success. Early in the afternoon, Lincoln entered the carriage with Mary for a last round of the hospitals before leaving for City Point. Two reporters dogged Lincoln down the steps with questions about Grant and just as the coachman lifted the reins, Sumner rushed up and laid a detaining hand on the carriage door.

"Mr. President, I *must* see you on the matter of that naval court decision. I can get no satisfaction out of Mr. Welles." He turned to the reporters. "May I ask you two gentlemen to step out of earshot? I have a matter of great urgency and privacy to talk over with the President."

The two reporters fell back but watched the group with rapacious interest.

"You mean you want me to set aside the sentence of those two Boston acquaintances of yours who've been convicted of defrauding the Government?" asked Lincoln, casually. "Well, drop in on me at lunch, to-morrow."

Sumner, flushed and impatient, shook his head. "In my opinion, Mr. President, you ought not to sleep on the case. If Abraham Lincoln had suffered unjust imprisonment as a criminal, degradation before his neighbors, an immense bill of expense, trial by court-martial and an unjust condemnation, he would cry out against any postponement of justice for a single day."

Lincoln sighed. "It's evident that in order not to be a miracle of meanness in your eyes, Mr. Sumner, I must take a great deal of trouble. Very well. If you'll come around at eleven to-night, I'll see you. I'd like you to write out your legal opinion on the case before then to take as little time as possible."

Sumner, with raised eyebrows, bowed, and the carriage moved on. Lincoln turned to Mary, winked at her solemnly and lapsed into his perpetual study of Sumner's character.

There was a frightful thunderstorm that night, but in the midst of it Sumner kept his appointment with the President. It was significant of the intense anxiety and preoccupation of the two men that neither mentioned the dreadful turmoil that beat at the windows. Sumner began at once to read a superbly prepared brief. It was half an hour after midnight when he finished.

"It looks to me as if you were right," was Lincoln's comment. "Leave the brief with me, Mr. Sumner. I'll write my conclusion before I sleep and you can have it as soon as I open shop in the morning."

"And when will you open shop?" asked the Senator.

"At nine o'clock."

"Thank you, Mr. President." Sumner rose and went out into the storm.

At three o'clock, Lincoln finished his reply. Promptly at nine o'clock Sumner appeared. He stood beside the President's desk and read what Lincoln had written, then with a softened face and a voice that broke with gratitude he exclaimed:

"Thank you! Thank you! A wonderful résumé indeed! May I send a telegram from your office here, saying the men are to be discharged?"

"Do so and I'll have Hay attend to it," replied Lincoln, reaching into his desk as he spoke for the envelope of Petroleum Naseby clippings. He wanted Sumner to go without any attempts at personalities. When he was ready to move on the Senator, he'd do so with one big jump. Until then—

"Let me read you something funny, Mr. Sumner," and he began to read aloud with great gusto. He had only started the second clipping when Sumner gave vent to an enormous sigh and departed. Lincoln grinned at John Hay and turned to the war dispatches. Lee had not yet made a move.

The visit to Grant was begun very quietly. The country, in its long-drawn-out agony over the siege of Richmond, must not be roused to undue optimism by news of the President's departure for the front. The party was small: Mary, Tad, the President, Crook, the bodyguard Stanton had bullied Lincoln into enduring. Also on the morning of the departure, March 23rd, there arrived at the White House a tall, fair-haired, handsome young officer, Captain Penrose, detailed by Grant to act as aide to the President.

The party of five drove to the wharf at one o'clock in a closed carriage. But alas for secrecy! A crowd had collected and there were anxious shouts as Lincoln walked up the gangplank of the *River Queen*. "Where are you going, Mr. President? . . . Is it peace this time? . . . Has Lee skinned out?"

Lincoln could only smile and wave his hand. He went at once to his little stateroom and did not emerge until they were well out into the river with the tug boat, *Bat,* snorting along behind and making a tremendous impression on Tad. Then, in a deerstalker cap, his old gray lounge suit and a blue cape, he joined Mary on deck. They watched the receding city till they could see it no more.

Toward night a cold wind rose, with rain, and they went into the little salon where the boat's captain hovered over them, anxious about their comfort. He'd had a partition torn out, he told them, and a berth of adequate length built for the President.

"I noticed it first thing, Captain." Lincoln stretched his long legs out with a sigh of comfort on the padded lockers that ran the length of the cabin. "You were mighty clever to remember my extra inches so kindly."

"I'm going to enjoy your housekeeping instead of my own, I know, Captain," added Mary, dropping into a rocker near the President. "Taddie's gone to the engine room. Will you tell the engineer and the sailors to send him to me if he's a nuisance?"

"Oh, any one can get along with young Tad!" said the Captain. "Will you give the steward your order for supper, Madam President?"

"Indeed I won't," exclaimed Mary with a laugh. "Didn't I tell you that's just what I want to avoid? We'll take what you're going to take, Captain, and you're to eat with us."

"Right!" agreed Lincoln. "And, Captain, I want you to be prepared to repeat to Mrs. Lincoln and my two guardian angels here some of those adventures with blockade runners you told me about last February."

The Captain looked pleased. "I don't need to repeat, Mr. Lincoln. I've had a whole new set of experiences since then."

"Good! I'm determined not to think of the war to-night. So hurry up the supper, Captain, and get my mind out of Washington and onto the sea in ships. I've all an inlander's love of sea tales."

The Captain of the *River Queen* was a really fine story teller. They kept him talking until midnight. Then Lincoln slept without dreams, ate a good breakfast, and slept again until noon. He was preparing himself for the final stupendous act of the drama. He would know in the next few days whether he was to witness the death struggle of the Rebellion or one of those tremendous coups of Lee's that would prolong the agony for another year.

CHAPTER XXVI

RICHMOND

THE James and the Appomattox come together at City Point. The little town was perched high on a bluff that overlooked the harbor thus formed. All the afternoon of the second day, the *River Queen* made its way up the beautiful James, which was crowded by the shipping that ministered to the Army of the Potomac. It was after dark when the boat made fast to its wharf. All that could be seen of the town were lights straggling upward, with a long row of them bordering the sky line.

Lincoln, lying in a deck chair, which he had occupied most of the afternoon, saw Captain Penrose leap to the pier, heard a sentry challenge him and a low-voiced colloquy follow. A moment later, Penrose came up to him and reported that General Grant wished to come aboard.

"Good!" Lincoln rose, his muscles stiffening to the load, and went into the salon where he stood by the red-covered center table waiting. Little Grant came in followed by a group of officers, Bob among them. The cabin was filled with the glitter of accouterments and the smell of leather and horses and tobacco. First a confusion of greetings; then Grant began his report. The Lieutenant-General seemed to Lincoln to be in better trim than he'd ever seen him before. He was very thin, but hard and brown and quick. The discipline of the many adversities of the past year had been good for him.

He was optimistic and had every thread of the gigantic pending operations gathered into a steady hand.   He was not underestimating the enemy, neither was he over-estimating him.   He said that Sheridan was coming in for a conference the next day and so was Sherman on a flying visit from Goldsboro, North Carolina.   And he said casually that there'd been no fighting worthy of mention, lately.

But Bob told his father in their one moment alone that what looked to his green eyes like battles were go-ing on all the time and he'd had the satisfaction of carry-ing messages under fire, several times.   So he'd not have to go into the ranks, after all.

Grant ended the interview by giving Mary an invita-tion from Mrs. Grant, now at City Point, to "visit about in the handsome new ambulance that was to be devoted to the ladies."   Grant's horse, Cincinnati, was again at the President's service.   Young Beckwith, his own tele-graph operator, was to report from now on to Lincoln. Beckwith's tent as well as Grant's office tent were now Lincoln's.   Grant was a gentleman.   He did these things with a quiet savoir faire that Mary said made her dis-believe half the stuff she'd heard about him.

Lincoln went up to Beckwith's tent the next morning. From its opening he could see the long curved lines of the Rebel entrenchments which stretched between Peters-burg across the river and Richmond, thirty miles north. After an exchange of telegrams with Stanton, he visited General Meade's headquarters.   Here for two hours, from a little hilltop, he watched what Meade called a light skirmish—shells bursting, thin lines retreating and melting away.

The war council was held on the *River Queen* that evening.   Sheridan and Sherman both were there.   Lincoln was deeply stirred at seeing these two again. He thought they looked more gaunt and weatherworn than any of the other generals. They were more nervous, like racers held in unwilling check. He liked Grant's manner with them. To these men, he was no autocrat but a brother-in-arms.

Rain and wind were having their way with the *River Queen*. The light on the war maps was uneasy. The grizzled heads bent over the table on which the maps were spread were now in shadow, now in full yellow glow. Lincoln walked the floor a good deal, though with difficulty, as his imagination took hold of the details the soldiers discussed so dispassionately.

Once he interrupted to say, "I hope this will all be accomplished with as little bloodshed as possible."

The stern faces were lifted to his, somewhat confused and blinking.

Grant answered after a moment. "You tell me the country's in a mood where anything less than entire success will be interpreted as disastrous defeat. That kind of success will cost a good deal of blood, I'm afraid, Mr. Lincoln." Then laying a broad finger on the outworks of Petersburg, he continued the sentence the President had interrupted.

All in all, he felt strengthened by the conference. He knew everything now. Stanton had had no chance to censor this. His last remark to Grant that night was:

"Keep me informed. Don't let me be in suspense and I'll come through as well as the rest of you."

"That's why you have Beckwith," replied Grant crisply.

Sherman was returning to Goldsboro that night. He went out before the rest, saying with his face shining, "This will end it!"

End it—and the heartache and the thousand shocks!

But Hamlet did not express the war mood. It took Macbeth for that. Lincoln read himself to sleep with Macbeth that night.

Nature herself provided a terrible back drop for the first movement of Grant's advance. A thunderstorm of unprecedented severity swept down the James on the night of March 29th and the Lieutenant-General took advantage of its confusion and fury to start the great advance. Lightning fought with bursting shells. Thunder contended with the roar of artillery. The *River Queen* strained and groaned at her moorings. Tad refused to go to bed but cried himself to sleep on the sofa in the salon. Mary, wrapped in a shawl, her face blanched, sat beside him all night. Bob was out there with Grant! Lincoln knew that the strain was too much for her and wanted her to go to bed, but she couldn't.

Wrapped in his cape, he paced the deck all night, going inside only occasionally to look after Mary. The tumult without suited his mood. Nothing could so nearly express the four years' accumulation of agony and of unalterable purpose as this night. He shook with exaltation, muttered broken prayers and expletives.— "Blow wind! and crack your cheeks!"—"Oh, ye lightnings and clouds, bless ye the Lord!"—"And thou, all shaking thunder, strike flat the thick rotundity o' the world."—"Lay on, MacDuff—! . . ."

But as the hours wore on, the clamor became torture. Death, out there! Death and suffering.—For a long time he wept silently and as a dawn of battle shot gray lifted the river and the hills from fitful eclipse to steady, dull visibility, he pulled off his cap and lifting his face to the shell-ravaged heavens, pleaded that this be the final eruption of blood and fire.

That day and the next, as the rains forced the army to

construct corduroy roads as it moved, the firing slowed
down. Lincoln began to urge Mary to go back to Washington, taking Tad. She would not hear of this. She
proposed to remain in order to prevent the President
from going to the front and to be near Bob if he were
wounded. Lincoln did not argue the matter at any
length. He was too deeply immersed in following
Grant's movements as Beckwith reported them. However, after a third sleepless night, Mary was so exhausted
in mind and body that her own good sense told her to
give in to her husband's advice. But with a pathetic
heroism she insisted that Tad stay and never leave his
father for an instant.

"But it's no place for Tad," protested Lincoln, uneasily. "He'll see sights and sounds that'll give him
nightmares for the next year. This is no place for a
child."

"No, it isn't," agreed Mary. "And war's no work
for human beings. But since we're all in it, Tad must
pay with the rest of us. I admit I'm no good here but
I think if Tad's with you, you won't run as many risks
as if he weren't."

With a shake of the head and a sigh, Lincoln gave in.

Mary left on April first and on that day he moved up
to a tent next to Beckwith's on the bluff. Tad had a cot
beside his father's, but Lincoln was grateful to note that
the child did not take his mother's orders too literally.
He spent the afternoon with the Grant children, while
Lincoln on Cincinnati rode slowly over the deserted battle lines, viewing the still unburied dead, blue and gray.
After all, Grant did not keep him fully in touch now with
his movements. Perhaps it was impossible. Yet suspense here was less difficult to bear than in Washington.

The bombarding of Petersburg continued without ces-

sation. He grew so habituated to the uproar that when
it suddenly ceased on the night of the second he woke
from a light sleep and went into Beckwith's tent. The
young operator, wrapped in an army blanket, sat beside
his candle and chuttering instrument. Lincoln in trousers
and cape stood over him waiting. It seemed an hour
before Beckwith looked up to say in an uneven voice:

"Petersburg has fallen, Mr. President!"

"Almighty God, I thank thee!" murmured Lincoln and
returned to his cot. The ring of fire around Richmond
was complete.

He really fell asleep now and did not rouse till Crook
came in long after sunup to tell him that Captain Penrose
was waiting to take him to visit Grant in Petersburg.

He told himself as he rode the fifteen miles to Petersburg that it ought to be utterly impossible for him to
realize that this nightmare city actually had given up the
ghost. So long had it held out against all attacks, so
often had it proved the Waterloo of officers on whom he
had built great hopes, that this success ought to seem
like a dream. But not so. His brain never had been
clearer or his nerves steadier, his imagination quicker.
He was not weary—this for the first time in many, many
months.

Petersburg was utterly silent and utterly deserted.
Not a living creature in street or window, not even birds
in the ragged trees or flies on dead things in the gutters.
The National Army had gone on in pursuit of the retreating rebels. Grant with a few members of his staff
awaited the President on the piazza of an empty house.
He said that as he had come into the town that morning
the Appomattox bottom at the north end of the city had
been packed with the Confederate army.

"But I hadn't the heart to turn the artillery upon such

a mass of defeated and fleeing men. I hope to capture them, shortly."

"That's right! That's the spirit!" ejaculated Lincoln. He stood with one arm around Bob's neck. "I thought you'd forgotten me, General."

"No! You couldn't have thought that!" Grant smiled. "But you've had so many disappointments and I couldn't be sure this was coming so quickly."

He spoke then of his desire that the Army of the Potomac should have the reward of its four years' struggles and actually take Richmond, rather than the Western armies. He was quiet and business-like, utterly unlike a conquering hero. He was impatient to be off after his army, now several miles in advance, and Lincoln let him go. With Crook and Penrose he rode slowly back the fifteen miles, across the trenches that had protected the city. They were full of dead. Poor fellows!

He had reached City Point and was slowly pushing his horse up the long road to the bluff-top when a messenger came at a gallop to meet him. He thrust a telegram into Lincoln's hand. The President halted his panting horse and tore open the message. It was from Grant.

Richmond had fallen.

He wiped his spectacles, put them in his pocket, and looked up and down the river.

Peace!

He had a physical sense that a load was being lifted from his shoulders. A dogwood tree in early bloom by the roadside suddenly impinged on his consciousness. Dogwood no longer need break his heart. He'd stand no more knee-deep in its blooms plucked from soldiers' kepis—

Crook touched his arm. "There's Vice President Johnson riding up ahead of us, sir."

A door in Lincoln's mind opened and reconstruction crowded in. He felt irritated. Could he not be allowed to savor this moment to the full? "Johnson?" he asked. "What's he doing here?"

"He came down yesterday, Mr. Lincoln. There are a number of parties here from Washington. I've heard that Representative Hooper is in a tug below with the Secretary of the Treasury."

"I don't want to see them, not Mr. Johnson or any of the rest, Crook. I came down here for a rest and a change. And Grant's seen that I've had it, God bless him!"

He pushed on up the hill, to the telegraph tent. There was a telegram from Stanton, dear old granny. "Ought you to expose yourself to the consequences of any disaster to yourself in the presence of a treacherous and danger-ous enemy like the Rebel army?"

He laughed aloud as he wrote his reply. "Thanks for your caution, but I have already been to Petersburg, stayed with Grant an hour and a half, and have returned here. It is certain now that Richmond is in our hands and I think I will go there to-morrow. I will take care of myself."

Ship bells were ringing now. The river was pande-monium with the shrill of whistles and shouts of soldiers and sailors. Tad came tearing up shooting a pistol into the air.

"Wichmond's fallen, fallen, fallen!" he chanted.

His father hastened out of the tent. Tad with a pistol always made him uneasy.

"How much money do you want for that cannon, Tad-die?" he asked.

"You went off to Pete'sburg without me!" cried Tad reproachfully, firing another shot.

"Give me the pistol, Tad," insisted Lincoln.

"Will you take me with you if you visit Wichmond?" bargained Tad, dancing about with the smoking weapon dangling from his hand.

"Yes! Yes! Anything!" exclaimed his father.

"And a dolla'," added Tad.

His father gave him the money and told Crook to lose the pistol. Then he seized Tad's dirty hand firmly in his own and took him down to the *River Queen* for supper. He decided to send Tad back to Washington with Hooper, if the Representative was returning soon.

But the next morning, before he could get in touch with Hooper, the *River Queen* had joined Admiral Porter's fleet and the visit to Richmond was in process. The fleet steamed up the river to Drury's Bluff. Here a wreck had blocked the narrow channel. Lincoln and Tad were transhipped to the Captain's gig, manned by twelve sailors. They were very close now to the death that made the James horrible, bodies of men and horses —Tad clung to his father's fingers but made no comment.

The trip was almost too much to bear. The shore, for a quarter of a mile before they reached their landing place beside Libby Prison, was packed with negroes. They were not noisy. But a continuous, rich murmur rose from the dusky lines, broken occasionally by soft cries:

"Massa Lincum, the sabior of the land! Mass' Lincum—Lincum—Lincum—"

Too much for a man's heart, this. He felt half suffocated.—The wharf was packed with soldiers and marines, with Admiral Farragut hovering about, smiling tensely. Six marines armed with carbines, then the President with Admiral Porter and Captain Penrose on his

right and Crook clinging to Tad's other hand on his left.
Behind, six more marines. Absurd precaution, when
any window might hold a gun. He felt like an intruder
—an unwelcome, hated alien in a foreign country. He
was sorry he had come.

They began a march up the middle of a street. It was
thick-bordered with spectators, that pinkish border so
familiar. People clung to the telegraph poles like ants
to grass stalks. The sun was hot and almost obscured
by smoke. The Richmondites had tried to burn their
own city. There was an appalling, a sickening silence,
an utter stillness, through which the tramp, tramp of
their own feet sounded loudly. It was a march through
border lines of hate. He wished he hadn't come.—This
view of the wreck of Jeff Davis' dream was a hurting
thing. Suddenly he felt unutterably weary.

CHAPTER XXVII

"GOD'S IN HIS HEAVEN"

THERE was a group of people standing on the wharf when the *River Queen* made her moorings at City Point the next day. Tad recognized its members with a shout that roused the waterside:

"Motha'! Senata' Sumna'! Goody! Goody!"

A moment later, Lincoln was greeting Mary's party: Sumner, the Harlans, Marquis de Chambrun. He was so tired! Why had Mary done this? She told him why under her breath. Stanton had complained to her that the President was jeopardizing his life daily, but he wouldn't make arrangements for her to come back. So she had organized this party and Stanton had been obliged to move. They were going to visit Richmond and then bring the President back with them to Washington.

"I don't suppose you had any idea of Sumner and me working each other over a little, crowded together on the *River Queen?*" Lincoln whispered, half amused, half irritated.

Mary looked up at him pleadingly. "Abra'm, promise me that you'll be nice to the Senator!"

He looked down at her and said, half wonderingly, "Mary, it comes to me for the first time what Grant has given *me*. Do you know there isn't a resentment in my heart toward any one in the world? The same God that brought peace to this distracted country isn't going to let Sumner's crazy notions rend it. God is going to let me bind the nation's wounds in my own way. You needn't worry. It's going to be easy for me to be nice to Sumner."

Mary stared up to him and suddenly blinked back tears. She patted his arm and turned to her guests.

Lincoln was upset by the news the party brought of a bad accident to Secretary Seward. His jaw had been broken in a runaway. It was time for him to get back to Washington. He did not care to accompany the group to Richmond; to hear Sumner and the Marquis and Mary chattering in French while death muttered all around them.

Sam Hooper and Alice called on him soon after the others departed. Nice fellow, Hooper, with no fanatical notions about anything. Mrs. Hooper had mellowed too. He invited them to come to supper to meet Mary's guests on their return. Sumner's face when he beheld Alice Hooper ought to be worth any price paid for the experiment!

But as it happened, the President did not behold the meeting between the two. The party returned from Richmond in mid-afternoon and Sumner arranged for a visit to the army hospitals. Crossing the wharf, he met Alice. She was followed by a maid, carrying a great basket of the sour pickles so passionately craved by the wounded. They had just landed from the skiff that had brought them from Hooper's boat.

"Alice!" ejaculated the Senator, standing for a moment as if frozen.

"Senator!" she returned, looking extremely handsome in the dark blue silk cloak and tiny white bonnet she was wearing. Simple clothing merely enhanced her beauty.

Sumner rushed forward and took her hand. "You're not surprised to see me?"

"No!" shaking her head, "Mr. Lincoln apprised us of the tremendous fact of your presence when he invited us to supper to-night."

"Don't laugh at me!" he begged. "I can't bear it. May I go with you, wherever you may be going?"

"If you wish—I'm on my way to one of the hospitals where they say there's a large number of our Boston boys. If you'll take the basket, Becky can return to the boat," smiling up into his face. "It's a long time since we've had a tête-à-tête."

"I've a vehicle of sorts out on the road, driven by a colored Jehu," said Sumner, taking the basket with alacrity and piloting her carefully among bales and crates to a decrepit victoria drawn by a mule scarcely more unkempt than the old negro on the seat. "This is hardly up to your father's Morgans, but it's the best I could lay hands on," he continued. He handed her gravely to her place and ordered the colored man to find a route to the hospital unknown to ambulances. Then he stepped into the carriage. "So I'm to have the pleasure of being with you at supper to-night? Strange the President didn't mention it."

"He said that if we surprised you, the look on your countenance would be worth any price the experiment might cost." Alice looked up at him, eyes twinkling.

"And what did he mean by that?" with a puzzled scowl on his pale face. He was looking very much worn.

"He didn't explain himself," replied Alice. "He can't know how we last parted, so he couldn't have been anticipating a public reconciliation. In fact, I'm not sure that there will be or has been a reconciliation. Let's see! Our last quarrel had to do with my telling you

what I thought of your defeat of the President's bill!
I still am unchanged as to that, Senator."

"Don't! I beg of you, Alice. Let's not mention politics. Let's sing a Te Deum together that Richmond has
fallen and then let's talk only of our two selves."

Alice looked from the disreputable mule to the disreputable darky and from the darky to Sumner in his
blue broadcloth coat and fawn-colored pantaloons. The
thought of herself and the immaculate Senator chanting
together under such chaperonage was too much for her
risibilities and she bubbled over with laughter. The old
darky looked round sympathetically.

"That's right, Miss!" he said, "you-all be joyful in de
Lawd dis ebening! You'se a-riding with the Holy
Ghostes self that helped the Sabior of the niggers to dis
day of Jubilee. Yaas'm." He turned back to the mule
which had come to a halt during this apostrophe. "Git
up, Judas," he urged.

But Judas was aweary. He had halted under a budding tulip tree in a quiet lane where the westering sun
could not strike him and where there was a matchless view
of the harbor with the long half-moon of war vessels
sheltering the wharves. He slumped well down between
the shafts and went to sleep.

Sumner leaned forward impatiently but Alice touched
his arm. "This is the South. There's no hurry. Let's
see what happens."

The Senator looked down at the little hand and leaned
back with a sigh of deep content.

The darky did not move for a full minute. Then
he turned round with a rueful twist of the lips under the
grizzled white beard. "I reckon I might just as well tell
you-all lady and genmun that I cayn't get Judas goin'
lessen I build a fire under him or lessen I go get old Peter

to hitch to his forelock and drag on him. Peter bein'
my brudder's mule."

"How long will it take you to fetch Peter?" asked
Sumner.

"Not mor'n half a hour, Mass' Sumner. I'd be
obleeged if I could work it that way, cuz burning his old
hide do make him kick." The old man's voice was very
pleading.

"Very well! But you must move rapidly," agreed the
Senator.

"Yassir! Faster'n Uncle Robert Lee's hoofin' it from
Gineral Grant!" clambering down and making off over a
fresh-plowed field.

"What a glorious mischance!" exclaimed Sumner, toss-
ing his felt hat to the seat opposite. "Dear Alice!"

"I deserve no credit for it, Senator!" protested Alice.
"But I'll admit I'm very well content. Do you think
there's any chance that Judas will come out of his coma
and start? Our Jehu has left his reins dragging."

Sumner rescued the knotted ropes that answered for
reins and hung them within easy reach over the whip.
"I shall be grievously disappointed if he starts before
Jehu's return.—Alice, coming down on the boat from
Washington I spent much of the night on deck thinking
of you. Somehow, under the stars, it was impossible to
concentrate on affairs of state. My mind was filled with
your lovely self. And thinking so, free of all the irrita-
tions inseparable from Washington, I realized that I'd
played a petty part with you."

She looked up at him, her face a little sad. "Dear
Senator, you're never petty. You were merely true to
yourself. It was I with my ambitions that was petty.
You and I both have our arrogances and our egotisms,
Senator, but I see some things clearer than you do. I

shouldn't have criticized your splendid career. It was putting my own little dreams ahead of your big ones."

"No! No! You shall not say that!" cried Sumner. "Let's not talk of it. Let me tell you of my love for you and how it's filling me more and more with an unrest that will not be stilled. Let me ask you again to be my wife! Give me yourself to cherish and adore and take me as I imperfectly am. Alice! Alice!"

She sat quite still, her head in the little white bonnet bowed. Faint bugle calls came from the ships below. There was a smell of new earth. Robins and red birds called.

Then Alice said in a low voice. "I shall not be a perfect wife, Charles, but I love you dearly, dearly and admire you extravagantly."

Tears filled Sumner's eyes. He slipped his arm around her waist and drew her gently against him. And then he kissed her; at first softly but in a moment with the passion that told of the breakdown of the dam of loneliness and frustration built by the years. For a moment she was only tender with him and then, as the years passed from him and she saw the youthful beauty that age had only covered in his face and not destroyed, she kindled to his fire.

The sun had set when the colored Jehu appeared, dejected and empty handed.

"Pete, he done balked too," he reported. "Reckon I'd better get that fire started."

"Mercy, no!" cried Alice. "How far is it back to the wharf?"

"About fifteen minutes' walk, Miss," replied Jehu, hopefully.

"Then, Charles, let's walk," suggested Alice. "I feel the need of expansion, as you would say. The man can bring the basket back to me, when Judas permits."

Sumner tossed a bill to the smiling darky and gave Alice his hand from the carriage. He did not release it when she was beside him and with the grinning Jehu watching they strolled off into the dusk.

Sumner began to press Alice to agree to an early marriage. From his point of view there could be no reason for more than a few months' engagement. But here the amenability that had marked Alice during their two hours together showed signs of hardening. The Hoopers, she protested, would feel badly if she were to marry so soon after the death of Sturgis.

"In fact," she went on, "they're going to oppose any marriage at all. They're quite content with the present arrangement. So we mustn't think of the wedding before another year. And you're so tied here that after we're married, I shall expect never to get abroad again. Mr. Hooper plans to take us all over to London this summer and leave us for six months."

Sumner groaned. "Alice! You almost make me want to be Minister to England."

"Well, why don't you be? No! Don't be cross, dear!" as she felt his fingers stiffen. "You shall be and do whatever you wish. Keep right on fighting the darkies' fight for them. Kill yourself in another struggle in the Senate, if it'll make you happy! I warn you now, though, that I'll not invite Fred Douglass to eat at our table."

"There'll not be another Senatorial struggle," declared Sumner firmly, "unless Mr. Lincoln precipitates it. And after he ceases to be Commander-in-Chief, he'll have no authority whatever. No, that fight is finished."

"And do you think he'll try to precipitate another struggle?" asked Alice, casually.

"No, I don't. I never saw a man more thoroughly whipped than he was, last month. They tell me he was actually despondent. And I know he's made no move since. In fact, he can't move now, without Congress. He can't appoint military Governors and cause them to call elections. No, thanks to killing that iniquitous bill of his, Congress is now in the saddle."

"You mean you're in the saddle with Congress riding postillion fashion," laughed Alice. "Do you see the rim of the moon behind the masts of those ships, Charles? It looks like Holland. I'm afraid we're going to be very late for the President's supper. We must not delay to dress."

They boarded the *River Queen* just as the party was sitting down at the table. Lincoln, eyeing them keenly as they stood together in the doorway, wondered just why Alice had wished to rob him of his surprise. He was half minded to joke her about it. But although Sumner was extraordinarily whimsical and cordial at the supper table and Alice so gentle that her father-in-law eyed her wonderingly, no mention of the obvious situation between the two was invited by either Alice or Sumner.

When supper was over, Lincoln went out on the deck. He wished very much to go up to Beckwith's tent but wasn't sure that Mary wouldn't feel he was neglecting the guests. There was a full moon on the river. Its enchantment softened the brutal paraphernalia of war to delicate beauty. Even the distant sounds of Grant's pursuit of Lee lost some of their suggestiveness in competition with this enthrallment of the eye. As Lincoln stood by the rail in contemplation, Sumner joined him.

"Mr. Lincoln," he said in a low voice, "Mrs. Hooper and I wish that you and Mrs. Lincoln shall be among the first to know of our great happiness."

The President took the proffered hand in a mighty grip. "I saw it on your faces when you arrived! All the good things in the world be showered on you, Senator! Your wife will be a beautiful and gifted lady."

In the moonlight, he saw that Sumner's face was indescribably softened and moved. "I can't believe that after all these years, I'm to know the bliss of marriage," he murmured.

Lincoln dropped his hand on the Senator's shoulder. "You'll be the handsomest couple in Washington, by Jings, and I shall certainly dance at your wedding. When will it be, Senator?"

"That's the one fly in the ointment," replied Sumner with a sigh. "Mrs. Hooper wishes to postpone it for a year." He gave the President Alice's reasons.

Lincoln shook his head. "Too bad! But I reckon she'll give in if you let her see how you feel about it."

"I don't want to be selfish in my demands," said the Senator. "She has been so generous with me."

"Didn't insist that you lay your future career in her pretty little hands, eh?" asked Lincoln, with a smile.

"No! No!" protested Sumner. "Strange as it may seem to you, Mr. Lincoln, she cares for me without reference to my career."

"Now, why should it seem strange to me?" asked Lincoln.

Sumner leaned against the rail, facing the President. "To tell you the truth, sir, I've felt that since February you've hated me."

"Oh, come now, Senator! Allow me a little slack! You knocked my dearest hopes higher than a kite. Trumbull and I felt as if a cyclone had been playing tag with us. It's a wonder I didn't return the ring and all your letters! Instead of that I got your friends out of jail for you!"

Sumner smiled slowly. "It was a fair fight, Mr. Lincoln."

"Absolutely! And the best man won. Trumbull says he's through," with a chuckle.

"And you?" asked Sumner.

"I'm telling you frankly, Senator," sighed the President, "that I never felt so beaten in my life. I have no more ideas than an egg. I'm certain of just one thing. I'm going to keep your friendship. I've gotten very little to take away with me out of Washington, Senator. But I'm doing my best to take that. Friendship isn't as precious to you as it is to me."

Sumner's face contracted with pain. "Don't say that! I don't deserve it, truly. Friendship means much to me. It's all I've had."

"I think you've been careless with a good many of your friendships," insisted Lincoln. "With mine, for instance. But I won't let you go. Sometimes I'm surprised when I examine my feeling for you, Charles, because I reckon I've never had before or will have again just that kind of a liking for any one. I suppose a lean, sallow, cadaverous fellow like me is bound to be attracted by your handsome looks. I couldn't have the same liking for you if you were a little, slim, consumptive man like Stephens of Georgia. I like your prideful way of comporting yourself.—'Why, man, he doth bestride the narrow world like a Colossus and we petty men walk under his huge legs and prowl about to find ourselves dishonorable graves.'—And there's your glorious voice. Makes mine sound like a rabbit's squeak."

"No! No! You embarrass me, dear Mr. Lincoln!" Sumner's eyes were full of tears.

Lincoln, watching him, felt his whole heart go out to the Senator. There was something pathetic, something

that tugged at all his sympathies about Sumner. He
felt that same almost overwhelming gush of pity and love
rising within him against which he had fought at Hamp-
ton Roads. But he didn't strive against this.

"Charles! Charles! You're a very noble figure of a
man! I wish I were one of the monarchs of old who
could tap a loved favorite on the shoulder and make him a
knight! Sans peur et sans reproche. I know a little
French, myself. That's it! It's your integrity, Charles!
That's the core of your charm for us. I'd rather my
boys had it than any other single quality. We all rest on
your integrity, Charles, as on the Everlasting Arms."

"Don't! Ah, don't, Mr. Lincoln!" Sumner's face
worked. "You overwhelm me with your generosity.
Me, who have worked against you, thwarted you, beaten
you." He took a step across the deck and turned back
holding out both his hands. The tears were running
down his cheeks. "Mr. Lincoln, I will be Secretary of
State for you!"

Lincoln could feel himself grow faint. He clung
speechlessly to Sumner's hands. The leap of relief in his
breast was physically painful. *Sumner out of Congress
giving Lincoln a free hand with reconstruction!* "Is that
a promise, Charles?" he finally gasped.

"Yes! You must give me a few months to arrange my
affairs."

"Take all the time you want!" Lincoln paused, still
holding the firm fingers in his own. "You and Grant between you to-day have given me perfect happiness. I've
had only one other hour as great. That was when I
signed the Emancipation Proclamation. Go down to your
Alice now, Senator, before I weep!"

Sumner gripped Lincoln's hands and obediently turned
away.

Shortly after this the Hoopers left, and the *River Queen* started back to Washington.

Lincoln's mood of exaltation demanded expression. He went to his cabin and procured the beautiful quarto volume of Shakespeare that Mary had given him on his last birthday. Then he joined the group in the cabin. Mary looked up with a smile.

"We're debating Jeff Davis' fate," she said.

"Judge not, that ye be not judged," he replied, soberly. Then he seated himself under a lamp and opened his book. "If you all are in my frame of mind, Shakespeare alone can satisfy you. And of Shakespeare, only Macbeth."

"Oh, not Macbeth!" cried Mary shuddering. "Give us something gentle and tender, Mr. Lincoln, like Tennyson or Longfellow."

"Like 'Resignation,' I suppose--" smiled Lincoln and he repeated aloud:—

> " 'There is no flock, however watched and tended,
>   But one dead lamb is there!
>   There is no fireside, howsoe'er defended
>   But has one vacant chair—'

No! No! That's too tame! Give me Macbeth. . . .

> " 'Duncan is in his grave;
>   After life's fitful fever he sleeps well.
>   Treason has done its worst; nor steel nor poison,
>   Malice domestic, foreign levy,
>   Nothing can touch him further. . . .' "

He adjusted his spectacles. "That has teeth! Let's have the witches next. You should have seen them at work on the night of March 29 over Petersburg."

He read for an hour in his dramatic fashion, then closed the book. After all, Macbeth was a tragedy and his was no tragic mood. He went on deck for one last look at the serene beauty of the night. Mary followed him and they stood together by the rail in silent communion.

After a moment, Lincoln said, "Mary, Sumner has filled my cup to overflowing."

"You've made up?" cried Mary.

"Well," smiled the President, "you might call it so. You know that a hundred times the last two years I've tried to woo Sumner and I couldn't. But to-night, without thinking of a thing except my honest love for him, I wooed and won him." He told her of their conversation and of its extraordinary climax, ending with the remark, "I don't yet see why he came to my arms!"

"Oh, but I do, Abra'm! He thinks, as I've told you before, that you're finished. He thinks you're powerless now to hurt his cause."

Lincoln laughed softly. "Then I wooed him under false colors because I am certain that as soon as Andy Johnson and I get our heads together we can pull the teeth of the Vindictives.—No, not false colors either. I love Sumner and he knows it."

"Yes," murmured Mary, "at last, thank God, he knows it."

She leaned against him. Lincoln put his arm about her, pressing her warm body against his side, and in deep happiness they watched the sliding Virginia shore.

PARTIAL LIST OF BOOKS CONSULTED

CHARLES FRANCIS ADAMS: An Autobiography. Boston, 1916.

JEFFERSON DAVIS: A Memoir by His Wife. New York, 1890.

EDWIN MCMASTERS STANTON, *F. A. Flower*. New York, 1905.

LINCOLN AND SLAVERY, *I. N. Arnold*. Chicago, 1866.

LINCOLN'S PLAN OF RECONSTRUCTION, *C. H. McCarthy*. New York, 1901.

BUTLER'S BOOK. Boston, 1892.

PRIVATE LIFE AND PUBLIC SERVICES OF SALMON P. CHASE, *R. B. Warden*. Cincinnati, 1874.

TWENTY YEARS OF CONGRESS, *James G. Blaine*. Norwich, 1884.

MEMOIRS OF ROBERT E. LEE, *A. L. Long*. Philadelphia, 1886.

MEMORIES OF THE WHITE HOUSE, *W. H. Crook*. Boston, 1911.

THROUGH FIVE ADMINISTRATIONS, *Crook-Gerry*. New York, 1907.

AN AIDE-DE-CAMP OF LEE, *Major General Sir Frederick Maurice*. Boston, 1927.

ABRAHAM LINCOLN, *Lord Charnwood*. New York, 1917.

MEMOIR OF LAST YEAR OF WAR FOR INDEPENDENCE OF CONFEDERATE STATES, *Jubal A. Early*. Lynchburg, 1867.

RECOLLECTIONS OF CIVIL WAR, *C. H. Dana*. New York, 1848.

LIFE OF SEWARD, *Frederic Bancroft*. New York, 1900.

RICHARD HENRY DANA, *C. F. Adams*. Boston, 1890.

WASHINGTON IN LINCOLN'S TIME, *Wort Brooks*. New York, 1894.

PERSONAL MEMOIRS OF P. H. SHERIDAN. New York, 1888.

THE STORY OF THE WHITE HOUSE, *Esther Singleton*. New York, 1907.

DIARY OF GIDEON WELLES. Boston, 1909.

GENERAL BUTLER IN NEW ORLEANS, *James Parton*. New York, 1863.

MEMOIR AND LETTERS OF CHARLES SUMNER, *E. L. Pierce*. Boston, 1877.

CHARLES SUMNER: Works. Boston, 1872.

UNPUBLISHED CORRESPONDENCE OF CHARLES SUMNER. Harvard University Library.

LIFE OF HENRY W. LONGFELLOW, *Samuel Longfellow*. Boston, 1886.

ABRAHAM LINCOLN: A History, *Nicolay* and *Hay*. New York, 1886.

PERSONAL TRAITS OF ABRAHAM LINCOLN, *Helen Nicolay*. New York, 1919.

LINCOLN AND MEN OF WAR TIME, *A. K. McClure*. Philadelphia, 1892.

CONGRESSIONAL GLOBE: Part I, 2nd Session, 38th Congress.

PERSONAL MEMOIRS OF U. S. GRANT. New York, 1885.

SIX MONTHS IN THE WHITE HOUSE, *F. B. Carpenter*. New York, 1866.

THE LIFE OF JOHN HAY, *W. R. Thayer*. Boston, 1908.

CHARLES SUMNER, *Moorfield Storey*. Boston, 1900.

MEMORIES OF MANY MEN AND OF SOME WOMEN, *B. Field*. New York, 1873.

LINCOLN AND SEWARD, *Gideon Welles*. New York, 1874.

LINCOLN AND STANTON, *W. D. Kelley*. New York, 1885.

RECOLLECTIONS OF PRESIDENT LINCOLN, *L. E. Chittenden*. New York, 1891.

EDWIN M. STANTON: Life and Public Services, *G. C. Gorham*. Boston, 1899.

THE WAR BETWEEN THE STATES, *A. H. Stephens*. Philadelphia, 1868.

THE LOST CAUSE, *E. A. Pollard*. New York, 1866.

BATTLES AND LEADERS OF THE CIVIL WAR. The Century Company's War Book. New York, 1884.

PHOTOGRAPHIC HISTORY OF THE CIVIL WAR. New York, 1911.

REMINISCENCES, *Perley Poore*.

OFFICIAL RECORDS OF UNION AND CONFEDERATE ARMIES: Series I. Washington, D. C.

ABRAHAM LINCOLN: Complete Works. New York, 1920.

LIFE AND LETTERS OF FRANCIS LIEBER. 1882.

LIFE AND LETTERS OF LORD LYONS.

LIFE OF CHARLES SUMNER, *Chaplin.*

GENEALOGY OF HOOPER FAMILY. Boston.

MEMOIRS OF WILLIAM T. SHERMAN. New York, 1875.

FROM CHATTANOOGA TO PETERSBURG, *W. F. Smith.*

RECOLLECTIONS, *John Sherman.*

POLITICAL RECOLLECTIONS, *Julian.*

CORRESPONDENCE OF J. L. MOTLEY. New York, 1889.

HISTORY OF THE UNITED STATES, *J. F. Rhodes.* New Yor
    1899.

HISTORY OF THE UNITED STATES, *John Fiske.* Boston, 1894.

SHORT HISTORY OF THE CONFEDERATE STATES, *Jefferson Davi
    New York, 1890.

LIFE OF LORD JOHN RUSSELL, *Sir Spencer Walpole, K.C.B.*

ANDREW JOHNSON, *Clifton R. Hall.* Princeton, 1916.

LIFE AND TIMES OF HANNIBAL HAMLIN, *Hamlin.* Cambridg
    1899.